D0811668

JAMES HORWITZ

ASBURY PARK PUBLIC LIBRARY
ASBURY PARK, NEW JERSEY

TC

Thomas Congdon Books
E. P. DUTTON & CO., INC. | NEW YORK

"Back in the Saddle Again," by Ray Whitley and Gene Autry, copyright 1940, © renewed 1967. Used by permission of Western Music Publishing Co.

"Blood On the Saddle," by E. Cheetham, copyright © 1936 and 1964 by ABC/Dunhill Music, Inc. (BMI). Used by permission only. All rights reserved.

"Bob Dylan's Blues," by Bob Dylan, copyright © 1963 by Warner Bros. Inc. All rights reserved. Used by permission.

"Buffalo Bill's," by E. E. Cummings, copyright 1923, 1951 by E. E. Cummings. Reprinted from his volume, *Complete Poems 1913–1962,* by permission of Harcourt Brace Jovanovich, Inc.

"The Cisco Kid" © 1972 and 1973, Far Out Music, Inc., reprinted by permission. Written by Sylvester Allan, Morris "B.B." Dickerson, Harold Brown, Charles W. Miller, Leroy "Lonnie" Jordan, Lee Oskar, Howard Scott.

"The Legend of Wyatt Earp," by Harry Warren and Harold Adamson, copyright by Four Jays Music.

Portions of this book originally appeared in *Rolling Stone,* Issue 146, October 25, 1973.

Copyright © 1976 by James Horwitz
All rights reserved. Printed in the U.S.A.
First Edition
10 9 8 7 6 5 4 3 2 1

No part of this publication may be reproduced or transmitted in any form or by any means, electronic or mechanical, including photocopy, recording, or any information storage and retrieval system now known or to be invented, without permission in writing from the publisher, except by a reviewer who wishes to quote brief passages in connection with a review written for inclusion in a magazine, newspaper or broadcast.

Library of Congress Cataloging in Publication Data

Horwitz, James.
   They went thataway.

   "Thomas Congdon books."
   1. Western films—History and criticism. 2. Moving-picture actors and actresses—United States—Biography. I. Title.
PN1995.9.W4H6   791.43'0909'32   76–13883

ISBN: 0-525-21683-9

Published simultaneously in Canada
by Clarke, Irwin & Company Limited, Toronto and Vancouver

for my parents,
who always gave me
movie money
and never once
asked for the change

and
for the Gloucestershire
lady . . .

THE FRONT ROW KID

"The past went that-a-way. When faced with a totally new situation, we tend always to attach ourselves to the objects, to the flavour of the most recent past. We look at the present through a rear-view mirror. We march backwards into the future."

—Marshall McLuhan

Buffalo Bill's
defunct
     who used to
     ride a watersmooth-silver
          stallion
and break onetwothreefourfive pigeons just
          like that
          Jesus

he was a handsome man
       and what i want to know is
how do you like your blue eyed boy
Mister Death

—e.e. cummings

The Front Row Kid

"I'm back in the saddle again
Out where a friend is a friend
Where the long-horned cattle feed
     on the lowly jimson weed
I'm back in the saddle again.

Ridin' the range once more
Totin' my old forty-four
Where you sleep out every night
Where the only law is right
I'm back in the saddle again."

The Front Row Kid rocks back and forth in time to the music.
He knows the words by heart and sometimes sings along or
whistles. Trail dreaming . . . Over a mountain pass, along the
rim of a canyon, silhouetted against the Western sky, across
the dusty plains, through the sagebrush and the cactus, past
the dry water holes. Light in the saddle, he rides the range
under the sun, and when it begins to dip low in the sky, he tips
his Stetson down over his eyes and gallops on. Heading West.
At night he follows a certain star and listens to the darkness,
a coyote, a rattler, a hoot-owl, the thumping of his old horse's
hoofbeats, the sound of his own voice. The wide-open spaces.
And from time to time he comes to a town. Dry Gulch, Waco,
Cactus Creek, Silver City, Hadleyville. They are all the same.
A dusty street, a saloon, a hotel, a sheriff's office. He's a stranger passing through; he could be anyone. A cowhand, a hired
gun, a drifter, a gambler, a bounty hunter, a tinhorn, a tender-

3

foot, or The Lone Ranger. He rides, he ropes; he sometimes
has to fight. He shoots straight and rolls his own cigarettes.
He's a man. Whoopi-tii-yii-yaa. He goes his own way. Back in
the saddle again . . . until his mother calls from the kitchen that
it's time for dinner and he must hang up his six-guns, "Lone
Ranger" model .44s with the mock silver bullets, and turn the
record player off. Come back from where he has been a Wild
West Cowboy-Hero to where he is only a small-town boy, a
Front Row Kid.

But the trail dreaming doesn't stop. Not even for dinner.

"Drink your milk, cowboy," his mother says, pointing to the
full glass with the picture of Hopalong Cassidy on it.

"Ecch!" says the Front Row Kid, wrinkling his nose and
pushing his fork across the Gene Autry dinner plate, moving
around the mixed-up remains of green beans and meat loaf
and a pool of catsup, the better to see Gene Autry and Champion the Wonder Horse in full gallop.

"You know what will happen if you don't."

"What?"

"Your teeth will fall out, for one thing."

"Don't care," the Kid says, flashing two buck front teeth
with a wide-open space between them. And imagines a showdown in the saloon of some sagebrush town. Backing out
through the two swinging doors. Daring anyone man enough
to stop him, to draw down on him. Making a flying mount onto
his horse and riding out like the laughing wind to another
town, another challenge. Tall, silent, and heroic. Terrific.

"And for another," his mother says, heading him off at the
pass, "no movies on Saturday." Bang! Shot right out of the
saddle. Bush-whacked.

"O.K.," he says, surrendering, coming out with his hands up.
"But make the galloping."

His mother begins to tap her hands slowly on the dinner
table. Ta-ta-tump. Ta-ta-tump. Making the sound of galloping
hoofbeats. The Kid reaches for his glass. And begins to gulp
down the milk. She taps faster. Ta-ta-tump. Ta-ta-tump. Faster
and faster. While he gulps to keep up, to get ahead. Ta-ta-
tump. Gulp. Until the glass with Hopalong Cassidy's picture on
it is empty.

"There," she says, "that wasn't so bad, was it?"

"What about the movies on Saturday?"

"We'll see."

The Front Row Kid wipes his mouth on the sleeve of his cowboy shirt. And wishes it was already Saturday . . .

The Saturday Matinee. Action-packed, rootin'-hootin'-and-a-shootin' double-feature Western movies. Saturday afternoon trail dreaming. Cowboy-struck and hooked on the myth, the Front Row Kid could not get enough of it. The mountains and canyons and prairies. The Indians and the Cavalry and the horses. The thrill of the showdown, the shoot-out and the punch-up. The villain with the smarm and the smile and the thin mustache. The bush-whackers, the desperadoes, and the crooked bank presidents; the cattle barons, the rustlers, and the claim-jumpers. The double-dealing, back-shooting, two-timing, yellow-bellied sidewinders. The dirty varmints. The Bad Guys in the black hats. The Frontier Folk, the sodbusters, the nesters, the sheep herders and the homesteaders, all paunchy and righteous. The rancher's daughter, the dancehall girl, and the prim little schoolmarm from back East who got in the way of the action and sometimes in the way of the Good Guy. Ah, the Good Guy. The Cowboy-Hero. Galloping across the screen 20 feet tall. The one who put things right, who rode like the wind and fought like a mountain lion and never had his white Stetson knocked off, who beat everyone to the draw and never let you down. Not ever.

The Saturday Matinee. If you were the Front Row Kid, coming up before rock 'n' roll, and you had not yet discovered the fantasy possibilities of baseball and girls, for one thin dime you bought the best of all possible worlds and believed in the Western movies. Life without them was unimaginable, empty, dull. It was more than an event, those three or four hours in the dark looking up. It was a living daydream. A ritual. An idea. Better than a birthday party. Better than recess. Better even than a 500-pound hamburger and a chocolate sundae as big as your house.

The Saturday Matinee. Just to be able to pay your dime at the ticket booth and walk into that lobby at one o'clock on a

Saturday afternoon, to slip through the crowd of kids at the refreshment stand and plunk your extra nickel down on the glass-top counter for a Mars Bar or a Coke or a box of popcorn popped before your very eyes and still warm in the box (with plenty of salt and butter). And then to enter the dimly lit theater, to walk or skip or run down that long aisle, past rows and rows of kids from all over town squealing and scuffling, whistling, laughing, bouncing up and down on their springy cushion seats, meeting and greeting each other, down to that front-row seat. Then to sit yourself down, almost dizzy with excitement and anticipation, your elbows propped on the arm rests, your toes tingling and your brain doing cartwheels. To wait out the last few unbearable moments until the time, looking up at the ceiling so high above you covered with mock clouds and stars like night, turning around in your front-row seat to look back at the balcony so far above and behind you and watch the candy wrappers and paper airplanes come sailing down until the ushers below, done out in uniforms like the Phillip Morris midget, shine their flashlights up toward the garbage-bombers, trying to keep everyone's excitement in check but knowing that it is impossible and not trying very hard because there are just too many of us. And then to have the lights go down into darkness like a blanket being draped over our shoulders, and all the kids who have been crawling between the rows or running up and down the aisles hurry to their seats as the pitch and roll of the cheering and whooping fills every corner of the darkness, knowing what is coming next but unable to hold on to our excitement one second longer, we burst, as the great red curtain folds away, and the Eagle flies! Republic Pictures Presents. . . . Yeeaaahooo! Ride 'em cowboy!

What could be better than that? To be transported on the instant to all the plains and prairies and cowtowns of the Wild West and to actually see the Cowboy-Heroes doing their stuff, riding, roping, fighting, shooting . . . winning. See them take chances and face challenges without flinching. See them do the right thing at the right time, save the day and then ride out of town, into the sunset, as if they had done nothing unusual, just what had to be done. And to sometimes hear them sing a cowboy song. That was something to look forward to all week, to talk about and think about and dream about if you were a Front Row Kid. Not to be missed. No matter what.

All the brave cowboys. Our first and best heroes. As certain of them and their ultimate victories as we were unsure of ourselves and the world we were coming up in. The miracle riders. So tall and handsome and straight and strong. So brave and able. So easygoing and at home on the range. So much better in every way than anyone else we knew or ever heard of. Who cared if the West wasn't *really* like that?

Our belief in the Saturday cowboys was solid, undoubting, perfect. And "all the money in the world" was not too much to bet on what we knew they could do. And we knew they could do just about anything because they were man enough and not afraid. They were a perfect fit for the Front Row Kid's imagination. An imagination that was only just beginning to reach out, to peek into strange dark corners, to stand up on its own two feet, to run, to risk to fly, to believe and make-believe. If not to ask "why?" at least to wonder "how?" and "what if . . . ?" Mothers, fathers, teachers, and policemen, the guy in the battered hat who owned the corner store where you bought your popsicles and comic books, the Frightener, who lived in the shack behind your yard and scared the daylights out of Front Row Kids playing too near his bushes, in fact every grownup around said "don't" or "can't," said "no" and "impossible" and "be quiet" to Front Row Kids. But when John Wayne leaped from that stagecoach to the front team of horses going full gallop, when Gene Autry and Champion outraced a train, when Hoppy laughed off a threat and stood his ground, when Tim McCoy turned his twinkle-eyed but deadly stare on a saloon full of strangers, when Joel McCrea sat up tall in his saddle listening for a sound on the trail or sat cross-legged at his campfire drinking coffee out of a tin cup, alone in the dark, they were saying "do" and "can" and "try." And when the music started up behind the chase or the fight, it only confirmed the possibility of the impossible. You could almost feel yourself growing taller and stronger right there in your front-row seat. They put a man-sized boot print on your brain at a time when there were still very few tracks up there to mark the fact that anyone had passed that way. And they left, every Saturday, a pretty clear trail to follow, a trail that gave hope of full days and fantasies and the promise of one day being man enough to fit your own footstep into that boot print, to make your own trails. What little we knew or could imagine, at the age of 5 or 9 or 12, of grownup things, of bravery, honesty, courage, justice, even death, we learned from them, from their example. We believed in them. They were ourselves as we someday hoped to be.

"When I grow up, I'm going to live in Texas."

"Me, too."

"There's ranches out there, you know, and horses and maybe Indians."

"We could be Texas Rangers, huh? Or drive cattle."

"We don't have to decide until we get there."

"Does your mom know?"

". . . ?"

Not that we actually hoped to become cowboys. It was already too far along into the twentieth century, with too many Buicks on the road and too few covered wagons, for a dream like that to hold up. All the buffaloes were in zoos. There were buses and tall buildings. And airplanes overhead that didn't fit the dream. We knew vaguely what year it was and almost certainly that it was too late. No, the best we could hope for was to be cowboy-like. Tall, heroic Good Guys who feared nothing, who could not be bossed or bullied or beaten up, who came and went as we pleased without having to ask our moms whether we could or not. We might, indeed, go West when the time came to go. Perhaps, with luck and if there were any left, we might even save a rancher's daughter in distress. We would certainly not have to drink milk if we didn't want to. And, of course, it almost went without saying, we would live forever . . .

In the meantime, we lived from Saturday to Saturday. And in the days between "played" cowboys as if our lives depended on it. Galloping around the big back yard with our hats flopping off our heads and our six-guns blazing, puckered lips dry spitting to make the sound of gunfire. Ptchoo! Ptchoo! Falling to the ground and getting up again. "You're dead. I gotcha!" "I'm not dead. You missed me." Wearing down the grass between the house and the garage where we galloped in our cowboy boots until it would never grow again, even years later. Lying in ambush in the bushes and trying not to give ourselves away as we slapped mosquitoes off our faces, pretending they were rattlesnakes and practicing not being afraid. Our fistfights always accompanied by grunts and groans and a triumphant musical soundtrack. Ta-dum. Ta-da. Take that! And that! Ta-dum. Ta-da. But never actually landing a blow for real. Only drawing blood when we caught our spurs in the spokes of our bikes and skinned our foreheads or our knees on the cement in front of the garage/sheriff's office/ saloon. "You're crying." "No I ain't. I got something in my eye." And getting up again and galloping off. Climbing the apple trees out in the back yard/lonesome prairie and having our guns fall out of the holster when we were way up on top. Sometimes tying up the girls from the neighborhood to the same apple trees to see if they were man enough to get themselves loose. And sometimes catching a glimpse of their underpants but not knowing exactly what to do about that. "Hey, you're not supposed to look!" "Who's looking?" And we were our own heroes.

Front Row Kids and small-town boys, every glorious day was full of shouting and shooting and thundering hoofbeats, barroom brawls and jailbreaks, stampedes and stagecoach journeys through the Badlands and the Indian Territory and daydream cowtowns of our back yard. As if we would never run out of breath or time or Cowboy-Heroes to imitate. As if the day would never come when one of us would say: "Let's play baseball. I got a new catcher's mitt for my birthday." Or: "I don't feel like playing today. I gotta go to the library." Or: "Count me out. Raeanne and me are going skating." What? As if the day would never come when the back yard would be just the back yard, when our week-by-week supply of new frontier fantasies and Wild West Tales would vanish, when the theaters we went to, the Time, the Strand, the Mode, the Star, would not be showing action-packed double-feature Western movies for a dime (or even a dollar!). When Gene and Roy and Hoppy and Tex and Rex and Sunset and Cisco and Buck and Tim and "Lash" and "Wild Bill" and "The Durango Kid" and Randolph Scott would not be riding across our Saturday afternoons. Or worse yet, and unimaginable, as if the day would never come when we no longer cared if they did or not . . .

But eventually and inevitably we do grow up, grow older, move away from our back-yard cowtowns, our Saturday fantasies left behind by events and the passing of time, swapped or dropped or traded off for other fanciful dreams and promises, of love or money or magical powers. But at the bottom of the saddlebag, buried under layers of years, there are still the images that will not go away of those perfect Cowboy-Heroes.

I won the West when I was 5. I was the Front Row Kid. And now, on the other side of 30, too old for playing cowboys in the yard, I thought it a good idea to travel forward backward for a while, to sniff around the edges of that memory and try to find my Good Guy Cowboy-Heroes. See if they were still alive and what they had to say for themselves. What they could possibly have to say to me, the Front Row Kid who had cheered so loudly for them on so many Saturday afternoons, bought the comic books that had their names on them (and hoarded them like gold), wore the shirts and boots, cowboy hats and six-guns that carried their brands, ate the cereals they recommended, only drank milk from their "official" glasses and dreamed of a life to be lived, modeled on their example, that would be nothing but a continuous string of white-hat Good Guy heroics. I haven't won anything since I was 5. And the world outside the Saturday matinee has not been what it promised to be, glorious, romantic, and full of heroes. The Saturday Matinee and the Cowboy-Hero are dead as a doornail and buried in Boot Hill. But not, perhaps, entirely forgotten. Still rattling around like loose nostalgia-change in the secret pocket in which a Front Row Kid keeps his best memories. And if the pocket has a hole in it, and some things have, over the years, fallen through, and you have to dig down into your socks, well, you never can tell what you might find.

There is a story about a man who loses a silver dollar and goes down on his hands and knees, searching for it under the light of a street lamp. He searches there for some time. A passer-by walks up to him and asks what he is doing.

"I'm looking for a silver dollar that fell out of my pocket," the man says.

"Been looking long?" asks the passer-by.

"Seems like years."

"Well, where did you lose it?"

"Up the road," says the man, pointing into the distance, toward the darkness.

"Why're you looking here?"

"Because," says the man, "the light is better."

And so it is when you are looking up lost or faded memories, sifting through the blur of myths and fantasies. Everything changes everything else. And time changes memory most of all. You have to sometimes look where the light is better. And travel back to a time before your time. Crazy as it sounds. Talking backward is the hardest part. Listen: ".diK woR tnorF eht llits ma I."

Chelsea Cowboy

Some days are better than others. And some days can only get better, starting out as bad as they can possibly be. Like that day Gerald Ford pardoned Nixon. Deceitfully disguised as a Sunday School Sermonette, a kind of dial-a-prayer sneak attack on the unsuspecting, it oozed out of the telly on a quiet Sunday morning when nobody was looking, when the Good Guys were still sleeping off Saturday night, and the others were in church praying for miracles. The way it was done was the nearest thing to tiptoeing out into a completely deserted street at 4 o'clock in the morning and whispering it to a lamppost. Pssst. I, Gerald Ford, hereby grant full and complete pardon to Richard M. Nixon for any and all crimes he committed against the United States during the time of his Presidency. Shhhh. It was not very heroic. And with the possible exception of waking up to find you are lying in bed next to a dead body, the worst way to start the day. But after the first waves of nausea subside, you can take some comfort in the fact that the day can only get better. It seemed to me like a good day for getting out of town, for saddling up and going in search of my old Cowboy-Heroes.

Time and events had turned decidedly weird since the days when the Front Row Kids had had Good Guys to cheer and a steady and seemingly endless supply of examples of courage and grace to measure against.

And Gerald Ford, missing only the bolt through his neck to complete the creature feature, said: "The national nightmare is over."

After years of Vietnam and paranoia, cops and robbers, the

Hunchback of San Clemente, and now this, I was feeling fantasy starved and deprived. Even the loco weed didn't help. It was becoming more difficult to pluck those old hero visions out of thin air. And I was beginning to wonder if I was the only one in the world who still bothered to remember them. Or had, perhaps, never outgrown them. It was almost as if I had this permanently fixed rearview mirror in my head that I liked to check from time to time, a quick glance out of the corner of my eye, to remind me where I'd been and where I was coming from. I had no idea where I was going. But then who does?

I turned the television dial looking for an early morning Western movie.

I had been hanging around for some days, in and out of my $9-a-day room at the Chelsea Hotel on Twenty-third Street in New York City, mostly watching television and winos. And listening to the famous Chelsea roaches walk around my room in their golf shoes. I had moved in hoping to find myself surrounded by the echoes of some earlier Chelsea time and to light up a literary fantasy or two, but this once rich and fine cultural landmark had slipped quite a way down the backside of the hill since the days when Thomas Wolfe, Dylan Thomas, James T. Farrell, Brendan Behan, and O. Henry had called it "home." Or even since Bob Dylan wrote "Sad-Eyed Lady of the Lowlands" there. As far as I could tell, they had taken the best fantasies with them when they checked out. In recent years (say the last decade or so) the Chelsea Hotel had become more or less a halfway house for Warholesque weirdos and various other off-the-wall sight gags. Queers, drag queens, loitering pimps, dope dealers, and dwarfs. Clifford Irving stopped there awhile on his way to the Federal jug after his Howard Hughes flim-flam got blown out of the water. During my short incumbency, a noted and colorful New York artist whom I never heard of had died at his easel in the studio he occupied on the top floor. And if you climbed up to the roof, you could see Peggy Lee practicing piano for her comeback and singing to herself in a tiny rehearsal room in the building next door. The Chelsea had become like one of those hotels they have in

Paris where Sartre and Simone de Beauvoir and Bud Powell and Jack Hatfield (who?) *used to* live. It was a ghost of Christmas Past. It was not the sort of place you would expect to find a Bible in every room.

The television in my room looked as if it had been picked up by a sharp-eyed bellboy who'd seen it fall off the back of a furniture van. The antenna had probably been snapped off a parked car and used in a street fight. I had been watching the television for a week before I even realized it was a color set. And then it was like watching those old 3-D movies without the special glasses. Triple images of red, green, and blue. I felt more nostalgic than annoyed. Some folks who lived in the Chelsea would have found it psychedelic. Mostly it just hurt my eyes. Nevertheless, I watched it continuously, for hours, triple-headers and all, in the hope of seeing a good old Western on the Late Late Show. Or at the very least an old John Garfield movie. And wondered, during the program interruptions, if I was really as stupid as the people who made the commercials seemed to think I was. Could anyone be *that* stupid and still live? At least at the Saturday Matinee there were no commercials to interrupt the fantasy. Only Previews of Coming Attractions. I would have kicked the television in the head, put it out of its misery on the very first day, but then I would have missed out on *two* John Garfields, a great Randolph Scott oldie, a Joel McCrea, and *The Man Who Shot Liberty Valance.*

It was finally television that had ambushed the good old Western movie as it galloped into the Fifties and put a bullet in its back. The wonderful Cowboy-Hero of the Saturday Matinee was a tired gun by that time, after 50 years in the saddle. Not as quick on the draw as he had once been. He died, twitching, on a 10-inch screen in the middle of the living room. And now the Cowboy-Hero only rode, like a ghost, on the Late Late Show, his exploits perforated with used-car commercials and cheered by insomniacs.

Somehow it was not the same. They were not 20-feet tall on that tiny screen. In the early Fifties, when so many of the B-Western cowboys went over to Saturday morning TV to save themselves from having to look down the muzzle of oblivion, the picture was often hazy. Every time a bus came up the street outside, the television buzzed with the gear changes. And if you put that rainbow-tinted plastic sheet across the screen to give the illusion of color, you couldn't see anything at all. At the best of times, when ours was still the only set in the neighborhood, there were, perhaps, six of us Front Row Kids gathered around. Not exactly a full house. Sometimes I watched alone. Eating homemade popcorn. There was no ticket booth. No refreshment counter. No drinking fountain to meet at between shows. No aisles to run up and down. No ushers to pester or to shine a flashlight in our faces. And not really a front-row seat to speak of. The fantasy was cramped for space, jammed into a little box in the corner of the living room. And finally the reruns ran out. To be replaced by made-to-order television cowboys who mostly talked in the saloon and rarely rode a horse for more than 30 seconds. And although the Kids would continue to watch until their eyes went funny, *American Bandstand* seemed to have more interesting fantasy possibilities. Mary Ann. South Philly. I'll give it a 65. It's got a good beat you can dance to. But the words ain't so hot. Shoo-bop. Shoo-bop. A-wop-bop-a-loo-bop. A-lop-bam-boom.

Now there was only the Late Late Show if you wanted to see the genuine article, the Cowboy-Hero doing his stuff in the wide-open spaces. Not Gene Autry and Roy Rogers and Tim McCoy—their pictures were almost completely out of circulation. Museum pieces. And not considered "adult" enough for the Late Late Show. But there was Randolph Scott and Joel McCrea and John Wayne and Audie Murphy to fill the gap between commercials. And on occasion there was John Garfield, who was not a cowboy but beat the pants off all the tough guys Hollywood ever invented. If you couldn't get a Western, old John Garfield movies were worth staying up late for.

But the Westerns were the best of all. They took me out of that hotel room without my ever having to leave it. Without television, a Front Row Kid couldn't see a good old Western with a Cowboy-Hero anywhere these days. Unless you rented a projector and knew of a place where you could get old 16 mm. prints for less than $50 a showing. And even then nobody would believe that's what you were doing.

There was a time a few years back, living in Paris and feeling a little French fried, when I could go to the Dragon Cinema in the Latin Quarter and the Napoleon behind the Arc de Triomphe and see a Western all day, every day, for a month. The French, who have always taken Hollywood seriously, respecting even its trivia, called it "Le Festival Western." Every day you could see a different Western. Joel McCrea, Randolph Scott, John Wayne, Audie Murphy, and more. It wasn't Hoppy, Gene, and Roy stuff, but it was good enough for a Front Row Kid in Paris who was looking for a little home on the range to supplement his diet of Godard, Resnais, Truffaut, and vin rouge. You could see *My Darling Clementine, She Wore a Yellow Ribbon, Decision at Sundown, Comanche Station, Wichita, Four Faces West, Bend of the River, The Man From Laramie, The Tin Star, Drums Across the River, The Unforgiven, 3:10 to Yuma, The Man Who Shot Liberty Valance, High Noon, The Left-Handed Gun, Man Without a Star, Ride the High Country,* and *Lonely Are the Brave.* And a dozen others. Thirty Westerns in 30 days. And when the cycle ended, it started over. You could go into the Napoleon at 2 in the afternoon (if you were awake that early) and stay until midnight. Watch the Western that was showing that day five times in a row on a single 3 franc ticket (plus a small pour boire for the usherette who shouted and called you a dirty bastard and would not give you back the stub until she got her tip). And if it was a film you especially liked, *Comanche Station, She Wore a Yellow Ribbon, Ride the High Country,* or *Lonely Are the Brave,* you could go over to the Dragon the next day (they staggered the program by a day) and watch it five more times.

While I lived in Paris, I must have seen *Lonely Are the Brave* close to 50 times. A modest beauty of a film about the last lonesome cowboy who doesn't know or much care that he is an anachronism on horseback in the middle of the twentieth century. Not just an ordinary oater. It ought to get Kirk Douglas into heaven even if nothing else does. I have seen it, in all, perhaps 100 times. (I've lost count over the years.) In Paris, London, Philadelphia, and the Forty-second Street cockroach palaces, in my home town sitting in the same front-row seat where, years earlier, I had first become the Front Row Kid, and on the Late Late Show. I love that movie. Even more than I love *Ride the High Country* or any movie Gene Autry ever made. Perhaps I am like those little old ladies who went every afternoon for years to see *The Sound of Music.* Whatever it is, I still cheer like a Front Row Kid when Kirk Douglas fights the one-armed Mexican in the cantina; when the desk sergeant who is locking him up in the jailhouse asks: "Are you sure you're John Burns?" and Kirk answers back: "Sure enough to bet you can't prove I'm anybody else"; when he breaks out of jail by squeezing through the hack-sawed bars; when he shoots down the pursuing helicopter with his Winchester; when he reaches the top of the mountain and rides hell-for-leather into the trees and out of rifle range, safe and free at last. And at the end, when he is trying to ride across a busy highway in the middle of a late-night downpour, and he is run over by a diesel rig carrying a load of toilets from Missouri to New Mexico, I feel a sense of loss that is something more than grief. And on those Paris midnights I would walk out of the Napoleon or the Dragon with a lump in my throat and melancholy rising.

"Tu viens, cheri?" the whores along the Rue St. Denis would say, and wink at me as I walked by. But I was already well away on the trail of a different fantasy. Le Festival Western would get me through the night. And anyway, I couldn't spare the 50 francs.

But that was a few years back and in another country. These days you had to take your chances on the Late Late Show. Like some cockeyed game of Russian roulette, you just spun that dial, put the set to your head, and fired. Some nights you were lucky. But most nights you blew your brains out. Rory Calhoun and Rod Cameron were no substitute for Randolph Scott. It was not easy to be a Front Row Kid again if you were living in the Chelsea. Or anywhere. I expect, by now, they have closed down Le Festival Western in Paris. Replaced it with Le

Festival Kung Fu. Or Le Festival du Cinema Erotique. It is not the same thing. But these are, after all, the weird Seventies. Where the present is forgotten even while it is happening. And the future looks grim.

The Past is a condemned building with more junk stored away in its attic than can ever be uncovered and reclaimed. Nostalgia is now. The Twenties Look. The Fifties Sound. The Thirties Trivia. It is clodhopper shoes and bright-red lipstick and Jay Gatsby lounge lizard suits. It is Bette Midler singing "The Boogie-Woogie Bugle Boy." It is Rock 'n' Roll Revivals. And Humphrey Bogart Seasons. It is *Give 'Em Hell, Harry.* And Coolidge-Hoover Economics. It is yo-yos and the Mickey Mouse Club. And Paul Newman-Robert Redford movies filled with old cars and honky-tonk pianos. But nostalgia is artificial memories. Like trick photography. Like new furniture painted over to *look* old. Because time whips along too fast these days, and nobody wants to be left behind in the rush toward amnesia.

Of course, some things are not worth remembering and some old songs not worth singing. They weren't so hot the first time around. Who would want to bring back polio season, for example? Or World War I? Or Black Thursday, October 29, 1929? And bring back the Nazis? Never again. God forbid. And for all the romantic and nostalgic images called up by yester-year, there is something to be said for indoor flush toilets. Who wants to shit in the winter in an outhouse? Or live in a hobo jungle by the railroad tracks? The 5¢ cigar ain't never coming back. Nor the 30¢-a-pound steak. But were the Twenties really such a terrific time? Or the Thirties? Or the Fifties? Was 1969 such a good year? Or 1846? It may now be chic to *look* like Rosie the Riveter, but how many girls want to work all day in a defense plant packing parachutes?

What is worth reviving? What better lost? What well remembered? What best forgotten? Should we bring back the birch? Bring back the banjo? Bring back hanging? What makes Bogie revivable? And John Garfield movies hard to find? How does Wendell Corey rate even the Late Late Show, while Hopalong Cassidy gets the dustbin?

I thought about this for a long time. Brooded over it. And wondered, as I flipped the dials on my battered set, if much of the fault did not lie in television. That little box of tubes and gadgets, sitting like another person in the room, demanding to be watched. An alternate nervous system. A substitute brain. Making video idiots out of all of us. Chopping our fantasies off at the knees by shrinking them to postage-stamp size and making us squint to see them. Chasing the Cowboy-Hero off the range and replacing him with sit-com trash, cops and private eyes. Surely the sight of a man on horseback riding across the prairies beats the pants off anybody huddled over the steering wheel of a Ford Mustang. At least both the man and the horse are alive!

After checking all the channels, I decided there was nothing on. Watching *Yoga for Health, Meet the Press,* or another Van Johnson-Wendell Corey creeper was not my idea of a good time. Anyway, the "Gerry Ford Show" had turned me right off. It was too hot in the room to read. I couldn't go back to sleep. It was Indian summer outside. I decided to get up, get myself together, go up to Times Square and take in a movie.

I put on my jeans, grabbed my denim jacket with the "Texas Cattlemen's Association" badge pinned to the collar. The badge, a genuine cowboy relic, had been given to me by a Front Row Friend. It had come to me pinned to a photo of John Wayne, age 4. A funny picture of Duke with a round baby face, curly blond hair, and wearing a frilly white dress, with his fat little baby hands sticking out of the sleeves. You could never have guessed from the photo that this fat child, who looked like a girl, would one day grow up to be John Wayne, the man who shot Liberty Valance and uncountable numbers of other black-hat Bad Guys and what seemed to be the entire Imperial Japanese Army.

John Wayne. I could not abide the big guy's Seventh Cavalry politics. He has been leading that particular charge for 25 years. And the spiritual dilemma he presents frustrates me. I go to all his films. Even *The Green Berets.* Because, well, John Wayne is John Wayne. But I have to go to his movies alone because nobody I know would be caught dead at one. My friends look at me as if I were some sort of neo-Nazi or war criminal. It creates psychic confusion and takes some of the fun out of it.

The Man Who Shot Liberty Valance had been a genuine Late Late Show treat the other night. Seeing the Duke striding around in a giant high-crowned Tom Tyler-type Stetson saying things like: "Liberty Valance is the toughest man south of the picket wire . . . next to me," and finally sending the crazy villain to Boot Hill, making the West safe for James Stewart and the pretty girl, a Front Row Kid just can't keep from cheering. But then the vision creeps in of all those blue-haired Republican Committee women screaming their throats hoarse, and there is John Wayne stirring them up from the high platform and Richard Nixon swearing, "I am not a crook!" And the Front Row cheer sort of chokes in the back of your throat. Say it ain't so, John.

But the Marion Michael Morrison baby picture was funny. And the "Texas Cattlemen's Association" badge was a rare gift. With luck there might be a John Wayne Western showing up in Times Square.

I took a fast look around the hotel room, not expecting to find any of my stuff there when I returned; then I went out and shut the door behind me. Hoping the lock would hold. I was wearing my "Wild Bill Hickok" hat. A wide-brimmed pancake affair with a studded leather band. The kind of hat I imagined was worn in the Old West by the checkered-vest types who never went outside the saloon except to walk over to the whorehouse. I usually only wore it when it rained or threatened to. It had been a good buy in a Forty-second Street hat store that specialized mostly in pimp fedoras and Borsalinos, the kind of hats that, unless you were a 6-foot-tall black man with your game well together, wore you instead of the other way around. The "Wild Bill Hickok" suited me better. And if I got a few funny looks when I was wearing it, if some of the street corner cruisers mistook me for the "Midnight Cowboy," that was their problem. It was my "Wild Bill Hickok" hat and even if it wasn't exactly a ten-gallon white Stetson, it helped me keep in touch with the Front Row Kid fantasy. And it was a damn good bad-weather hat. So what if I looked a little peculiar?

Down in the lobby Chelsea life was going on as usual. A French couple were trying to cash a traveler's check with the desk clerk. The mademoiselle was fashionably trendy and immaculate in the way all French girls are in Claude LeLouch films, in a pair of breathlessly tight flare-bottom jeans and a little tight beige sweater that did not come down to her navel. Her hair was long and Saint-Tropez sun-streaked and looked gently wind-blown even indoors. Her monsieur was a lot older than she was and looked constipated. The desk clerk's French was not quite up to the transaction. Someone was shouting inside the phone booth near the out-of-service elevator in the way some people still do when they are talking long distance. A longhaired freak sat on the naugahyde banquette in the lobby, grinning amiably at nothing in particular, his hair flying out in all directions like a cartoon cat with his finger in a light socket. The colored bellboy pushed an empty Seventh Avenue garment-district trolley through the lobby. (No doubt its original load of mink coats had long ago been fenced, and it served now as a baggage carrier.) Standing just inside the front entrance was a guy dressed in a sailor suit with a small telescope in his hand. There were half a dozen colored silk scarves flowing out from under his blue blouse. He was not a sailor in any navy you ever heard of, but he was definitely at sea. And he scowled at a guy coming in from outside who was in pajamas and toting a Sunday *New York Times*. So I didn't feel at all conspicuous in my "Wild Bill" hat. I could have ridden through the lobby on horseback, herding little dogies while singing "Home on the Range," and nobody would have remarked. Every one of us would have been arrested at the Plaza. Except the French girl. She just might have gotten by on her good looks. She was probably a heroin courier.

And we all could have painted our bodies in stripes like a barber pole and ridden camels up Broadway for all anybody in Times Square would have cared or even noticed. Next to that open-air lunatic asylum, the Chelsea Hotel was as straight as the Yale Club. Coming up from the subway onto Forty-second Street, you are immediately hit with the full catastrophe of humanity. Pimps, whores, junkies, drunks, cops, robbers, bum boys, and transvestites. All the leaners, staggerers, and street screamers on promenade. Hustling, bumming, or simply hanging out, eating garbage and waiting for something to happen to somebody else. Once the show-biz and neon heart of America, Times Square crawls. It is a sordid mess. But still fascinating in its way. If you like raw weirdness. It is about as far away from Cowboy-Heroes as you can get. There are no white-hat Good Guys on this street. Although from time to time there is a high-noon shoot-out. It starts suddenly, ends quickly, and life goes on all around it.

I walked along Forty-second Street with my "Wild Bill Hickok" tipped down low over my forehead, not feeling much like a Cowboy-Hero, sidestepping casualties, and checking out the marquees of the theaters to see what was showing. Forty-second Street was where the double feature was making its last stand. And the marquees of nearly a dozen cockroach palaces hung out over the sidewalk, with running lights flashing around them and the odd block letter put up upside-down. On good days a flicker freak could have much to choose from. But Front Row Kids were no longer as lucky as they might once have been. I had seen *Deep Throat* back in the early days of the wrinkled raincoats, before it became a fashionable thing to be caught seeing. I did not want to see it again, even in a double feature with *The Devil in Miss Jones.* I wasn't in the mood for that stuff. And I did not fancy Kung Fu or any of the half-dozen "blacksploitation" films, which effectively eliminated almost all the theaters from my choice of possibilities.

What I was in the mood for, of course, was a double-feature Western show. But I would settle for a single Western and hope the second feature was at least bearable. If it was good, so much the better. As it happened, and such was my luck, there was only one Western showing on the entire street. It was not a John Wayne. It was an Italo-Franco-Germano-Spano co-production number, *My Name Is Nobody,* starring a languorous Henry Fonda and a synthetic Italian who called himself Terence Hill and was about as genuine and authentic a

Cowboy-Hero as Marcello Mastroianni. I took it as a sign of the times. That such a crossbreed Western could actually pass itself off as the real thing could only mean that I was making my search for the old Cowboy-Heroes very late in the game. I had a moment of serious doubt. But quickly brushed it off, paid my $1.75 to the woman in the bullet-proof ticket booth, and went inside. I didn't care or even bother to notice what the second feature was.

It was bright enough inside the theater to read a book. I walked down the aisle to a front-row seat. There was the heavy sour smell of stink foot in the uncirculating air. Like a second-class compartment on the Orient Express on the third night outbound from Paris, full of Turkish workers. In the aisle seat in the front row there was a guy freaking out. Bare-chested, his shirt rolled up and tied around his waist and his trouser legs rolled up to his knees, he leaped out of his seat, did a little dervish dance in front of the screen with his arms over his head, howled some gibberish, and slumped back down in his seat. Meanwhile, Terence Hill rode across the screen on the back of a mule and blasted everything in sight. I had arrived in the middle of the film and didn't have a clue what was going on. Except that a great many snorting and grimacing desperadoes seemed to be getting shot full of holes and bleeding all over the place. Henry Fonda looked old and hemorrhoidal but spoke in his own voice. Everyone else was dubbed.

These mumbo-jumbo crossbreed Westerns were mutants. Like the weird grotesques who will emerge from the fallout and the rubble 100 years after the H-bomb end of the world. They bore only the faintest resemblance to all those generations of Cowboy-Hero Westerns that had gone before. More than the spirit of the thing was lost in the translation. They had bent the Cowboy-Hero all out of shape with boredom and gross brutality. They were not the sort of image a Front Row Kid could wrap his fantasies around. Unless, perhaps, his secret dream was to be a freeway sniper or a mass murderer. There was more numbness than nobility in the Cowboy-Heroes of Clint Eastwood, Lee Van Cleef, Bud Spencer, Terence Hill, and the other spaghetti Westerners. They clanged with psychotic menace and an oppressive joylessness. As I watched Terence Hill blow away another deformed and seemingly mentally retarded Bad Guy, I could not help wondering if, indeed, no Westerns at all might not be better than *some* Westerns. Had it finally come to this? I got up from my seat, careful not to rouse the strange man in the aisle seat who appeared now to be asleep, his head dangling at a sharp angle over the back of his seat as if his neck were broken, tipped my "Wild Bill Hickok" over my eyes, and walked out. It was only the third time in my life I had walked out of a Western in the middle of it. Mercifully, I had long ago amnesiaed the names of the other two. I needed air badly.

I headed down toward lower Manhattan to look at the water and the Brooklyn Bridge and to sit for a while in the Paris Bar down on Peck Slip in the fish market, which was usually deserted on a Sunday afternoon. I needed to think about some things. The Paris Bar was as good a place as any for that. The Paris Bar only came to life at night when the fish market was going. During the day it just echoed emptiness like those old ghost-town saloons. It was a good place to go to talk backward to yourself. I am sentimental about the past, but I did not want to rush back into it without thinking it over. After all, I *was* a little too old for playing cowboys in the yard.

Was this the blast from the past I really wanted to go in search of? If I was looking for the Ultimate Truth in the rearview mirror, might I not find it somewhere else? On some other voyage of discovery? There was someone in another country with truths to tell, whom I hadn't seen or heard from in half a decade or so. Could I possibly find out where she had disappeared herself to? That particular trail had gone cold long ago. But had once, by chance, run right through the Paris Bar where I was heading. Hell with it. Maybe I ought to just go back to my room at the Chelsea and watch television into eternity. It had been over 20 years since the last posse of real Cowboy-Heroes had ridden off into the sunset. Who was still alive? What did they have to say? And frankly, Scarlett, who gave a damn? If the Front Row Kids today only had Disney's talking Volkswagens and Italo-Franco-Germano-Spano Cowboy-Heroes and late-model John Wayne to cheer, then they were truly fantasy-deprived. Would they even know a Cow-boy-Hero if they saw one?

The question met its answer. A block from the Paris Bar two small raggedy dead-end kids, who were lugging one of those "velvet" paintings in a broken wooden frame, stopped to stare at me. They were probably around 10 years old, and the frame was almost as tall as they were. They were having trouble keeping it off the ground and at the same time seeing over the top. I could not see the picture clearly at first. They had the thing turned around and upside-down and hanging half out of the frame.

"You from Texas?" one of the boys asked me in the same tone of wonder he might have used to a Martian.

"What?"

"You from Texas, huh?" He looked me up and down. From my boots to my "Wild Bill."

"Maybe," I said. What the hell?

"What's that badge?" the other kid asked, taking a finger out of his nose and pointing it toward my jacket.

"Texas Cattlemen's Association," I said.

"You from Texas police?" asked the first.

"Gee," said the other.

I didn't say anything. I thought it was funny and ironically appropriate for these dread-filled times that these two boys, who could have been Front Row Kids, who could have been *me*, would automatically and instinctively think "cop" and not "cowboy." The first kid came around from behind the paint-ing, leaving the little nose picker to hold it up by himself. It was pretty clear which kid would have been Smiley Burnette every afternoon in the back-yard cowtown, and which one would have been Gene Autry.

"D'ya have two guns?" asked the bold one.

"No, just one."

"One?" He sounded disappointed.

"You don't need more than one." I said. Who did I think I was? Randolph Scott?

"You have one of those belts?" The boy's hand went around his waist by way of sign language.

"Yup."

"You ever shoot anyone?"

"Nope." Pure Gary Cooper!

"Gee," said the sidekick, picking away. "Rob any banks?"

"Yeah. Do they have a lot of bank robbings over there in Texas?"

"Not just Texas," I said. "Fellow'll rob a bank wherever he finds one." The conversation was getting peculiar.

"Can you arrest people in New York?"

"No. There are more than enough police in New York to do that." As if I could arrest anybody, anywhere!

"What kind of cigarettes they got over in Texas?" Cigarettes! Did they think I was G.I. Joe? Hey Joe, got cigarettes? Chocolate? In a minute they would be asking me if I wanted to buy their sister.

"Same as here," I said. "It's all the same country."

"Yeah, but it's far."

"Pretty far." I had never been there.

"You going back there today?"

"Not today."

"You stay around here? In New York?" The little dead-end kid would have made a good cop. He was naturally nosy.

"Maybe. You boys live around here?"

"Over there." He pointed to a block of flats across a junk-yard.

"You wanna buy a painting?" asked the kid who was holding it up.

"Where did you steal it?"

"We didn't," said the first kid. "We're selling it for three dollars. A guy told us to sell it."

"Let's see it."

They helped each other turn it around without falling over it. Velvet paintings were the sort of thing you won at the county fair for knocking over milk bottles. They were usually grotesque pictures of Martin Luther King, Jr., JFK and Bobby, Pancho Villa, Mexican señoritas, or bare-breasted African queens. This particular one was none of those. It was a bizarre painting of John Wayne in his *True Grit* disguise! Complete with eye patch! I nearly shit. Its failed three-dimensional effect

made it so ugly and weird that it was almost sickening. It was
also terrific. Rooster Cogburn! Was it an omen? Some peculiar
signal to help me come to a decision? Or merely sheer dumb
coincidence?

"Holy shit!" I said to keep my jaw from hitting the pavement.

"You like it? You wanna buy it?" The first kid was coming
on like a pitchman in front of a strip club. The other one just
stood there, stroking the velvet.

I wanted to buy it. In its awful way, it was irresistible. It was
perfect.

"Do you kids know who that is?"

"Nah," said the little pitchman.

"The Lone Ranger," said the sidekick.

We all looked at it as if waiting for it to speak, to say its name.

"Three bucks," said the kid again. It didn't matter to him
who it was. "You wanna buy it?"

"No." I didn't need it. I knew who John Wayne was.

From the direction of the Paris Bar a guy staggered toward
us.

"Hey, Jimmy," the kid called to him. "Ya wanna buy a painting?" They lugged the thing away to show him, leaving me
standing there. No sale.

"My name ain't Jimmy," I heard the guy say. "It's Willy." He
would never buy the thing, either.

"So long, boys," I called to them. And considered for a moment waving my hat to them like Tom Mix would have done.
I decided not to. It would have been foolish.

Back at the Chelsea in the early evening the street creepers
were out like crows in a wheat field. They pretty much
minded their own business and did not have a lot to say. Mostly
they just stood around the street trying to focus and cop small
change from strangers. One old guy, in full wino trim, a
grease-stained old Eisenhower jacket, a pair of shiny trousers,
and rubbish-heap sneakers, was drawing some attention to
himself by going out into the middle of the street and pointing
his backside up at oncoming buses while he beat a rhythm on

the concrete with a set of drumsticks. It was only a matter of time before the cops would come and close down his show.

Coming down Twenty-third Street from the corner deli with a tuna-fish sandwich to go, my path was blocked by a man in an old N-1 jacket and a leather cap. He looked to be in his late fifties, but you couldn't really tell with these guys.

"Hey, Chelsea cowboy," he said. "Can you spare some change for a fellow?" He had a sipping bag in his hand. His lower jaw protruded slightly, and you could have set fire to his breath.

"Why not?" I said. I gave over a quarter and put a finger to the brim of my "Wild Bill Hickok" in a kind of salute. He snapped a return salute.

"Where's your horse, cowboy?" he said to show me he was not completely whacked out and had a sense of wry humor.

"Parked it at a hydrant. Got towed away."

"Nah," he said. "You're no cowboy." He twisted the sipping bag around the neck of his bottle and looked me over. "Lemme guess . . . betcha yer a writer."

I felt a little foolish. "Sort of," I said.

"Ah hah!" he said with a triumphant flourish. "Thomas Wolfe. Brrrendan Bee-han. Dylan Thomas." He jerked his thumb over his shoulder toward the Chelsea. They were the names on the commemorative plaque at the entrance. Fine writers who had spent some time at the Chelsea and done battle with the roaches. I was a little surprised he knew of them. New Yorkers, even sober ones, are not known for paying attention to that sort of thing. (I had once asked a grounds-keeper at Yankee Stadium who the plaques in center field were for. He couldn't tell me. "I only work here," he had said.)

"Well, not exactly," I said. He had lumped me in pretty heavy company.

"Whadda ya write about?" It was a strange conversation to be having with a dero who had just cadged your small change.

"Cowboys," I said. What the hell. There are times when I will talk to anybody who will listen to me. "Western-movie Cowboy-Heroes," I said. In one ear and out the other. What he said next was most unexpected.

"Fred Thomson." He grinned as if he had just said the magic

word and was waiting for the duck to come down with the money. "Ever hearda him? He was before your time."

"Yeah. I sure have." Fred Thomson, the silent-movie Cowboy-Hero who was almost as popular as Tom Mix and wore a giant Stetson like the Arby's Roast Beef sign. You had to go a long way back to come up with his name. Son-of-a-gun!

"Buck Jones!" he said. Now his blurry eyes were alight, and he was grinning with the funny pride of someone who knows he has faked you right out of your socks by telling you something you never thought he would say. Not your usual wino gibberish, his grin seemed to say. Gotcha that time!

"One of the best."

"That's right. That's right. There was a real cowboy for ya. Got killed in the Coconut Grove fire. Died a heeero!" He was becoming excited.

"Yeah, yeah," I said. "That was in 1942." I was getting pretty excited myself.

"Bet yer surprised I know about that. Didn't think I'd know that, didja?" This was *definitely* not the usual wino gibberish. "Wanna know how I know?"

"Sure."

"I know because I was there."

"No shit."

"Yeah. In Boston. Where it happened. During the war that was."

"Right." I was amazed.

"Yeah. I was stationed up there. In the navy, you know. Couple of us guys was drinking at a joint right down the street when that fire started. We went over to see it. That was the night Buck Jones died. I'll never forget that night." So this guy had his own rear-view mirror.

I didn't know what to say to that. Buck Jones. One of the Big Four. Went all the way back to the days of Tom Mix. Only Tim McCoy was still alive. Someplace.

And here was an old wino who probably had trouble remembering most things, telling me he was there, standing in front of the Coconut Grove in Boston on the night Buck Jones died.

"Hey, man, what was it like? What happened?"

"Oh, it was something. I'll say that. A big fire. We were all out there. A little drunk, you know." He grinned. "Somebody said the Grove was burning down, and we all went over to see it. Maybe help out, bein' as we were navy men and had some service puttin' out fires. It was a tragedy, you know. Really terrible. All those people gettin' burned alive in there. It was in the winter. Around Thanksgivin' or somethin'. The water from the hoses was freezin'. And that Buck Jones, he died a hero tryin' to rescue people out of it. It was a big fire. A helluva fire. I oughtta know, bein' in the navy."

The guy was right. Buck Jones, a Cowboy-Hero since the Twenties, had been on a war-bond drive and personal-appearance tour. He just happened to be at the Coconut Grove Night Club doing some celebrating when the holiday trimmings in the place caught fire. The club was gutted in no time. Whoosh. It was a little before my time, but it was one of those things a Front Row Kid just naturally knew about.

"Wow," I said, sounding stupid.

"Ya gonna write about that?"

"Maybe." I wanted to sit him down in the Horn & Hardart and pump him for details. I'd even buy him a wedge of pie.

Just then a police hurry-up wagon pulled up to the curb to take the old drumstick beater out of the middle of the street. Ducking under his flailing drumsticks, the cops picked him up by the armpits and carried him along. A small crowd gathered to watch it. A colored guy with a sipping bag began to applaud. The bag slipped out of his hand and smashed on the pavement. "Sumbitch," he said. And one of the cops gave him a menacing look that said there was still some room in the wagon. My eyewitness decided it was time for him to be shuffling along.

"Listen," he said, "d'ya think ya could . . ."

I gave him another quarter. He shook my hand. We exchanged salutes as before. "Good luck, mister," he said. "Hope ya get yer horse out all right."

"See ya later, pardner," I said.

The day, in its weird way, had definitely gotten better since its disappointing start with the unholy pardon. I went into the Chelsea to pack my gear. I would be checking out in the morning. If my 1961 Dodge Seneca, the last of the big-fin jobs, held out, I was heading West.

The Old Cowtowns
They Ain't What
They Used To Be

Shane: "Joey, tell your mother there aren't
any more guns in the valley."
Joey: "Shane, come back!"

The old Dodge threw its exhaust somewhere between St.
Louis and Kansas City, in the middle of nowhere at 4 o'clock
in the morning. The shit kicker at an all-night Kansas garage
couldn't fix it, so he rigged up a bent-wire coat hanger to keep
it from falling into the road.
"How far to Dodge City?"
"About 250 to 300 miles."
"It's a bigger state than I thought."
"There's nothin' in Dodge."
"I just want to see it."
"I think you'll be disappointed."
"I *know* I will be."
The old Dodge roared out of the station like a bronchitic
dinosaur. There was no chance I'd fall asleep at the wheel with
all that racket. I could get it fixed in Dodge City.
Dodge City. A magic name to trail-herding cowboys, buffalo
hunters, dancehall girls, tinhorn gamblers, and every Front
Row Kid who ever imagined a wild and woolly cowtown. A
must stop if you happen to be heading West in search of old
Hollywood Cowboys. Just to see it.
I had stopped off along the way from New York at my home

32

town to try to shake loose some of the old visions of the days when I galloped around my back-yard cowtown. And to collect my cowboy junk from a trunk in the basement where my parents kept my childhood all these years on the odd chance that someday I would want to go down there to have a look at it. Parents do that. In some ways they remember your childhood better than you do. And they keep it in a trunk in the basement and on the walls in the upstairs hallway. All the old cowboy junk. The old, dusty, cracked leather cowboy boots with the Hopalong Cassidy spurs, the battered cowboy hat, the lunch pail. Old phonograph records of Gene Autry singing "Back in the Saddle Again," "Home on the Range," and "Tumbling Tumbleweeds." Old Lone Ranger comics. A set of Hopalong Cassidy books (revised Mulford editions). And pictures of me in my cowboy outfit, at the age of ten or so, pointing my six-gun straight ahead at the camera like George F. Barnes in *The Great Train Robbery.* I am fat and silly-looking in these photographs. "You were the cutest little cowboy," my mother said. And we had a few laughs over the memory of it as I threw the stuff in the trunk of the Dodge. I may never look at it again. But I might as well have it with me. As long as I'm going that way.

For a moment I debated whether to take along the shoe boxes full of old baseball cards. But they do not really fit into the picture. Baseball came a little later, along with girls and school dances and pimples and anxieties. "Sell them," I said to my mother, "and send me the money."

So now I was tooling along the flat nothingness of east and central Kansas with a trunkful of cobwebbed Cowboy-Hero memories. And hoping I wouldn't be too disappointed by Dodge City. The roar of the busted muffler was driving me crazy. In earlier times it would have stampeded all the buffalo on the plains. But they were long gone, butchered to build the railroad. If this had once been the heartland of the Wild West Tale, the end of the Chisholm Trail, the land of rustlers and gunfighters and two-gun marshals, it didn't look much like it now. And neither did Dodge City.

Wyatt Earp would not have recognized Dodge City, Kansas.

He and "Doc" Holliday and Bat Masterson would have thrown their arms around each other and wept.

Coming upon the outskirts of Dodge City on Kansas 56 in the early evening, you smelled the place long before you saw it. The choking odor of manure hung over the plains like a cattle driver's saddle blanket after three months on the Santa Fe Trail. Pee-yew. Dodge City was bracketed by giant fertilizer processing plants that pumped stink into the air day and night. Between them, Dodge City sat under a cloud, in putrid parenthesis. Yeccch! A perpetual reminder of Dodge City's hay-daze, 1875–1885, when three million head of cattle passed through its stockyards on the way to the meat markets and shoe factories back East. And thousands of rowdy cowpokes crossed horns with the Dodge City "Peace Commission," and not all of them lived to carry the tale back down to Texas. And out of those cow pies and shootouts countless Wild West Tales and Western movies were fashioned. I held my nose and drove on into Dodge.

The main drag was called Wyatt Earp Boulevard. It ran parallel and right alongside the tracks of the Atchison, Topeka & Santa Fe. Smack in the center of town on Wyatt Earp Boulevard was something called "the World Famous Boot Hill" and a replica of old Front Street. I tried hard to fantasize the old cowtown as I drove along Wyatt Earp, to imagine myself a stranger who had just ridden in off the trail ready for a bath, a bottle of whiskey, and a dancehall girl. The fantasy refused to fly. Dodge City, flat, low to the ground, and mostly open spaces, seemed a sleepy little town. Far removed by something more than miles and time from that old Dodge City of the Wild West Tales.

Down the street, an *American Graffiti* car-hop drive-in seemed to be the liveliest place in town. I drove up with my muffler growling and my stomach rumbling. The parking area was crowded with motorcycles and hot rods. And high school heroes and spotty-faced teen-age girls who looked at me as if they thought I was crazy; I had the feeling they were giggling at my hat. I wondered what it must be like to live in a town where the main street is called Wyatt Earp Boulevard and the only place to go at night is the local hamburger stand. I downed a cheeseburger that was awful and a coke that was flat and drove away in search of the oldest hotel in town. I was dead tired and half deaf.

I found the Lora Locke Hotel three blocks east of Boot Hill on the corner of Central and Gunsmoke. Gunsmoke!?! The Lora Locke was a wonderful, gloomy old brick hotel. The ghostly lobby was wide open, and from the first floor you could look down on the leathery railroad switchmen in bib overalls playing checkers. The whole place echoed with your footsteps. But nobody looked up or even seemed to notice. As if they had been frozen in some vague distant past. Perhaps not as far back as Wyatt Earp but a long time before that hamburger stand got built. A fine old place, the Lora Locke was by no means elegant, but it was dignified in its creaking silence. Just the sort of hotel you would expect to find in Dodge City, even if Dodge City turned out to be not quite what you expected. I bought two pulp magazines and rented a room with a bath for 10 dollars.

On my bed I opened one of the pulps to an interview with Gene Autry. But I was too tired to read it, so I just looked at the pictures. There were shots of Gene and Champion the Wonder Horse in action right out of a Front Row Kid's best memories. And a page of pictures as he looks today. Old and round as a barrel. The rest of the magazine was full of pictures of stagecoaches and bullet-riddled gunfighters. I could barely keep my eyes open. I fell asleep looking at the pictures. And drove 3,000 miles in my dreams. All the miles I had come and all those I had still to go.

Dodge City morning was cool and fresh. The sun was up; the sky was clear blue without a cloud in it. And the air did not stink of shit. I took the Dodge to the Dodge City garage. And went on foot exploring.

Boot Hill and "historic" old Front Street were monstrous fakes. As I knew they would be. But I didn't mind that. What distressed me most was that the place seemed to be dedicated not so much to the memory of that rough-and-tumble Dodge

City of the Wild West Tale, Wyatt Earp, "Doc" Holliday, and
Bat Masterson, but to the television series *Gunsmoke*. To
"Doc" and "Miss Kitty" and that big lunk "Matt Dillon." Shee-
it, I reckon. Here was an old and famous prairie cowtown with
genuine links to real trail herders, gunfighters, and frontier
marshals. And the giant statue standing like a tower in the
middle of the mockup Front Street was of Marshal Dillon. My
disappointment was keen. I wanted to register a complaint
with someone. I stared up at the giant statue. It looked as tall
as a smokestack, but I was unmoved. It was dressed in Marshal
Dillon clothes, but the rifle the big hands were supposed to be
curved around had disappeared, making Marshal Dillon appear to be a limp-wristed cowboy indeed. And whoever built
the thing slipped up even more outrageously by putting him
in shoes instead of cowboy boots. It was too much for an old
Front Row Kid to endure. To have come all this way to find
the Dodge City of my fantasies had abdicated its traditions to
crypto-Disneyland fakery and boob-toob Cowboy-Heroes.
How fucking sad.

Behind the false fronts of false Front Street a casual tourist
will find the predictable souvenir parlor, a somewhat jumbled
Western museum with exhibits of an old-time bank, a frontier
doctor's office, an 1870 general store, a barbershop, an apothe-
cary shop, and a frontier marshal's office. There is also an
"old-fashioned" ice cream parlor that features 14 different flavors. And at the "Long Branch Saloon" you can buy
3.2 beer and "sarsaparilla" (Kansas is a "dry" state) and for a
nickel see *Thru a Knothole;* or, *The Bathhouse Exposed, The
Dance of the 7 Veils,* and Clean Clara in *Nymph in the Nude*
in an old-fashioned peep show. On a wall in the Boot Hill
Museum there are framed photographs of honorary Boot Hill
marshals: Duke Ellington (??), Joel McCrea, Tex Ritter, Rex
Allen, Tim Holt, Roy Rogers, James Arness, Hugh O'Brien,
and a 1966 picture of Congressman Gerald Ford in a baggy
suit.

In the museum, though, there was an old newspaper carrying a small ad: "J. H. Holliday, dentist, very respectfully offers
his professional services to the citizens of Dodge City and

surrounding country during the summer. Office at room no.
24, Dodge House. Where satisfaction is not given money will
be refunded."

It looked genuine enough. I wondered how many of "Doc"
Holliday's patients had asked for their money back.

As I walked away from Front Street, the Santa Fe came
barreling through town. And I waved my "Wild Bill Hickok"
hat at the engineer. Then I went to look for the marshal of
Dodge City. Maybe he could help me call up a Wyatt Earp
daydream. On the way I stopped in front of City Hall to look
at a memorial plaque:

> In honor to all
> veterans of Ford
> County who lost their
> lives in the Vietnam
>   conflict
>   dedicated
> November 11, 1973
>   by
> American GI Forum
> American Legion
> Boothill Marines Inc.
> Disabled American Veterans
> Veterans of Foreign Wars
> Veterans of WW I

There were eight names engraved on it. Even Dodge City
had helped to pay the blood bill on that gross Asian Wild West
Show.

It seems there is no marshal of Dodge City. And the sheriff
was out. The desk officer in the sheriff's office let me speak to
the under sheriff. Name of Horton. He came out, friendly-like,
wearing black-rimmed glasses and a blue-gray zipper jacket
with a Dodge City/Ford County Sheriff's Department patch
on one shoulder and an American flag patch on the other. A
pearl-handled and deadly looking silver-blue .44 Magnum
peeked out from under his jacket. After quickly explaining to
him that I was just passing through on a private tour of Wild

West cowtowns, he decided there was no need to frisk me and
led the way into his office.

He told me that Charlie Basset was the first sheriff of Ford
County, from 1873 to 1878. And that Bat Masterson was the
second. Then he hauled out a pack of photographs of all the
former sheriffs of Ford County.

"Tourists come to Dodge and want to know if I'm Chester
or Matt Dillon," said Under Sheriff Horton, expecting a laugh
out of me but getting only a grimace. "TV's been a good deal
for Dodge. Gunsmoke used to be called Walnut Street, but we
changed it when the show came on. And we had a big deal
with Matt Dillon and Kitty coming to town for the occasion.
Wyatt Earp over there used to be called Chestnut Street until
about fifteen years ago."

"Why change it?" I asked him.

"Oh, for the tourists, I guess," he said. "We've had about two
hundred and fifty thousand tourists. They used to run more,
but Interstate Seventy is a hundred miles north, and that cuts
it down. People don't like to get off the Interstate. Didn't used
to have all this stuff. The original Front Street's been torn
down for years. Burned down. It was actually a couple of
blocks over from the one we got now. The community decided
to put up this new replica of Front Street as a tourist attraction
and a historical thing. Folks who come into Dodge want to see
something of the Old West, you know."

"But it's mostly *Gunsmoke* and Matt Dillon," I said, register-
ing my protest. "There never was a marshal named Matt Dillon. He never existed. It strikes me as being peculiar." You
can't protest too much to an under sheriff with a .44 Magnum.

"Well, you know, that show's been so popular I guess folks
kinda expect to see something to do with the characters they
seen on TV. And you know, that Kitty, Miss Kitty is a real fine
lady. Amanda what's-her-name?"

"Blake."

"Amanda Blake. She was here when we named the street.
Signing autographs and all that. She didn't put on any airs. The
kids like to see that, I guess. Anyway, it's been good for the
town."

"What kind of town is Dodge?"

"Oh, pretty quiet. Not like New York. People here like to take things quiet. The county's over a thousand square miles. About sixteen thousand people. Mostly agriculture and some cattle. And the big fertilizing plants."

"No shit," I said without thinking.

"There's still some cattle rustling, you know. A while back, not too long ago, we had forty head stolen and one horse. Horse started out a stud and ended up a filly. Fellow had a semi he was taking the cattle to Omaha in. Stopped for a cup of coffee and this other fellow just drove off with his livestock. Took off. Sold 'em, bought himself a T-Bird, and took off. The horse wound up down in Mountain Home, Arkansas. The fellow got himself arrested down in Tulsa. We get that sort of thing from time to time. There's no compulsory brand inspection and anybody can take fifty head and run 'em in the sale bins. I'll tell you, though, the biggest crime we got around here is check bouncing. Haven't had a shootin' for a month or so, I guess. Had a stabbin' here couple of months ago. Nothin' like the old days."

"What prompted the shooting?"

"A woman," the under sheriff said in a way that made you think there couldn't possibly be any other reason for a shooting and that it was a stupid question.

I didn't know what else I wanted to ask the under sheriff. And when he leaned back in his chair and hauled out two kilos of grass just confiscated in a drug bust, and I thought I detected a slight snarl in his tone as he talked about rounding up dopers, I figured it was time to be moseying along. The conversation reminded me that I was carrying. Gulp.

"Well, I guess I'll be going now," I said, getting up and shaking hands. "Thanks for the information."

"Not at all. Hope you like our little town. You stayin' long?"

"Not very," I said.

He walked me out to the front door and waved me off. I decided not to put on my hat until I had turned the corner.

Shortly after high noon I was back in the saddle. Driving past the manure factory on the outskirts of Dodge City. Out-

side of town there were genuine Santa Fe Trail ruts permanently worn into the earth by all the cattle drives that used to
end up here in the heart of the Wild West Tale. A long time
ago.

If I drove without stopping and was not attacked by Comanches in Indian Territory, I figured to make Tombstone, Arizona, by the following night. Giddyap you old Dodge Seneca!

Everybody has his "spiritual place," his fantasy place. Some
town or stretch of land or mountain peak that triggers, by the
mere thought of its name, a range of magical fantasies. It may
be a place you once lived in and loved. Or a place you have
never seen but have read about or heard tell of in legends and
myths, or have only seen in the movies. It may be some place
like Khartoum that holds the magic. Or Fort Lamy in Chad.
It may be Nepal or New Orleans or an island in the Pacific. It
may be associated in your imagination with an ancient time
long gone. Or written up on the front page of tomorrow's
newspaper. As much as anything else, this place, wherever it
is, is an idea in your mind. A kind of soul place through which
you can keep in touch with your personal make-believe. A
place to place your daydreams. If you have never actually
been there except in your imagination, the chances are good
that if you ever do go, the sense of disappointment will be
bitter. Reality may even ruin the thing for you altogether. But
sometimes the fantasy becomes even richer if you've walked
the dusty streets or climbed the thing or maybe just laid over
for an hour at its airport while changing planes. For me Paris
is one of those places. It has me by the life, and I will never
get free of it. And do not wish to. Another place and name that
rings magic is Tombstone, Arizona. But Tombstone, unlike
Paris, I had never visited except in daydreams and Wild West
Tales. And I did not wish to go there any other way until I
drew a line on the map and headed southwest from Dodge
City. What the hell. It was on the way to wherever it was I was
going.

I had seen *My Darling Clementine* enough times. And
Gunfight at the O.K. Corral. I knew the name and legend of

Wyatt Earp and "Doc" Holliday since my first Front Row Kid days, the way an English schoolboy knows King Arthur and the Knights of the Round Table. I had watched the TV series and knew the theme song: "Wyatt Earp, Wyatt Earp/ Brave courageous and bold/ Long live his fame and long live his glory/ And long may his story be told." I had fought the Clantons and the McLaurys in the back yard in front of the garage. I bought this Wild West Tale completely and counted it among my favorites.

Wyatt Earp had seemed to me a Knight and a glorious Cowboy-Hero. I preferred him to all the other real-life Westerners whose exploits had become legendary, and who symbolized those old frontier days of virtue and violence. Of course, like all the rest, Earp had been completely whitewashed and sanitized. There was nothing in the legend about whorehouses, gambling, and pistol-whipping. And when the legend hit the movies, that clinched it. A 20-foot-tall Henry Fonda could never be mistaken for a pistol-whipping bully. And even later, when a little truth crept in, showing Earp to be, if not a licensed killer, at least a cold-blooded, cynical, and corrupt lawman who cared more for his 25 percent interest in all the cowtown's gambling and whoring than for order and good citizenship, the truth only made him all the more interesting. And the truth made Earp's gun buddy, "Doc" Holliday, nothing short of fascinating. A crazed and consumptive ex-dentist turned professional gambler and killer with a death wish. A psycho gunfighter whose weirdness made him fearless. Wyatt Earp called "Doc" Holliday the "most dangerous man alive." And Earp would know. The two of them made quite a pair. In truth and in make-believe, a hell of a lot more interesting than Paul Newman and Robert Redford ever could be. And their legend would forever be linked to that magical frontier place, Tombstone.

Coming down to Tombstone from Dodge City as Earp and Holliday had done in 1879 (except that they did not travel in a Dodge Seneca with Elton John singing to them on the car radio), I was ready for whatever Tombstone turned out to be. It was enough that it was there. And if I should find it to be nothing more than a Howard Johnson's/McDonald's oasis without one fantasy vision to be squeezed out of it, I didn't think I would mind all that much.

Easy riding through Oklahoma. Indian Territory of the Wild West Tales. You begin to see the kind of scenery and landscape that was so familiar from all those Saturday Matinees. And much of it hasn't changed a great deal since the trail-herding days. If you ride the back roads and two-lane blacktops, there is nothing out on the wide-open spaces but the odd cow sitting by a fence. If you squint into the sunset, you can almost see bands of Comanches riding along a ridge or a cowpoke slouched in the saddle coming in from the range or a rancher's daughter tearing along in the distance in a runaway buckboard with Gene Autry galloping to the rescue. And as you drive through the one-horse towns like Laverne, Oklahoma, where they do not know what year it is and there is a giant banner stretched across the main and only street reading, "Welcome to Laverne. Home of Jane Jayroe Miss America 1967" and Elton John gives up the airwaves to Johnny Cash singing "Ragged Old Flag," you are unmistakably traveling backward to where the Wild West Tale still holds. And you don't look out of place driving a 14-year-old car and wearing a "Wild Bill Hickok" hat. And when you walk down the street while the car is getting gassed up, you don't have the paranoid, tingling fear that some stranger is going to rush at you and hit you upside the head for your small change. On the other hand, you don't want to go into a bar wearing a "McGovern for President" badge because you never can tell with these cowboys. Or perhaps it is just my imagination. Like any foreign country, you have to spend some time here to know what the natives are really like.

Texas. White stripe on the highway. Driving across the stovepipe in the middle of the night, that is all you see under a big sky. And the head- and taillights of a continuous convoy of big rigs hauling their loads through the night. You could be anywhere. When you've seen one Interstate you've seen them all. From what little I already know about Texas, that LBJ was born there, that JFK was shot there, and that Mission Control lives there, I do not burn to stop and stay awhile. Best to leave Texas to the Texans. And let Larry McMurtry write about the shit kickers and the last picture show. Horseman, pass by.

New Mexico is better. The sun comes up behind me. The hills are painted.

I pull into a tiny joint in a place called Truth or Consequences for breakfast at dawn. I do not usually bother with breakfast. But who can resist a place called Truth or Consequences? The gas gauge registers E-minus. There is nothing in the tank but fumes. And I am vibrating with wonder and fatigue.

At the counter sits a big leathery cowboy, dressed in well-worn denims, shit-covered pointy-toed boots the size of gunboats, and a straw summer Stetson. He is eating a stack of flapjacks as high as a mountain. I sit down a few stools away. In awe of the image. The waitress, bee-hived and big-hipped, with Maxwell House eyes and an upside-down nametag, NƎƎᴚOᗡ (it looked right-side-up to her), came up with a menu and a glass of water.

"Morning?" she said, as if she were no more sure of it than I was. "Coffee right away?"

"Why not? Sure." I never drank the stuff. Hated coffee.

"Be anything else with that?"

"Same as him," I said, pointing my thumb toward the cowboy.

"You bet," she said, and went off to fetch an order of flapjacks. Or to cook them herself. I didn't know.

Out of the corner of my eye I watched the cowboy put away his breakfast. His hands were enormous. A hunk of flapjack dripped syrup off the end of the small fork held in his fist. His face under the Stetson, which he did not bother to take off while he ate, looked like the old Santa Fe Trail ruts. His neck was red. He made the Marlboro Man look like a fairy ballet dancer. He had the air about him, the way. He might have stepped right out of a Wild West Tale. He probably still believed them. My flapjacks came about the time he was finishing his. It was too late to try to strike up a conversation. I don't know what I would have said. And whatever it might have been, unless he answered "yup" and "nope" and "mebbe," I risked ruining the fantasy. He dismounted from his stool and went out picking at his teeth. "See ya later," he said to the air. Perfect. Too much. I thought of asking DOREEN about him, but I didn't want to find out he was a used-car dealer. The early-morning cowboy of Truth or Consequences, N.M.

Old HWY 80 dips from Lordsburg, N.M., down to Douglas, Arizona, on the Mexican border and climbs up to Tombstone through the back door. Off into the distance for part of the way are the Chiracahua Mountains. They are not as splendid as the Rockies or the Grand Canyon up north, but they make a genuine Wild West Tale heroic landscape. Geronimo and Cochise once hung out here, and those tribes of Apaches who were made out to be the trickiest and most crazed and bloodthirsty of the Saturday Matinee injuns. It was a misleading and false depiction ("the only good injun is a dead injun"), warped and dishonest. But we bought it as Front Row Kids and sometimes slept in our beds buried deep in our blankets against the chance that some wild Apache might tiptoe in on moccasined feet in the middle of the night with designs on our scalps.

I parked the Dodge on the side of the road and climbed up into the rocks. I had been driving like a mad fucker, but there was no hurry . . .

I am the only person around here as far as the eye can see. The sky is blue with a few clouds like smoke signals rising above the far hills. In the distance across the flats the Chiracahuas in sun-haze and soft focus look like the land of the moon. Wyatt Earp must have seen them like this and been glad he left Dodge City. The Indians knew them like the back of their hands. There are no Howard Johnson's as far as I can tell. And it is silent as prehistory except for the flies buzzing and the crackling of the brush and undergrowth. And there are cactus and mesquite and tumbling tumbleweeds and all that good Wild West shit. I can see how the Wild West Tale could only have come out of land like this. And how the lonesome cowboy could be seen as a heroic figure moving across it. It is a long way from the winos and weirdos of Twenty-third Street. I enjoy sitting on this rock in the middle of the wide-open spaces. And that surprises me. As a rule, I prefer crowds and bus fumes to emptiness and fresh air. Maybe all this Front Row Kid fantasy stuff is getting to me.

Tombstone. The name rings with 100-year-old echoes. Forty-five hundred feet up. In plain view of the Dragoon Mountains (another Cochise stomping ground). It was born out of a silver prospector's bearded weirdness and a lucky strike. "All you'll find is your tombstone," the soldiers at Fort Huachuca were said to have teased old crazy Ed Schieffelin as he set out to pickax his way around the San Pedro hills. So when he made his strike in September of '77, he named his first silver claim "the Tombstone." Word of it spread like rolling thunder and earth tremors throughout the Southwest. In no time at all, Tombstone was a boom town. Miners, prospectors, cooks and drummers, hustlers, fortune hunters, con men, gamblers, and gunmen dropped whatever they were doing and rushed to the silver strike like whores following armies. And the whores came, too. Along with thousands of other no-gooders, ne'er-do-wells, and some businessmen and good citizens who fancied their chances. Tombstone never slept in those days. And, inevitably, Law, too, came to Tombstone. Wyatt Earp and his good buddy John Holliday (who had heard the dry air of Arizona Territory might be good for his health). By January 1881, there were over 14,000 people settled in Tombstone, with more than a few of them dealing in some kind of trouble.

The Earps (Wyatt, Morgan, Virgil, James, and Warren) and ready-for-anything "Doc" Holliday had come down from Dodge in '79 with the hope of opening a stage line and tearing off a good piece of all that action and loose money. The stage deal fell through, and Wyatt bought into the gambling concession that rattled away day and night in the Crystal Palace Saloon, while Holliday settled himself more or less permanently behind a card hand at one of the poker tables. But the Earps soon figured out that the way to put a hammer lock on the spoils of the silver town was to be the Law. Wyatt was already a U.S. marshal, and when the job of Cochise County sheriff suddenly opened up (along with the head of the previous sheriff, who had used it to stop a bullet from the .45 of Curly Bill Brocius), Earp wanted the sheriff's star to go with his marshal's badge. He lost out, however, to a certain Johnny Behan, who was owned by Ike Clanton, a grisly rustler who already had a blood feud going with the Earps. Virgil Earp was the town marshal, and the family would have had the territory wired if it weren't for Clanton and *his* sheriff. Tombstone was that kind of town.

On October 26, 1881, the Earp-Clanton feud was settled with dreadful finality. By city charter and territorial ordinance, guns were banned inside the city limits. On that day, Ike Clanton was caught packing a piece inside the line, Virgil Earp's turf. He was disarmed by Virgil and Morgan, who also thumped him for good measure. Wyatt pistol-whipped Tom McLaury, a Clanton crony, and ordered them to hightail it out of town if they knew what was good for them. Surprisingly, the Clantons, who were mean as junkyard dogs and just as smelly, decided to take their advice. But not fast enough to suit the marshals. Later in the day, Morgan, Virgil, and Wyatt Earp and "Doc" Holliday came a-gunning for their enemies. They found Ike and Billy Clanton, Tom and Frank McLaury, and Billy Claiborne saddling up at the O.K. Corral. Sheriff Behan tried to stop the inevitable, but the Earp boys brushed him aside, and he disappeared himself from the scene as fast as he could go. This was to be the last dance of the bloody ball, and the Earps and Holliday had Clanton names on their dance cards. Ike Clanton, being unarmed, declined the invitation and Billy Claiborne split. And then it began.

There was no leaping and running about the way Burt and Kirk did it in that good picture *The Gunfight at the O.K. Corral.* Nothing fancy. The hard-noses just stood there, face to face and 20 feet apart, and blasted each other. In half a minute the shooting match was over. Three dead. Three wounded. Wyatt had killed Frank McLaury. Morgan got Billy Clanton. And "Doc" Holliday's sawed-off shotgun had air-conditioned

Tom McLaury. Morgan, Virgil, and Holliday were wounded. Wyatt Earp was not even dusted. They were all subsequently arrested and tried for murder. They beat the rap.

And Tombstone had itself a Wild West Tale that was more celebrated and glorious (and glorified) than any other event that ever took place in all the cowtowns of the West. And Wyatt Earp became a Cowboy-Hero and a symbol. It is hard to believe, but Wyatt died of old age, with his boots off, in Los Angeles in 1929.

Tombstone. "The town too tough to die." I liked it the minute I saw it. I drove down Allen Street. It had the look and feel of 1881. Obviously restored but not in the fakery of Dodge City's old Front Street. Tombstone's "frontier" street was not *in* the center of town. It *was* the center of town. The sidewalks were plank wood and covered by overhanging roofs held up by wooden posts every few yards. There was the Crystal Palace Saloon on the corner of Fifth and Allen. The Oriental Saloon (now a steakhouse but looking much the same as it must have originally) was across the street. Bat Masterson and Luke Short (late of the Dodge City "Peace Commission") had dealt faro in that saloon, and Wyatt Earp had had 25 percent of the action. Billy Claiborne, who had sat out the gory waltz at the O.K. Corral, was killed in front of the saloon by the Oriental's bartender, "Buckskin Frank" Leslie. There was the Bird Cage Theater nearby, the date of its original construction, 1881, engraved over the door. Up and down the street there were saloons where old saloons had once stood. And they were open for business. Even the drugstore, the supermarket, and the souvenir shops seemed to fit in. This was not Disneyland. This was "the place." Although they obviously encouraged the Wild West fantasy by design, it was close to what I had hoped I would find. And as I drove down Allen Street near Third, there it was. The O.K. Corral. The old Front Row Kid was freaking out!

I parked on a side street and walked out to the edge of town, which was not very far. It was coming near to sunset. The sky in the distance over the Dragoons was layered in red-orange and purple. It was as quiet around me as it must have been at

the O.K. Corral on the Thirty-first second. The air was fresh
and cool with the promise of quickly going to cold. Behind me,
back along Allen Street, the lights were on in the saloons.
There was nothing moving outside. It was as if I was standing
in backward time. For the moment, at least, I was *in* the
rear-view mirror.

"Fuck my old boots," I said to myself, not having the words
just then to speak my thoughts. Tombstone had taken me by
surprise.

I stood there for a while kicking up dust with my boot and
getting a little cold. Then I walked back to Allen Street to the
O.K. Corral, strode up and down in front of the locked gate
a few times, wondered if I ought to call somebody I knew back
in the world from the pay phone nearby, just to let a friend in
on my secret, then sat down on a wooden bench with my back
up against the Corral fence. And waited. For what? I couldn't
say. For the Clantons to show up? Or Wyatt and "Doc" Holliday? Or Henry Fonda and Victor Mature? Burt Lancaster and
Kirk Douglas? For a gunfighter? Or another tourist? For nothing and nobody?

The street was empty, deserted and quiet except for piano
music coming out of one of the saloons down the line. I waited
around for half an hour. No gunfighters turned up. Everything
was peaceful. They must have all been home watching television. A Chevy Nova with the markings of the marshal of Tombstone on its door and with its party hat turned off tiptoed down
the street past the O.K. Corral on a casual night patrol. It
turned the corner and did not come back.

I strolled up the middle of the street from the O.K. Corral,
heading for the Crystal Palace Saloon. Coming toward me was
a boy on a bicycle. Slowly, steadily, I walked a straight line in
his path. Looking out at him from under the brim of my
"Wyatt Earp" (formerly "Wild Bill Hickok"). As he approached, Draw! You yellow-bellied sidewinder. Reach for
your shootin' iron, hombre. And the sound of our gunshots will
wake up the dead and gone ghosts of old Tombstone. And
scare the piano player at the Alhambra Saloon right off his
stool. Closer and closer we came, down the middle of the quiet

street. Make your play, coyote! Closer. Closer. Face to face showdown. Let's see how fast you really are, you old rattle-snake. Now! Draw! The kid on the bike looks up from 10 yards down the street. Our eyes meet for a second in the dim light of Tombstone. Tlink! Tlink! The boy rings the bell on his bike, and I step out of the way.

The Crystal Palace Saloon claims to look exactly the way it did when Virgil Earp's town marshal's office was on the second floor and Wyatt Earp ran a faro game in the saloon. The long bar runs almost the entire length of the room. At the back there is a little stage with footlights for the dancehall girls and "painted" ladies to entertain the bar flies. There are half a dozen people drinking and talking. I belly up to the bar and order a Coca Cola. In the Saturday Matinee such an order would have been an open challenge for every gunfighter in the place to call me out into the middle of the street. Of course, in the movies I would have beaten them all to the draw and then come back inside to finish my "sodey pop." And a dancehall girl, the most beautiful one in the place, with fiery eyes and dirty thoughts, would have come up and hung on my arm.

"Stranger in town?" A fellow with a few days' growth of beard and a greasy cowboy hat was leaning down the bar toward me. I wondered if he was the town drunk.

"Yup," I said. He knew I was, of course. Tombstone is a toy town, so small they must know who the strangers are about 3 seconds after they cross the city line.

"I knew you were," he said. "There's only about fifteen hundred people who live here, and you ain't one of them. Unless you've just moved in in the last few days. I've been on vacation the last few days."

"Nope. Just passing through."

"Used to be only about five hundred people living here. There wasn't no highway. And only one street. The rest was dirt roads. Fixed 'er up in 1963. It's a nice little old town now. You think you're a cowboy?"

"What?"

"Said ya think you're a cowboy?"

I didn't answer. I pushed my "Wild Bill Hickok" a few inches along the bar. I didn't see any neon lights strung on it.

"Reason I asked is because it seems everyone who comes to Tombstone, the minute he sets foot in town, thinks he's a cowboy. Like something comes over him. Seems like he takes to walking different and everything. Now me, I was born here, around Bisbee."

I wondered if this geek had been watching me the whole time from behind a tree.

"I guess it's the town," I said. "The way it looks."

"I think it's from watching too many cowboy movies and reading them Western books," he said, tipping back his last drop of drink. "Whatchu drinkin'?"

"Coke."

"What the heck you drinkin' that stuff for?"

Was this the Saturday Matinee? Were we going out in the street in another minute?

"I'm driving," I said. But I offered to buy him a drink.

"I'm going over to hit the Alhambra," he said. "I got a lot of catchin' up to do from my vacation."

I sat alone in the Crystal Palace for a while longer, trying to call back the Wild West fantasies of the place. It was no good. They had fled. It didn't matter.

It was too late to check into a motel. Outside, Tombstone was dark as a grave and just as quiet. I drove out to the edge of town and went to sleep in the back seat of the Dodge. In the morning I discovered where I had spent the night. In Boot Hill! All around me were tombstones.

Time to go. I point the car west. Toward Los Angeles and Hollywood. Where the Western movies came from . . . and where, for 50 years, the Cowboy-Hero rode the range in Wild West tales too good to be true but also too good not to be believed. Moving pictures! And 20-foot-tall Cowboy-Heroes!

THE WILD WEST TALE AND THE HOLLYWOOD COWBOYS
(talking backward in the rear-view mirror)

"I've always acted alone. Americans admire
that enormously. Americans admire the cowboy leading the caravan alone astride his
horse, the cowboy entering a village or city
alone on his horse . . . a Wild West Tale, if you
like."

—Henry Kissinger

The Trail Blazers

The Western movie made Hollywood. Without the Western movie there would have been no Hollywood.

The Wild West Tale with its miracle riding Cowboy-Hero is the American Myth. The National Fairy Tale. It is about a world that never *really* was but *ought* to have been, is not now but *should* be. It is the Frontier Experience transformed into something glorious and fantastic and romantic. The Great American Adventure. Historical fact and far-out fantasy. Where the Ultimate Truth meets the Ultimate Doubt and beats it to the draw.

It was no accident that the first American movie to tell a tale told a Wild West Tale.

Edwin S. Porter's *The Great Train Robbery,* made in 1903, could not miss. It was a natural. The frontier fling had only just ended, and America was beginning its love affair with the memory of it. It was as if, with the passing of the last frontier, America sensed there would never again be anything quite like it. There was an eagerness, a never-to-be-satisfied hunger for things Western and for Wild West Tales. The movies, with their magical powers of illusion and make-believe, would permanently preserve the fantasy and make it larger than life. The "flickers" and the Frontier Fantasy were made for each other.

Edwin S. Porter was a pioneer. From the giant close-up of George F. Barnes looking like Mustache Pete and firing his six-gun right at the audience, through the train robbery to the final posse chase and the rousting of the robbers in their roost, Porter's Western was dramatic and full of action. If the Front

Row Kids *believed,* even momentarily, in the reality of what they were watching, that was the main thing, that was what counted.

The Great Train Robbery was not made in the West but on a stretch of track of the Delaware and Lackawanna Railroad near Dover, New Jersey. But it showed wide-eyed America what the movies could do when they got their hands on the Wild West Tale. And this was only the beginning. Soon enough, the Western movie, like the frontier it glorified, would go West. And the Cowboy-Heroes of its Wild West Tales would dwarf anything the Old West had to offer.

On board Porter's train was another pioneer. But nobody knew it at the time.

While casting *The Great Train Robbery,* Porter was approached by a man looking for work who claimed he could ride like a Texas Ranger. His name was Max Aronson, but he called himself G. M. Anderson. Porter planned to use him as one of the bandits. Until he discovered that Aronson-Anderson could not only *not* ride like a Texas Ranger, he could barely mount up and hope to stay on a critter's back long enough to get comfortable. Porter did not, however, send him packing in disgrace but relegated him to the "cast of thousands." (There are Western movie aficionados who claim that in the sequence in which the passengers are robbed, the man who makes a break for freedom and falls to the tracks with all the theatricality of a dying swan is, in fact, G. M. Anderson.)

But if G. M. Anderson couldn't ride and couldn't act, he was, nevertheless, no dummy. This first taste of the movie business made a believer out of him. He liked what he saw, and what he saw was possibilities. And the motion-picture field was not exactly what you would call overcrowded. Anderson got a job at Vitagraph as an actor and production assistant, learning the business and moving up to direct some one-reelers of his own. Eventually, around 1907, he went West. To Chicago. Where he joined the Selig Polyscope Company, an outfit run by Colonel William Selig, which was fast and furiously turning out one-reelers. Although the center of the film industry, such as it was, was still New York City and most of the product was being cranked out in the studio-lofts of New York or the "plains" of New Jersey. Chicago was becoming the major motion-picture center west of the Hudson.

The Great Train Robbery had, inevitably, generated interest and a demand for more of the same, more Westerns. Aware of public demand and of the Western movie's possibilities, Anderson got the idea to take a Selig crew out to Colorado to make some Westerns in a more authentic setting. After all, Chicago was already halfway West. Selig agreed, and Anderson made the films. But Selig was not much interested one way or the other, and the films that came out of the trip were not much good and not very successful. Anderson left the Selig Company and went into business with an old friend, George K. Spoor, who was a Chicago movie producer. They called their outfit the Essanay Company.

Anderson believed that the Western movie was not just a passing fad, that it could only get bigger and better and the making of Western movies was a good business bet. But this time he would go even farther West. Chicago was really not much better as a location for Westerns than New Jersey. And the weather was lousy. Anderson knew where to find a place in the sun. It was as far West as you could go. The scenery was terrific. It was warm all year around, sunshine every day. And it was virgin territory. California here I come.

At the end of 1908 Anderson established a West Coast studio for Essanay in Niles, California. He was a pioneer. The first motion-picture settler. A one-man advance guard who scouted the West and brought the first dream-dispensing fantasy factory to California. The others would follow in a rush like the days of '49. Griffith and Ince. Chaplin and Sennett. DeMille and Lasky and Laemmle and Louis B. Mayer. And all the others, coming into films by way of vaudeville and music hall, the rag trade, the fur business, the market and the merry-go-round, who would turn Hollywood into that special place of make-believe.

G. M. Anderson's move West would guarantee him at least a footnote in the cinema history books. What he did when he got there should (but, alas, often doesn't) give him a permanent place in the Hollywood Wax Museum of Movie Pioneers. Or at the very least, the Hollywood Cowboy Hall of Fame. Anderson was determined to make Westerns in California. It was his reason for going there in the first place. But the Westerns he had made up to that time, as well as those made by other producers, were missing something, an element that would carry them out of the shadow of *The Great Train Robbery*, something that could focus the concentration of the audience and capture their imagination. Some thing. Some twist. Some figure. That was it! Some figure. Some body. Some presence that would hold the focus and carry the load. Some central figure to identify with, to follow. Some character around whom the story could unfold and through whom the action is reflected, the drama justified. The Western movie needed a hero. The dime novels had their Hickoks and Earps and Buffalo Bills. Wister's *The Virginian* had its slow-talking, quick-drawing cowpoke. The Western movie needed a central figure to fill the screen with his presence, to carry the story and to bring the audience into the theater and, once inside, into the action. That was it. A Cowboy-Hero. Son-of-a-gun!

Anderson knew it would work. He searched the beaches, the orange groves, and the music halls of Southern California looking for a likely actor. He found none. And decided to take the job himself. He would produce, direct, and star in his own Westerns. Star! The magic word! The name above the titles!

He wasn't exactly a natural hero type, what would later be regarded as "star material." By this time he was no youth, and he was not even handsome. He was beefy and heavy-set as a tree trunk. Decidedly clumsy of movement, without fluidity or grace. He still could not ride like a Texas Ranger. But he projected a presence on the screen, with his solid body and cold stare. And, after all, there were no other "stars" in that particular firmament against whom he would suffer in comparison. He was the first. All the others would come after him, suffer or surpass comparison to him. He would be the first Hollywood Cowboy-Hero. And the first Hollywood Star. He would change the game.

Anderson found his Cowboy-Hero in a Peter B. Kyne story

called "Broncho Billy and the Baby," a sentimental story about a hard hombre redeemed and reformed by love and a small baby. G. M. Anderson purchased the story for 50 dollars and became "Broncho Billy," the "good badman." It was a giant step for motion picture make-believe and supplied the vital element that would make the Western movie Hollywood's longest-running and most popular moving fantasy, for fifty years its backbone and bread and butter. "Broncho Billy" Anderson made nearly 400 one- and two-reelers from 1910 to 1915. Such movers and shakers as *Broncho Billy's Adventure, Broncho Billy and the Rustler's Child, Broncho Billy and the Maid, Broncho Billy's Sentence,* and *Broncho Billy's Oath.* All of them full of action and romance and featuring "Broncho Billy," the good badman, in the center of the screen. The Cowboy-Hero.

But if "Broncho Billy" Anderson can be said to have triggered a Western movie revolution, like all revolutions it was merely a moment, a turning point in a process of continuing change. "Broncho Billy" himself would be left behind by new and better Hollywood Cowboys who would follow his trail across the screen and the imagination, galloping faster and farther and offering richer Front Row Kid fantasies than he had. In a way, it would be like that familiar Wild West Tale in which the young gun learns his tricks from the old one and then, inevitably, beats him to the draw and sends him to Boot Hill. Some of them were already mounting up and taking aim at "Broncho Billy" even while he was still riding high. That G. M. Anderson would, in life, outlive many of the Western stars who came after him is an irony. Anderson died in California in 1971, in semi-obscurity. "Broncho Billy," on the other hand, was shot out of the saddle by the first serious Cowboy-Hero who came along to challenge him. And that man would be the first Hollywood Cowboy to become a towering giant in the imagination of America's Front Row Kids.

William S. Hart is a name to conjure with. Calling forth images of cowboy heroics even in the minds of Kids who never saw him, hadn't a clue what he looked like on the screen or

what his Western movies were about, Front Row Kids of future generations who had not yet been born during the time
he was King of the Hollywood Cowboys. Perhaps only Tom
Mix, the Cowboy-Hero who would eventually replace Hart
when he became too old and slow on the draw, would equal
or surpass him as a magic name. Hart was one of those cowboys
who left an afterglow so that if the subject of silent-movie
Cowboy-Heroes ever came up, even a Front Row Kid from the
late Forties would instinctively, automatically think: William
S. Hart.

The image of William S. Hart, slightly horse-faced and glow-
ering, crouched behind a pair of six-guns, is as evocative of that
era from World War I up to the Roaring Twenties as the figure
of Charlie Chaplin in baggy suit and derby hat, the Keystone
Kops tearing around in circles, or Harold Lloyd hanging from
a flagpole, as much a symbol of that time as the Doughboy
marching, smiling, off to the European holocaust, the sputter-
ing, put-putting Model T Fords that were seriously beginning
to crowd the horse and buggy off the roads, the bucket of beer,
the penny candy and Woodrow Wilson.

Hart pulled the Western out of the two-reel doldrums and,
taking up where "Broncho Billy" left off, permanently fixed
the Cowboy-Hero in the very center of the action and turned
him into a kind of rough-edged Knight of the Prairies. Hart's
films were exceptional for their aura of realism and authentic-
ity of background. That, mixed with a good dose of romantic
sentimentality, gave his stories and the character he played a
kind of ruggedly poetic flavor. His were the first Western
movies to be taken seriously. It was this romantic realism that
John Ford, at that time just beginning to direct two-reelers,
would eventually refine and develop into a classic Western
movie style and attitude.

William S. Hart was no born cowboy, was not, in fact, a
Westerner at all, having been born in 1870 in Newburgh, New
York. He trained to be a stage actor, but he had a love for the
"Old West" and developed particular and definite ideas about
the historical reality and significance of America's Frontier
Experience. (His father was a traveling miller, and the family

lived for a time in Wisconsin and the Dakotas when he was a boy.) His first cowboy roles were in the stage productions of *The Squaw Man* and *The Virginian*. But on the boards he was no Edwin Booth or Barrymore, and his stage career was essentially an up-and-down affair, with oblivion a definite prospect by the time he was in his forties.

As the story goes, he saw his first Western movie while in Cleveland on tour with a theatrical road show. He was amazed and impressed by the film and, at the same time, outraged by its phony and innacurate depiction of the West. He decided that, given the chance, he could do better. As he wrote years later in his autobiography, *My Life East and West*, his future was revealed to him at that moment as if in a vision: "The opportunity that I had been waiting for years to come was knocking at my door . . . rise or fall, sink or swim, I had to bend every endeavor to get a chance to make western pictures." Autobiographies are notoriously hindsightful and hyperbolic. But in Hart's case, the dream-wish did propel the reality, and when he made his way to California, he got his chance. And he did not fumble it.

Thomas H. Ince, an old friend from his stage-acting days, was a big deal in Hollywood's fledgling film industry, producing Westerns for the New York Motion Picture Company, when Hart looked him up in 1914. Ince had been making Westerns that were strong on realism, even bringing to Hollywood the riders and ropers of the famous Miller Brothers 101 Ranch Wild West Show and building a Western movie "location" in the Hollywood foothills called "Inceville," complete with Wild West town, ranch and wide-open spaces (the prototype for the locations known as Lone Pine, Chatsworth, and Pioneertown, permanent Western settings that would thunder with hoofbeats and gunshots during the Western-movie salad days of the Thirties and Forties). Ince was fussy and particular about production in ways that were, as yet, unheard of in the film business. Organizing, scheduling, budgeting, scripting, shooting. He was another of those Hollywood Pioneers.

Ince did not exactly jump up and down with excitement

when Hart renewed their old acquaintance and hit him up for a job in Westerns. But business was not too good. The Western, though popular, was beginning to bore with its sameness of tone and style and story line. (Even "Broncho Billy" had gone about as far as he could go.) So Ince and Hart struck a deal. Hart would get a chance to show what he could do in an Ince production. And if, indeed, Hart could cut it, so much the better. Ince put him in two short films as the villain, and then, in response to Hart's appeals, gave him a starring role in *The Bargain,* a five-reel feature co-written by Hart. Then followed, one right after the other, three more films in which the hero Hart would portray for the next 10 years was already beginning to be formed.

William S. Hart would be the "good badman," after the fashion of "Broncho Billy." But where Anderson's hero had been essentially a stick figure, a skeleton portrayal, Hart would develop and refine, give new dimensions of breadth and depth and significance to his own Cowboy-Hero. Tough, humorless, hard-nosed, and with a potential for violence that ticked away like a time bomb behind his eyes, Hart's cowboy had a hero's heart beating away under that villainous exterior. The embodiment of the "Code of the West." Incorruptible. A man of honor. Deadly in vengeance. Chivalrous in love. Responsive to truth and beauty. A Cowboy-Hero who reflected Hart's personal vision of what the West was like or ought to have been. And if Hart had any doubts in the beginning about his "vision," his performance, and whether he was on the right track, they were quickly settled by success.

The Bargain was boffo box office! Ince had turned the Hart package over to Famous Players for distribution. The dynamo operation of Jesse Lasky-Sam Goldwyn-Cecil B. DeMille had produced the first full-length Hollywood feature film in 1913, *The Squaw Man,* starring Dustin Farnum, and if anyone could make Hart a household name, Famous Players was the outfit to do it. When Ince realized Hart's potential as a Cowboy-Hero, he quickly put him under contract, without (in true movie-mogul fashion) letting on to Hart the deal that was going down with Famous Players nor indicating the enormous success he expected to have with Hart's films. Hart eagerly signed with Ince as an actor-director for a salary of $125 per week, which was, even in those early days, daylight robbery. Hart was still a greenhorn in the business of Hollywood. But he would learn. For him, the main thing was being able to make his Westerns.

He began directing two-reelers. He was not a great director. (Some would say he was not even a good one.) But even in the early two-reelers, he was working on that William S. Hart Cowboy, getting him down, fixing him in the center. The stories all revolved around his hero. All other characters played second fiddle. He used dramatic close-ups of his scowling (or mean or determined or love-struck) hero to dominate the screen and the action, to pop the eyes of the Front Row Kids. There was action and drama from the start. And that romantic realism that would become his trademark. And there was, from the very beginning, a Don Quixote-like innocence about his Cowboy-Hero. And an undertone of sentimentality in his Wild West Tales. At first, and at its best, this sentimentality gave another dimension to his character and his stories. Later on it was overdone and became a burden, a dead weight that would sink him.

Time and again the chord would be struck. The "badman" reformed by the love and virtue of the pretty heroine. The tough hombre who is devoted to his sister or the memory of her. Or who finds God and religion and quits his low-down ways. Or who loves his horse and therefore can't be all *that* bad. (Hart was the first Hollywood Cowboy to feature his horse, a pinto named "Fritz," as a kind of partner in the action.) The violent and dangerous and humorless tough guy crying real tears in giant close-up or dying for the good cause clutching a rose in his iron fist. All of this was as much a part of the William S. Hart image as his high-crowned Stetson, his leather wrist cuffs, and the sash he wore around his waist under his gun belt.

Hart's was a Cowboy-Hero with enormous appeal. The two-reelers increased his popularity, and when he began to make full-length features, he was right up there with Douglas Fairbanks and Charlie Chaplin and Mary Pickford. A Hollywood Star.

When Ince, Griffith, and Sennet combined to form Triangle Productions in September 1915, Hart went along. And his successful Westerns pulled their coals out of the fire more than once during the next two years when their big production non-Westerns flopped at the box office. Although Hart would get no thanks from Thomas Ince.

In 1917 Ince, Griffith, Sennett, Douglas Fairbanks, and Hart left Triangle and went over to Paramount (Adolph Zukor-Jesse Lasky). It was a move upward for Hart, as Paramount was already becoming a giant Hollywood studio. And he was, no doubt, delighted to get out from under Ince's supervision, his coolie wages, and all the other grievances and objections that had poisoned their relationship. (Ince hated Hart's horse, Fritz.)

At Paramount, over the next eight years, Hart continued to turn out the kind of Westerns he had become famous for. Serious, realistic, and romantic. *The Narrow Trail. Selfish Yates. Square Deal Sanderson. Wagon Tracks* (concerning a covered-wagon journey, which was so successful it encouraged Paramount to produce James Curze's *The Covered Wagon,* the first genuine epic Western). *The Toll Gate.* And more.

By the early Twenties Hart was making bigger films and fewer of them. But he was slipping. There were definite signs of cinematic hardening of the arteries. The films were now noticeably sluggish and targets for the damning criticism "old-fashioned." The Western movie was moving along. Hart, as hard as he spurred his pony, was standing still. And standing still, in Hollywood, is the same as going backward. Zukor and Lasky, who knew how to read a form sheet and bet a winner, now saw Hart as a mudder trying to run on a fast track. He was about to be scratched. He made one more film for Paramount, *Singer Jim McKee.* It was a dog. And then he was through. They told him he could continue to star in Westerns, but from now on *they* would be in the saddle, choosing his scripts and his directors, strictly supervising his productions. They must have known he would say no.

Hart made one last Western, *Tumbleweeds*. In 1925. Not for Paramount but for United Artists. It was his first and only epic. With a Cherokee Strip land-rush sequence as mighty and impressive and extravagant as any stampede sequence ever filmed. And he gave one last performance of the William S. Hart Cowboy-Hero. Older now, but still stern and moral. The dominating presence who leads the way and gets the girl in the end. But Hart was, by now, beating a dead horse. He was showing the Front Row Kids and the Hollywood producers that he was alive and kicking, that he was still a giant. But Tom Mix, Buck Jones, Hoot Gibson, Ken Maynard, Tim McCoy, Fred Thomson, Harry Carey, were the new giants, remaking the Moving Picture Cowboy in their own images. And William S. Hart was a dinosaur.

As good as it was, United Artists did not care for *Tumbleweeds*. Nor take much care with it. They fudged its distribution, booking it in the flea pits and neighborhood theaters, losing it in the crowd. Hart sued, as any proud and famous Cowboy-Hero would have done, and eventually won a judgment of $500,000 against lost earnings. But his triumph was off screen and took place long after the last William S. Hart reel had gone by.

William S. Hart had been the first giant Hollywood Cowboy-Hero. He was, in many ways, a strange man. A romantic, a Victorian, with a wide streak of moral purity that showed strongly in his characterizations, his stories, his ideas. He wanted to be accurate about the West. But what he did—and he must have known this would happen—was to add a nobility, a poetry to the symbolism of the Wild West Tale. The after-image of his Hero would remain, hovering like a noble ghost, on the edge of the screen and over the front-row seats.

William S. Hart died in Los Angeles on June 23, 1946 and was buried not on the lone prairie but alongside his parents, his sisters and brother in Greenwood Cemetery in Brooklyn.

Tom Mix and the
Miracle Riders

The Roaring Twenties. The moguls were in their place, becoming entrenched in their domains of power—Lasky, Zukor, Laemmle, Louis B. Mayer, Fox, the Warner brothers. The Great War was over. The ablebodied were back home again, flapping and frivolous and in search of make-believe. The Chicago White (black) Sox had thrown the World Series to the Cincinnati Reds for small change, bus fare to oblivion. Warren Harding was hanky-pankying in the maid's quarters of the White House, while Calvin Coolidge stared for hours at the pigeons on the White House lawn. And Tom Mix was King of the Cowboys.

Tom Mix was a Moving Picture Cowboy of a different cut and style, with other ideas and notions about the Wild West Tale and Hollywood make-believe, a Cowboy-Hero more suitable for the flash and fancy and flamboyance of the new times than the stern and sober William S. Hart. If Hart's Cowboy-Hero had been the "good badman," tight-lipped, a little cold-blooded, yet possessing a poetic nobility, Tom Mix's vision was of the Cowboy-Hero as Daredevil. Miracle Rider. White Knight. Tom Mix was the first of the Rhinestone-and-Neon Cowboy-Heroes. A Hollywood, Show-Biz Cowboy.

Flash and action were the center-core of the Tom Mix Wild West Tale. As a hero-figure, no Hollywood Cowboy that came after would equal him. And as a personality, no Hollywood Star of *any* kind could compare.

Hollywood was fast becoming the land of the tinsel dream. The movies had not yet come near their potential for charging up front-row fantasies. But with each new step, each new

A GUIDE TO EXHIBITORS
PUBLICITY AND ADVERTISING MATERIAL

CAUGHT ON THE JUMP!

A runaway team dash madly down a dangerous road, bearing in the wagon behind them a terror-stricken girl. An intrepid horseman, following in the rescue, comes abreast the team, and shouts a command. Only by a perilous leap from wagon into strong, waiting arms can the girl's life be saved. She takes the leap. Is it strange that romance was born in that embrace? The horseman is

Tom Mix IN THE WILLIAM FOX Production Fighting for Gold

A rapid-fire drama of the West   A play that grips the imagination

Scenario by Charles Kenyon   Directed by Edward J. Le Saint

BLANK THEATRE—All Next Week

AD ILLUSTRATION NO. 1

experiment, each new success, the moguls and the stars were learning. Learning that the folks who paid their money at the box office not only wanted a hero to follow and identify with *on* the screen but expected the stars, in their off-screen lives, to continue to project the fantasy, the actions, the glamour, the romance, the larger-than-life heroics. They expected Hollywood itself to become part of the make-believe it produced. The power of the motion picture was in its ability to fuzz the line between truth and illusion. And once blurred, where is the line redrawn and restored? Why not just keep it blurred if it's good for business? In this business of keeping the make-believe working and well oiled (and printing money), Tom Mix would show Hollywood the way.

He was just the man for the job. Better than Chaplin or Fairbanks or Mary Pickford or Buster Keaton or Sennett or Rudolph Valentino. Tom Mix put show into the business and made business out of the show. The Hollywood Cowboy would never be the same after him. Nor would Hollywood. Not only did Tom Mix create a Cowboy-Hero larger than life, he also made his *life* appear larger than life. And thereby obscured, if not completely obliterated, the line between dreaming and waking, reality and make-believe. For the Front Row Kids, the fantasy would be limitless.

Tom Mix invented . . . Tom Mix. He was all showman. If moving was what the motion picture did best, his movies would move faster and with more action, stunts, cowboy heroics, and excitement than all the rest. And if any other Hollywood Cowboys aimed to pass him, they would have to move faster. It hardly seemed possible. He fought like a cat and rode like the wind. He never passed up a chance for that extra bit of flash. Rearing his horse Tony up onto its hind legs. Jumping him off and onto moving trains. Or across chasms that appeared to be just that bit too wi. . . .de. Performing flying mounts and running dismounts. Twirling his six-guns. Waving his hat. Always that extra something, that "bit of business" to make the action and the image more exciting, more fantastic. Dressed (unlike Hart's dusty, dreary saddle tramps) to the nines in fancy-button cowboy shirts, hand-tooled boots, and a high-crowned Stetson hat. And (most unlike Hart) always smiling. As if he were having fun. Cutting an image across the screen that glowed in the dark. But more than that, he *became* the Cowboy-Hero he portrayed, working up a lifestyle and personal history to reinforce the make-believe he put on the screen. And if the suit of Truth was, in reality, a little drab in color, with the sleeves and pants too short, well, he soon cut the fantasy cloth to fit the image and grew into it. Tom Mix was a studio publicist's dream. He rode into Hollywood on a custom-built legend.

"He was the goddamnedest liar that ever lived," said the great Western movie stuntman Yakima Canutt, who began his own movie career in the silent days and knew the Tom Mix of both life and legend. "But never did he lie to hurt somebody," Canutt said. "It was always done in showmanship."

The Tom Mix *invented* by Tom Mix was born in a log cabin near El Paso, Texas, on January 6, 1880. His great-great-grandfather was a Cherokee Indian who translated the Bible into the Osage language. His father was a captain in the Seventh Cavalry. He learned to ride and shoot and throw a rope almost before he could walk. He had little formal education as a boy, but at 14 went off to Virginia Military Academy, where he became an athletic star. He spoke Spanish and four Indian dialects fluently. When the Spanish-American War broke out in 1898, the future Cowboy-Hero quit school, enlisted in the artillery, and was sent to Cuba where he fought in the battle of Guaymas and was later shot in the mouth by a sniper. An adventurer, he was now a gunfire-baptized warrior as well, and after the war he went to the Philippines to help put down a native insurrection. And taking off after that to join the 9th Infantry in China during the Boxer Rebellion, he marched with the victorious allied army into Peking. Badly wounded in China, he was shipped home. But still hungry for adventure, he next went to Denver to break horses for the British Government, eventually taking the stock to South Africa in time to fight in the Boer War. Back in the United States again, he went West where he was a guide to Teddy Roosevelt during one of that crypto-cowboy's hunting expeditions, served as sheriff of Montgomery County, Kansas, Washington County, Oklahoma, and Two Buttes County, Colorado. He was also a United States marshal in Montana, New Mexico, and Arizona. And a Texas Ranger. As a Texas Ranger, he single-handedly captured the Shonts Brothers, a notorious gang of rustlers and desperadoes, despite being shot in the back during the fight by an Indian woman. Turning in his lawman's badges, he headed down Mexico way where he joined Francisco Madero's band of revolutionaries, survived a firing squad, and participated in the capture of Juarez, where he caught a bullet in the leg. Returning once again to the States, he rode an old horse named Blue to Hollywood where he broke into the movies. Somewhere between all the fighting and law enforcing he managed to find time to become an all-around champion cowboy, and when he hit the movies, he could do everything, riding, roping, bronco busting, shooting better than anyone else around, and became, naturally, a Star.

It was a wonderful and exciting background. Breathless. Full of fighting and heroics and great escapes. It was a life guaranteed to inspire dreams in any Front Row Kid. It was fantastic. It was a pack of lies!

Will the real Tom Mix please stand up?

The real Tom Mix was born in Mix Run, Pennsylvania, which is nowhere near El Paso, on January 6, 1880. His father was a lumber miller whose family had settled in that little valley along the Susquehanna River back in 1804. The Mix clan were neither Texans nor cavalry men. He learned to ride and shoot rabbits as a boy, and when he was 10, the Buffalo Bill Wild West Show came to the local fairgrounds. Like any other Front Row Kid who ever saw that great showman and buffalo bullshitter, he dreamed Cowboy-Hero dreams. At the time, those dreams were only in his head. As a teen-ager, Mix was tall, broad-shouldered, and good at outdoor sports, especially football and bicycling. He never was a football star at Virginia Military Academy because he never went there. But when he was 17, he took a train to Hartford, Connecticut, and won a Fourth of July bicycle race. He would always be a fresh-air fiend and a physical-fitness buff.

In 1898, the day after war was declared with Spain, Tom Mix enlisted in the army (he lied about his age) and was assigned to Battery M, 4th Regiment, United States Artillery, whose mission was to guard the DuPont powder works on the Delaware River against the possibility of a Spanish attack on Philadelphia. Needless to say, soldier Tom Mix saw no action during the war. Any wounds he may have suffered during his posting with Battery M could only have come from falling off a bar stool on Pea Patch Island in the Delaware. Fact is his entire military career was uneventful. After the Spanish-American War ended, he was transferred to Battery O at Fort Monroe, Virginia, where he made the rank of sergeant. He did not go to the Philippines to fight insurrection. Although he did participate in the evacuation of Fort Monroe after an outbreak of yellow fever hit the National Soldier's Home. It was not exactly hero stuff.

After his honorable discharge in 1901, he re-enlisted, hoping, perhaps, to get into the Boer War. Some U.S. Army regulars were given leave to go to South Africa as "volunteers," but no U.S. Army records indicate that a First Sergeant Thomas E. Mix was among them. What is known and a matter of record is that during that period Tom Mix met and married Grace I. Allin from Norfolk. His first wife. In his lifetime, officially and legally he would have five wives. Informal arrangements, however, probably pushed the count into two figures. As for his military career, it did not exactly end with a star-spangled bang, as the legend would have it. But with a whisper. In October of 1902, Tom Mix, future Cowboy-Hero and reputed gallant warrior, deserted his post at Fort Hancock and took off with his wife for the West.

Tom Mix's days on the range were far short of the rootin'-tootin', sharp-shootin' cowboy legend he made out of them. In Oklahoma Territory, deserter Tom Mix got a job as a drum major in the Oklahoma Cavalry Band. No musician, he paraded around in front of the marching band decked out in a fancy gold-braided uniform. It was Mix's start in "show," if not in "business." In 1904, the band went to St. Louis for the World's Fair, where Tom met Will Rogers, a rodeo clown with the Zack Mulhall Wild West Show. Mix was one of the first of many future Hollywood Cowboys who would fall under the friendly spell and the corn-pone homespunnery of Will Rogers, who was always ready with a plug of tobacco and some sagebrush philosophy to offer any aspiring show-biz cowboy. Will Rogers is reputed to have once said: "Invest in land. It's the one thing they won't be making any more of."

At the close of the World's Fair, Rogers headed East, soon to become a star of the Zeigfeld Follies, while Tom Mix went back to Oklahoma and swapped his fancy marching band uniform for an apron and a wet rag. He quit the band and took work as a bartender. Those old Cowboy-Hero dreams were still only in his head. Tom Mix did serve (in addition to mugs of beer) as a deputy sheriff and night marshal of Dewey, Oklahoma. But he was no Wild Bill Hickok or Wyatt Earp lawman. The job mostly just called for guiding stumbling drunks to the calaboose and making sure the door of the dry goods store and the barber shop were securely locked at night. It is possible that he helped to round up some rumrunners after the Territory gained statehood and went "dry." Whether he ever became a Texas Ranger and captured the Shonts Brothers is anybody's guess. After he became a Hollywood Cowboy, he was given "honorary" membership in the Rangers.

Legend aside, the real testing ground in which Tom Mix learned the tricks of his trade and out of which came his big show-biz break was the Miller Brothers' 101 Real Wild West Ranch. The Miller Brothers (Colonels Joe, George, and Zack) operated one of the great and famous Wild West outfits of the early years of the twentieth century. Named for the Bar-O-Bar cattle brand, it spread out over 101,000 acres of Oklahoma range. It was a showpiece Real Wild West Ranch and home base for a fabulous Wild West Show in the tradition of Buffalo Bill and his Congress of Rough Riders. Through its years of big-time operations, it would be the "school" for more than a few rodeo champions and Hollywood Cowboys, and its ranch hands and authentic Wild West flavor would be used as background for many of the Western movies of the early years.

It was over a bar Tom Mix was tending in late 1905 that he

met Colonel Joe Miller, who offered him a job out at the 101 for a wage of $15 a month. It was just the sort of thing the 25-year-old bartender who hated working indoors was looking for. He could be outdoors, among real cowboys, learning the ropes. And he could afford to marry wife number two, Miss Kitty Jewel Perrine. (The marriage did not last long.) He was not much of a cowboy when he reported to the 101 Ranch for the 1906 season. Compared to the rough and woolly cowhands on the place, Mix was a rookie, a relative tenderfoot. But he was big, athletic, and good-looking in his boots and Stetson hat. He spent his first season herding "dudes," city slickers who came out from back East to "play" cowboys and cowgirls, to pass their vacations acting out their own Front Row Kid fantasies in an authentic setting. It was a good chance for Mix to learn the cowboy life and to show off what he was learning to an eager and impressionable audience. In the Wild West Show, because he was still not up to big-time rodeo standard as a bronco buster, bulldogger, or all-around stunt rider, he took the part of the horsethief the "good guys" dragged around the arena floor at the end of a rope. But everything he picked up during his time at the 101 Ranch (including the many mouthfuls of sawdust) he would put to good use in the movies on the way to becoming King of the Moving Picture Cowboys.

Over the next three years, Tom Mix practiced. He worked his way up to being a pretty fair cowboy, and around the beginning of 1909 he went off with his third wife, Olive Stokes, to join up with the Widerman Wild West Show in Amarillo, Texas. After a short time, they quit and formed a show of their own to play the Alaska-Yukon-Pacific Exposition in Seattle. It was a moderate success, with Mix performing a fancy rope-trick act and billing himself as "Tom Mix, Champion Steer Thrower." He was far from a Cowboy-Hero, but he was getting the hang of it.

After closing down his own show, Mix joined up with Will A. Dickey's Circle D Ranch Wild West Show and Indian Congress and found that the Circle D was under contract to the Selig Polyscope Company to supply cowboys and Indians for movie Westerns. By this time he was well past the "drugstore cowboy" stage and the film people decided to use him as an off-screen wrangler. He was now very close to realizing those old dreams in his head. And his big chance came when Selig Polyscope was filming *Ranch Life in the Great Southwest* near his old stomping grounds of Dewey, Oklahoma. It was a short, "realistic" film depicting working cowboys on a roundup. And Mix charmed or bribed or conned the director into letting him within camera range during a bronco-busting sequence. Colonel William Selig liked what he saw, and Tom Mix had his ticket to ride.

The Selig Company was after quantity more than quality, and their Westerns, largely one-, two-, and three-reelers, were shot quickly (usually three to four days) on outdoor locations. The stories had simple plots and as much action as could be crammed into the short running time. Mix signed a personal contract with Selig in 1910 and thereafter wrote and directed many of his own films. In 1913 Selig moved his operations out to Hollywood, and Tom Mix went with him. His Selig films varied in quality (he was, at best, only a competent producer-director), but his popularity as a movie cowboy was increasing, and his films never failed to include spectacular action scenes that showed off Mix's remarkable riding, roping, shooting, jumping, and fighting talents. The special Tom Mix Cowboy-Hero was coming into focus.

In 1917 the Selig Company went to the wall financially and Tom Mix signed with William Fox, then an up-and-coming-but-not-quite-there movie mogul. Colonel Selig had never really understood or appreciated what he had had in Tom Mix, and William S. Hart was still King and not about to be bush-whacked by a two-reel cowboy. But William Fox was a twentieth-century fox and knew the difference between gold and tinhorn. And Tom Mix was ready to make his run for the money.

After one two-reeler for Fox, Mix jumped up to full-length features, and Hart could have looked over his shoulder and seen the Miracle Rider gaining on him. Tom Mix was an immediate success in his Fox films. His theatrical and showy approach to Western movie make-believe was a perfect fit for the end of a somber decade and the new times that were fast coming on. The Front Row Kids responded by pouring their precious pocket money into the Fox box-office tills. They made Tom Mix the hero that those dreams in his head always promised him he would be.

By 1920 Tom Mix was top gun. His fictitious past heroics became part of the package, and the eager Front Row Kids, to whom his Westerns were more and more consciously directed, bought the total image, absorbed it into their fantasies, and clamored for more. Here was a white-hat Cowboy they could really identify with. On the screen he was all fun and breathless action. Riding fast. Fighting fair. Living clean. He was the first Hollywood Cowboy whose "Code of the West" was: Patriotism, Courage, Kindness to Animals, Courtesy to Women and Old Folks, Cheerfulness, Clean Teeth and No Smokin', Drinkin', or Cussin'. And he was, so it seemed, a genuine war hero and ex-lawman. Gosh! Terrific!

And if that wasn't enough, he lived the magnificent and gaudy life of a Hollywood Star that was guaranteed to make his fans' mouths water. Tom Mix gave a lesson in the business of show business to the country and to Hollywood. When the money started pouring in, his life took on the style and opulence of fairy-tale royalty. By 1922 his salary at Fox was $17,500 per week (almost $1 million a year, with income tax practically zero). And it was gladly paid by William Fox because without Tom Mix Westerns in those years, Fox would have been picking peaches in the San Fernando Valley and sleeping in a lean-to. Tom Mix was his Babe Ruth. And 20th Century-Fox was the lot that Mix built. Tom Mix also built himself a palatial mansion on Summit Drive in Beverly Hills, with a giant swimming pool and gardens, a maze of rooms and rooms and rooms (some of them so cavernous you had to practically send a telegram if you wanted to communicate with someone at the other end), a seven-car garage, all parking slots filled with the most expensive and flashy automobiles a piston-driven fantasy could imagine and money could buy, including a white-chromed Rolls Royce with a silver-inlaid saddle on the hood and a custom-built Cord Roadster with a set of longhorns on the radiator and the TM brand gold-leafed on the doors. In fact the TM brand was everywhere. From the massive iron gates that opened on to the mile-long private road that led to the mansion's front steps to the silver-studded saddles he collected, the diamond-studded spurs, the $30,000 diamond-studded platinum belt buckle he used to hold up his tailor-made Western pants on showy occassions, to the monogrammed handkerchiefs he kept in his pocket to blow his nose in. He entertained like a Roman and spread his money around like bird-seed. His life style became legend, and nobody could possibly mistake Tom Mix for any other Hollywood Star or Cowboy-Hero.

And he did work hard for his $8 million. He made over 75 features. Going out to authentic locations in Wyoming, Arizona, Utah, Death Valley, to give his films maximum production values. In his 10 years with Fox he did most of his own stunts and daredevil feats. And bruised his body and broke his bones more than a few times. His athletic ability was his pride, and if he could do the "gag" as well as, if not better than, the professional film stuntmen, he would go ahead and do it, and in close-up so that there would be no mistaking Tom Mix for a stand-in. When he did use a stunt double (a broken Tom Mix bone or fractured skull was a thought to make William Fox shudder), the rider who actually performed the death-defying leaps and hell-for-leather galloping along the edge of a cliff was sworn to secrecy. The Front Row Kids were not to know. For Tom Mix, his showmanship was also his pride. To keep the image shining and in full view, he went out on public appearances between film commitments, a piece of Tom Mix-style showmanship that would become standard procedure for all aspiring Hollywood Cowboys, whether they could twirl a rope or sing a song or just had to stand like a cigar-store Indian in the middle of a mob of fans. He even went back out with 101 Wild West Show for part of the 1924 season. In 1925 Tom Mix and his Wonder Horse Tony went on a personal-appearance tour of Europe, and the Germans, the French, the Dutch, and the English went crazy.

For Tom Mix life was all go. It had to be because he was King of the Hollywood Cowboys with a title to defend against all comers. Unlike Hart, who for most of his career had been more or less unchallenged by competition, Tom Mix's phenomenal success naturally and inevitably started a trend. And with the success of James Cruze's *The Covered Wagon* in 1923, the first serious, large-scale epic Western, and *The Iron Horse,* John Ford's first important Western, which came out the next year, the Western movie was back in the saddle of popularity after a temporary eclipse in favor of comedy and romance. In fact, Westerns were the only certain money-makers, paying the studios' overhead, while the more lavish and extravagant A-Feature dramas and romances too often turned out to be box-office clinkers. Hollywood could not afford *not* to make Western movies. The result was, not surprisingly, that Tom Mix saw potential Cowboy-Hero rivals popping up at him from behind every bush and tumbleweed.

One of Tom Mix's main rivals, who would be a mighty and much-loved Cowboy star for twenty years, was bred in Mix's own home corral, the Fox Film Company, under his very nose. Buck Jones (born Charles Fredrick Gebhart back East in Vincennes, Indiana) was ironically a creation of Tom Mix's own showmanship, impetuosity and ego. Tom Mix knew that he was Fox's main meal ticket, that every new piece of equipment, each nail pounded in the construction of a new soundstage, was bought with the profits his Westerns were putting into the Fox bank accounts. And he wanted his contracts to reflect that worth in higher and higher salaries and fringe benefits. Fox would eventually pay him the highest salary of any star in Hollywood. But William Fox was a mogul and not a philanthropist. And from time to time Tom Mix had to throw a temper tantrum to get what he wanted and felt he deserved. To keep him in line and show him who was boss, Fox decided to create and promote a second Cowboy-Hero to nip at Mix's heels and, in the event that Mix should take it in his head to quit in a huff over some future salary fight, to replace him as top Fox Cowboy. He chose Buck Jones for the part. And Buck Jones's success would pleasantly surprise Fox as much as it doubtless riled Mix.

Buck Jones was well built and handsome, with a strong,

serious face that called to mind William S. Hart. (Except for Hart himself and Harry Carey, John Ford's favorite leading cowboy, Jones was the only Cowboy-Hero of the Twenties who seemed more serious than flamboyant.) Buck Jones knew his way around action. At 17 he joined the army and served two hitches in the cavalry, with duty along the Mexican border during the days of Pancho Villa and later in the Philippines where he was wounded by a sniper. (One hears the distinct echo of Tom Mix's make-believe.) He joined the Miller Brothers 101 Ranch Wild West Show in 1913 and toured as a rodeo rider (hear that echo-cho-ho-o?), meeting and marrying along the way his one and only wife, Odelle. For a while he had a job test-driving racing cars at Indianapolis Speedway. But he was a rider, not a racer, and it was with Ringling Brothers Circus that he first came to Hollywood. He broke into movies as a $5 a day stuntman in Universal's short Westerns, moving over to an independent outfit called Canyon Pictures where he worked in a Western series starring Franklyn Farnum (a fairly nothing cowboy), and finally landed a job at Fox in 1919 as a $40 a week double and stunt rider, at which time William Fox tapped him on his big he-man shoulder and said: Hey you! You're just the man I'm looking for. What's your name? I'm gonna make you a Star!

Buck Jones's first starring Western was *The Last Straw* in 1920. It was a hit with the Front Row Kids. And William Fox discovered that he had something more in Buck Jones than just a stick to hit Tom Mix over the head with. Over the next eight years, Buck made more than 60 movies for Fox. They were all fast-action, good-humored Westerns after the fashion of Tom Mix, but Buck Jones was more low-key than Mix and less flashy in his simple buckskin gear or plain dark cowboy shirts. He seemed to take his acting as seriously as his image. He did, however, have his own famous co-starring white horse, "Silver," and a nationwide fan club of 4 million "Buck Jones Rangers" who loved him best and packed the theaters when his films were showing. He pulled down a salary of $3,500 per week. And if he wasn't exactly King of the Cowboys, he was certainly not just another pretender in the manner of Bob

Custer, Bill Cody, Buddy Roosevelt, Jack Hoxie, Neal Hart, Jack Perrin, and the other saddle stiffs who were trying to cash in on the cowboy craze of the Twenties. Buck Jones was one of the Miracle Riders who gave Tom Mix a merry chase across the decade. And would keep on riding right into and through the next one.

Buck left Fox in 1928 to form his own Buck Jones Productions, but his first independent film, *The Big Hop,* was a big flop, caught in the gap of Hollywood's change-over to talkies, and he was forced to abandon the venture. It was the start of a stretch of bad luck for Buck. Being a popular and public Cowboy-Hero with a background in rodeos and circuses, he put together the "Buck Jones Wild West Show" to tour the country and keep his star shining. But he had barely got the show on the road when the Depression fell on him like a ton of cow flop from a very great height and wiped him out. Flat busted. For a while it looked as if Buck Jones had come to the end of the trail after a good run through the Twenties. But Buck bounced back. Working for $300 a week (one-tenth his former salary), he took what he could get. And eventually got to Columbia where he became that studio's top cowboy and re-established his career and fat salary checks. For another decade he rode at the front of the pack, still a big-time Cowboy-Hero.

Three generations of Front Row Kids followed Buck Jones and cheered for him. Through the silents and the talkies. From 20th Century-Fox to Columbia, Universal, and Monogram. He was a Cowboy-Hero until he died.

Buck Jones was killed on November 28, 1942, burned to death in the flash fire that gutted the Coconut Grove Night Club in Boston. Buck got out all right but, Cowboy-Hero to the end, went back into the flames to help rescue others. Almost 300 people died. Including one of the best of the white-hat Good Guys.

Another of the Good Guys who gave Tom Mix a run for the money, helped the Twenties roar, and captured the fancy of the Front Row Kids was Edmund Richard Gibson. Called

"Hoot." Hoot Gibson was another up-from-stuntman Cowboy-Hero. But unlike many, Hoot was a genuine cowboy from the plains of Nebraska who punched cows in Wyoming, rode the rodeo circuit, and won the title "All-Around Champion Cowboy" in 1912 at the Pendleton Roundup. Flushed with success and not a bit shy, he went to Hollywood to be a cowboy star. If "Broncho Billy" could do it, Hoot must have thought, then anyone can. As played by Anderson, "Broncho Billy" couldn't even ride a horse, let alone a bucking bronco. But it was not so easy, even in those early Hollywood days, to break into pictures. A fact that would be learned the hard way by a million ambitious cowboy types and small-town girls with pretty faces who would come out to Hollywood over the years, clutching their spurs or their tap-dancing shoes, and never got to see the inside of a studio except on the 25¢ tour.

Hoot was luckier. But not right away. He was a virtually invisible extra in *The Squaw Man,* then went to work as a wrangler and stuntman. The pay was $2.50 to bite the dust disguised as an Indian and $5 to fall in the same heap dressed as a cavalry man. It was all the same to Hoot, who would just as eagerly and with careless enthusiasm hurl himself off a cliff if he knew there was a camera turning down at the bottom to record the flight and the splat! Eventually he was spotted by Harry Carey, who dusted him off, encouraged him, and fixed him up with stunt-double work and supporting roles in his own popular two-reelers. In 1917 a better break came. He co-starred with Carey in a Universal film called *Straight Shooting,* which was John Ford's first feature as a director. It was a very good Western for those early days, and Ford was definitely going places as a Western movie director. Hoot Gibson, athletic, handsome in a boyish way, with a quick smile and a mouthful of prominent teeth, seemed well placed in the scheme of things to come. Until the war reared up and Hoot had his ticket punched for France. He served two years in the Tank Corps before he could get back to Universal and pick up where he left off with Carey and Ford. He worked steady for two more years, and in 1921, with Tom Mix by now firmly in the saddle as King of the Cowboys, Hoot made *Action,* his first

star-billing full-length cowboy feature. It was directed by John Ford. It was a hit. And instantly put Hoot Gibson in the running as a big-time Hollywood Cowboy.

The head of Universal, "Uncle Carl" Laemmle, was one of Hollywood's Founding Father-figures and, standing 5 feet 2 inches, an industry giant. A German refugee who "off the boat got" without two pennies to rub together, he built Universal up from nothing and was, above all, a clever and hard-bargaining businessman. But he loved the make-believe he was producing. And of all the motion picture make-believes, he loved Westerns the best. It was only natural that, with the great success of *Action*, he would come to love Hoot Gibson. Hoot would be Universal's first big Western star, Uncle Carl's Ace to play against Tom Mix's Royal Flush. Universal had already established a cheap, fast-moving, and efficient Western movie operation, with good young directors like Ford, Western types like Carey and Hoot, and hard-working, low-salaried crews that turned out tight little Westerns, one right after the other. With Uncle Carl spurring them on and keeping a watchful eye on everything that moved on his lot (and probably wishing he were a 6 feet 2 inch cowboy). Hoot had learned Western movies on Uncle Carl's two-reeler assembly line. Now he would be Laemmle's Number 1 Cowboy.

Universal (which meant, of course, Uncle Carl) looked after him, promoted him, and as hit followed hit, rewarded him. Hoot Gibson's salary hit $14,500 a week, and he lived like a caliph, with a Hollywood mansion, sports car, private planes, and a fairly continuous supply of dancing girls. Universal gave him his own production company (a standard fringe benefit for all big-time Cowboy-Heroes), and Hoot put his own distinctive brand on his films, as any Hollywood Cowboy had to if he hoped to stand out from the competition. His Westerns had plenty of fast action, but his own specialty was lighthearted humor and he often quite unself-consciously cast himself as a goof or a boob rather than as a Mix-like white knight of the range. And although, while he was in the chips, he lived the flash Hollywood Cowboy life, throughout his career he always tried to keep his image on the screen that of an ordinary range-riding cowboy. Having genuine cowboy roots, Hoot was opposed to the flamboyant and fancy-geared screen cowboy. It was a matter of principle and pride as much as good "theater."

"Most of my movies were comedy-drama rough-and-ready stuff," he was quoted as saying years later about his Western movie career. "There hasn't been a comedy-drama since I quit. I got out of jams logically. My movies didn't have much violence. That's bad for kids. Instead of fighting the villain physically, I'd trick him.

"I did all the stunts myself. I wasn't a phony cowboy. . . . I never wore loud clothes, but what real cowboys wear—overalls, shirt, a hat. I stuck my gun in my belt instead of in a fancy holster. I never featured a horse. I used five of them, and they didn't have names. I never sang . . ."

In all, Hoot made over 300 films and made and lost about $5 million. He was cold-cocked by the Depression, bad investments, dry water holes, and perpetual handouts to deadbeats and hangers-on. All the usual catastrophes that seem to hit those who suddenly find themselves with enormous wealth, a good heart, and a dumb head for business. But when each piece of money was gone, he'd go out and make some more.

He carried on cowboying into the talkies, left Universal and went to work mostly for the independent companies who were churning out Westerns for the Saturday Matinees of the Thirties. The quality of his work fell off a good bit from his great days at Universal, but he kept making Hoot Gibson Westerns and was one of the Big Four until he retired in 1936 (a retirement that was hastened by the enormous impact on the Front Row Kids of the singing cowboy, Gene Autry, against whom Hoot could not hope to compete). In the early Forties he came back, a little old and fat, for the Trail Blazers series at Monogram, with Ken Maynard and Bob Steele, two of the great old greats. He pulled down a salary of $4,000 a week on those.

But then it was over for Hoot. He retired to Nevada to live out his days on the dry desert, entertaining his friends and "greeting" old fans and high rollers at the Last Frontier Hotel and Casino in Las Vegas. Watching other people lose their money. In 1959, for sentimental reasons, John Ford cast him in a small part in *The Horse Soldiers.* They say he handled himself well, but most of his performance ended up on the cutting-room floor. He died of cancer in 1962 at the Motion Picture Country Home and was buried in Inglewood Park Cemetery in his cowboy gear. All the Hollywood Cowboys turned out to pay their last respects because for 40 years the name Hoot Gibson had signified "Cowboy-Hero" almost as much as the name Tom Mix.

Ken Maynard was the next Cowboy-Hero to come bucking out of the chute in pursuit of Tom Mix in the Twenties. And if he never did quite catch Mix as a National Fantasy (who could?), Ken Maynard nearly did out-Daredevil him and did, in fact, outlast him in the business, staying in the saddle until the middle Forties, long after Tom Mix had heard the final buzzer sound.

Ken Maynard was wild and a dreamer. He brought a kind of hot-blooded daring to his role as a Cowboy-Hero. The idea of being larger than life suited his personality, matched his own private image of himself. He could be tyrannical, uncompromisingly demanding of himself and others. He was powerful, impetuous, undisciplined, stormy, brash, sarcastic, belligerent, had a hair-trigger temper and an ego that made even the largest white ten-gallon Stetson a tight fit. And he was a demon-black drinker. But he was romantic and sentimental, played half a dozen musical instruments, sang loudly if not well, wrote music and poetry, and loved to draw. And he was totally committed to motion-picture Cowboy-Hero make-believe. He was, perhaps, the most complex of all the men who galloped across the imagination of America's Front Row Kids. As exciting to watch and to cheer as any white-hat Good Guy, there was an edge of darkness in his nature, something short-fused and explosive that zinged the nerves with hints of danger. Not the sort of thing Front Row Kids expected to find in their straight-shooting, righteous Saturday afternoon heroes. Certainly there were no such indications of complexity in the high-polished, glittering image Tom Mix had created. Nor in the goofiness of Hoot Gibson or the semi-seriousness of Buck Jones. Some of the people who knew and worked with Ken Maynard came away with the feeling that he was, well, maybe just a bit crazy.

His high-spirited personality, with its potentially explosive mixture of recklessness, fantasy, and controlled tension, was best reflected on the screen in the action sequences and the almost incredible stunt riding and horseback tricks he performed on his golden Palomino, Tarzan. There seemed to be nothing he wouldn't dare to do on a horse. And in big close-up so that nobody could cry Fake! Ken Maynard's screen trademark was the running insert, that most dramatic and exciting of all Western-movie action shots, in which the camera, mounted on a camera car, races along at close range with the galloping horseman. It was the most striking example of both Ken Maynard and the Western movie doing what they did best. Moving! Ken would come barreling down the road on Tarzan, as if he and the horse were one, with the camera keeping the same breathless pace, holding Ken in the center of the frame, larger than life, while the Wild West scenery whipped along in the background. For the Front Row Kids the involvement was total. Except that their seats were firmly nailed to the theater floor, they would swear they were galloping right along with their Cowboy-Hero. That illusion of being part of the action on the screen was, after all, at the heart of motion-picture Wild West Tales, and only the very best Hollywood Cowboys could make that illusion work for them as well as Ken Maynard did.

He could take jumps and hurdles on that horse of his that you wouldn't want to take in a biplane. There was no angle in the saddle he couldn't maintain long after any good rider would have passed out or fallen off and broken all his bones. He could hang upside-down while going flat out or lean waaaaay back in the saddle and snatch an object (or even a man) off the ground. Any kind of flying mount or dismount was merely exercise for Ken Maynard. Like a walk in a safe park on a lazy afternoon. No sweat. It is said that he could slide off

one side of the saddle, with Tarzan going full gallop, pass himself underneath the horse's body, and come up and into the saddle again from the other side. Ken Maynard on horseback was almost too exciting. Here was a Miracle Rider trying to extend the edges of physical possibility, seriously exploring the limits of what he could control. And at the same time presenting to the Front Row Kids a smiling, good-natured, morally pure, straight-shooting, and unambiguous Cowboy-Hero to idolize and emulate.

As much as the gaudiness of Tom Mix showmanship reflected the spirit of the Twenties, so did, in its way, the public grin and private grimace of Ken Maynard. The Roaring Twenties, for all its flapping and frivolity, was essentially a schizo-frenzied era. On the one hand was the moral tradition of small-town innocence, temperance, and the Protestant work ethic (the Volstead Act and the Bible) that the Cowboy-Hero symbolized better than any other figure of fantasy. On the other there was a "new" morality, gin-soaked abandon, manic gaiety, free-wheeling criminality, and a national giddiness that seemed to give license to outrageous extremes. The Twenties echoed with the sound of those two hands clapping, and Ken Maynard, a man of extremes who was both Cowboy-Hero and wild man for most of his life, loved the sound ringing in his ears.

Ken Maynard began his pursuit of applause when he ran away from his home in Indiana at the age of 12 to join a wandering Wild West Show. His father brought him back. But at 16 he went away for good (with his father's blessings) to join a touring carnival. Except for a turn in the army during World War I (not in combat but in civil engineering), Circus World was his life for the next 10 years. And would always be in his blood, as it stays in the blood of anyone who has ever been a "carny." There was something freebooting and exciting about circuses and Wild West Shows that appealed to all the Cowboy Heroes who came up in the Twenties, most especially to a man like Maynard who was so good and happy in the Big Top spotlight. He worked them all, from rinky-dinks to three-ringers, even, apparently, the Buffalo Bill show itself during one of the last years before Cody died, broke and broken. In 1920 Ken Maynard won the title "Champion Cowboy of the World" and the next year was headlined as the top rider for Ringling Brothers Circus. He earned $40,000. And was encouraged by Buck Jones, who caught his act out in Los Angeles, to make a run at the high-powered spotlight of Hollywood.

He spent the next two years riding and rowdying, with no producers rushing to push him near a camera. His riding was too hairy for their cautious taste. And he seemed to get into fist fights whenever he was in the same room with an open keg. He did get one bottom of the billing walk-on in a Fox Western. But for the most part he just hung around Tom Mix's ranch, exercising his elbow when he wasn't putting all the other cowboys to shame with his trick riding. He was a better horseman drunk than most of them were sober.

Finally, in 1924, he got his chance to ride as co-star in a big-time feature film. Not, however, as a Cowboy-Hero but as the most famous American rider of them all, Paul Revere. The film was *Janice Meredith,* the million-dollar history-drama William Randolph Hearst produced for the greater glory of his number-one girl, Marion Davies. Maynard collected $1,000 a week and was off and riding.

After a series of low-budget Westerns for a small independent studio, Ken Maynard rode out the silent Twenties as the top cowboy at First National, matching his Cowboy-Hero image against anything Tom Mix could do. And as a daredevil horseman and furiously freewheeling stunt rider, he clearly outclassed Mix. Even Maynard's horse, Tarzan, was amazing. The golden Palomino could dance, count, shake his head yes or no, grin, laugh, roll over and play dead, ring a fire bell, tie a knot, save Ken from just about any disaster—burning buildings, tumbling rivers, dangerous precipices, or the clutches of treacherous black-hat Bad Guys—take any kind of fall and get up again, even act as matchmaker between Cowboy Ken and the rancher's daughter. Everything except recite poetry and sing "Home on the Range."

In 1929, after 19 Westerns at First National, he got a good offer he could not refuse from "Uncle Carl" Laemmle and moved over to Universal. And the films he made for Uncle Carl would bring him his greatest wealth and fame. However, the freedom and responsibility and recognition would cause the demons of his dark booze-and-ego-driven nature to howl louder and make the wildman in him more difficult than ever to control. Eventually he would become impossible to work with, raging and fighting when things didn't work out the way he wanted them to. But until he finally went out of control, Ken Maynard was luckier than many of the Hollywood Cowboys of the silent Twenties who were forced to put their money where their mouths were when the movies began to talk.

After his first series at Universal was completed and his contract was not renewed because Uncle Carl was still doubtful that sound and action could mix in Wild West Tales, Ken rode for three years for Tiffany and for World Wide, independent "Poverty Row" studios that were eager to rush in and take a chance on action talkies with a Cowboy star of Maynard's caliber. It was a step down from the Big Time, but at least Ken was working. Riding hard, as if his life depended on it. And eventually it paid off royally in another contract with Universal.

Once again at home on Uncle Carl's range, Ken was given his own production company and an absolutely free hand to make whatever kind of Western movie struck his fancy.

Next to his First National silent Westerns, this second Universal series should have been his most memorable and best work, giving him the stature in the Thirties he had had in the Twenties. Finally he had what he'd been fighting for, the power to do what he wanted. But what did he want? He laced his films with music—songs and his own accomplished fiddlin'. (During his first Universal tour, in the film *Sons of the Saddle*, he had become something of a sound Western pioneer. The first movie cowboy to put songs in his films.) And when he wasn't singin' or fiddlin', he was in the saddle, tearing around at full speed as he had always done.

But with all his freedom, he still chafed and chomped at the bit over the way Universal did things, its assembly-line productions, and the pressure of the responsibility he felt to get his work done. He was drinking more and harder now than he had ever done before, arguing and raging on the set and off, threatening to shoot people who didn't see things his way. All the admiration and satisfaction that should have been his for all his years as a top-ranked Cowboy-Hero, he was smashing to smithereens in his black fury to achieve . . . perfection?

There is a story that after completing *Smoking Guns,* the last and most bizarre and confusing of his elaborate Universal Westerns, a ragged-nerved and nearly freaked-out Ken Maynard was called into Uncle Carl's office.

"Ken," said the tiny, white-haired Uncle Carl, "you have made me a very bad picture. Why didn't you spent two or three thousand dollars more and make it a good picture?"

"Mr. Laemmle," said Ken in a smoldering and bitter rage, "I have made you *eight* very bad pictures." And promptly walked out of the office, off the lot, and out of his contract. It would be his last big deal.

His next job was for Mascot Pictures, another Poverty Row independent. Nat Levine, head man at Mascot, hated Ken Maynard's guts but wanted him to star in *Mystery Mountain,* a 12-chapter serial, and to follow it with a full-length feature. Ken's relationship with Levine was maddening and soul destroying. He howled threats on the set, drank constantly, and held up production with hours of quarreling and bitterness. Levine, who never spent a penny more than he had to, to get by, who cut every production corner to ensure maximum profits at minimum expense, regarded Maynard as an uncontrollable madman. The serial, however, was a financial success. And through some miracle of pure will and determination, the feature Ken made for Mascot, *In Old Santa Fe,* was one of the best of all his Western films, with an easygoing naturalness to his performance that revealed nothing of the self-destructive turmoil he was going through. Not by accident, *In Old Santa Fe* featured three musical numbers by Nat Levine's latest personal discovery, Gene Autry. No doubt Levine swallowed his own personal hatred for Maynard and endured Ken's furies because he wanted to use Ken's still-enormous Front Row Kid popularity to introduce his new singing cowboy.

In Old Santa Fe would be his last good film. But he probably didn't give a damn. After 10 years of constant work, pushing himself to the edges of his physical and mental possibilities, he was becoming less and less interested in the films he was making. He could not give up the spotlight and the applause, but the energy spent on keeping his place and his integrity, the fighting and the bitterness (and the bottle), only added despair and disappointment to his load of psychic confusion. In his subsequent films for Columbia, Grand National, Colony, and Monogram over the next 10 years, there was no longer much opportunity to do the things he had become famous for. He was not the Daredevil he once was. Some of the action sequences in these films were stolen from his own better days, stock footage from his great silents and his best early sound Westerns!

As if to speed the downward spiral of his career, he organized the Diamond K Ranch Wild West Show to tour the country and get back to his beloved free-wheeling carny roots. The Show busted out almost before it began and he lost everything.

His final series of films, "The Trail Blazers" series made at Monogram in the early Forties with Hoot Gibson and Bob Steele, were fun to make because he and Hoot were old pals and drinking buddies. But, still true to his own peculiar nature, he hated Bob Steele, fought with the producers, and walked out on the contract before the series was completed. His last starring Western was *Harmony Trail,* made in 1944 for Ascot Pictures. It was the bottom of the barrel for Ken.

During the next 30 years, Ken Maynard, one of those who had been daring and confident enough to pick up Tom Mix's challenge, just slipped off sideways into drunkenness and oblivion. During the Fifties and Sixties he sometimes traveled the rodeo circuit with his third and last wife, Bertha, a former circus tightrope walker whom, in the full-blown romanticism that was also part of Ken's nature, he loved more than his life. For 28 difficult years she devotedly helped him with his life, his memories, and his drinking problems. When Bertha died in 1968, he was left alone in the trailer in the San Fernando Valley where they had lived together, and where he wrote poetry and was visited by friends who remembered him. He died on March 23, 1973, of old age, tired of life and of being alone. He had been one of the best of the breed. At least one Front Row Kid, out of millions, was there at the funeral at Forest Lawn in Orange County, California, to mark the passing.

Of all the morally pure, acrobatic, and straight-shooting Cowboy-Heroes of the Twenties, an ex-Presbyterian minister and track star, Fred Thomson, probably made the nearest run against Tom Mix in Hollywood Cowboy popularity and Front Row Kid appeal.

In those days, Hollywood had two faces—one public, one private. The first one was of easygoing, carefree laughter, glamorous diamond-studded fantasy, a living daydream of wholesome and heroic possibilities, beautiful women and handsome men performing on the screen and in real-life America's dream-wish of fame, success, love, wealth, power, and good times. The other face, shocking and distasteful, was of a hairy-toothed vampire whose heavy-lidded bloodshot eyes and sleazy, twisted smile hinted of outrageous perversion, depravity, greed, sex, drugs, and murder. It was Hollywood's private face of creepy-crawly nights and wildness. It was not the one Hollywood wanted to show the public and certainly not the one it wanted to project on a 20-foot-tall screen. The scandal potential was bad for business. It was enough to make producers and investors twitch, break out in spots, run for their lives. But it was no easy thing trying to keep its scandals out of the bright glare of sweeping crisis-crossing spotlights.

In 1921 there was the infamous Roscoe (Fatty) Arbuckle rap. Perhaps Hollywood's primo scandal of the Roaring Twenties. A roly-poly comedy star, Arbuckle was one of the public's darlings. Until the Labor Day weekend of that year. After an all day and all night bootleg whiskey and bathtub gin-drinking party in the St. Francis Hotel in San Francisco, a pretty young girl named Virginia Rappe pegged out under mysterious cir-

With comic Charlie Murray in The Pioneer Scout.

cumstances (most likely an infinite number of overindul-
gences). Fatty, who had been the last man in the bedroom
with her, was arrested and charged with manslaughter. It
became a front-page, banner-headline affair. Pornography
and death. The public response was a thundering burst of
moral outrage mixed with a hot-breathed interest in every
sordid detail, both real and imagined. Fatty was eventually
acquitted. Nevertheless, the industry and the public stoned
him as a sinner and banished him to oblivion as if he were
Frank the Mad Axe Man or the dreaded ague spreading pesti-
lence. He never appeared in another picture, and those he had
already made were yanked out of distribution despite their
popularity and buried in quicklime. Round-faced and ruined,
Fatty Arbuckle became the personification of the hairy-
toothed vampire and was purged for the sake of Hollywood's
other face. But the memory lingered on. Hollywood of the
Twenties needed a good-sized rug to get all of its dirt under
and out of sight.

While Fatty Arbuckle was undergoing his ordeal by trial and
innuendo, film director William Desmond Taylor was murdered under circumstances even more dubious and mysterious than the Arbuckle/Rappe case. Taylor's murder was never
solved, but the death-breath of the hairy-toothed vampire
blew scandal all over the careers of two pretty and popular
actresses. Mary Miles Minter, who had been promoted as a
possible successor to Mary Pickford, was discovered to have
been fairly desperately in love with the unfortunate and
rather disreputable director. (There was evidence that he was
also fooling around with Miss Minter's mother!) And Mabel
Normand, delightful and lovely star of Mack Sennett comedies, was found to be the last person (save for the undiscovered
murderer) to have seen Taylor alive. Neither woman's career
survived the association.

Drugs made the headlines and put egg on Hollywood's face
in 1923 when Wallace Reid, All-American hero and clean-cut
Griffith and DeMille leading man, freaked to death in the
madhouse. A junkie for some time before his death, he was
only one of many Hollywood bright lights whose eyes could

have revealed what their lips would never admit in public, that they were strung out on junk and pills even while they performed before the cameras. Hollywood in the Twenties was Morphine Alley, Coke City, and in the secret opium dens of L.A.'s Chinatown were probably more celebrities, clunked out and smiling vacantly, than you would find at a world premiere at Grauman's Chinese Theater.

It was not a happy time for the fantasy factory. And making things even worse for the hero-worshiping American public, across the continent in Washington, D.C., President Harding's Teapot Dome corruptions added their fetid odor to the general air of unwholesomeness that blew in gusts through the Roaring Twenties' good times. For the sake of its own survival Hollywood felt a heavy obligation to put its best face forward. To protect and insure the business of the business, the industry created an organization called the Motion Picture Producers and Distributors of America, Inc. And brought in ex-Postmaster General and politico Will Hays to run it, with primary responsibility to police the morals of Hollywood and to regulate the industry.

The establishment of the Hays Office led directly to the imposition of the rigid, narrow, infantile, growth-stunting directives of the Production Code of Ethics that governed for nearly 40 years what motion pictures were permitted to show.

And every studio put a morality clause in their contracts to give themselves a tight guarantee that if the private indiscretions of their star players did not altogether cease, at least they would be carried on in a deep and dark hole in the ground, preferably some place absolutely out of the public's sight, like Borneo or the North Pole, where all screams of agony or ecstasy would be muffled beyond all hearing.

Under these circumstances, the Hollywood Cowboy as he appeared in the Saturday Matinee, with his unquestionable white-hat Good Guy image of moral purity, virtue, honesty, bravery, health, vigor, and handsomeness, devoted above all to justice, the Good Cause, and his horse, was the ideal figure to represent Hollywood's happy face in the movies. Tom Mix was, of course, perfect for the part. Hollywood could not hope for anyone else as near-perfect for a Cowboy-Hero. Unless it was an ex-Presbyterian minister, champion athlete, and Boy Scout. Fred Thomson was almost too good to be true. Just what the censors ordered. And the Front Row Kids flocked to see him do his stuff.

Fred Thomson was a local boy. Born in Pasadena. He was the son of a preacher and, quite unlike most Hollywood Cowboys, a college graduate. He earned a B.A. degree at Occidental College in Los Angeles as well as the college letter in three sports, football, baseball, and track. Track was his specialty, that sport of the ancient Greeks, with its rigorous training and discipline and where the competition is as much against yourself as it is against the other guy. Thomson twice won national track and field titles. And broke Jim Thorpe's world decathlon record. There was no trace of Wild West Show or rodeo roustabouting in Fred Thomson's pre-Cowboy-Hero past. After college he attended the Princeton Theological Seminary, was ordained a Presbyterian minister, and named pastor of the Hope Chapel in Los Angeles. Later he became pastor of the Presbyterian church in Goldfield, Nevada, and served a term as State Commissioner of the Boy Scouts. The Reverend Fred Thomson was straight as a pine and squeaky clean.

In 1916 he joined the army as a chaplain. He was not exactly a warrior. He won his "red badge of courage" in an interservice football game in which he broke his leg. It would prove to be his lucky break. While recovering in an army hospital, he met Mary Pickford and script writer Frances Marion, who found him to be handsome, charming, and refreshingly cheerful. When the war was over (he had eventually gone to France), he returned to California, looked up Frances Marion, and married her. It would soon be the end of Bible beating for the Reverend Fred. And the beginning of the Big Time.

His wife and their friends urged him to try the pictures. C'mon, Fred. You can do it. There's nothing to it. Finally seduced and persuaded by the possibilities of motion pictures for good, clean entertainment, he took the plunge. No walkons for him. He entered at the top, as co-star and leading man to Mary Pickford in *The Light of Love.* His starting salary was

$2,000 per week. After starring in a Universal serial, *The Eagle's Talons,* in 1923, he knew that Westerns were for him and that he wanted to be a Cowboy-Hero. The moral stance of the Cowboy-Hero coincided perfectly with his own feelings about the way things ought to be in the world.

Thomson began his full-time Western movie career at FBO (Joseph P. Kennedy's studio), and his films were a great instantaneous success. The Front Row Kids (and even their parents) took to this dashing, upright, and stylish Hollywood Cowboy as they did to none of the others except Tom Mix. He gave them exciting stunts, light humor, chaste romance, and whenever possible, a minimum of violence. His films were aimed directly at the Kids and were intended to be good clean fun and wholesome entertainment, without any trace of sordidness or cynicism. He fought bulls and mountain lions, jumped from rooftops and moving trains, even swung from chandeliers. He had a horse called "Silver King" who did everything a "wonder horse" was supposed to do, including the unbelievable. (In *Thundering Hoofs* Silver King supposedly buries a dead body, fashions a wooden cross and plants it on top of the gravesite along with a pot of flowers!) Fred Thomson was very definitely in the show-biz cowboy tradition established by Tom Mix. On screen he was outfitted more lavishly and flamboyantly than all the rest. And off screen, he lived in a $650,-000 mansion in Beverly Hills, with closets full of cowboy paraphernalia and show-biz clobber. The former Reverend Fred seemed to know instinctively the value of "show." And it paid off handsomely for him. In little more than six years (living relatively tax-free as well as scandal-free) he earned $2.5 million.

Following his success at FBO, he formed Fred Thomson Productions to make his own films for Paramount distribution. They were lavish and extravagant in their production (not quickies), with plenty of gloss and glamour. But their aim was always sheer entertainment. With Boy Scout ethics at the core. In *Jesse James,* the outlaw-hero did not commit even one bank robbery! But his fans didn't seem to mind Fred Thomson sanitizing this historical Wild West figure. *Jesse James* brought in over $1 million at the box office. It was also the only one of all his films in which the Cowboy-Hero dies at the end.

In his Paramount films Fred Thomson was at the top of his form, the peak of his career. He was a phenomenon. The future looked to be without limit for Fred Thomson. There was no doubt about it. But *Jesse James* was to be Fred Thomson's last film. Like the Cowboy-Hero he portrayed in that film, Fred Thomson died at the end of the picture. But unlike Jesse, Thomson died with his boots off, of tetanus, from stepping on a rusty nail. On Christmas night, December 25, 1928. Had he lived, he surely would have ridden right into the sound era, triggering Front Row Kid fantasies and memories for years to come. He was that good and that popular in his lifetime. As it turned out, 50 years after his big run, the name Fred Thomson rings no bells. Except as the right answer to the trivia quiz question: After Tom Mix, who was the most popular Cowboy-Hero of the Twenties?

And then there was Colonel Tim McCoy. Elegant gentleman. Indian Agent. Soldier. Cowboy-Hero. The last (and longest-lasting) of the Big Four—Buck Jones, Hoot Gibson, Ken Maynard, and McCoy—who rivaled Mix. The man who knew more about the West (certainly about the Indians) than any Hollywood Cowboy. Who came out to Hollywood to instruct the movie makers in what the West was really like. And stayed to perform topnotch Wild West Tale make-believe. The only Cowboy-Hero that Metro Goldwyn Mayer, *the* top-drawer glamour studio of Hollywood, ever put under contract. A Cowboy-Hero with his own unique personality and image. Not to be mistaken for anybody else. If William S. Hart was the "good badman." And Tom Mix was the Rhinestone-and-Neon Cowboy. If Ken Maynard was the Daredevil. And Hoot Gibson the Ragtime Clown. Then Colonel Tim McCoy's image would be the "Man of Destiny." In basic black. He wasn't every Front Row Kid's idea of a Cowboy-Hero. Only the smart ones'. Tim McCoy, with his cavalry officer's bearing and a twinkle in his eye, was a Cowboy with . . . class.

Timothy John Fitzgerald McCoy was born in Saginaw, Mich-

igan, when it was still a horse-and-buggy town. In 1891. It wasn't the West, but there were plenty of cowboy types to be seen. Horse catchers and wranglers from Wyoming and Montana who brought herds to sell in the horse-poor Midwest. A boy could catch Wild West Fever just as quickly and surely from these cowboys as he could from Buffalo Bill's Wild West Show. Young Tim McCoy caught a permanent dose. It was not something he would get over when he grew up. In his sophomore year at St. Ignatius College in Chicago, he went to every performance of the Miller 101 Ranch Wild West Show for a solid week, then he quit school, boarded a westbound train, and got off in Lander, Wyoming. With $5 in his pocket. And a passion to become a cowboy.

It was 1907, but Wyoming was still fairly wild. He found work pitching hay and digging fencepost holes. Then, just as he had hoped, as a cowboy among cowboys. He rode in the last of the great Wyoming roundups. Eventually, as much a Wyoming cowboy as if he had been born there, he homesteaded a piece of land and built up a ranch. It would, in time, become a 5,000-acre spread.

During those years of making his home in Wyoming and learning to be a cowboy, Tim developed his great respect and love for the Plains Indians. The Arapahoe and Shoshone Indians—or what was left of those tribes after years of white "civilizing"—lived together in the Wind River country where Tim worked, trying to maintain their old ways and mind their own business. They were fascinating and impressive people. McCoy spent a great deal of time among them. Mastered their sign language so that he could communicate with them. Eventually he would come to know as much about them as they knew about themselves. The Arapahoe adopted him and gave him the name "High Eagle." Later, in his Hollywood days, no Tim McCoy Western would ever depict the Indians as "crazed, bloodthirsty savages" or "red devils," as inhuman or stupid or inferior. Only Tim McCoy, out of all the Hollywood Cowboys, could have said, without sarcasm, cynicism, or condescension: "Some of my best friends are Indians."

When World War I broke out, Tim McCoy volunteered to

recruit a band of the toughest hard-riding cowboys he could find in Wyoming to make up the cavalry troop that Teddy Roosevelt wanted to take to France. The old Bull Moose egomaniac hankered for a replay of his famous "Follow me, boys!" charge up San Juan Hill. Romantic as the notion was, it was not one of Teddy's best and most practical ideas. Lucky for McCoy, the idea was filed and forgotten. He and his cowboys would have undoubtedly been ground to hamburger in the first charge. As it turned out, Tim applied to officer's candidate school instead, was commissioned a captain, and went to France as an artillery officer. He came out of the war with the rank of lieutenant-colonel and the close friendship of Major General Hugh Lenox Scott, last of the great Indian fighters, former Army Chief of Staff and authority on the language and customs of the Plains Indians.

As an aide to Scott, Colonel McCoy traveled all over Wyoming with the general, visiting army posts and talking to Indians. In their travels they traced the route of Custer to the Little Big Horn. And in their sign-talk with the Indians they learned that two old Arapahoe, Water Man and Left Hand, had been in the famous fight and were still alive. Colonel Tim, with an interpreter and a stenographer, powwowed with them. McCoy's research helped to set the record straight on Custer's folly at the Battle of the Little Big Horn.

When Scott became head of the Board of Indian Commissioners, Tim McCoy was appointed adjutant general in Wyoming with particular responsibility for Indian affairs in the state. He was by then an acknowledged authority on the Indians and got his picture in the papers when he found and brought out of hiding Wavoka, messiah of the "Ghost Dancers," that strange, fanatical, and mystical Indian religion that had swept the Plains tribes in the 1890s and so frightened the shit out of the white eyes that the Wounded Knee massacre was perpetrated in the hopes of destroying it and its influence. But neither Wavoka nor any of the Wyoming Indians had anything to fear from Tim McCoy. And Hollywood had much to learn from him.

In 1922, when Famous Players-Lasky began production of

the first epic Western, *The Covered Wagon,* with a cast of hundreds, vast cinematic frontier panoramas, and grand-scale epic sequences, including a wild river crossing, buffalo hunt, and an Indian attack, the natural and logical choice for technical advisor and supervisor of the hundreds of Indian extras was Tim McCoy. Who else? The only sign language any of the producers knew was dollar-sign language. Who would talk to the Indians? Tell them where to stand and when to fall off their horses? Tim McCoy came to Hollywood. And brought his Indians with him. Camping them, wives, braves, papooses, tents, cook-fires, and dogs, in Cahuenga Pass in the Hollywood Hills.

When the history-making Western premiered at Grauman's theater, Tim and the Indians performed a live prologue on stage, complete with Indian dancing, a short history lesson, sign-talking, and 50 Indians in full feather. To add poignancy to the prologue, one of the Indians was a Mrs. Broken Hand, who was in fact a red-haired white woman who had been captured as a child and remained with the tribe. And another was a Little Big Horn survivor. The film became a box-office hit. The prologue, which was performed nightly for eight months at Grauman's, was fascinating and popular. And Tim McCoy was in show business.

After serving as technical advisor on two more FP-L Westerns, McCoy caught the sharp eye of Irving Thalberg, boy wonder and head of production at M-G-M. Thalberg's wit and taste and literate sensibilities were responsible for making Louis B. Mayer's studio the class of Hollywood. It was the studio of Garbo and Gilbert, Ramon Navarro, Lillian Gish, Norma Shearer, and later, Lionel Barrymore, Jean Harlow, and Clark Gable. It did not, as a rule, "stoop" to Western productions. As if those compact, quickly made, strightforward, and fairly limited vehicles did not fit M-G-M's grand vision of itself. But the astute and alert Thalberg must have gone in disguise to see *The Covered Wagon,* Ford's *The Iron Horse,* and more than a few Tom Mix, Buck Jones, and Hoot Gibson Westerns. And while he sat there in the dark, he was counting the house. He decided to get in on it. And Tim

McCoy seemed to be his sort of Cowboy-Hero. He had the M-G-M style about him. In 1926 Tim McCoy signed a long-term contract with M-G-M. He would be their first and only resident Cowboy-Hero.

Thalberg, knowing enough about Western movies to know that he didn't know anything at all about them, but knowing that Tim McCoy knew more about the West than anybody around his lot, put McCoy together with the director, W. S. "Woody" Van Dyke, one of M-G-M's pros, in the hope that the two of them could come up with a good Western to launch McCoy's Cowboy-Hero career.

That first film was *War Paint.* It was filmed in Tim McCoy's own "back yard" in the picturesque terrain around Lander, Wyoming, using Tim's Indians. The story concerned a handsome cavalry officer who had been adopted into the Arapahoe tribe and given the Indian name "White Eagle" (familiar?), and who, because of his closeness with the Indians and great regard for them, goes among them to put down an uprising that has been instigated by a rebellious young chief. After defeating the chief in a mano a mano knife fight, McCoy convinces the other, less hot-blooded chiefs (by talking in sign language) that because they are not wild and bloodthirsty savages but a great people with their own gentle way of life, a war with the white man would be a slaughter they could not hope to survive. Peace is the answer. Give peace a chance. The treaty is made, and Tim wins the fort commander's daughter for his efforts. It was not the usual Cowboy-and-Indians Wild West Tale. It was a personal film for McCoy. And he looked after the image of the Indians while still cutting a dashing figure for himself as the white-hat Good Guy.

His next series of films were not, strictly speaking, Westerns in the manner of Mix and Maynard, Jones, and Gibson. Rather, M-G-M's big idea of a Western. Lavishly mounted, period-costumed, historical, colonial frontier Wild West Tales. Not your run-of-the-mill, galloping and shoot-'em-up, action-first-and-forever Westerns. They were intended to be something more than just Westerns. M-G-M was, after all, M-G-M. Let the other fellow do the nickel-and-dime assembly-line programmers. This series of M-G-M Wild West extravaganzas gave McCoy's Cowboy-Hero image the added lustre of a "sense" of American history. And he usually got to wear a uniform, which is what he looked best in. *Winners of Wilderness, California* and *The Frontiersman* were Wild West Tales intended for grownups.

But then a bit of corporate weirdness took place. In the production offices and the executive washrooms at M-G-M discussions were going on, pressures applied by Harry Rapf who was in charge of McCoy's productions. Are we supposed to be making Westerns here, Irving, or what? Is McCoy supposed to be a Cowboy-Hero or ain't he? Don't worry about it, Harry. Yeah, but Irving, look at Mix. Look at Fred Thomson. Shouldn't we be trying to get a piece of *that* action? I've seen them, Harry, but McCoy is different. *We* are different. M-G-M is no shlock house, Harry. I know, Irving, and you're no Uncle Carl. That's for sure, Harry. You can say that again. But I think we're missing out here, Irving. I'll give it some thought, Harry. That's all I'm asking, Mr. Thalberg. We'll see, Harry.

Apparently Thalberg did give some thought to what Harry Rapf was saying. Because Tim McCoy's Westerns began to change, to become less historical and more cowboy-like. The thrust was toward pulling in the Front Row Kids rather than the general movie-going audiences. However, Tim McCoy could never and would never play an ordinary cowpoke. He had too much style, with his military bearing and the air of an aristocrat about him. He was through with historical period pieces but would continue to play cavalry officers, Texas Rangers, Pony Express riders, government agents. And in the rest of his M-G-M westerns, the special Tim McCoy image began to emerge. The straight and immaculate, lightning-fast-on-the-draw Good Guy. The icy stare that froze the hearts and gun hands of the Bad Guys. The sideways glance, almost a twinkle in his eye, that told the Bad Guys they didn't have a chance and would be wise to throw in their hand before he made them look foolish. The black shirt, big white Stetson hat, and white horse that would become part of his trademark. These films put Tim McCoy right up there in the Big Four.

Being an M-G-M player, McCoy might have become more than a Cowboy Star. If Harry Rapf hadn't gotten his way with Irving Thalberg. But McCoy was never that hungry to be a Star Star. There were other things he could do with his life. He was still a reserve colonel in the army. He had a ranch and a home in Wyoming. He was no dummie. And so when sound came to Hollywood and all the studios freaked out, and M-G-M did not pick up his option, Tim McCoy went to Europe and then back to Wyoming. Figuring he had had a good time and a good run in Hollywood. He didn't expect to go back. He was disappointed that Louis B. Mayer had given him the bullet. But he would survive. Something would turn up.

And it did. A call came out to his ranch from Universal Studios. Uncle Carl wanted Tim McCoy, and only Tim McCoy, to be the Hero of what would be Hollywood's first talking Western serial. He would not take no for an answer. McCoy was surprised and flattered. He packed his kit and went back.

The Indians Are Coming was a cracker-jack, 12-chapter serial that combined elements of Wild West Show and dime-novel melodrama with much action and end-of-chapter cliff-hanging. After making a second serial for Universal and turning down an offer for a third (who wanted to be a serial king, anyway?), Tim went over to Columbia Pictures to work for Harry "King" Cohn, the monster of Gower Gulch, who had built Columbia up from nothing through sheer brass-knuckle intensity, a tightwad, and a tyrannical determination. While the major studios fluttered in hesitation, Harry Cohn charged. He had picked up Buck Jones, who was down on his luck after the Crash! and put that fine cowboy's career back on its feet. He knew there were good profits to be made from low-budget Westerns. And that Tim McCoy could do the job.

McCoy made 24 Westerns at Columbia from 1931 to 1935, picking up the cool and self-possessed image he had begun to establish during his M-G-M days. Still the marshal or the ex-officer or the undercover agent with the lightning-fast draw and the fearless style and grace. It was the one sure thing the Front Row Kids count on. When "King" Cohn tried to upgrade McCoy into non-Western action films and put him to playing a modern-day cop or fireman, forest ranger, or auto racer, the kids and the critics would not sit still for it. Tim McCoy was a Cowboy first and always. In his final series of Westerns for Columbia, he was not only back in boots but added a dramatic touch to his image. He traded in his white Stetson for a black one. For the rest of his cowboy days he would be the white-hat Good Guy who dressed completely in black, from the tip of his pointy-toed boots to the top of his high-crowned Stetson hat. Mix and Maynard had sometimes worn black, and a black shirt had become McCoy's trademark in his silent Westerns. But no Good Guy had ever gone over the line entirely. On Tim McCoy, black was beautiful. A dynamite image.

McCoy's Columbia Westerns were his best and most popular after the great M-G-M silents. They were also the last he would make for a major studio. Moving from there down the line to the independent Western factories. Puritan. Monogram. Victory. Back to Monogram. The budgets diminished, the schedules became tighter, the production values that had made the silent Westerns so outstanding were sacrificed for speed and economy. His Victory Films series were filmed in three to four days for a measly $8,000 ($4,000 of it went to pay Tim's salary). But Sam Katzman, the lowest of the low-budget producers, who was so tight he squeaked when he walked, didn't care how the films looked as long as they each brought in a sure $60,000 profit. Tim McCoy, on the other hand, did care. He took his low-budget Westerns as seriously as all the others he had made. The Front Row Kids would at least get a good Tim McCoy, icy stare and all, even if the saloon sets he was standing in wobbled visibly in the background.

In his films for Puritan he developed the character of Lightning Bill Carson, government lawman, enforcer, and avenger, who often went among the Bad Guys disguised as a Mexican, a Chinaman, a barfly, or a dusty prospector. But when the time came for the final showdown, and he came on in his spic-and-span black outfit, his flowing neckerchief, and his elaborate, hand-tooled gun belt, there was not a single Bad Guy (or Front Row Kid) who did not know that Tim McCoy was still a Cowboy-Hero who meant business.

McCoy's luck turned momentarily sour in 1938 when Tim,

"THE
ROUGH
RIDERS"

PRESENTED BY
Monogram
PICTURES

"FORBIDDEN TRAILS"

BUCK JONES · TIM McCOY
RAYMOND HATTON and "SILVER"

Produced by SCOTT R. DUNLAP · Directed by ROBERT N. BRADBURY
ORIGINAL SCREENPLAY JESS BOWERS

after three successful tours headlining for Ringling Brothers-Barnum and Bailey Circus, put together his own Wild West Show and took the inevitable pie in the face. The show lasted a month on the road and cost Tim close to $500,000. But by 1941 he was back in the money. Buck Jones and Monogram had a scheme for a series of "trio" Westerns starring Buck, Tim, and old-time professional sidekick Raymond Hatton. They would be *The Rough Riders.* And they would be terrific. Slick, fast-moving, and stylish. Buck Jones, in buckskin, riding a white stallion. Tim McCoy, all in black (save for a big white scarf), aboard a black charger. Hatton, the old codger, wore a battered hat and vest. Tim and Buck, in all their Cowboy-Hero dignity and glory, together against the Bad Guys! The old Front Row Kids, who knew them in the Twenties, would watch them do their stuff with a lump in their grownup throats for the passing of Cowboy-Hero time these two formidable Good Guys represented. And the new Kids, who might be seeing them for the first time, would just cheer like crazy because every Front Row Kid knew the real thing when he saw it. And at the end of each film, when the three Good Guys rode off alone in their separate directions, Tim McCoy to Wyoming (where else?), Buck Jones to Arizona, Ray Hatton to Texas, and waved their hats and called, "So long, Rough Riders!" there wasn't a Front Row Kid in the theater who didn't wish he were going with them. The smart ones, if given their choice, would surely have followed Tim McCoy.

When contract time came up for a second *Rough Riders* series in '42, Tim McCoy decided not to sign, and instead, at the age of 51 and still an active reserve colonel, went off to war to fight against the *real* Bad Guys. Only a real war could have gotten Tim McCoy out of the saddle.

When he returned in 1946, Buck Jones was dead. And the Western movies as Tim McCoy had known them were dying. And so he retired. But not out to pasture. In the early days of television, he had his own show, which featured his old movies as well as his pride and joy, Wild West history lessons and Indian stories that included sign-talking with his great Indian friend Iron Eyes Cody. The show won him an Emmy. He appeared in three films during the Fifties and Sixties. As the cavalry colonel in *Around the World in Eighty Days.* As a crusty one-armed general in *Run of the Arrow.* And as a circuit judge in *Requiem for a Gunfighter.* But the pace of his life was too slow to suit him. In 1962 he joined the Tommy Scott Wild West Show as the headlined cowboy attraction. For the next 13 years he was on the road 300 days out of the year, performing a sharp shooting and a bullwhip act and galloping around the arena to the wonder and delight of the Front Row Kids whose great-great-grandfathers had cheered Buffalo Bill. Even in his eighties, he was as cool and sure and ramrod straight in the saddle as ever. The last of the breed. The last and, for many, the best of the Big Four who came roaring out of the Twenties in hot pursuit of Tom Mix. Colonel Tim McCoy is not dead.

Buck Jones, Hoot Gibson, Ken Maynard, Fred Thomson, Colonel Tim McCoy. These, then, were the rivals of Tom Mix in the Twenties. And so, too, in their own way, were Valentino, Greta Garbo, Barrymore, Douglas Fairbanks, John Gilbert, Clara Bow, Lon Chaney. Rivals either for Cowboy-Hero fame or Hollywood rhinestone-and-neon Stardom. Charles Lindbergh was his competition, too. And Babe Ruth and Dempsey and Tunney. And, over in Paris, Ernest Hemingway, who knew a thing or two about heroes. And soaking himself in the fountain in front of the Plaza Hotel and wishing it were 100-proof gin, F. Scott Fitzgerald. Candidates for the daydreams and fantasies of the growing and the grownups who looked ceaselessly for something better happening somewhere else.

And how did Tom Mix fare against his competition? He beat them like a gong throughout the Twenties. First there was Tom Mix. And then there were all the rest. Tom Mix really was the king of that age. Whether you were a cowboy fan or not.

The Big Four were younger men than he was. But none of them passed him on the fly, made him obsolete or old-fashioned the way he had done to Hart (and Hart to "Broncho Billy"). Tom Mix was the one. Fact is that although there would be Cowboy-Heroes over the years who made more money than he did, perhaps even better (certainly different) Westerns than he made, no single cowboy would change the Western on him and put him out of it. Each of the Big Four had his own distinct personality and separate image. But they were all operating, more or less, in the Hollywood Cowboy-Hero tradition that Mix had fashioned. Action. Quick-draw make-believe. Aimed at the Front Row Kids. With only a sideways glance at Wild West reality. And no desire to imitate that reality. But to create a Wild West unreality that was better. Certainly more fun. And as the number of Cowboy-Heroes grew who were not flashes-in-the-pan or bums-of-the-month, Tom Mix met them all head-on, putting his best work up against theirs. As great and exciting and terrific as any of the Big Four or Fred Thomson were, they would still play second feature to Mix's *Riders of the Purple Sage, The Rainbow Trail, The Great K and A Robbery, The Outlaws of Red River,* or *The Horseman of the Plains.* And if there was still any doubt about who was number one, Tom Mix was the only Hollywood Cowboy who could keep a Wild West Show or a circus on the road longer than a split second, long enough to show a profit.

After years of maximum glory at Fox, Tom Mix left the studio in 1928. It was, depending on where you were standing, a case of: You're getting on, Tom. Hang up your spurs. Talkies are coming. Thanks for everything, including our studios. We'll name a sound stage after you. Get lost. Or: You can't fire me. I quit!

Tom Mix was already 48 years old when he went over to Kennedy's FBO to make six features for the ex-bootlegger. There was no way these films could have matched up to his best at Fox. But good and bad no longer had anything to do with it. The Front Row Kids (including, apparently, the young Kennedy boys) paid their money at the box office because he was Tom Mix. That was enough. It was the Depression that really unsaddled him. He took the full blast of the Crash! right in the pocket. He lost over $1 million, his gaudy palace in Beverly Hills, and his Arizona ranch. He decided to retire from films. And hit the road as the center ring attraction of the

Sells Floto Circus. Pulling down a salary of $10,000 a week.

His legend would continue to flourish during the next decade, although the Thirties were pretty hard on the life and body of the real Tom Mix. He smashed his shoulder to bits in a horse fall during his Wild West act, which developed into arthritis of the back. In 1930 he was bagged by the IRS for back taxes. And Victoria Forde Mix (wife number four) gave him the bullet on the grounds that he was "slipping around." (There were rumors that she actually shot him during one of their arguments.) He bounced back in 1932 by marrying Mabel Ward, a daring young girl on the flying trapeze who performed with the Sells Floto Circus. The Tom Mix body, though, continued to take a pounding. An injured leg and bruised side from another horse fall. A concussion. A serious attack of peritonitis. A broken leg. And there were all those bone-wearying miles and one-night stands with the circus.

In 1932 he took a break from all the broken bones and bruises to return to moving pictures. Uncle Carl Laemmle (who else?) signed him up for nine "talkies" at Universal. The critics and the smart alecks would say of these films that Tom Mix was not the man he once was, that he was old and stiff and out of it, that his voice was bad and he slurred his words. But the critics were talking through their hats. Tom Mix's sound Westerns were pretty good. And, better still for Universal and for Tom, they were popular. He may have been 53 years old. But when he came wheeling in on Tony, Jr., reared him up on his hind legs, and waved that ten-gallon white Stetson, Tom Mix was still King of the Cowboys.

The Universals should have been his last farewell. But in 1935 Nat Levine lured him back for a Mascot serial, *The Miracle Rider.* It was popular with the Front Row Kids. But it was junk. Why did Tom Mix do it? He gave as his reason: "I was mad at the conditions I saw and read about every day. Criminals on the loose. Boys and girls learning Communist propaganda in the schools. Crime filling the newspapers. Finally I figured out a way that I could help by returning to the screen with a picture with some good old-fashioned virtues and justice." Maybe so. But his urge to fight Communism was strengthened some by Levine's offer of $40,000 to take the part. Tom Mix needed the money. He had acquired the giant Sam B. Dill Circus for $400,000 and turned it into the Tom Mix Circus (admission: 25¢ for children, 60¢ for adults). But bread *and* circuses were a tough combination for anyone to make in the middle Thirties. The Tom Mix Circus folded its tents for good in 1938 after three seasons of diminishing returns. And that was the end of that.

On October 12, 1940, after a personal appearance in Tucson, Arizona, the day before and an all-night booze-up with some old buddies, Tom Mix climbed into his custom-built Cord Roadster with the longhorns mounted on the radiator, floored the thing, and headed north up U.S. 80. He was dressed in a fancy white cowboy-style suit, wearing a diamond-studded belt buckle, a pair of hand-tooled boots, and a white ten-gallon Stetson hat. In his pockets he carried $6,000 in cash and $1,500 in traveler's checks. There were two metal suitcases in the back ledge of the Cord. About 18 miles outside Florence, Arizona, that afternoon, going full throttle and feeling good, he did not see a crew of highway project workers who were digging up the road. The car swerved once or twice, went down a dry wash, up the other side, and turned over. One of the metal suitcases flew out, hit him in the back of the head, and broke his neck. When they pulled him out from under the car, there was not a mark on him, and his fancy Cowboy-Hero suit was immaculate. Tom Mix was dead.

You Ain't Seen Nothin'
Like the Mighty Bs
(A Gallop Thru the
Thirties and the Forties)

Tom Mix and the Big Four had shown the way. As soon as Hollywood adjusted to the new realities of the Thirties and to the sound of its own voice, came the stampede. Cowboy-Heroes galore. More of them than ever before. More than a Front Row Kid could keep track of. Dozens to choose from. Some of them just passing through on the way to something else. Or to oblivion. Distinguishable only by the way they creased their Stetsons. Others, the best of them, distinctive and unique. Bound to ride in the hearts and fantasies and full view of the Front Row Kids for 10, 15, 20 years. Almost forever. It was the age of the B-Western.

B for Budget (low)? B for B-Class? B for Bad? B for Better? B for Best? And also B for Boom. But rarely B for Boring. Certainly the best thing that could possibly have happened to the Front Row Kids of the Thirties and Forties. And to Hollywood.

In 1929 the bubble had burst. Tom Mix, Buck Jones, Hoot Gibson, Ken Maynard, and hundreds of other big-time stars found their pockets shot full of holes. The Squeeze and the inevitable Doldrums hit the movies along with everything else. The moguls were hurtin'. It was dues time in Fake City. Buddy, can you spare a dime? Jesse Lasky, warhead of Paramount Studios and one of the founding moguls of Hollywood, boarded a train in New York one afternoon, the boss of a giant film empire. And got off three days later at Union Station in

Los Angeles out of a job. He had gotten the bullet while riding the Super Chief with his feet up. The big studios lurched in shock as the money went funny. Little outfits collapsed altogether. Change was coming down. And nobody knew for certain what was going to be. The talkies had just begun. Money had been invested. Chances taken. It all looked dodgy. People wanted to look away from the grim realities of failure, bankruptcy, foreclosure, knuckle-scraping poverty, hungry ugliness. They looked to Hollywood to show Good Guys winning, to let them see heroes and pretty girls. And when they *could* spare a dime, they spent it in the movies. And the Western movies with their Cowboy-Heroes were the best bet. Hollywood pulled itself up by its bootstraps. And rode horseback out of the Depression into a boom time.

At first the moguls were doubtful, hesitant, gun-shy. Sound equipment was expensive and awkward. Productions were leaden, static, full of jabbering dialogue. Action seemed to have no natural place in this kind of setup. Hedgers like Carl Laemmle at Universal tried to work both sides of the street by making dual-version Westerns. Chicken producers cut back on their Westerns altogether. Big silent-picture stars (cowboy and otherwise) found themselves chopped off at the ankles, retired before their time to the Motion Picture Country Home because, their bosses told them, their voices squeaked! They were supposed to be hero types, and they sounded like sissies. Or else they delivered their lines as though each word was a separate block of concrete that came out of their mouths with agonizing, tongue-tied effort and then dropped straight through the floorboards. Things were tough all over. But there were Front Row Kids out there in the midst of the Depression eager to spend their dimes on anything with a cowboy in it. Hollywood could not afford to completely give up on Western movies.

In 1929 a fairly grand-scale talking Western called *In Old Arizona,* directed by Raoul Walsh, turned into one of the biggest box-office hits of the year. And Warner Baxter, its star, won the Academy Award for Best Actor for his performance as The Cisco Kid. In the same year, a lanky and slow-talking

Montana cowpoke type named Gary Cooper made a hit in the first sound version of that irresistible Wild West Tale, *The Virginian.* The next year, 1930, Raoul Walsh was back again with *The Big Trail,* which was a flop but starred a big, boyish dude who was called Marion by his mother, "Duke" by his friends, and who called himself John Wayne. And there was King Vidor's *Billy the Kid* with Johnny Mack Brown, a one-time All-American football hero. 1931 was the year of the epic *Cimarron,* the only Western ever to win the Academy Award for Best Picture. And also the year the Front Row Kids got their first good look at another long and lanky, iron-jawed, wry and dry, serious action cowboy, Randolph Scott, who starred in a Western aptly titled *Lone Cowboy.*

And there were a band of fine Cowboy-Heroes out of the silent Twenties, who already had a following of Front Row Kids who loved them and would go to see them in action if they only had the chance, Hollywood Cowboys too good to go to waste who refused to get the message that they were washed up. Just behind the Big Four, Buck and Hoot, Ken and Colonel Tim, there were men like George O'Brien, Tom Tyler, Harry Carey, and Bob Steele.

With new stars coming up, ready cowboys like the Big Four, and eager Front Row Kids, the future of action Westerns in the early Thirties came down to the question of producers willing to put their money (what they could beg, borrow, or steal) on the line. If the major studios were reluctant (with the exception of Uncle Carl at Universal, who loved his Westerns), the independent producers of Poverty Row were more than willing. They were hungry. For them, the B in "B-Western" would stand for Bread and Butter.

Hollywood in the Thirties was full of independent film companies with names that sounded big as seven million bucks, but in truth most of them had barely enough small change to cover the rent on their office space. Names like Allied, Liberty, Tiffany-Stahl, World Wide, Victory, Resolute, Puritan, Metropolitan, Majestic, Mayfair, Progressive, Tower, Peerless, Chesterfield-Invincible, Producers Releasing Corporation, Grand National, Mascot, Monogram. Most of them based their

scuffed-shoe operations around Gower Street and Santa
Monica Boulevard, a few blocks south of Sunset. They seemed
to have gravitated there because the office rents were low.
And because that was where the Big Daddy of all the independent companies, Harry Cohn's Columbia Pictures, was
located, the studio that would be their model of success. Because the indies were there, the area became known as Poverty Row. And because they survived by turning out as many
Westerns as possible at the lowest cost, the area was called,
with affectionate sarcasm, "Gower Gulch."

Gower Gulch was only a shout away from Sunset Boulevard,
but it was not in that diamond-studded world. It was more like
hustle or die. The Gulch had established its image as the hard
side of the Hollywood street after a notorious shooting incident involving a couple of crazed would-be cowboys. One
high-noon day in the Twenties, Black Jack Ward (a ne'er-do-
well) drew down on Johnny Tykes (a no-account) near the
corner of Gower and Sunset and blasted him. It was the dreadful final solution to some long-running feud they had had (over
money or women or dope?). As much as anything that went
down on Poverty Row, this shoot-out gave Gower Gulch its
reputation as a wilderness.

But there was work down there. If you could get it. And by
the Thirties the Gulch was a round-the-clock hangout for
buckaroo cowboy types parading around the streets and bars
in pawn-shop cowboy gear, telling themselves, as they waited
to be cast in something, that Montana Gary Cooper got his
start in a Gower Gulch posse. If you fancied your chances in
the saddle, the doors of the Gower Gulch producers were the
ones you knocked on. If you could find them. And if they had
a door.

Many of the fly-by-night producers of Poverty Row were
indeed that. Hustling a picture deal with them one day, you
would have to be Phillip Marlowe or Sam Spade to have even
a hope of finding them the next. They would be long gone
before their morning mail (usually bills) was delivered. Keep
dark, seemed to be their m.o., and keep moving. Sometimes
they clicked, and all the pieces they were juggling fell into

place. Mostly they were the fringers, looking to tear a fast and profitable piece off the action Western action. With, at all times, an up-to-date timetable of trains and buses in their coat pockets. Just in case they had to disappear themselves over the state line to Ely, Nevada, or some Mexican bean town.

Such was the business of the business in the early Thirties that the fly-by-night Poverty Row producers, if they had nerve enough and a bit of cash, could leap where the majors hesitated to step. They had no studios with crushing overheads, no big investments in equipment, sound stages, or feather-bedding personnel. Of course, they also owned no giant coast-to-coast theater chains to guarantee distribution of their product. What they did have was the freedom that comes with having nothing to lose.

It was in the Thirties that the double-feature came into fashion. Times were hard, and the folks wanted as much as they could get for their precious dime. Two for the price of one was almost like getting something for nothing. By 1936, 85 percent of all movie theaters in the country had double-feature policies (not to mention bingo, banko, and amateur nights), but there were not enough Garbo, Harlow, Cagney, or Dietrich films to go around. *Somebody* had to fill those double bills. Action Westerns were the answer, and the Gower Gulch gang jumped right in with both boots. The big studios weren't making Westerns the way they had done in the Twenties. There was no William S. Hart at Paramount. No Tom Mix at Fox. After Tim McCoy was dropped by M-G-M, there would never again be a full-time Cowboy-Hero working at that studio. If the indies could fill the bill with fast and cheap cowboy movies, they could corner the market.

Traveling light and shooting fast, a Poverty Row producer could turn out a Western in a week's time for $10,000 and be almost certain to bring in a $50,000 profit in rental fees. Thus the Bs were born. And led by Universal and Columbia, the two independent studios with the biggest guns, B would stand for bonanza and for bucks.

Although Gower Gulch production companies came and went, appeared and disappeared, now-you-see-'em-now-you-don't, like the Queen of Hearts in the three-card trick, they helped to keep the Western movie alive during the early Thirties and established its Saturday Matinee patterns.

In 1933 there were 19,000 theaters in America needing films to show (in the world there were 30,000, including 77 in Lithuania). Gower Gulch producers and a few majors who were slowly wising up (Fox, RKO, Warners) turned out 84 Westerns with genuine and terrific Cowboy-Heroes (not to mention all those bottom-of-the-barrel pictures that featured outright stumblebums). By 1936–37 the number was up to 131, starring all the old faces and some new ones. If your local theater changed programs twice a week, and you could afford to go that often every week for a whole year, you still would not see all the Western movies there were to see.

It has been said that there are but seven basic Western plots: the railway story, the cattle empire story, the ranch story, the outlaw story, the revenge story, the cavalry versus the Indians story, the "law and order" story. The wonderful B-Westerns would work every one of them in a thousand variations. They would become so well known to every Front Row Kid that they became part of their very lives, the games they played, the dreams they dreamed, their idea of life.

The Front Row Kids loved them. And even if the films were all very much alike, they were also different because each Saturday was different and had never been lived before. The story variations (or lack of them) did not really matter all that much. As long as each story had a Cowboy-Hero smack in the middle of it. And if the whole process could be said to have turned into an assembly line, with the same predictable faces in the background and the same background in the background, at least the Front Row Kids knew what they were getting for their dimes. They were never disappointed. And in 20 years of B-Westerns, they were frequently surprised with something new and better than anything that had gone before.

1935, to pick one year out of the 20, was full of surprises. New faces and new twists that would drive the Front Row Kids crazy with excitement and delight. The country was still socked into the Depression, with FDR's schemes to save the day, NRA, WPA, CCC and all the other initials, being shot down by a Supreme Court whose justices were old enough to remember the covered wagon days of '49. But at least the Front Row Kids were getting a New Deal. For one thing, 1935 was the year of Hopalong Cassidy. Oh boy!

Was there ever a Cowboy-Hero of Front Row Kid fantasy who cut a figure as magnificent and beautiful (yes, that's the word for it) as Hopalong Cassidy? White-haired Hoppy, dressed all in black from hat to boot, save for a checkered neckerchief held in place by a longhorn slide. Two pearl-handled six-guns on his hips. The big black Stetson with the vertical dent at the top of the crown. That wonderful voice and laugh that was as deep as a well and as clear and sharp and fresh as an ice-cold winter day when there was no school. Galloping to glory on "Topper," his white-as-the-clouds stallion and charger. He was Knight, Saviour, and Boy Scout, surrogate father and all-around Hero. At least the way he was played by Bill Boyd.

The original Hopalong Cassidy was created by Clarence E. Mulford, a Brooklyn marriage-license clerk who at the time had never even seen the West. Mulford wrote a 6,000-word short story called "The Fight at Buckskin," which he sold in 1907 to *Outing Magazine* for $90. Later he developed the idea and the characters into a highly popular series of Wild West novels, over twenty of them. Mulford's hero was, in fact, a cowpoke named Buck Peters. Hopalong Cassidy was his side-kick, a foul-mouthed, whiskey-drinking, tobacco-chewing or-nery galoot who spit a lot and walked around on a gimpy leg (Hop-a-long). Not exactly what you would call a natural Cow-boy-Hero character.

In 1934 Harry "Pop" Sherman, a long-time hustling pro-ducer (he was the man who found the $100,000 needed to save D. W. Griffith's *Birth of a Nation* from abortion), bought the rights to Mulford's novels. And Paramount, wanting to get into the B-Western business as a profitable prop for its studio over-head and expensive big-time productions, cut a deal with "Pop" Sherman to finance and distribute a low-budget Cassidy

series. Sherman, looking for a star who needed money badly enough not to want a whole lot of it, picked Bill Boyd, who was, in that respect, typecast for the part. He was flat busted and looking for his lost movie career down the neck of a bottle. But he was no cowboy.

Bill Boyd was born in Ohio in 1898. As a youngster, he moved with his family to Tulsa, Oklahoma, where his father was killed in an explosion on a construction job. At the age of 13, Boyd quit school, and over the next few years worked his way back East to Akron and then back West again. He was an odd-jobs man. Grocery clerk, surveyor, car salesman, rubber plant worker, lumberjack, oil-field laborer, hotel keeper. He finally made it to California in 1918 as an orange picker and a chauffeur. Handsome, strong, prematurely white-haired, he married an heiress, developed a taste for expensive lounge-lizard suits, and got his first acting job as a bit player in a Cecil B. DeMille production. He caught DeMille's eye and was signed by Famous Players-Lasky to a $30 a week contract. Under DeMille's direction, he became a silent-movie matinee idol, starring in such films as *The Volga Boatman, King of Kings, Yankee Clipper, Two Arabian Knights.* When sound came in, he was over at Pathe, where his good voice earned him $2,500 a week and starring roles in popular films like *The Leatherneck* and *The Painted Desert.* (Clark Gable got good notices as the villain.) He lived the Hollywood high life, with a Beverly Hills mansion, a Malibu beach house, a ranch in the hills. When he wasn't working, he was gambling, drinking, and partying. He was big-time Bill Boyd. Intoxicated by success.

Until a case of mistaken identity smashed his career flatter than a tortilla. It seems there was another popular actor in Hollywood by the name of William Boyd who was just as much a big-time wag and partygoer as Bill. One wild werewolf night in the early Thirties, the other Boyd (William) threw a booze-and-bimbo party that got out of hand. His home was raided by the cops. The scandal made the next day's papers. But with Bill Boyd's picture to go with the front-page story. Overnight his career was snuffed out. And he wasn't even at the other Boyd's party. He was later quoted as saying: "He (William Boyd) was the only guy in town who behaved worse than I did. But I got blamed for everything *both* of us did." From then on, until "Pop" Sherman came to his rescue with an offer he could not refuse, Bill Boyd's Hollywood career was strictly "on the rocks." He was surviving, intoxicated now by failure, on bit parts in Gower Gulch Westerns.

At first Sherman wanted him to play Buck Peters. Boyd liked the Cassidy character better. And persuaded Sherman to let him play that instead. With a few major alterations on the original Mulford model. No longer would Hopalong Cassidy be a cussing, whiskey-breathed, tobacco-stained old reprobate. He would be a black-outfitted, white-horsed do-gooder. The picture of gallantry, chivalry, honesty, justice, morality, and good-natured Christian decency. Who was also quick on the draw. And walked on two good legs. Who needed Buck Peters with that kind of Cowboy-Hero around? It was as if Bill Boyd, coming off the drag end of a life of self-destructive excess and wallowing in the wreckage of a once-promising career, believed that by changing the nature and character of the cowboy he intended to play, by cleaning up Hoppy's act, he could affect a kind of psychic and spiritual transformation of his own life and lowdown ways. And sure enough it worked. For Hoppy and for Boyd. Wonder of wonders, Bill Boyd *became* Hopalong Cassidy. And Hopalong Cassidy became, in the very first film, *Hop-Along Cassidy,* a sensation. That old Bill Boyd was dead. Long live Hopalong Cassidy.

It would be the longest-running continuous characterization in the history of show business. (The Cisco Kid and The Lone Ranger may have run longer, but with half a dozen different Kids and Rangers.) The Hoppy films were also the first in what would become a trend in B-Westerns. The "Trio" Western. Because Boyd was no youth and not a natural action-cowboy (in the first few films he was only shown aboard the magnificent Topper in close-ups, with the horse's hoofs firmly nailed to the floor—stuntman Cliff Lyons did the actual riding), it was decided to give him *two* sidekicks for support. One to handle the comedy. One to do the strenuous fighting and pursue the rancher's daughter. The part of the old codger,

"Windy Halliday," would be performed to absolute perfection by George "Gabby" Hayes, the best of all the B-Western professional sidekicks. When Hayes left the series to go to Republic, the part of "Windy" was permanently retired (like Lou Gehrig's uniform—nobody else could ever hope to fill it), and Andy Clyde, another professional old codger, was brought in to play "California." The young buckaroo, called "Johnny Nelson" and played by James Ellison in the first eight films, became "Lucky Jenkins" thereafter and made Russell Hayden, who would play the part for over five years, almost as popular as Boyd. The "Trio" trend would be picked up by Republic in its *Three Mesquiteers* series and with the *Rough Riders, The Trail Blazers, The Range Busters,* and *The Frontier Marshals* at Monogram during the late Thirties and early Forties. But the Cassidys were probably the best of the lot because, well, they had Hopalong Cassidy in them.

The Hopalong Cassidy series was also much better than most B-Westerns in that Harry Sherman's productions were filmed with more care, longer shooting schedules, and higher low budgets than most of the others. No back-lot locations for "Pop" and Hoppy. Whenever they could, they went out to the wide-open spaces, to the mountains, the snows, the forests, the plains, and the deserts for authentic Wild West backgrounds. To make the final, action-packed chases and fights even more exciting, Sherman hit upon the extra-added touch of lacing these scenes with a rousing, agitato musical soundtrack (another "first"). As if the sight of Hopalong Cassidy galloping over the hills and across the screen was not enough to drive the Front Row Kids wild with excitement, the music pulled them right out of their seats into the action.

Pop Sherman produced 54 Hopalong Cassidy Westerns for Paramount over a period of 10 years. They made a fortune for that studio. And from the start, Boyd/Cassidy was in the top 10 of Western movie money-makers (usually number two on the list neck-and-neck with a certain singing cowboy). In terms of national recognition, the name Hopalong Cassidy was right up there with FDR.

By 1945 Sherman had had enough of Hopalong (and of

Boyd). It was getting more difficult to make good B-Westerns for less than $100,000 (which was a little out of the Hoppy range), and he didn't want to make bad ones. Fact is, Pop Sherman wanted to make good A-Westerns, more substantial productions with first-class Cowboy-Heroes like Joel McCrea. But Hopalong Cassidy was Bill Boyd's life. He took over production himself and turned out a dozen more over the next two years. But the smell of death was on the deal. They were quickies and not really up to the mark Sherman had achieved. And in 1947, the bottom fell out of the Hopalong Cassidy market. To Boyd's dismay and frustration the time had come when he couldn't even give the damn things away. After all the years of being Hopalong Cassidy in his own mind as well as on the screen, Bill Boyd was facing the dreadful prospect of going from hero to mug a second time. It was not his idea of a good way to go. After all, he *was* Hopalong Cassidy, and Hopalong Cassidy would not have succumbed to tough luck and the fact that nobody wanted him around anymore. Hopalong Cassidy would go to glory with both guns blazing. Somehow. Hold the Last Sunset!

Boyd had one shot left in his six-shooter. And before he would point it at his own head and pull the trigger, he would fire the shot into the future. And hope to hit something. He hit Clarence E. Mulford.

Mulford's reaction to what Boyd and Sherman had done to his fictional creation had been something less than joy. It is said that upon seeing the first Hopalong Cassidy film at his local movie theater, Mulford passed out in the middle and had to be revived with smelling salts. But old Clarence not only came to but eventually came around. When his novels were reissued to coincide with Hopalong's rising popularity, they were also rewritten to coincide with the Boyd-Sherman vision. And Mulford apparently lived happily ever after, only, perhaps, wishing he had hit them up for more money for his good idea. As it happened, he did reserve, in the original contracts, all television rights—either a crackpot notion of his at the time, or he was something of a prophet. Back in 1934 television was little more than a science-fiction weirdo's dream. By the late Forties, television had arrived, and except that there was almost nothing to see on it, it looked to be the wave of the future. Bill Boyd recognized it as his last best chance to ride to glory rather than slink off sideways into oblivion. If he could only get the television rights away from Mulford.

Sherman and Paramount didn't seem to care if they never saw another reel of Hopalong Cassidy film cluttering the vaults and executive offices. Boyd already owned the 12 films he had produced. And as far as the world cared, he was welcome to them. Fuck you, Hoppy, *and* the horse you rode in on. The folks in Hollywood who thought they were so smart thought Boyd was a bit tetched in the head, certainly in the grip of an unhealthy obsession, as he went about gathering up all the rights and all the negatives of every Hopalong Cassidy film ever made. Was he planning to spend the rest of his days projecting his old films for himself? Or was he on to something?

He sold his ranch, moved into a tiny one-bedroom bungalow in the Hollywood Hills, mortgaged his car, hocked everything he owned, begged and borrowed every penny he could to raise the money for Mulford's television rights and everything else that went with Hopalong Cassidy. He gambled everything he had to save Hopalong. It cost him $350,000. At the end he was, once again, flat broke and hoping.

And then . . . bull's eye. In November of 1948 he talked the local Los Angeles NBC station into televising one of his Hopalong Cassidy films. The station paid him a rental fee of $200. Bill Boyd's last bullet hit like the shot heard 'round the world. Within the year, Hopalong Cassidy films were playing on over 60 stations around the country. NBC paid him $250,000 for the weekly showings. Television went through all 66 films, and he went back into production to make 52 half-hour shows especially for TV. In 1950 he spun off a Hopalong Cassidy radio show to 500 radio stations and a comic strip for the funny pages of 125 newspapers. And he mined a merchandising mother lode. Everything from comic books (over 20 million distributed), records ("Hopalong Cassidy and the Singing Bandit" had prerelease sales of 200,000), Front Row Kid cowboy paraphernalia, bathrobes, raincoats, pajamas, lunch pails, bars of soap, and the Hopalong Cassidy drinking glass. Whatever it was, if it had the Hopalong Cassidy-Bar 20 brand on it, it sold out. Once again Bill Boyd had come back from Nowhere. And this time even bigger than before. Hopalong Cassidy was the hottest thing since sliced bread (which he also merchandised on a deal with a national bakery). He became the first television Cowboy-Hero. And he stopped traffic in front of Macy's, which Gene Autry could never have done. In 1950 he made $1 million. At the peak of this almost incredible revival in the early Fifties, Hopalong Cassidy Productions and William Boyd Enterprises grossed over $100 million in business. Things could not go on like this forever, of course, but satisfied that he would be leaving the game a hero and not a bum, Boyd finally sold out all his interests for $8 million and retired himself to Palm Desert, California, in 1955. Only coming out for some circus appearances and to lead the Rose Bowl Parade.

Hopalong Cassidy died September 12, 1972 in a hospital in Laguna Beach, of Parkinson's disease, congestive heart failure, and cancer. Perhaps his ride was eased somewhat by the satisfaction of having given a new generation of Front Row Kids an exciting and delightful Cowboy-Hero surprise. Just as he had done for their fathers before them back in 1935.

Meanwhile back at the ranch. 1935. The year of Hopalong Cassidy was also the year of Republic Pictures. And the year of the Singing Cowboy. Gene Autry.

Republic Pictures was the king of the Cowboy-Hero studios. There would not be a single Front Row Kid from 1935 to television whose heart did not beat faster, whose imagination did not catch fire, and whose Saturday afternoons were not made infinitely richer in Cowboy-Hero fantasies by the mere sight of the Republic Pictures Eagle, flapping its wings and perched on that rugged mesa among the clouds, as the curtain slowly parted and everything was revealed. M-G-M might have its growling lion. Fox its sweeping spotlights. Columbia its torchbearer. And Universal its airplane circling the globe. The Front Row Kids pledged their allegiance to that bold

Eagle and to the Republic Pictures for which it stood.

What the other independent and Poverty Row producers had hoped to do (and had at least begun before dropping by the wayside over the years), Herbert J. Yates and Republic Pictures would continue and succeed at beyond anyone's expectations. At Republic, B-Westerns would finally come to stand for Business. Herbert J. Yates had big ideas.

Yates, like Uncle Carl and Harry Cohn, was another of those 5 feet 4 inch demon businessmen. A former tobacco executive with the American Tobacco Company and Ligget & Meyers (and a lifetime tobacco-chewer), he became a small power in the film business when he formed the giant Consolidated Film Laboratories from several small labs he had been operating. During Hollywood's hard times, just about every film company in town was in debt to Yates and Consolidated. Yates was no philanthropist. His dream was to be a mogul. The way he read the future of the business, low-budget action production could be done more efficiently, more cheaply in the long run, and more successfully if some of the little guys with borderline operations got together. Yates was a merger shark. With Consolidated as an ideal financial base, he wanted to swallow up the competition. Looking around for the best possible setup, he saw that Mascot and Monogram already had the knack of shoestring production down pat, that Nat Levine of Mascot also had a lease (with option to buy) on the old Mack Sennett studio in North Hollywood, and that Monogram had John Wayne. So Yates called in the due bills against Monogram, Mascot, Liberty (another small Poverty Row show), and merged the three operations into Republic Pictures, a single company over which he ruled as Head Mogul.

Republic would be home range for at least a dozen first-class Hollywood Cowboys: Gene Autry, Roy Rogers, John Wayne, "Gabby" Hayes, "Wild Bill" Elliott, Bob Steele, Johnny Mack Brown, Don "Red" Barry, Sunset Carson, Allan "Rocky" Lane, Rex Allen, the Three Mesquiteers, and The Lone Ranger. Someone to fit every Front Row Kid's fantasy. Singing cowboys or straight. In one-man shows, pairs, or trio. More cowboys in the yard than the Pendleton Roundup. Republic was a veritable General Motors of B-Westerns and action films.

Filling the screen behind the Cowboy-Heroes there would be a virtual stock company of supporting players, black-hat Bad Guys like Roy Barcroft and Charlie King, Indians (Iron Eyes Cody, Chief Thundercloud), pretty Peggy Stewart, who was many a rancher's daughter, and townfolk whose faces would be almost as familiar to the Front Row Kids as the faces of their heroes but whose names would be a blur. As well as the best wranglers, riders, and stuntmen in the business. And to keep the assembly line well oiled and constantly moving, Republic had a payroll of contract directors (Joe Kane, William Witney, Spencer Bennett, John English, Allan Dwan, George Sherman, John Ford's Argosy Company) who could turn out slick, action-packed, and tight-budgeted features in less time than it took Cecil B. DeMille to shoot one scene of his flatulant extravaganzas. As well as crack technicians and production crews that were the envy of every major studio in the industry. The fastest clapper-boards in the West.

In addition to the Westerns, Republic cornered the serial market. In 10 years the studio turned out 66 Saturday Matinee cliffhangers: *The Adventures of Red Ryder, Zorro, King of the Royal Mounted, Captain Marvel, Dick Tracy.* And more. And the most famous and successful serial of them all, *The Lone Ranger.* And *The Lone Ranger Rides Again.* They probably earned close to $1 million for the studio. Unfortunately for Yates, he had only the screen rights, for 7 years, and no radio, television, comic-book, and lunch-pail rights. He might have become a trillionaire. Who *was* that masked man?

Yates was determined to have something for everybody. But of all Yates's big ideas, the biggest idea, the one that would be the most successful and make all the others come true, was not really his idea in the first place. Nat Levine not only brought low-budget knowhow and an option to buy a studio into the deal with Republic. It seems he also had a singing cowboy he wasn't exactly sure what to do with.

Coming into 1935, the Western movie seemed to be heading into a long yawn. The popcorn concession was down. There was the Big Four, of course, but they were beginning to show

signs of age. Tom Mix had come back for his last comeback in the serial *The Miracle Rider,* and the best that could be said about it was that it was embarrassing. The Front Row Kids, even if they didn't show it, were crying out for some new twists, new faces. The Hays Office and the Catholic Legion of Decency were howling about violence and filth in the movies. So that was out. And nobody yet knew that Paramount was about to spring Hopalong Cassidy on the Kids. Nat Levine huddled with Yates. A singing cowboy?

> I got this singing cowboy, Herb, and maybe we can do something with him. He ain't no Caruso, and he can't ride like Maynard. But he's pleasant. We can always use a stuntman for the hard stuff. He's already sung a song or two in that Maynard picture, and nobody got sick. I don't know, Nat. Don't you think it's a little unusual? Nah, it could be terrific. Just what the doctor ordered. It could really set us up, Herb. You think so, Nat? What have we got to lose, Herb? It's only money. Yeah, Nat, *my* money. What's a few bucks here and there, partner? That's funny coming from you, Nat. If he was a horse out at Hollywood Park, I bet you'd bet him, Herb. Think of it as ten thousand dollars on a thirty-five to one shot and all the other nags are pulling brewery trucks. What'd you say his name was, Nat? Autry. Gene Autry. Gene Autry? Sounds kinda like a fairy to me. I don't think so, Herb. He had a million-seller record a few years back. I think the name will ring a bell. You think so? I think so, Herb. Who knows in this business? A singing cowboy? Oh, well, what the hell? Like you said, Nat, it's only money. Gene Autry. Gene Autry. Gene Autry. You know, Nat, if you say it often enough, the name kinda grows on you. A singing cowboy is a damn good idea. I'm glad I thought of it, Nat. Yessir, Mr. Yates.

And indeed it was a damn good idea. For the Front Row Kids. For Republic Pictures and Herbert J. Yates. For Gene Autry. For everyone except Nat Levine. For a while he held the title of president and head of production at Republic. But by 1937 the feisty little producer was out of the picture. Back to scraping together independent productions for whoever was interested in his ideas. But he had already had the best idea he would ever have. And in the end only the trivia freaks and Hollywood Cowboy aficionados would give him the nod of recognition for it or even remember that it had been his big idea in the first instance.

Gene Autry would change the image of the Cowboy-Hero as drastically and surely with his guitar as Tom Mix had done with his fancy shirts. He gave it a twist that not even Hopalong Cassidy would be able to supply. Until now there had been just Cowboy-Heroes. And they were divided into good or bad. You liked a certain one, or you didn't. Now they would be divided into the singers and the nonsingers. The singers would beat the talkers to the draw at the box office. And in reply to the purists' howl: Cowboys? Cowboys? You guys ain't cowboys. You're warblers! The West was never like that. The singing cowboys shot back: It's *all* make-believe. So what's the diff? Race you to the corral. Last guy in is a wooden Indian.

Gene Autry made Republic Pictures. Just as Tom Mix had made Fox, and Rin Tin Tin had kept the wolf from the door at Warners. But neither one of *them* could sing worth a damn.

Gene Autry was born in Tioga, Texas, on September 29, 1907 (a birthdate he shares with Lord Nelson and Clive of India,) and if he was not exactly a cowboy, at least he was no city slicker. At 15 he traveled with an outfit called the Field Brothers Marvelous Medicine Show, peddling patent medicines. And later hitched up with the railroad as a telegraph operator in Sapulpa, Oklahoma, where he tapped out Morse code and sat around singing cowboy songs to himself. Tom Mix was King of the Cowboys and Gene Autry was Nowhere.

But there must have been a silver bullet somewhere with his name on it because he got a lucky bit of encouragement out there when Will Rogers (that old corn shucker) came into the telegraph office to wire his column back to the Eastern newspapers. "Son," he said (or some such Will Rogers homespunnery) upon hearing Autry strumming and singing when he should have been tapping, "go East and get yourself a recording contract." Whereupon Autry saddled up and went to New York City, where he lugged his guitar up and down Broadway singing his cowboy songs to the rhythm of record-company doors slamming in his face. But he did not lose heart. The echo of Will Rogers's encouraging words were louder in his ears than all the tin pan alley rejections. And the skies were not cloudy all day.

Back home on the range in Oklahoma once again, he landed a radio show in Tulsa called the "Oklahoma Yodeling Cowboy," from which he gained experience, exposure, and eventually, a record contract. With a friend, Jimmy Long, he co-wrote a little ditty called "That Silver-Haired Daddy of Mine." It was not half bad. It sold a million, and Gene Autry was off and galloping. First to Chicago where he did a radio show on WLS in the morning and played the tanktowns of downstate Illinois at night, accompanied by his country-bumpkin pal Smiley Burnette. And finally, in 1934, he made it to Hollywood.

Lucky for Gene, he was corraled by Nat Levine. Levine eased him into the Ken Maynard serial and the feature *In Old Santa Fe* to break up the action with a couple of songs. Then put him to star in that most peculiar serial *The Phantom Empire*. About a singing cowboy with his own radio show who discovers an H. G. Wellesian futuristic underground kingdom beneath his ranch. For 12 chapters Autry sings his songs and fights off the strange armor-plated creatures from the mysterious kingdom of Murania, who look a bit like walking aerosol spray cans. It was a far-out serial for 1934. The following year, when Mascot merged with Republic, the time for Nat Levine's big idea had finally come.

Tumbling Tumbleweeds. Autry's first Republic Western came in a gusher. Pay dirt. Never mind that as a cowboy he looked like a wooden Indian. Or that he recited dialogue like Zeppo Marx. He'd improve. And you couldn't fault his singing. That nasal twang of his had undeniable charm. And being a little tenderfoot-hesitant and camera shy didn't hurt the Cowboy-Hero image one bit. The Front Row Kids went nuts for it. The horse opera was born, and Gene Autry, the singing cowboy, became a movie star. Just like that. Overnight.

His popularity was astounding, incredible, enormous. Republic couldn't turn out Autry films fast enough. It hardly mattered what they were called. Or even what they were about. As long as Gene Autry continued to pluck that guitar out of nowhere and sing a few cowboy songs before and after he rounded up the Bad Guys (and sometimes even during!). And for comic relief there was Smiley Burnette, fat and familiar in his checkered shirt and floppy hat with the brim turned back, making deep-throated frog sounds.

Autry pictures were a strange mixture of elements, Wild West Tales out of time. There were cowboys and horses chasing Zephyrs, Hudson Hornets, and Studebakers and being buzzed by low-flying aircraft. They were crossbreeds of the Old West and the day before yesterday. With the Cowboy-Hero playing anything and everything from a radio cowboy to a ranch foreman with 500 head of cattle to drive to market. But always singing. And always, no matter what, going under his own name. He was the first Cowboy-Hero to be so bold. Not Tom Mix nor any of the Big Four used his own name. Gene Autry was always Gene Autry. No doubt following Herbert J. Yates's reasoning that if you say the name often enough, it kinda grows on you.

By 1937 Gene Autry was the top Western star in Hollywood and the only Cowboy-Hero in the box-office Top Ten. Right up there with Clark Gable. Republic Pictures was singing all the way to the bank, its saddlebags filled with money. And when Autry wasn't making pictures, he was traveling around the circuit with a musical Western show, going to all the small and medium-sized towns on the map, singing "Home on the Range" to his horse, Champion, getting to know all the little theater owners who showed his films, and making the name Gene Autry a household word.

Autry's amazing and almost unprecedented success naturally bred a posse of imitators. Some of them almost as good as he was. Some of them collosal no-talents who, under any other circumstances, could not have gotten a job with Western Union delivering singing telegrams. They only made Autry look that much better. The best of the breed and Autry's only real rival was Roy Rogers, who was invented by Herbert J. Yates for the same reason William Fox invented Buck Jones.

To box Autry's ears a bit and show him who was range boss and who was the hired hand.

Those who knew Autry best would say that he was a businessman first and a Cowboy-Hero afterward. His eye was always on the main buck, the best deal. And he could count the house as well as any Hollywood mogul. Certainly as well as Yates. Down to the last 10¢ admission. His films were making a fortune for Republic, and Yates was still only paying him a measly $5,000 per picture. What kind of shit was this? It didn't add up. It was daylight robbery. Unfair labor practice. Exploitation. Indentured servitude. No way to treat the biggest Cowboy-Hero in America. Whoa! Hold the horses! Autry went on strike. Just like the lunch pailers at General Motors. Unless he got a raise, he would not set foot in front of a camera. Not even so much as a yodel. But Herbert J. Yates was still no philanthropist. He was a movie mogul. And nobody puts the squeeze on a movie mogul. Not even the most popular singing cowboy in the world. We'll tie his spurs together. We'll drygulch him. We'll invent a new singing cowboy, and Gene Autry can sit in the corral until the cows come home. Who does he think he is, Rudolph Valentino?

So they search the stables and come up with a fresh-faced kid from Duck Run, Ohio, by the name of Leonard Slye. He'd been hanging around the lot with the Sons of the Pioneers. Had even been in a few Autry films. And though his voice seemed to come from somewhere near the back of his head and out his eyeballs, he could sing a cowboy song. He had also played in two Charles Starrett Westerns over at Columbia under the name of Dick Weston. Starrett was Columbia's top cowboy, replacing Buck Jones and Tim McCoy in Harry Cohn's stable and pushing Hopalong Cassidy as a very popular straight-action Cowboy-Hero. But such was Autry's impact that even the action-all-the-way Cowboys had to have somebody in their films who could sing a few cowboy songs while the hero stood around listening and tapping his foot. Charles Starrett was good enough not to need any yodelers slowing up his action. But you couldn't buck the fashion. Anyway, Dick Weston did not exactly stop the show. And never would if he

went on calling himself Dick Weston. The name was definitely not a bell ringer. No matter how many times you said it. It would never do for the Cowboy-Hero being groomed to challenge Gene Autry. It made him sound like a newsboy. It was too blah. They decided to call him Roy Rogers at Republic. And gave him his own horse to sing to. His first film was *Under Western Stars* in 1938. It did not exactly light up the skies.

Gene Autry's fans would accept no substitutes. Republic's ploy turned into a range war. The little theater owners in Autry territory sent Republic's junk back unshown. And the cry went up from the Front Row Kids throughout the land: Gene Autry. He's our man. If he can't do it, nobody can. Come back, Gene Autry. Yates had no arguments against the uproar. Autry won the showdown—a raise to 10 grand—and was quickly back in the saddle again. But Roy Rogers would catch on. By 1939 it was a two-horse race.

And for a while even a three-horse race if you wanted to count Woodward Maurice "Tex" Ritter. The singing cowboy with the most distinctive voice of them all. That slightly mournful east Texas twang and drawl that could send a physical tingle down a Kid's or a grown man's spine. Tex Ritter sang hundreds of cowboy songs in over 70 Westerns. From 1936 to 1946. Most of those years as the number-three Singing Cowboy.

But unlike either Autry or Rogers, Tex's songs were actually integrated into the stories. Not just tacked on every 10 minutes or so when things got dull. He never played a radio cowboy or a traveling medicine show singer breaking into song routines for no good reason. He only sang cowboy songs in situations in which a genuine cowboy might legitimately sing them. Around a campfire or on the range while herding cattle. In the bunkhouse or at a Sunday-go-to-meeting. And the songs were generally country-and-Western tunes, not the show-biz production numbers that Autry and Rogers liked to feature.

Tex Ritter hung up his spurs in 1946. But not his guitar. Tex stayed on the road for 25 more years as one of the Kings of country-and-Western music. A C & W Hall of Famer and Grand Ole Opry star. Being a singing cowboy and not just a

Cowboy-Hero, Tex could still keep on keepin' on after his career as a cowboy star was over. And he was probably more popular during the years after he left the screen than he ever was on it. Even after being trounced in a run for the Tennessee Republican Party nomination for U.S. Senator in 1970. He was still on the road when he died of heart seizure on January 2, 1974 while visiting one of his band musicians in prison.

Tex Ritter had been, in fact, the first rival to Gene Autry. And although he never did reach the peaks that Autry and Rogers rose to, he stayed close behind for longer than anyone else. And he did sing the theme song in *High Noon.* A film he did not appear in but in which his voice is as dramatic as the weary face of Gary Cooper. Tex Ritter was number three. And perhaps the reason he didn't try harder was that he was a good ole boy and probably not as hungry to become a millionaire as "Hertz" and "Avis" over at Republic.

From 1939 onward, while everybody else also ran, Gene Autry and Roy Rogers went at it hammer and tong. So as not to miss any promotional opportunities, many of Autry's film titles were pegged on his hit records: *South of the Border, Mexicali Rose, Back in the Saddle, Red River Valley, Boots and Saddles.* In more than a few the story was secondary, merely a device to get from song to song. But the Front Row Kids did not seem to mind. Gene Autry was, as the title of one of his films had it, *Public Cowboy No. 1.*

And Roy was number two. Until Republic could settle on a distinctive personality for Roy, who looked *so* young with his fresh face, his films followed the Autry lead. In many cases being virtual remakes of Autry films. Same story. Same cast. Sometimes the same songs. Giving "Gabby" Hayes to Roy for a sidekick in 1940 helped establish his identity. And just to make certain there would be no confusion over which singing cowboy was Roy Rogers, they eventually gave him Dale Evans. (a.k.a. Fanny Butts—they would marry in 1947.) Roy's popularity steadily grew. When Autry began his CBS radio show, *Melody Ranch,* in 1940 and became practically synonymous with Doublemint Chewing Gum, Roy lined up a show on NBC for Quaker Oats. If Gene had merchandise out with his name on it, Rogers followed. Matching him cap pistol for cap pistol, lunch box for lunch box. Dogging Autry's bootsteps all the way. But never really catching up.

Until Autry dropped out of the competition to enlist in the Army Air Corps in World War II. (He didn't have to go, he wanted to.) Then Republic Pictures pulled out all the stops to make Roy Rogers "King of the Cowboys." They jumped his budgets up to $250,000 and produced musical numbers more extravagant than Autry's had ever been. Roy took off on the personal-appearance trail that Autry had blazed in earlier times and flooded the marketplace with his brand-name merchandise. For as long as Autry was out of it, flying transports over the Hump, Roy Rogers had the range all to himself. It was all the same to Yates, as Autry and Rogers were a two-headed coin for Republic to flip. Yates could not lose.

Out of the Air Corps in '45, Gene Autry returned to Republic long enough to sue Herbert Yates (who was claiming that Autry owed him three years on his contract for the time overseas) and sleepwalk through a final series of musical Westerns. Then he took his business over to Columbia, where he got a better deal. He could produce his own pictures and take home half the profits. Autry made six films a year for Columbia, including some of his very best: *The Cowboy and the Indians, Rim of the Canyon,* and *Strawberry Roan.* With smaller budgets at Columbia, the musical numbers were less absurdly theatrical than the Roy Rogers extravaganzas, the stories were tighter, and the action faster and tougher. And he beat Rogers in the record business, too. Writing more than 200 songs in his career, Autry lassoed nine gold records (sold over 40 million in all) and topped it off with the most unlikely hit of all for a singing cowboy, "Rudolph the Red-Nosed Reindeer." They say his wife Ina May talked him into that one. And if that wasn't enough, with "Peter Cottontail" Autry put his brand on the Easter bunny.

In the early Fifties, like Hopalong Cassidy, Autry galloped right into television. Because of a dispute with Yates over the television rights to his old Republic films, Autry decided to produce his own made-for-TV films. His company, Flying A productions, cranked out the *Gene Autry Show,* and a new generation of Front Row Kids, glued to the toob, discovered the singing cowboy. Predictably, Roy Rogers turned up on another channel, adding a dog and a battered jeep to his entourage.

By the middle Fifties, singing cowboys had just about had it and were limping off to the last roundup. The last of those in the Autry-Rogers tradition would be Rex Allen at Republic and Jimmy Wakeley at Monogram, who were not bad but came along too late in the day. And then it was all over. For nearly 20 years the singing cowboys had been a phenomenon and a delight. But Elvis would soon be finishing them off with a karate chop to the throat. And the "adult" Westerns of the Fifties would be the kiss of death to their kind of Kid-oriented cowboy heroics. But it was all the same to Autry. He simply changed horses and became a corporate cowboy.

Flying A Productions supplied the early days of television with not only Autry's show but half a dozen others, including *The Range Rider, Annie Oakley, Young Buffalo Bill,* and *Death Valley Days.* Autry rode off on a corporate roundup, herding hotels and oil wells, film companies, and music companies into his corral, as well as collecting a string of radio and television stations that stretched across the frontier from Phoenix to Portland. And in 1961 he bought the California Angels baseball club. His Los Angeles radio station, KMPC, had been broadcasting the Dodger games, but Walter O'Malley, that most artful Dodger, lived too far away to pick up the station on his radio, so he took his business to KFI, leaving KMPC down wind. But Autry, a baseball freak from way back who once tried out for the St. Louis Cards, wanted baseball games for his station, and when the American League expanded, and the Angels were created out of thin air, Autry and his associates popped out of the trees one Friday afternoon armed with nothing more than a letter of credit and a radio outlet. By Sunday Gene Autry was owner and president of his very own baseball team. There is, apparently, no truth to the rumor that he bought the team just so he could get autographs from the players. Autry has always taken the business of busi-

REX ALLEN
THE ARIZONA COWBOY

HILLS OF OKLAHOMA

A REPUBLIC PICTURE

REPUBLIC PICTURES CORPORATION · · · HERBERT J. YATES, PRESIDENT

with ELISABETH FRASER · ELISABETH RISDON

ROBERT KARNES · FUZZY KNIGHT · ROSCOE ATES

Directed by R. G. SPRINGSTEEN · SCREEN PLAY BY OLIVE COOPER AND VICTOR ARTHUR · STORY BY OLIVE COOPER

ness seriously. His accumulated business enterprises bring in an estimated gross annual income of $40 million. In this, Gene Autry has left his old rival Roy Rogers (and just about everybody else but Howard Hughes and the Rockefellers) far back in the dust. Nat Levine and Herbert Yates could never have imagined just how much gold there was in them thar hills when they first turned this singing cowboy loose on the Front Row Kids in 1935.

With Gene Autry and Roy Rogers leading the way, it seemed that Republic Pictures could not miss. From the very beginning in 1935 through the late Forties, the studio had an almost infallible cowboy touch. It was almost as if the production office was wired into the imagination of every Kid in the country, as if it knew what the Kids wanted even before they did. You could trust the Republic Eagle to fill your Cowboy-Hero fantasies. You didn't have to waste time (or your precious dime) shopping around.

Yates seemed to have it all ways. And might have gone on forever. Except that he didn't believe in television. Even after it fell on him. And sometime along in the Forties he sealed his fate and iced the studio's future by falling head over heels for a big, lunky Czechoslovakian ice skater named Vera Hruba Ralston. He was in love and wanted to make her a star. Other moguls had done it with their bimbos. Alas, poor Yates. Vera Hruba Ralston was pretty enough, but her English was barely up to the job of ordering lunch at a soda fountain. Trigger was better. For the sake of the soul, everyone should have at least one thing in this world that is, to him, worth losing everything for. For Yates it was Vera. And he lost everything. Hari-kari would have been quicker and less messy. Every film he made with Vera Ralston, and they were big-budget jobs financed with B-Western profits, was a towering flop and a financial disaster. Eventually the works came tumbling down.

Between suits and countersuits over television rights to Gene Autry and Roy Rogers Westerns and a feud with the Screen Actors Guild over residuals that Yates refused to pay that led to a kiss-of-death Guild sanction against the studio,

Republic Pictures did not have a chance. The studio was dead long before it finally keeled over. The Fifties would bring new styles and trends in Western movies that Yates could neither accept nor understand. Serious Westerns with brains and dramatic tension that came from within the stories and the characterizations, not from continuous galloping this way and that. The Good Guy did not necessarily wear the white hat. He certainly did not wear a fancy shirt. Things were no longer that clear-cut. But Yates only knew from action, action, and more action. And he could not run with these new Westerns.

Nor could any of the other independent studios that had been surviving on action Westerns. Monogram hung on through the Forties with its Buck Jones-Tim McCoy *Rough Riders* series. And had fair luck with the Ken Maynard-Hoot Gibson-Bob Steele *Trail Blazers.* Johnny Mack Brown did the best he could in dozens of Westerns with diminishing budgets and qualities. And Jimmy Wakeley made a pretty fair singing cowboy. Duncan Renaldo was popular as *The Cisco Kid.* (He would be unforgettable on television.) But the series that really paid their rent was not even a Western. The Bowery Boys with Leo Gorcey and Huntz Hall.

Producers Releasing Corporation (P.R.C.) also rattled along through the Forties, more dead than alive. The only good and interesting thing to come from P.R.C. in that period was the strange and bizarre "Lash" LaRue. Dressed all in black, sporting his low-crowned black Stetson at a rakish angle, and snapping a bull whip, "Lash" LaRue was, well, you might say, uh, ahead of his time. The first Velvet Underground Cowboy-Hero? "Lash" LaRue's P.R.C. films were made in three to four days on budgets that would cover a magazine subscription but not quite stretch to a train ticket out of town. They had nothing to recommend them to even a desperate Front Row Kid. Except "Lash." He had a certain something. You could not quite put your finger on it. He made the Front Row Kids a little uncomfortable in their seats. The black gear. The whip. The sharp nasally voice. The droopy eyes. The vague resemblance to Humphrey Bogart. "Lash" LaRue seemed to hint at things the Front Row Kids did not yet know anything about.

For a Cowboy-Hero of a certain weirdness, who came along very late in the game and in a series of rock-bottom Westerns, "Lash" LaRue would be remembered long after P.R.C. was flushed down the toilet.

As the Forties became the Fifties, the B-Western was fighting a losing battle to stay alive. If Republic, the King of the Bs, could not make it, then nobody was going to. And Republic, with all its internal problems, seemed to be in the grip of a death wish. Yates in his passion was like Captain Ahab in the wheel house. Stardom for Vera was his White Whale. Westerns could not save Republic this time because Yates could not and would not make the kind of Westerns the Front Row Kids wanted to see. The Fifties were going to be a most peculiar time of our time. With Commie hunting. And cold warring. And smiling Ike. And rock 'n' roll. And Uncle Miltie. And Mickey Mantle. Suburbia coming down. And Sputnik going up. And Marlon Brando changing the Front Row Kids' way of walking. Republic Pictures stood for B-Westerns. And B stood for Best. But eventually time and events, television and changing tastes would turn the Republic Eagle into a dinosaur. And then B stood for Boot Hill. And that was the end of that.

Empty Saddles

"There was blood on the saddle and blood all around
And a great big puddle of blood on the ground
A cowboy lay in it, all covered with gore
And he never will ride any broncos no more."

The Fifties came in under a giant mushroom-shaped cloud. And the simple, straightforward, Front Row Kid-oriented tradition that had been so exciting for so long was bombed out by technology, the telly, and an incipient paranoia that chilled the spirit. That glorious Cowboy-Hero of a million Saturday-afternoon fantasies suddenly seemed to be galloping over the plains with the damning word IRRELEVANT branded across his forehead and stitched on the back of his fancy shirt. What good were his wonder horse and pearl-handled six-shooter against the dreaded H-Bomb? And when the villain is not the black-hat Bad Guy with a thin mustache but (gulp!) an invisible conspiracy, who does the Good Guy Cowboy-Hero beat to the draw in the middle of the street? Come out and fight, *whoever* you are! Could the rancher's daughter be one of *them?* Eeeek! And where is the wonder in a 10-inch-tall Cowboy-Hero riding across the television screen in the corner of the living room, with a potted plant on one side of him and a satin-covered couch on the other? Once the Cowboy-Hero had been shrunk from 20 feet to 10 inches, how soon before he disappears himself altogether?

In Hollywood, the good old Cowboy-Hero no longer fit the bill or paid it. He seemed to have lost his power and symbolic significance as *the* American Hero. And as a financial proposition, action Westerns were dodgy. The cost of making them quickly and cheaply and half decently for double-feature Saturday Matinees had risen since the war beyond the possibility of profit. What had been done in the past for $20,000 could no longer be done for less than $60,000. (Even then it would still *look* like $20,000.) $150,000 was more like it if a producer wanted his Western to have real sky and more than three Indians. But then where would he show it? Theaters were emptying out faster than a whorehouse in a raid. And the customers were not coming back. Television had the country by the eyeballs. The double-feature was fast becoming extinct. Why go out and spend good money at the movies, the thinking went, when you could sit at home and watch Uncle Miltie, Sid Caesar and Imogene Coca, Dave Garroway, Ed Sullivan, Pulitzer Prize Playhouse, and Kukla, Fran and Ollie? For nothing. Free. Gratis. And without the fear of being jostled by juvenile delinquents.

And when the B-Western went down, television was right there to take up the slack. Hopalong Cassidy, Gene Autry, Roy Rogers, Rex Allen's *Frontier Doctor. The Lone Ranger, The Cisco Kid, The Range Rider, Judge Roy Bean, 26 Men, Tales of the Texas Rangers, Wild Bill Hickok, Tombstone Territory, Wyatt Earp, Bat Masterson, Maverick, Sugarfoot, Cheyenne, Wanted Dead or Alive, Have Gun Will Travel* (wire Paladin), *Bonanza,* and the monster, *Gunsmoke,* were all in the picture at one time or another. But, of course, it wasn't the same. Johnny Mack Brown, former Alabama All-American touchdown hero who became one of the better action-all-the-way Cowboys of the thirties and forties, was once quoted as saying: "The films we made had a good plot and a lot of action. We had people tumbling over cliffs and swimming rivers. TV does the whole thing in a room, and they film it in two days. They just let their characters talk. We really showed them riding to the pass . . . In TV all you've got is talk. You got New York actors in Western hats who don't know what a cow is standing around talking . . . Where's the flying, riding, falling—the thrills of the Old West? The clean, outdoor pictures that were athletic and exciting and American, that were born and raised

American?" Good question, R.I.P., Johnny Mack.

The film that had the sad honor of being the last of the B-Westerns was *Two Guns and a Badge,* released in 1954 and starring Wayne Morris as the Cowboy-Hero. He was fat and looked like an alcoholic. *Sic transit gloria mundi.* R.I.P. For the fifties there would be a new kind of Western movie, bigger and slower. And a new Cowboy, puzzled, neurotic, a little unsure of his position, who, more often than not, rode into town not as a Knight but as an object of suspicion and mistrust. He did not gallop across the plains in search of wrongs that needed righting. And it wasn't so much the "Code of the West" that inspired him to fight at the jangle of a spur. Mostly he rode around the wide-open spaces in search of his own identity and fought only to achieve it or maintain it. It was a question of survival in a world he never made but was the only one he knew. His violence was awesome, but strictly personal. And often he was its victim, dying right along with the Bad Guy. He was still, of course, a man of Honor and his Word and was unbeatable at the quick draw. But he was no longer a Boy Scout. When he went into the saloon, he drank whiskey not milk or sarsaperilla. And sometimes he got drunk and staggered, and his dignity sometimes took a battering, although his integrity could never be doubted. His shirt was often more dusty than fancy. His Stetson, if it was white, was no longer a simple symbol signifying moral purity. Battered and sweaty, it was just something used to keep the sun out of his eyes or sometimes to water his horse (a horse with no name!). The new Cowboy-Hero could be ruthless, violent, mean, selfish, and unsportsmanlike, taking advantage wherever and however he could. He was still tall in the saddle, but he rode with confusion and contradiction as sidekicks and with ambiguity rolled up in his bedroll. Whether he was better or worse than what the Front Row Kids were used to, he was certainly different. Tough, troubled, balancing passion and cold-bloodedness, he was more the lonesome cowboy than ever before. As the country became more and more capsulized in the Fifties, folks enclosed alone in their too big cars, or sitting in small, tight groups, or alone in front of a little box in the living room rather than together by the hundreds in a movie theater downtown in the world and sharing a common fantasy and dream-wish, the Cowboy-Hero became more and more a symbol and a reflection of society's sense of alienation and insecurity. This was complex and serious stuff. If you listened real close, you could probably hear Tom Mix turning over in his grave.

Hollywood, when it even bothered with action Westerns, went with the strictly A-Westerns, the big features. They could hardly afford to do otherwise. You could not pull the people away from their television sets for just any old thing that galloped. They came out, if they could be bothered, only for something special or interesting that might be worth the $1.50 it would cost them. They would not come out for a guitar strummer with bewhiskered sidekicks who did not kiss the rancher's daughter even once and fired 47 rounds from his six-shooter without reloading and who never got his hat knocked off and was so sure of himself. They wanted realism with a dose of sex and brutality. They wanted psychotic Bad Guys and neurotic Cowboy-Heroes. They wanted to feel at home. Or at the very least see technicolor wide-open spaces.

Fact is, there was almost no such thing as a Cowboy-Hero anymore, in the sense that Gene Autry or Tim McCoy or Tom Mix were Cowboy-Heroes, and you followed them from film to film because they were in the center of the piece, and that was the main thing—and the more Cowboys the merrier. Western movies now came individually wrapped, and you couldn't be sure of what was in the package until you paid your money. The name on the marquee out front was usually a big-time he-man star: James Stewart, Henry Fonda, Gregory Peck, Gary Cooper, Glenn Ford, Robert Mitchum, Burt Lancaster, Kirk Douglas. They were actors more than Cowboy-Heroes. The next time you saw them, they might be an Air Force officer, a Philadelphia lawyer, a cop, or Doris Day's boy friend. You had to take your Western movies one at a time.

And more often than not, they were becoming directors' Westerns or writers' Westerns rather than Cowboy-Hero Westerns. It was a trend that began in the Forties with serious but often inflated and pretentious films like Hawks's *Red*

River, Ford's *My Darling Clementine,* William Wellman's
dramatic and intelligent *The Ox Bow Incident,* and the Vi-
dor/Selznick flatulent, passion-bloated *Duel in the Sun.* The
Fifties would see better and sometimes wonderful Westerns
with brains. Anthony Mann's films starring James Stewart.
Anything Budd Boetticher touched. Ford's *The Wagonmaster.*
The Man without a Star with Kirk Douglas's eyeballs rolling
crazily. *Shane,* which was highly romantic but ultimately ridiculous. Marlon Brando's sado-psycho *One-Eyed Jacks.* And
the great one, *High Noon.* They were meant to be taken
seriously and deserved to be. But they were not exactly what
you would call Cowboy-Hero stuff. And the Front Row Kids
couldn't even get in to see them without a letter from their
mothers swearing they were a lot older than they looked.

The only genuine, full-time Cowboy-Heroes in the saddle
were Joel McCrea and Randolph Scott. John Wayne, who,
even if he wasn't making Westerns all the time, *seemed* to be.
And Audie Murphy who was in a world of his own.

The great attraction of 50 years of Hollywood Cowboy-
Heroes was their ability to embody—on-screen and off—the
heroic dream-wishes of the Front Row Kids and to feed those
hero fantasies. Tom Mix, the most popular of them all, embel-
lished his own life story with incomparable heroics, the better
to enhance his Cowboy-Hero image. By rights, then, Audie
Murphy should have been the ultimate Cowboy star, for the
little Texan was no make-believe hero.

Audie Murphy, the Farmersville, Texas, orphan, went off to
World War II before he was even old enough to vote. He came
back after the war, the most decorated soldier in the history
of American arms. A genuine, no-doubt-about-it Hero. He had
won the Medal of Honor, the Distinguished Service Cross, the
Silver Star with Oak Leaf Cluster, the Legion of Merit, the
Bronze Star, the ETO campaign ribbon with seven battle
stars, a Presidential Unit Citation, Expert Infantryman's
Badge, the French Legion of Honor Chevalier, the Croix de
Guerre with two palms, the Fouragere, the Purple Heart with
two Oak Leaf Clusters. He was still not old enough to vote.

His heroics made laughable everything the bluff and blow-

AUDIE MURPHY GIA SCALA

RIDE A CROOKED TRAIL

CinemaScope in Eastman **COLOR**

Co-starring
WALTER MATTHAU
HENRY SILVA · JOANNA MOORE · EDDIE LITTLE

DIRECTED BY JESSE HIBBS · SCREENPLAY BY BORDEN CHASE · PRODUCED BY HOWARD PINE · A UNIVERSAL-INTERNATIONAL PICT

hard warrior John Wayne ever did in all the battles of the back lots against armies of Japanese extras. And in France and Germany Audie Murphy did his own stunts! Audie Murphy's battalion commander said of him: "You can just say he was the best soldier there ever was."

A real hero and a real Texan, Audie Murphy seemed a natural for a Cowboy-Hero. Instead, he turned up in Hollywood about the time it was undergoing change of life. If Audie Murphy performed wonders against the entire German Army, he did not do so well against the Hollywood vampires. Audie Murphy, the hero of World War II who had his picture on the cover of *Life* magazine with all his medals laid out in front of him, was seduced by Hollywood and then abandoned. They made a Cowboy-Hero out of him all right. He made over 40 films and $2 million during a decade in the fantasy factory. But at the end of it, he was lucky to have a suit that wasn't rumpled and enough walking around money in his pockets to keep the L.A.P.D. from collaring him on vagrancy charges.

Audie Murphy was not that bad. In an age of neurotic Cowboys Murphy was best in Westerns that focused on his disappointment and disillusionment with the life he was trying to make. As a baby-faced Cowboy-Hero, more than a little reluctant and shy, even a bit overwhelmed and wearied by having to do constant battle with the black-hat Bad Guys (who were usually *taller* than he was), there was, nevertheless, always an exciting and admirable strength and toughness beneath his quiet Texas drawl and hints of a wild and frustrated anger. *The Cimarron Kid, Drums Across the River, Walk the Proud Land, Destry, No Name on the Bullet, Night Passage, Seven Ways from Sundown,* and *The Texican* were not throw-away Westerns. Audie Murphy, mustachioed and slightly crazed, was without a doubt the best thing in *The Unforgiven,* a decent Indian picture that top-billed the usually preposterous and toothy Burt Lancaster. Stephen Crane's *The Red Badge of Courage* might have been written with Audie Murphy in mind, and it wasn't completely Murphy's fault that John Huston's film was a flop. And in the straight, non-Western role of Alden Pyle, the reluctant foreign-service officer attached to the U.S. Embassy in Saigon in Graham Greene's *The Quiet American,* Audie Murphy was fine. Although not a great film by any means, more folks should have gone to see it for a chance to see Audie Murphy out of the saddle and not bad.

Mostly, Audie Murphy was just not lucky in Hollywood. A fugitive from the law of averages during four years of war, the statistics caught up with him on the home front. His Westerns seemed to fall between two stools. Not quite up to the serious business of the brainy Westerns. Too good to be dismissed as just second-feature action stuff. And not having the mighty Cowboy-Hero box-office pull of a John Wayne, he could not carry the string of mediocre, medium-sized Westerns he starred in with the mere power of his presence.

"I had one hangup as an actor," Murphy would say in anger and despair and also a certain wistfulness after his Cowboy-Hero career had been rolled up and he was living deep in debt in the fixed-up garage of his estranged wife's house. "I had no talent. I didn't hide that. I told directors that. They knew. I didn't have to tell them. They protected me. I made the same movie 20 times. It was easy. But it wasn't any good. No one helped me. I never got to be any good. No one cared if I got any good or not. They used me until I was used up."

In 1960 he did a television series for NBC, *Whispering Smith,* which even he thought was awful and obsolete. "One of the cast committed suicide. He must have seen the rushes," Murphy said when a reporter interviewed him during his tough-luck days. It was just that the trend was definitely against him and the sort of thing he could do best. The opening show of the series was bumped off the air by NBC to televise a News Special on Alan Shepard, the astronaut.

Audie Murphy's bad luck inevitably went to worse luck. And finally to no luck at all. Almost $1 million in debt from bad investments, Murphy found himself under siege from creditors who slapped him silly with writs and summonses. He became a boozer and a pill head. Also a bully and a bar fighter. He suffered severely from insomnia and, once in a while, hallucinations.

In 1969 Murphy produced a small-budget Western in which

he played the part of Jesse James. The film was called *A Time for Dying*. He hoped it would get him back on his feet. It didn't.

In May 1970, Murphy took another thump when he was arrested on a charge of assault with intent to commit murder, assault with a deadly weapon and battery. It seems a girl friend of his claimed she had been attacked and abused by a Burbank dog trainer she had hired to teach her old dog some new tricks. Audie Murphy, a man of the West and a bit of a vigilante, went out to Burbank, drew down on the dog trainer, fired a few shots at him, and pistol-whipped him. Audie was ultimately acquitted but not before going through the strains and indignities of standing trial on the charges. Life for Audie Murphy had turned decidedly sordid.

A year later he was dead. At 11:40 A.M. on May 30, 1971, the pilot of a twin-engined Aero Commander radioed Roanoke Flight Service for permission to land. On board were three shady Teamster's Union business types and Audie Murphy, who was involved with them in a company that produced factory-built homes. The plane was never heard from again. It crashed into Brushy Mountain near Roanoke. There were no survivors. In three weeks Audie Murphy would have been 47 years old.

Murphy once said about Hollywood: "I'm strong. I'm too tough for this town. I won't let it break my heart. I won't let it break me. I'll fight it to the finish. I just wish it was a fight I knew how to fight."

Audie Murphy was buried in Arlington Cemetery next to a Vietnam vet. Scores of old army buddies turned up for the burial. No one from Hollywood was there.

Joel McCrea and Randolph Scott seem to go together in the mind. Men of few words but exuding a strength of character, a dignity, and a cowboy nobility that was in the tradition of Wister's *The Virginian* and William S. Hart, these two tall men riding, McCrea and Scott, the last and straightest of the great and true Hollywood Cowboys, brought the circle back around and joined the final loose ends of this 50-year phenomenon to

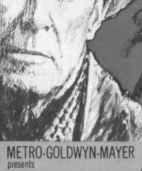

SHOWDOWN
IN THE
HIGH
SIERRA!

METRO-GOLDWYN-MAYER
presents
RANDOLPH
SCOTT

JOEL
McCREA

RIDE
THE
HIGH
COUNTRY

WITH
MARIETTE HARTLEY ·
WRITTEN BY   DIRECTED BY   PRODUCED BY
N. B. STONE, JR. · SAM PECKINPAH · RICHARD E. LYONS
In CinemaScope and METROCOLOR

its beginnings. They did not horse around with the Wild West Tale. No tricks and voom and things like that. No fancy shirts, guitars, or hand-tooled boots. Strictly serious and realistic in their approach, they gave the Front Row Kids the kind of Cowboy-Hero that might conceivably even have existed somewhere in the Wild West. Or at the very least, they portrayed the kind of man it might be possible for a Front Row Kid to grow up to become. A man of grace and courage, honor and self-reliance and integrity. And a man of some wit and weirdness but also of grit and confidence, of bravery without bravado, who is not entirely fearless but is unafraid to face the Ultimate Truth: that life is not a dream, and "some things a man can't ride around." That is, after all, what the Code of the West and the Cowboy-Hero have been about through all the years of myth and metaphor. Through all the variations, from Hart to "Lash" LaRue, the constant core of the Front Row Kid fantasy was each cowboy's personal commitment to a way of being that put the "Hero" into Cowboy-Hero. Joel McCrea and Randolph Scott were simply two of the best examples of that.

They were rock-solid Cowboy-Heroes. Joel McCrea, tall in the saddle, his face wind-and-dust roughened but handsome, wearing a simple, undistinguished Stetson and a pair of jeans, the collar button of his plain cowboy shirt always done up at the throat, his voice deep and clear as a bell as he very calmly tells some Bad Guy who is just about to cross the line of his Code: "I wouldn't do that if I were you." Randolph Scott, just as tall in the saddle and at home on the range, almost always in that well-worn leather jacket and the Stetson with the chin strap, his white neckerchief knotted so the two long ends hang down in front. Always serious and straight-faced, drawling that Virginia drawl, a kind of remoteness in his manner, an icy-coldness in his tone. In many ways the Lonesome Cowboy, but alone with himself, you cannot help feeling, because he prefers the company. Randolph Scott never sings cowboy songs and sometimes *is* the Bad Guy.

They were a couple of tough hombres the villains never seemed to have the sense enough to "ride around." And they were around for a long time, Scott and McCrea. Until the very end. The Front Row Kids did not outgrow them but grew up with them. And unlike most other Hollywood Cowboy-Heroes, they got better with age.

Joel McCrea was a local boy. Born and raised in Hollywood. Went to Hollywood High and in a school show played the part of a bear while a little blonde girl named Harlean Carpenter played a squirrel. Just a couple of kids, he would grow up to be a Cowboy-Hero, and she would blossom into Jean Harlow, Bimbo-Dream.

McCrea learned to ride on the ranches in Ventura County and in the Hollywood Hills, graduated from Pomona College, and started in films as a wrangler and a bit player. In those early knockaround days he doubled for Greta Garbo in a riding scene in *The Torrent* and danced with her in *The Single Standard.* After a feature role in *The Jazz Age* in 1929 and *The Silver Horde,* he became something of a leading man in melodramas and light comedies until *Wells Fargo* and *Union Pacific* made him a Star and a Cowboy-Hero. As a Star, he was picked by Hitchcock for *Foreign Correspondent.* ("Joel McCrea is the only man for the part," Hitchcock is supposed to have said. "It can only be Joel McCrea." Or something along those lines). And he showed remarkable versatility as an actor in the Preston Sturges classic comedies, *Palm Beach Story* and *Sullivan's Travels.*

But Joel McCrea was best as a Cowboy-Hero. In films like *The Virginian, Ramrod, Saddle Tramp, Stars in my Crown, Four Faces West, Wichita, Cattle Empire,* and even *Buffalo Bill.* He was tough and serious, could even be mean as hell. But he was charming and honorable, and he played his Cowboy-Heroes as if they were men, not comic-strip characters. And that was the best part.

And so it was with Randolph Scott, who began his career as a Cowboy star in 1931 and would never really be anything but that for 30 years. Born in Virginia, he could have been the Virginian. And although it was Gary Cooper and Joel McCrea who played the part in the movies, you could almost picture Randolph Scott saying: "When you call me that, smile." Al-

though only a madman would have called him a "son-of-a——"
in the first place.

He played Good Guys and Bad Guys, though as a Bad Guy
he was usually so good the Front Row Kids could almost not
bear to see him die. When he comes out of the church at the
end of *The Doolins of Oklahoma* and stands with his back to
the marshal who is just waiting there to gun him down, a Front
Row Kid could just cry out: "Run for it, cowboy! Get away! You
can do it!" And when he turns to face the fate that awaits him,
is shot down and dies against the white picket fence of the
church, a Front Row Kid just wants to cry. Randolph Scott
certainly had the way about him. After a while a Front Row
Kid could not help but warm to his coldness.

As a long-time contract Cowboy-Hero at Paramount, he
made a better job out of a series of Zane Grey Westerns in the
thirties than most other Miracle Riders, including Tom Mix.
And he made a fine Hawkeye in *The Last of the Mohicans*. In
the forties and fifties he rode the rounds between Universal,
Fox, Paramount, RKO, United Artists, Columbia, and Warner
Brothers. He beat up John Wayne in two Westerns, upstaged
Errol Flynn in *Virginia City*, built the railroad in *Santa Fe*,
and the telegraph in *Western Union*. Through these years he
starred in dozens of Westerns (with a few side trips into war
flicks that weren't so hot) and in the early fifties made Hollywood's Top Ten List (not the cowboy one but the *real* super-
star one). John Wayne was the only other Cowboy on it.

But the most outstanding series of Westerns he ever made
was the Ranown Cycle that he starred in and produced with
Harry Joe Brown in the middle and late fifties. *Seven Men
From Now* (not really Ranown but John Wayne's Batjac Productions), *The Tall T, Decision at Sundown, Buchanan Rides
Alone, Ride Lonesome,* and *Comanche Station.* They were
tight, serious, and remarkable. All directed by Budd Boetticher. All dealing essentially with the Lone Cowboy, whose
strength is in his aloneness, but who usually carries with him
dark memories of disastrous involvements. There is usually
regret and bitterness that he feels he must revenge or answer
to himself for, or he is confronted, as he goes about his own

business, with new involvements he cannot avoid. He is sometimes a tragic figure, sometimes philosophical, sometimes ab-
surd. But he meets his challenges head-on with courage and
style and a sense of awful and awesome inevitability. Because
he must, in order to maintain his own identity and the way he
wants to live. There is no avoiding the fight. The villains, who
may well be his equal in all things except serenity and discipline, will force him to it.

The Ranown Cycle were tough and almost chillingly austere
Westerns. The hero in them was exactly suitable and right for
the existential fifties. And an aging Randolph Scott was just the
man for the job. Tom Mix could not have made them on the
best day of his life, nor could Tim McCoy and Buck Jones. And
Gene and Roy would never have dreamed of trying. On the
other hand, Tom Mix did not live in these weird and puzzling
times, with bomb shelters in the back yard, missile gaps, and
a creepy-crawly technology that changed forever the way
people lived and the dreams they dreamed. And these times
were tumbling helter-skelter into even weirder times. Come
the sixties and the seventies, the Good Guys would be blown
away where they stood. Far from having a Cowboy-Hero or
two to cheer and admire and take as a model of courage and
grace under pressure, a Front Row Kid would be hard pressed
to find an honest man in the crowd of sociopaths, violent
madmen, crooks, and political worms without conscience or
dignity. And the Kids would hit the road in search of some one
thing or other person they could trust and not fear. And their
own parents would end up fearing *them.* And nothing would
make much sense in a time gone completely out of whack.

If the Cowboy-Hero was doomed to ride off into the sunset
along with all the other Good Guys of a less ambiguous age, it
is fitting that the last one of that kind of Western movie with
that kind of Cowboy-Hero should turn out to be *Ride the High
Country,* with Joel McCrea *and* Randolph Scott in it together.
Each in his own well-worn Cowboy-Hero image that had by
now been aged and broken in to a perfect, comfortable fit.

A humorous and graceful and modest and ironic Western
directed by Sam Peckinpah before he went funny and O.D.'ed

on technicolor blood, it is a Wild West Tale about two ex-lawmen and gunfighters, now out of place and time with a West that has turned the century on them and no longer has much use for the sort of thing they do best.

Steve Judd (McCrea) and Gil Westrum (Scott) sign on for one last ride to the high country to bring a shipment of mining-town gold down to the bank. Judd takes on the assignment because it is a job (better than bouncer at a whorehouse) and the sort of thing he could once do with his eyes closed. (Now he has to go off into the bathroom so the banker doesn't see him reading the contract with his eyeglasses.) "I expected a younger man," says the banker. "I used to be," says Judd. "We all used to be." Once taken on, he sees the job as a personal commitment to the bank and, more important, a commitment to himself and the strict Code of Honor he has always lived by. Westrum, with his young sidekick, goes along ostensibly to help his friend with the job, but really to help himself to the gold. Hard luck and age have led him to abandon the Code that he, too, had once lived by.

Essentially it is a journey film. The trip up to Coarse Gold and the trip back down to the bank. With much talk about the "old days" along the way, as Westrum tries to soften up Judd for the ripoff with reminders about how they both have nothing much to show for their lives spent risking their necks. And Judd coming back with how he only wants to regain his self-respect and when he dies to "enter my house justified." At the mining town they collect the gold and "rescue" the daughter of a crazed preacher, an innocent girl named Elsa, who rode up with them intending to marry a roughneck villain but changes her mind . . . too late. The plan is to take her back down to her father and then take the gold down to the bank. Westrum, of course, has other plans for the gold and the Hammond Boys, the smelly bridegroom, and his crazy brothers have other plans for all of them.

Coming down the mountain, Westrum takes the money. But Judd is waiting for him. He will endure almost any indignity (frayed cuffs, bad eyes, old age), but not the one of allowing his friend to make off with that money. Westrum's act is a betrayal of the Code and of Judd himself, and he will see Westrum in jail and in hell for that. When the Hammond Boys make their first assault, he will not even give Westrum a gun to help fight them off.

Eventually Westrum escapes, and Judd and the young sidekick are left to deliver the girl to her father and make the rest of the journey. They ride right into a Hammond trap and are pinned down in a ditch, Judd damning himself and his old age for letting it happen. But Westrum is no villain. The Code and friendship are stronger than his desire to get away. And Scott comes galloping in, six-gun blazing, has his horse shot out from under him, and joins his friend in the ditch, bullets whizzing over their heads.

The moment is set for the last showdown in the last good Western starring the last of the great Cowboy-Heroes.

"Well, what do you think, partner?" says Randolph Scott to Joel McCrea.

"Let's face 'em head-on," says Joel McCrea to Randolph Scott. "Halfway. Just like always."

"My sentiments exactly."

And after taunting and cursing the crazy Hammond boys into coming out of their hiding places, the two Cowboy-Heroes rise up out of the ditch, tall, cool, with courage and style, and walk out to meet the three Bad Guys face to face in the wide-open spaces. It is a great and terrible moment as they stand there. ("Okay, old man," a Hammond cries, going for his gun, "start the ball!") Then, drawing their guns, they fire away. Until the Hammonds are finished, all three dead. And Joel McCrea lies in the dust, hit and dying.

"Don't worry about anything. I'll take care of it," says Scott, tending to his friend. "Just like you would have."

"Hell, I know that," says McCrea, holding on to his life for just a bit longer. "I always did. You just forgot it for a while, that's all. . . . So long, partner."

"I'll see ya later," says Randolph Scott to Joel McCrea.

Scott may have survived this last showdown, but he knows he is not going to live forever and will, in a manner of speaking, be seeing his partner "later." But in terms of all those 50 years of Cowboy-Hero time, there is no "later." This is the last and the end of it.

Joel McCrea and Randolph Scott both retired after *Ride the High Country*. There was one other fine Western that year, 1961. *Lonely Are the Brave*. In it, Kirk Douglas is the Brave Cowboy. But he is already an anachronism, a dinosaur. The time of the film is the present. And the Cowboy-Hero races for the "freedom" of the mountains pursued by sheriff's cars and walkie-talkie-toting deputies, and fires his Winchester at helicopters.

There would, of course, be other Westerns. Never again 100 a year. But a steady trickle. Clint Eastwood's spaghetti Westerns. Charles Bronson's armpits. Buckets-of-blood Westerns. The clever-dick *Butch Cassidy and the Sundance Kid*. And a fistful of others that would pass across the screen unremarked and largely unattended. The Front Row Kids would all be at some other cinema, watching *Deep Throat, The Godfather, Jaws* (chomp!), and Humphrey Bogart revivals.

There would be only one last great Cowboy-Hero image to get the Front Row Kids through the rest of their lives. John Wayne, with a black patch over his eye, a rifle in one hand and a six-gun in the other, his reins between his teeth, riding like thunder hard down on a gang of Bad Guys and shouting: "Fill yer hand, ya son-of-a-bitch!"

HEADIN' 'EM OFF
AT THE FREEWAY

"Well, the Lone Ranger and Tonto
Were ridin' down the line
Fixin' ev'rybody's troubles
Ev'rybody's 'cept mine
Somebody musta tol' them I was doin' fine."

—"Bob Dylan's Blues"

Hooray for Hollywood
(L.A. All The Way)

The Frontier ends in Disneyland Grotesque. The last Frontier
Line is the San Diego Freeway. Go any farther West and you
have to swim for it. At the end of the Santa Monica Pier, as far
West as you can go without getting your feet wet, you can play
Quick-Draw for 25¢ a shot against a mechanical cowboy whose
recorded voice bellows after every shot: "Haw haw! Ya missed
me, ya sidewinder. Try again."

You are in the land of gross excess weirdness. The land of
Amnesia and Sunshine Lobotomy. The land of total Concrete
Rejection. Where the Past has been paved over. Emptiness is
all around. And the neon wilderness sparkles like Woolworth
junk jewelry under perpetual good weather. To be in L.A. is
like being in the hole of a doughnut, with only the illusion that
there is even a doughnut around the hole. Anything bad that
anyone has ever said about Southern California is true.

Aerospace wastelands. Fast-food franchises. Millions of cars
bumper-fucking along 465 miles of runway/parking lot on a
constant shuttle between the shopping center and the front
door of home. Shrunken heads bobbing over steering wheels.
Good old bad news on the radio. Off-ramp anxieties. Miles and
time are meaningless. This is the land where old Hertz rent-a-
cars go to die wearing fresh paint jobs and with their clocks
turned back. "A genuine, one-owner good deal," the Okies
who run the used-car lots pitch the yobos. "Y'all kin drive 'er
away fer nineteen ninety-nine and I'll throw in two free tick-
ets to the Queen Mary. Ya won't get a better deal anywhere,
folks. Or else I'll eat a bug. I'll stand on my head."

Desolation Row. The Future. Los Angeles is America giving

the finger to the world. And saying: "This is how it will be, suckers!" You don't see people here. Only walk-ons. And all those shrunken heads in car windows. "Our sidewalks are cleaner than your sidewalks," a mayor of L.A. once said to the mayor of New York. "That's because nobody uses your sidewalks," said the mayor of New York.

What the hell are all those California Chambers of Commerce talking about? Did the Donner Party eat their dead in the snowed-in passes so they could live to come to this? Oh, Lord. What am I doing here?

I knew when I hit the San Diego Freeway at the end of the run from Tombstone that I was anywhere from 20 to 50 years too late to find whatever it was I was looking for out here. And the certainty of it rushed at me like the hot air out of a preheated oven when you whip the door open. I wanted to call the whole thing off. To abandon the old Dodge to rot in the Southern California sunshine, to be stripped of its wheels and all moving parts by roving bands of souvenir freaks and eventually be towed away by the Highway Patrol for causing an obstruction. While I caught the next low-flying fantasy going in the other direction. But I had already come too far in my time-warp traveling to turn back. Just because most of the good old Cowboy-Heroes were in Boot Hill, and the rest of them were retired out to pasture, and I was chasing ghosts across the continent was no reason for despair. Surely those men who made all my best Front Row Kid fantasies had left behind them some tracks to be followed. Somewhere out there under the California sun, I would find a trail that led to Gene Autry and Roy Rogers, Tim McCoy and Bob Steele, Charles Starrett, Johnny Mack Brown, "Lash" LaRue, The Lone Ranger, and The Cisco Kid, John Wayne, Joel McCrea, Randolph Scott, and the ghosts of Hopalong Cassidy and Tom Mix.

I turned the radio dial to a C & W station. It was Kristofferson singing "Loving You Is Easier Than Anything I'll Ever Do Again." Nice song. And the Front Row Kid, with one foot on the accelerator and one foot tapping to the tune, drove the last miles into Hollywood. With the L.A. morning coming down.

Coming down on Sunset Boulevard and Santa Monica and Hollywood (and Vine) and Wilshire. Coming down on Schwab's Drugstore and Tower Records and the Whiskey A-Go-Go, on the Rainbow Bar and Grill and the Roxy and the Troubadour. Coming down on Mann's (formerly Grauman's) Chinese Theatre, where bygone matinee idols pressed their foot and palm and buttock (and hoof?) prints in wet cement and gave their autographs to eternity. ("It's not for me," the guy who poured the concrete no doubt said, "it's for my grandchild.") Coming down on M-G-M and Paramount and Universal and Warner Brothers and 20th Century-Fox. Coming down on Dino's (who goes there, Kookie?) and the Classic Cat (all-nude review) and the Body Shop (home of the lovely Susann Douglas, topless contortionist). Down on all the fuck motels and used-car lots and banshee-screaming billboards. Coming down on the Hollywood Hills and the firetrap canyons. Coming down on the freeways and the beaches and the *barrios.* Coming down on Beverly Hills with its wide, empty streets, finely nibbled lawns, and gently junkie-nodding palm trees. L.A. morning coming down on all the saunaed, jacuzzied, wet barred, specialty decorated, sinfully luxuriated, king's ransomed, private-property-keep-out homes and mansions of the Hollywood Big Deals (maps available—75¢). Coming down, too, on all the little cupcake houses and stucco-walled two-room flats of the less blessed. Coming down on all the weirdos and crazies, Evangelists and Bible salesmen, babblers and screamers, failed Okies and ex-Prom Queens, comers and go-ers and hangers-on, pursuers of ridiculous dreams. L.A. morning coming down on all that L.A. weirdness. Coming down (thump!) on me.

Hollywood is Hollyweird. Once nothing but an orange grove in the middle of nowhere with no prospects. It became the center of the Universe Where Nothing Is Real. It was always an unlikely place. Where a goofy cartoonist could turn a talking mouse into a billion dollars. And shit-kicker cowboys rode to the bank on silver-mounted saddles. And a horse could

command a wage of $2,000 a week. Where lives were mea-
sured against box-office receipts. And could be made or ruined
on the majestic whim of a mogul who knew how to count.
Hollywood. Where there were more stars than in the heavens.
Money to burn. And greed to strike the match. Where make-
believe was real. What would our daydreams and fantasies, our
very lives, have been like without Hollywood and its virginal
beauties, its weird romeos, its Cowboy-Heroes? And if it
weren't for the fantasies they made here, who would come
here? I'd come to the source. But the fantasies had changed.
Hollywood make-believe was no longer riding the horse but
picking up after it. The glorious Cowboy-Heroes had long
since hung up their spurs and taken to the far hills, leaving no
forwarding addresses. Which way did they go?

"I'm sorry," said the woman who manned the switchboard
at the Screen Actors Guild on Sunset Boulevard. "We don't
give that information out. That's strictly confidential. You
know how it is. We have to protect their privacy."

"When was the last time anyone came in asking for Tim
McCoy's address?" I said, wanting to shove my list down her
throat. "Twenty years ago? I'd say half the world thinks these
guys are dead already, and the other half probably doesn't
give a damn."

I had come to the Guild offices with a list. Roy Rogers, Tim
McCoy, "Lash" LaRue, The Lone Ranger and Tonto, The
Cisco Kid, Bob Steele, Charles Starrett, Rex Allen, Sunset Car-
son, Don "Red" Barry, Allen "Rocky" Lane, Johnny Mack
Brown, Russell Hayden, Jimmy Wakeley, Monte Hale, Joel
McCrea, and Randolph Scott. I didn't have John Wayne on my
list because I wasn't sure I even wanted to see him. And as for
Gene Autry, I knew where to find him. Assuming, of course,
that he wanted to be found. So many others were dead that
the list seemed small compared to what it might have been 20
years ago. Mix and Hart and "Broncho Billy" were gone. And
Hoot and Buck and Ken Maynard. Hoppy and "Wild Bill" and
Tim Holt and "Gabby" and "Smiley" and Tex. So many of the
Good Guys.

"Those are the rules," she said. "We have to go by them. If

it was for work or something, we could probably put you in touch with their agents."

Agents? Managers? Front men? What year is this? I tried to explain what I was after and that I wasn't just an off-the-wall autograph-seeker.

"Just a minute," she said, cutting me off in mid-sentence. "I've got Charlton Heston on the line." You could almost see her coming to respectful attention behind her switchboard. As if she were speaking to . . . Moses? Charlton Heston could get those addresses out of her if he wanted them. She clicked off on Heston and turned back to me, a little surprised and annoyed that I was still standing there with my list, refusing to take no for an answer.

"We're pretty busy here," she said. "The only other thing I can suggest is that you write letters to these people. We'll forward letters to the addresses we have on file, and if they still live there, they can get in touch with you. So why don't you go home and do that?"

I had visions of sending messages out to sea in a bottle and never knowing whether they would ever be washed ashore. "Not another one!" I imagined Roy Rogers saying to his horse. "That makes 10 million fan letters and crank letters. I wish the Guild would stop forwarding these things."

"Maybe I ought to just hire a private eye to find them," I said. And had a new, more amusing vision of the Front Row Kid climbing a dark flight of stairs in some dingy L.A./Hollywood office building and knocking on Sam Spade's door. "Could you find my Cowboy-Heroes, Mr. Spade?" And Sam Spade would say: "Sure, Kid. Nothin' to it. But first I gotta find a Maltese Falcon for Mary Astor."

"You could always take an ad in the trades," the Guild protector of privacy said, by way of a farewell suggestion. "Everybody reads the trades."

I took her advice and ran a vague and ambiguous ad in the *Hollywood Reporter,* one of the trades (along with *Daily Variety*) that keeps the show-biz industry up to date on itself. They **are** read religiously every day, usually in about 20 minutes **while** someone is sitting on the toilet in the executive bathroom. They contain production news, sanitized executive gossip, projects in the works, and on the back pages, small ads for luxury properties in Malibu. The trades are not quite as interesting to read as wire tap transcripts from a whorehouse pay phone. Three replies broke the deafening silence that swallowed up my ad. Two of them thought I was casting a film. The other one was a phone freak who wanted me to describe all the ways I would do it to her and to "breathe like you're fucking me . . ." "You're the one supposed to be the breather, man," I said, "not me." And hung up. She did not leave a number and never called back.

I also took a dozen letters back to the Guild for forwarding. Friendly, hopeful letters requesting meetings with each Cowboy-Hero and asking them to reply by "phone, post, or pony express" if they could spare the time. Two of the letters came back almost immediately stamped "No Forwarding Address." One letter, to Allen "Rocky" Lane, took a little longer but eventually came back marked "Deceased." And the rest appeared to have been lost at sea.

I did not bother to send one to Johnny Mack Brown at all. He had died suddenly on November 14, 1974, at the Motion Picture Country Home out in the Valley before I could get the letter written. Too bad. I did not want to go to any funerals. I was the Front Row Kid at Ken Maynard's funeral in March 1973.

Not a professional mourner but a Western movie believer, I had gone, on that gray March morning, to Forest Lawn in Orange County. Out of curiosity and a curious desire to pay my respects. Also on the hope that Gene Autry might be there. I had been trailing the Singing Cowboy from Hollywood Boulevard to Anaheim for a magazine article and had not yet caught up with him. Since Autry had made his first Singing Cowboy appearance in a Ken Maynard Western, it did not seem unreasonable to assume he might turn up at the funeral.

Near the cemetery gate a fountain gently sprayed water into a pond. Next to it stood a sign, more like a monument, in the shape of an open prayer book. Printed boldly across the pages were the words:

FOREST LAWN MEMORIAL-PARK
CYPRESS
MORTUARY CEMETERY CHURCH
FLOWERS CREMATORY MAUSOLEUM
EVERYTHING IN TIME OF SORROW

In the distance, across crew-cut lawns, a fresh body was being let down for the last time. From the distance it looked like a garden party. In the deadening echo of acres of manufactured silence, you feel like a trespasser. It is a weird thing about graveyards.

Ken Maynard's survivors began to arrive. Mostly old farmers, friends, honchos, and trailer park neighbors. Four old cowboys dismounted from a Lincoln Continental. They were wearing Stetsons and cowboy boots. One was a big Indian in a beaded jacket and Western shirt. He wore one of those flat-brimmed, round-crowned hats the Indians used to wear in the movies to show they've gotten religion. He looked familiar. It was not Tonto. A TV news crew stood about in the antiseptic serenity trying to look inconspicuous with their camera gear hoisted on their shoulders. After all, Ken Maynard *was* a celebrity. That he ended his days a rummy living in a trailer in the San Fernando Valley did not alter the Hollywood historical fact that he had been one of the Big Four, a Cowboy-Hero for 20 years and right up there with Tom Mix. However, unlike, say, Valentino's funeral or Marilyn Monroe's, this was not going to be an orgy of Hollywood mourning.

And then it was time for the service to begin. The mourners moved somberly into the Church of Our Father. Neither next-of-kin nor family friend but just a Front Row Kid, I was the last one in and took a seat near the back. No one questioned me about who I was or why I had come.

Inside, the body of the dead Cowboy-Hero, Ken Maynard, lay in an open coffin in front of the pulpit surrounded by banks of flowers. The mourners, about 75 in all, settled down to a hushed mumble and then a silence. The old cowboys, each with a flower in his lapel, were the honorary pall bearers. They sat in the front-row seats. The organ music stopped, and the pastor's monotone began.

"In the beginning God created the heavens and the earth . . ." the pastor monotoned into the echo. "Ken Maynard is not here. Thank God he's not here. His body is here. But his spirit has ventured on . . ."

From time to time a mourner coughed or cleared his throat. Nervous noises in the presence of Death.

The pastor eulogized on. About the Old Testament. The Lord. St. Paul. About Ken Maynard. How he had run away from home to join a circus. Become a champion rodeo rider. And eventually a movie star. How undisciplined, brash, and profane he had been. Yet decent, intelligent, and honest. That he had been a bigger man in life than ever he was on the screen. That he had been a lonely man in the later years. And that he finally died. President Nixon sent a telegram . . .

And then the mourners rose up and walked to the front to view the body before reassembling outside on the lawn at the "place of interment." The old friends and trailer-park cowboys walked quickly and silently past the coffin. One old cowboy, accompanied by his wife, had come to Ken Maynard's funeral in full gear. White Stetson and fancy shirt, sky-blue Western pants with a red stripe down the sides tucked into hand-tooled red-white-and-blue cowboy boots with eagles on them. And two six-guns on his hips. A touch of show-biz. A gesture. Ridiculous? But not out of place. Bizarre? But not really funny.

And the body of Ken Maynard lay small in the casket. Old and wrinkled, dressed in a dark blue suit, hands crossed over his chest, surrounded by flowers. Hard to believe this man had once been the wild, romantic, daredevil-riding Ken Maynard of the Saturday Matinee. The Cowboy-Hero who seemed to laugh at broken bones and Death when he was in the saddle. Who wanted things to be his way and would fight the Devil and the whole world for what he wanted. But now dead and gone. Left behind by events and the passing of time. Finally, not even the most fearless quick-draw Cowboy-Hero can outdraw Mister Death. But as long as one Front Row Kid still had the fantasy to look to, there would be, perhaps, some life after death for a Cowboy-Hero.

I did not spend too much time looking down into Ken Maynard's coffin, and once outside, I hung around just long enough to see the thing put into the ground. Then I went off to Disneyland. But it was closed.

On the day I read about Johnny Mack Brown, I had no desire ever to watch another Cowboy-Hero going to Boot Hill. But I felt an added sense of urgency to catch the live ones before they went thataway.

Gene Autry

Gene Autry was the key. If anyone in Hollywood knew where the Cowboy-Heroes were hiding out, even where the bodies were buried, Gene Autry would surely be the one.

It was once said of Gene Autry that the two things he hated most in the world were children and horses. Whoever said it must have owed him money. Some Western movie purists say Gene Autry ruined the Western, made it ridiculous with all that singing and show-biz, turned it into horse opera. The Front Row Kids did not agree. They went nuts for Gene Autry. And he became a zillionaire from it.

"When Gene was at his peak," an old Autry pal once said, "he was getting may be forty, fifty thousand fan letters a week! And you know, when you're a big Hollywood star you get to know a lot of important people, Joe Kennedy, Sam Rayburn, LBJ, mayors, governors, presidents, business people, and you get a lot of business deals offered to you."

Autry may not have been the rider Ken Maynard was or as athletic as Fred Thomson, but he knew how to count better than anyone. Everything Autry touched turned to gold. He was now, very likely, one of the richest men in Southern California, which made him one of the richest in the whole damn country. And he could be as elusive as Howard Hughes.

Gene Autry had been my favorite. Other Front Row Kids would swear by Roy Rogers. Between the two of them there was a difference in style, in things you could not exactly put your finger on. In substance they were much the same, always winning and always singing. They were both streamlined, bastardized versions of the Cowboy-Hero in the Wild West Tale. (All Singing Cowboys were.) But Autry, it seemed to me, was the more legitimate of the two. It was an instinctive call. Not necessarily based on anything more solid than a kind of spiritual attraction. Between Autry and Rogers, as between a Buick and an Oldsmobile, you chose your favorite mostly by instinct. It depended, probably, on what vague image of yourself you had fashioned in your fantasies. For me, there was Gene Autry. He seemed the most appealing, the more interesting. Less fresh-faced and innocent. He seemed to me, looking up from the front row, to be more the man, while Rogers bordered on boyish. And I preferred the look of Autry to Rogers'. His white Stetson for one thing. And the fact that Gene only wore one six-gun. Rogers did have "Gabby" Hayes, whom I loved above all sidekicks. Wizened and scruffy and bearded, he was nothing short of beautiful. (And he endured good-naturedly the requirement that he wear low-heeled boots and walk stooped over so no one would realize that he was taller than Roy!) But I cared not a damn for the rest of Roy's entourage, Dale Evans and the horse, Trigger, and when Roy went on TV with the goofy jeep, he lost me completely. There was something Gee Whiz! about Roy Rogers that seemed to me too wholesome and without any mystery. He was, perhaps, trying too hard. I liked the vague hint of boredom and faint annoyance that crept around the edges of Autry's Texas/Oklahoma drawl. Of the two, Gene Autry seemed the darker figure. And he sang closer to key than Roy Rogers. As a kid, I listened for hours to my Gene Autry recording of "Back in the Saddle Again." Over and over I played it until the grooves were nearly worn smooth by the needle and the thing just barely squeaked out a melody on the old Victrola. My mother did not bother to buy me Roy Rogers records. She knew I wouldn't play them. Nor did I "play" Roy Rogers out in the back yard cowtown. Let one of the other kids be Rogers. I would be Gene Autry and beat him to the draw every time. For me, Gene Autry was the best. And Roy Rogers was the Oldsmobile.

In the spring of '73, I was driving down Van Ness Avenue in San Francisco when a Country-and-Western tune came on the radio.

"Gene Autry," my passenger said. "Why don't you write an article on Gene Autry?"

"Good idea," I said.

And went straight over to the editorial offices of a magazine I sometimes wrote for to suggest it to the bosses.

"Good idea," my friend the managing editor said.

I had been hanging out for some days at the trial of Ruchell Magee in San Francisco. Magee was the sole survivor of the Marin County Courthouse shoot-out, which was no Wild West Tale. And on trial for his life. And the spectators at the public trial were being I.D.'ed, photographed, body searched for hidden razors, Uzi machine guns, and pitch forks and menaced by para-commando-type police in baseball caps and those combat suits with all the zippers. Each guy carried a 3-foot-long solid-oak club that looked like a tie from under the Union Pacific tracks, and you just knew by the way they scowled that those goons would love, even better than fucking and drinking, to hit your head all over the tenth floor hallway. The times were already pretty far out of whack. And none of us was bound for glory. As I watched the proceedings from my front-row seat in the bullet-proof courtroom, the thought was more sorrowful than terrifying. It would be a great relief to leave the trial in the middle and trail down to Los Angeles in search of Gene Autry on an assignment that promised to take me back, spiritually, to the good old days of Saturday Matinees, if only for a few weeks. It would be a piece of cake.

Ah, if only it had been so.

"Mister Autry's out of town," came out of his secretary's mouth with the predictability of a recording each time I called his office. "I'll see what I can do for you, but Mr. Autry's very busy, and I can't promise anything. I'll mention it to him when he calls in, but he really doesn't like doing interviews, you know, talking about the old days. He's said it so many times in the past, I think he's probably tired of it. Why don't you call back at the end of the week?"

I suggested that I would like to drive down to Palm Springs, where his baseball team was in spring training, just to watch him do whatever it is he does there. This was met with a titter of amusement and no encouragement. I was, however, fixed up with a private screening of old Gene Autry films.

I sat in a small storage room at his TV station with a 16 mm. projector rattling away behind my right ear. I saw *Tumbling Tumbleweeds, Comin' Round the Mountain, The Old Corral* (with young Roy Rogers as a singing villain), *South of the Border,* and *Mexicali Rose.* Sitting by myself in that room with those movies, I was nearly overwhelmed. I had tears in my eyes from something more than the dust and close quarters. If anyone had been in there with me, I could not have explained it and would have said there was something in my eye. I had gotten closer to some things that afternoon. But not, it seemed, closer to Gene Autry.

I continued to trail Autry with no joy for several weeks that spring, including one sad high noon at Forest Lawn where he did not turn up among the mourners. Finally, thinking to call it quits and leave town but nevertheless wondering what he looked like 20 years on, I went out to Anaheim Stadium to the ball game. Autry's team, the California Angels, were opening their '73 season against the Kansas City team (whatever they were called). I knew Autry would be there. Perhaps I could catch a glimpse of him from the bleachers. Or meet him during the seventh-inning stretch. But the club P.R. man said that was out. The President of the United States was bopping up from San Clemente to throw out the first ball, and Autry would be with him. It was absolutely impossible. No chance. Forget it. I settled for merely watching the same ball game and went out to the stadium, anyway.

Cars started lining up at the stadium gates at 6. The pregame ceremonies were scheduled for 7:30. A POW fresh from Vietnam was going to throw out a ball, and there would be fireworks. Hot dog!

Anaheim Stadium was an armed camp that night. Inside the stadium security people were stationed at every ramp, talking into two-way radios and checking ticket stubs. Nobody would be getting near the President that night without signing a loyalty oath. Every thermos jug was suspect. The Secret Service was all over the yard with roving eyes and that little bulge under their Robert Hall suit jackets where the .357 Magnum was packed away. There was as much high-tension paranoia in the air as before an imminent coup d'etat, more electricity than at any Yankee-Dodger World Series game you ever heard of. And it was only Gene Autry's California Angels, a slapped-together American League cellar dweller, versus the Kansas City whatcha-ma-callits.

But with a yellow media pass flying in my buttonhole like a flag, I was free and cleared to wander all over the park, along concrete tunnels and passageways, up and down the official elevators. Free to find Gene Autry if I could or the President of the United States if I dared.

Down in the home-team dressing room, an immaculate anti-septic and brightly lit locker room that smelled vaguely of athlete's foot powder, I found the great slugger Frank Robinson getting into his uniform. He had been MVP in both leagues and was finishing out his fine career with the bottom-drawer Angels. His knees were all shot to hell, and he was in his middle thirties. He had, perhaps, one or two more seasons left to play.

Sports seemed to have replaced the Wild West Tale as the national myth and metaphor. And stars of the gridiron, the court, and the diamond had become the American Hero. Names like Johnny Bench, Joe Namath, and Kareem Abdul Jabbar made Sideline Kids' eyes water. Of course, there had always been the Babe Ruths and Lou Gehrigs, the Stan "The Man" Musials and Bob Fellers, Dempsey, Tunney, Louis, and Sugar Ray, Otto Graham, Jim Brown and "Red" Grange, Kramer, Budge, and Pancho Gonzales, Jesse Owens, Jim Thorpe, and such as that for the Kids to look up. And for the sixties, until he had become a self-parody, there had been Muhammad Ali, who was, as he himself had declared, "the greatest!" But something had soured in the Great Sports Sell of the seventies. A kind of gimmickery and P.R. manipulation had come into the thing. Or perhaps I was just too old and out of shape to appreciate the fantasy potential of the playing field. Besides, I had always been a better make-believe cowboy than a right fielder.

I went over to Frank Robinson, who was lacing up his spikes, and asked him, rather dumbly, what it was like to have a Singing Cowboy for a boss. He looked at me without really *seeing* me, and I had the feeling that if he had had a bat handy, I would have been his first RBI of the season.

"Well, he's a great baseball fan," Robinson said, looking over to Johnny Roseboro, the ex-Dodger catcher, to see if he was laughing.

I wished him luck on the season and hot-footed it toward the dugout. TV crews and photographers were crowded all around the Presidential box although there was nothing to take a picture of. Nixon was late. The POW, Major David Luna, USAF, stood in the box, dressed in air force blues, shaking hands with someone, looking a little overwhelmed.

Nixon had just recently hero-welcomed the Vietnam POWs, and there were more of them in Orange County than in any two other places you could name. Orange County was one of the few places you could still trot out a war hero to cheers rather than to an avalanche of rotten fruit and vegetables. There was neither much mileage to be gained nor free meals to be gotten by being a war hero these days. That particular hero fantasy had been napalmed to ashes and anti-personnel bombed to smithereens. And good-bye to all that.

Security cops hustled the press out of the dugout area. Shortly, the Hunchback of San Clemente would be standing in the Presidential box, grinning from ear to ear, a robot in a summer suit. With time to kill before the freak show, I take a ride up in the official elevator to have another go at the press box. They say the view is best from there. But my yellow media pass gets me nowhere. No peddlers allowed. The security guards are cross-checking lists against press cards. Only the local working press, officially assigned to cover the Angels, can get through to the free booze. Looks like the end of the line for me. Might as well get a hot dog on the lower level and go to my seat far from the front row. If I hang around this hallway too long, looking for Gene Autry, someone is going to put the collar on me. I'll end up watching the game from a holding cell in the basement. Freedom's just another word for nothing left to lose. I push the elevator button and wait, trying to make myself invisible . . .

A flying wedge of important-looking people and executive briefcases comes out of a door next to the press box, making for the elevator. A voice from somewhere behind me says: "Thanks, Gene." I turn around. Tumbling Tumbleweeds. It's the cowboy, looking tan, plump, and well-preserved, wearing glasses with light-colored frames, a beige cowboy-style suit with a checkered tie and brown-and-white cowboy boots. It's Gene Autry. Gulp!

The flying wedge rushes into the elevator. And on a whim I jump in after as the doors slide closed. It is a tight squeeze. I jam up against Gene Autry's stomach. Pushing my elbow into his middle. He sucks on his teeth. It is not exactly an embrace we are in. What to say? Ah, Mr. Autry, you were my hero when I was five? I've been trailing you for weeks? Say a few words about the old days before we get to the ground floor? Why weren't you at Ken Maynard's funeral? Sing a few bars of "Back in the Saddle Again"? What the hell *do* you say to an old Cowboy-Hero when you're jammed up against his stomach in an elevator, and he's on his way to see the President of the United States? Nothing.

The elevator stops at the basement level. As the doors slide open, Gene Autry, my Cowboy-Hero, straightarms me out of the way, sending me flying as the wedge hurtles me like a longhorn stampede. Bam! And I am still spinning round as they disappear into a room marked: NO ADMITTANCE.

Out on the field, both teams were lined up along the baselines. I hustled down the aisle until I found a spare seat. Not 20 feet from the President. So much for strict security. And there he was. The Zen Dog of San Clemente. And there was Gene Autry at his side, playing host, clutching his score card. A big night for the Singing Cowboy.

Richard Nixon cocked his arm and lobbed one down to the home team.

Play ball!

Nolan Ryan's first pitch was a strike. The crowd cheered. Gene Autry put a mark on his scorecard. It was not every day he got to sit next to the President of the United States (even such a bent one as Milhouse Nixon), but business is business. Autry was the man who paid Nolan Ryan for throwing strikes. Whenever a big contributor came to chat with the President, I watched Autry give up his seat and move two rows back. By the eighth inning I was colder than a motherfucker and had seen everything there was to see. The Angeles were leading and would probably win. Frank Robinson was out of the game, having hit a homer into the left field bleachers in the bottom of the second. Gene Autry was still being shuttled from seat to seat. And Richard Nixon was not doing anything at all, stonewalling.

After the game, having crashed the Press Club Bar at last, I ran into Gene Autry again. He was standing at the bar, drinking whiskey out of a paper cup and wiping his mouth and forehead with a paper napkin. Being congratulated on the Angels victory (there would not be many during the season) and his night with the President. He looked tired. His chin and jowls were sagging. But he was probably approachable now. After the weeks of trailing him, the brushoffs from his office, the end runs to Anaheim and Forest Lawn, he was finally not in a hurry to go anyplace. I could talk to him if I wanted to. Ask him anything that came into my head. Buy him a drink. Get his autograph. But it was not necessary to do any of these things. That good old Gene Autry was in my head, and I could call him up any time I wanted to simply by talking backward until I came to the memory. I took my drink and went over to sit by myself at a table in the corner. When Gene Autry left the room, I did not even see him go.

That was in the spring of '73. Since then, had I forgotten that small but significant Front Row Kid truth? That the Cowboy-Heroes are where they have always been? What I was doing here now in Hollywood was trying to reconstruct a dinosaur from a few old bones. Or was I just depressed that night at the ball game? Taken by surprise? Because here I was again. After many miles and some time. Back in the saddle. Traveling the same dreary freeways. Getting the same no for an answer. It was like a weird acid flashback. But with a difference. This time I was looking not just for Gene Autry but for all the Cowboy-Heroes left alive. And hoping Gene Autry could point me to them. We were not exactly good buddies. Just short-ride elevator companions. It was not as if any of them owed me anything for being a faithful Front Row Kid all these years. Or did they? I would have to think about that one.

I did finally get Gene Autry's autograph. It had been 25 years coming. It was in the form of a signature at the bottom of a letter he sent me after the magazine article came out. The issue had his picture on the cover. For two weeks the face of Gene Autry stared out from newsstands coast to coast. Right in there with all those *Time* and *Newsweek* cover photos of the Yom Kippur War and the Saturday Night Massacre. He could not have failed to notice.

> Dear James: [he wrote:]
>
> I have read your article . . . and I was amazed at what you came up with from a bio, a ball game and a brief encounter in an elevator.
>
> I thought it was a very good article and I want to apologize for not being able to give you more personal attention and time.
>
> If you should ever get back to Los Angeles and if my schedule permits I would like to get together with you for lunch or dinner.
>
> Most sincerely,
>
> (Autograph)
>
> Gene Autry

Well, fuck mah ole boots, pardner. I'm back! And I'll have the lobster if you don't mind. And a bottle of Dom Perignon '47 will do quite nicely, thank you very much.

"This is Mr. Autry's office calling," the voice on the telephone said. "Could you come up tomorrow morning about eleven? Mr. Autry will have some time then to meet with you."

"Eleven o'clock?" I said. "Sure. That's fine with me. I'll be there."

"You know where the office is, I presume," the voice said, a little gritty around the edges.

"I certainly do," I said. I had a vivid picture of it in my mind from the times I had been there in '73 when he was out or hiding.

There were many things I wanted to ask Gene Autry about. The old days. The day before yesterday. The Cowboy-Hero myth. Whether he ever believed it or not. Whether he did hate children and horses. What he thought about the old Nixon. What was his opinion of Herbert J. Yates. Of Roy Rogers. Of Clint Eastwood. Did he think the Angels were ever going to win the World Series.

Gene Autry's office is at KMPC, the L.A. radio station he owns. Part of Golden West Broadcasters. It is the linch pin of his operations. He is chairman of the board and president. The building takes up an entire block of choice real estate on Sunset Boulevard, and it is not inconspicuous. Painted white and illuminated at night by spotlights, it calls to mind the White House or something Mussolini might have built. Next door, occupying more valuable Hollywood acres, are the studios of KTLA-TV, Channel 5. Gene Autry owns that, too, and they still show reruns of his old Westerns. He used to own the Continental Hyatt House farther down Sunset. (It was called the Gene Autry Continental.) When he sold it out to the Hyatt chain, he only regretted no longer being able to take breakfast in the hotel coffee shop every morning. Autry at one time owned four hotels. Now the only hotel where he can get free breakfast is the Gene Autry Hotel down in Palm Springs, which is very fine indeed, probably the best hotel in that dry desert town full of rich golfers and old millionaires. But then, Gene Autry had long ago wiped the cow flop off his bootheels.

I was out front with the Dodge parked in the sun by 10:55 in the morning, thinking I should have said 4 P.M. and spent the afternoon in a topless bar. Eleven in the morning is not my idea of a good time. It is the sort of time when army physicals take place and daylight jewel robberies. It is neither lunch nor breakfast. It is certainly not suppertime. Good-bye the lobster and the Dom Perignon. I should be asleep. My head is in a state of dysfunction. I am trying to think. And I am thinking that when this is over, I will probably spend the rest of the day thinking of what I *should* have said but didn't think of.

I paid the meter up for an hour and walked boldly into the building. For a change I was dressed like a human. No "Wild Bill Hickok." No jeans. A turtleneck. Corduroy pants. The jacket from an off-the-rack three-piece suit. Who was I trying to impress? Who was I fooling?

"Can I help you?" A pretty receptionist intercepts me as I come through the door, tucking my notebook into the back of my pants behind my belt.

"Gene Autry," I say.

"You've come in the wrong doorway." *That* was something that had changed since the last time I was here. Autry's private entrance was now around the corner on the KTLA side past the guard gates. I hate offices.

Gene Autry's office is a secure suite of rooms, with his private territory being the last and biggest room down past two secretaries. It is large and comfortable, like a living room, with a thick red carpet on the floor and five or six soft-cushioned easy chairs around the room. One wall is covered with wood-paneled cabinets with a space that suggests the existence of a built-in bar. The room is full of Western art. In the center of the office on a coffee table there is a statue of a buckaroo wrestling a maverick or maybe a cow. A Fredric Remington oil hangs on the wall. On the corner of Autry's enormous dark oak desk stands the famous Fraiser bronze of the sagging and weary Indian on the drooping horse, "The End of the Trail." The desk is covered with copies of the *Hollywood Reporter* (I wonder if he read my ad?) and the *Wall Street Journal,* as well as a stack of important papers and three or four silver statuettes that appear to be replicas of the Republic Pictures Eagle. To the left of his own high-backed gray leather swivel chair is a bank of three TV monitors where he, like the President of the United States, can simultaneously watch all three

network news broadcasts, or perhaps the *Gene Autry Show* in
triplicate. Along the wall behind the chair is a shelf with half
a dozen books lined up. It is a fairly restful, darkly lit room and
probably soundproof. A nice place to hang out after a hard day
on the trial. Or 67 years in the saddle.

Gene Autry comes around from his side of the desk to greet
me. He is wearing a brown suit and an expensive-looking tie.
There is a Shriner's curved scimitar pin in his lapel. He looks
much the same as he did at the ball game. A bit less anxious,
but friendly. He rather resembles Hubert Humphrey.

"Howdy," I say to Autry, reaching out my hand to shake his.

And Gene Autry says something like "how's it going?" But
it slips right by me in my surprise at the sound of his voice. It
is a voice that I have never heard before. We did not speak one
word the last time we met (in the elevator). It is not the voice
that spoke in all the Saturday Matinees. And sang "Back in the
Saddle" for hours and hours on the old Victrola. Gene Autry's
voice sounds like a scuffle in a sand pit. It is raspy and quaver-
ing and weak. As though the voice had been pulled out and
then put back, wrapped in a sandwich bag. It no longer
twangs. It is a voice on its way to disappearing down a throat
that once sang wonderful cowboy songs but now seems to be
strangling on its own vocal chords. Gene Autry may well be
a zillionaire and all the rest of it, but there is something terri-
bly terminal and beyond saving in that voice I hear. As though
something more than time has ground it down to wood shav-
ings. It surprises me to hear it. And saddens me. And I hope
he doesn't notice my reaction to this unexpected fragility and
deterioration that I sense in the man who was my best Cowboy-Hero.

He motions me to a chair in front of his desk and slips into
the swivel chair.

"I'd like to apologize again for being so busy when you were
writing that story last year," he says. "I enjoyed reading it. It
was an interesting way of handling it."

"Well," I say, not knowing what to say, "I'm glad you liked
it."

"My schedule keeps me so busy I can't always find time for

that sort of thing. I've got a pile of letters right here," he puts his hand on the stack of important-looking papers, "that have just come in recently from people, writers asking me for interviews. I don't even know where half of them come from. And I know I won't have time to do them all. There just isn't time. And I've just concluded a deal with a publisher to do a book on my life, and somehow I have to find time to do that. It will probably cover most of the things these fellows want to know, anyway, so you can see the problems."

"Yeah, I can see that," I say. And indeed I can. He wants to keep all his best stories for himself. Gene Autry didn't get to be one of the richest men in town by giving anything away. It almost goes without saying.

"So, what can I do for you?" he asks, leaning back in his chair with his hands on the armrests.

I begin to explain to him that I have come out to round up all the Cowboy-Heroes that I can, to meet them and talk about this and that and the good old days. And that I am not having much luck finding them.

"I didn't find out where Johnny Mack Brown was until the *L.A. Times* announced that he had died," I say, wondering whether I ought to speak too much of death. "And I was in Europe when Tex Ritter died. I read about that in the papers."

"I didn't know Tex was sick," Autry says. "I was quite shocked. I always liked Tex. He had such bad luck. I don't know why, but he was just not lucky. I used to say that if he was drilling for oil, and there was oil all around, he'd drill the only dry hole in the field. But he was a real nice fellow, and it was too bad. You're right, though, about everybody dying. Cooper's gone and Gable and Ty Power. So many of the big names are gone. Joe Kane is still around. He directed a lot of my pictures and Roy's. And Roy was at the station the other week. He was plugging his new record and seeing some of the disc jockeys. I guess he's doing all right. I don't see him much these days, but I see his manager, Art Rush, quite a lot. Art is the one to see about Roy. He handles all Roy's business. If I see him, I'll mention it to him that you'd like to see Roy. Art's the one to see about that."

Roy Rogers had recently released a record. "Hoppy, Gene and Me." It was not great, but you could hear it on the C&W stations. I wondered if Autry got any tickles of satisfaction about Roy having to come to his station, disc in hand, to pitch Autry's disc jockeys for air play, but I decide not to say anything. Roy Rogers, it seems, is still eating Gene Autry's dust.

"That would be a help," I say. "The only thing I've heard about Roy besides his record is that he's got Trigger stuffed out at his museum."

"I heard about what he did with Trigger," Autry says. "I don't think I would have done that with Champ." He smiles at the thought of Trigger stuffed.

I tell him about Roy being quoted in a magazine saying that when he goes, he wants to be stuffed and put on top of Trigger, but Dale said she didn't want anyone doing that to her.

"Did he say that?" Autry seemed bemused.

I'm not sure if he's going to laugh or be sick. I change the subject to the old days when I used to go religiously to Gene Autry movies on Saturday afternoons. And how we often got Autry-Rogers double features.

"There was never any feud with Roy," Gene says. "That was just Republic publicity. They thought it would make it more interesting. Personally I never liked the idea. But Republic seemed to think it would sell more pictures. Hell, we were both making six to eight pictures a year, and they were doing very well. I always liked Roy. There was never anything like a feud."

"Show business," I say.

I ask him if he would mind me asking him a few things about the old days, although I know he will keep the best stories for himself.

"Well," he says, "I don't really have time today. And for the next few weeks I'm going to be pretty busy." I think I have heard this old song before. Autry runs down his itinerary. "I have to go up to San Francisco for a broadcasters' meeting, and then I'll be back for a few days or so. And then I'm out of town again. My secretary might be able to arrange something in a few weeks."

"I don't mind waiting." What the hell, I've waited this long.

He picks up a small calendar, looks at it for a moment, then decides he doesn't want to make any firm decisions. "Will you excuse me for a minute," he says. "I've got to get rid of some of this coffee." He comes around the desk past me and goes out through a door at the back of the room. I think I hear a toilet flushing. I sense that my time for today is fast running out.

"Tell me about yourself," he says, coming back into the room. "Where are you from originally?"

"Oshkosh, Wisconsin."

"I know Oshkosh. Used to play all over that area. I worked at WLS in Chicago before I came into pictures. And later on we used to go out there on personal appearances to promote the pictures. It's nice country. I'm sure I've been through Oshkosh. Gosh, I played country fairs and theaters around there for years. Many times."

"I remember seeing you in Milwaukee when I was a kid," I say. That was a lie. I don't ever remember seeing Gene Autry in person when I was a Front Row Kid except in my head. If he came through my home town, which I do not doubt, it must have been before my time. I would not have missed it or forgotten. I only say that to keep him talking. And it works.

"Yes, we did so many shows. I probably made more money doing rodeos and personal appearances than I ever made making pictures. We went all over the country. And I was in Europe in 1939. I was in Liverpool on a personal apperance tour when Hitler took Danzig. I think we broke all the attendance records on that tour. And you know, on that same tour was when I got 'South of the Border' and first recorded it. We were at the Theatre Royal in Dublin, and a couple of English boys came up to me and said they had a song they'd like me to do. It was 'South of the Border.' Well, I heard it and liked it and started singing it on the tour. Then we recorded it over there, and I bought the rights and it became a big hit for me. That was a very successful tour. And those French cab drivers! They'll take you for a ride. It's like talking to ball players. When you talk to the Cubans and the Dominicans, they don't understand anything. But when you get to talking money and contracts, they sure can understand pretty good." Autry has a good chuckle to himself over that.

We talk for a few more minutes about this and that. Hollywood. And about how times really have changed and you couldn't make a picture today for what they did over at Republic in the old days. And he agrees with me that the Cowboy-Heroes he and Roy and the others played in the Saturday Matinees were good examples for Front Row Kids to follow. And maybe something like that would come back. But he doubted it. I ask him about his health. (That voice bothers me.) He says it's "pretty good." And as for the chances of the California Angels winning the World Series in his lifetime, well, they were working on it, and he hoped for the best. We do not speak of Richard Nixon.

The hour passes quickly. On the button of noon he announces he has a business meeting coming up right away but that he is glad to have met me at last and that something might be fixed up in a couple of weeks for a bit more conversation and some questions. I should call his secretary about that.

We shake hands again, but he does not walk me out through the front rooms of the suite. I nod to the secretary on the way out.

I left the building and went straight to the bar across the street. It was dark and cool and empty. The girl who worked behind the bar was putting money in the juke box and selecting Frank Sinatra songs. I ordered a "hot" Bloody Mary and twirled the ice cubes with the stick for a while. So I had finally met and spoken to my number-one Cowboy-Hero. A fine thing. He had revealed no secrets. I was not going to hold my breath until our next meeting. Whatever I might still want to know about Gene Autry that I didn't already know, I would have to read in his book, if he ever does write it, and if he tells the truth in it. Still, I could not help liking Gene Autry, this old, round, rich man with the gurgling voice. Perhaps we should have arranged to meet in a topless bar.

Sunset Carson
and the Good Ole Boys

December 7. Pearl Harbor Day. Coming on to winter. Almost Christmas, fer chrissake! But you can't tell in Los Angeles, because every day looks the midsummer same out the window. It is only a matter of degrees. Like being at sea where there is not even a passing telephone pole to check your speed against. Standing still in time and space. And Thanksgiving. Dinner at Schwab's Drugstore, a tuna sandwich on toast, was not my idea of a good time. They say Lana Turner was discovered there, sitting on a stool at the soda fountain. Maybe so. Nowadays, the ghost of Nathanael West rattles there, along with the dead hopes of a thousand tap dancers from Keokuk and Topeka, country girls and homecoming queens who came out here to be broken on the wheel of ridiculous dreams. All those sad girls who entered laughing but had to suck cock for a walk-on in a B-feature and went regularly to Schwab's to wash their mouths out with ice cream soda. Success was, conceivably, worse than failure. A back booth at Schwab's seems like a good place to go on Christmas Eve to commit suicide. I was beginning to pray for rain.

Except for my visit with Gene Autry, I was not exactly moving right along on my roundup. Phone calls to the studios where the Cowboys once rode the range, Universal, Columbia, Fox, were met with dumb silence on the other end and invariably the reply: "Buck who?" "Tim who?" "Tex who?" "Joel Gray?" It was becoming very much like a bad knock-knock joke. It was as if what Stalin did to the Russian history books had been done to the memory channel of the film industry. Or perhaps it was just demon time. In Holly-

OREGON
TRAIL
A REPUBLIC PICTURE
starring
SUNSET CARSON
with PEGGY STEWART
FRANK JAQUET
JOHN MERTON • MARY CARR
Directed by THOMAS CARR
Screen Play by BETTY BURBRIDGE
Based on a Novel by FRANK GRUBER

wood, where all relationships are nothing more than 13-week seasons with options to renew, to be 30 years out of the picture seemed virtually the same as never having existed at all. And time, which does not appear to be moving at all, really moves with lightning speed toward wipe-out and invisibility and amnesia. Thirty years is a geological age. Randolph Scott, where are you?

William Witney was one of Republic Picture's top-notch contract directors. Along with Spencer Bennett, he was the king of the serials. He directed the Lone Ranger serial, Zorro, Red Ryder, King of the Royal Mounties, Dick Tracy, and dozens of Roy Rogers Westerns. He could certainly tell a fellow a thing or two about those days and the Cowboy-Heroes. I managed to reach Witney by phone as he was running out the door headed for Mexico. "It's been so long ago," he said. "You did them and you walked away. I don't really want to dredge up some of those memories." End of conversation.

Sol Siegel was an important producer at Republic, right up there with Herbert J. Yates. He produced many Autry films in the Thirties. His brother Moe was head of production for the studio. Sol Siegel is about as happy to talk about those days as he would be to contract Black Plague. "I've been trying to forget those films for thirty years," he said. Click.

Jay Silverheels played "Tonto" to Clayton Moore's "Lone Ranger" in two Warner Brothers features and all the half-hour television shows. Tonto was *the* Hollywood Indian. Jay Silverheels, full-blooded Mohawk. We learned how to say "kemosabi" from him. He looked out for The Lone Ranger. It has been said that when the Indian Movement raised Tonto's consciousness, he took a very dim view of his role. He said that always having had to ride three paces behind The Lone Ranger, on a smaller horse, and having to talk baby talk ("Me ketch-um plenty good smoke, kemosabi, ugh!") was demeaning and portrayed Indians as subhuman and imbecilic. For a while there, he was on the warpath. But The Lone Ranger is an institution, a Cowboy-Hero fantasy too deeply rooted over the years in the national consciousness. Jay Silverheels would always be Tonto. And Tonto would always be a "good" injun.

What is a Cowboy-Hero round-up, I thought, without The Lone Ranger and Tonto? Alas, my smoke signal to Tonto was blown away by his agent. "Oh," he said, "Jay wouldn't be interested in anything like that. Good-bye." He must have thought I was The Lone Ranger. Ugh.

And what *about* The Lone Ranger? The fabulous masked man? Who left a silver bullet as his calling card. And rode off on his white horse without waiting for thanks or a reward, crying: "Hi-yo, Silver! Away!" There have been many Lone Rangers since George W. Trendle created the masked Cowboy-Hero. When he first galloped onto the radio in 1933, Brace Beemer was the Ranger. And there was Lee Powell and Bob Livingston in the Republic serials. Jon Hall was the masked man for a brief interval. But the one who counted, in over 160 half-hour TV shows, was Clayton Moore. He was the man behind the mask. Perhaps only the William Tell Overture was linked more closely to The Lone Ranger than Clayton Moore. Ta-ta-dum Ta-ta-dum Ta-ta-dum-dum-dum. According to the terms of his contract with the Wrather Corporation, who owns the world rights to The Lone Ranger (as well as to Lassie and Muzak), Clayton Moore is forbidden to appear in public as The Lone Ranger *without* his mask. A photo of The Lone Ranger unmasked is about as hard to come by as a recent picture of Martin Bormann. And Clayton Moore is apparently just about as elusive. He is alive and well and living near Reno, Nevada. You can dial him direct (if you know his number, that is!). He was not wearing his mask when I phoned him. But he might as well have been.

"I'm in and out all the time, and I never know where I'll be," The Lone Ranger says. "I never talk about my private life, and I won't tell you anything about what went on, on the set. I will only talk about The Lone Ranger, and you can read all that in old interviews I've given over the years. You'd only be wasting my time and yours. Why don't you just pretend you had an interview with me. Make it up. Nobody will know the difference."

"But *I* will, Lone," I say to him. "I'll know the difference."

But The Lone Ranger is beyond persuasion, cajolery, or

bribes. He cannot even be shamed into unmasking. And I am forced to bite the bullet. Who *was* that masked man?

And if, as Gene Autry says, Art Rush is the man to see about seeing Roy Rogers, then I do not hold out much hope of seeing Roy Rogers. "Listen," a voice answering to the name of Art Rush says over the blind telephone. "I really don't know what to say to you. Roy's record is beginning to break big all over the country. Everybody's after him for interviews. It's just phenomenal. We can't seem to get on top of it. It's really mushrooming for him. And he's opening up some more Roy Rogers family restaurants. Why don't you call back after New Years?" I had the feeling I was being Hollywood snow-jobbed, finessed with P.R. I hadn't noticed signs of a Roy Rogers mushroom. The earth was not shuddering where I was standing. But perhaps I was standing in the wrong place. "You do understand how it is, don't you?" he said. Do I?

A newspaper clipping about "Lash" LaRue finds me talking long distance to the police department of Mountain View, Georgia. "Ah, kin y'all call back in about ten minutes?" the officer at the other end drawls. "We got a fahr on down heah." Fahr? Ten minutes later, when the smoke has cleared in the station house, an officer briefly explains the latest episode in the saga of "Lash" LaRue. Seems there was a call down to the local Mountain View Police on the night of September 26 concerning a cowboy type who was apparently drunk and disorderly at Whitmarres grocery store. Some old movie Cowboy was disturbing the other customers by quoting scripture and passing out old publicity photos of himself as he looked 20 years ago in black cowboy outfit complete with bull whip. "Well, Officer Bowdie answered the call," the Mountain View cop says, "and it was this 'Lash' LaRue feller. We was goin' to jist pick him up on the drunk charge and let him sleep it off. Until we found these heah three bags of marijuana 'n' pills on him. And we had to go ahead and charge him under the Georgia Controlled Substances Act. We also found a bull whip in his car." It seems old "Lash" LaRue is still the Cowboy-Weirdo. Is he still behind bars, or do they know where he can be located? "Well, he's jist been indicted by the Grand Jury on two felony counts for unlawful possession of marijuana and amphetamines, and he oughta be goin' ta trial over ta Superior Court in Jonesborough in a few months, I reckon. Far as I know he made bail heah the day after he was arrested and left town. Ain't seen him since." What is the punishment for the crime? "Well, if he's convicted, the marijuana felony could be one to ten years. And the amphetamines is a possible two to fifteen. It's a tough law we got down heah on that." I thank the officer, hang up, and tentatively scratch "Lash" LaRue off my list. As far as I knew, "Lash" had not been very lucky since his Cowboy-Hero days ended and had passed his years as, among other things, a bankrupt, a wino, and an Evangelist. Now he was an alleged doper facing a possible 15 years in the Georgia State Penitentiary. Of course, there was the possibility he might beat the rap. Or get a Presidential pardon from Gerry Ford.

To date, I had hit a run of dry water holes along the trail, and I was beginning to shrivel up. Until I heard about a gathering of B-Western freaks to be held in a place called Siler City, North Carolina. "Jest a buncha us gittin' togithah ta show some old films," said the Southern stranger. "But Sunset Carson might be comin' down. Least ways he said he might. He's got some business over ta Hickory, so he'll be in the area. And y'all are welcome ta come down if ya want to. Be glad ta have ya heah."

North Carolina? It was a long way from Sunset Boulevard. You could not get there by freeway. A long way to go to see old B-Westerns and maybe Sunset Carson. But what the hell. I had already come a long way and seen almost nothing and virtually no one. Besides, what better way was there to celebrate Pearl Harbor Day? I asked him what the weather was like down there. He said it was raining cats and dogs. *"Terrific,"* I said. Perhaps my luck was changing.

It is, indeed, a long way from L.A. to Siler City, North Carolina. And to the various domestic airlines that flap across the skies between LAX and Greensboro, North Carolina, the shortest distance between two points is a pretzel. When you finally arrive, by puddle jumper, in Greensboro, you have to check the local newspaper to make sure what day it is. Surrounded by daing-a-lainging Southern draaawls, I have the feeling I am in a foreign country. Siler City is 60 miles into the Outback. The only way to go is by Greyhound or by thumbing. Outside the airport it is pouring like a son-of-a-bitch.

I am just beginning to have vague feelings of jet lag and futility when a mighty cute little Southern belle appears out of nowhere and asks if I need a lift someplace. It can't be a come-on. Probably a case of mistaken identity. But she is serious. She says I looked lost. I guess it's just Southern hospitality. Her story is she came out to meet her boy friend who was coming in from Minneapolis. But he wasn't on the plane. She hasn't seen him for a month, she says, and she's "maghty damn frustrated." I don't say anything to that but thank her for the offer of a lift, tip my "Wild Bill Hickok" back to get a better look at her, and go along to her car. My tired mind begins to project X-films in place of B-Westerns.

On the way to the Greyhound bus station, I tell her I'm going to Siler City.

"Siler City? What in the world for? There's nothin' *in* Siler City," she says. "Jest nothin' atawl."

And I tell her about the gathering of cowboy movie freaks and that Sunset Carson might be there. She says she has never heard of Sunset Carson and that it seems like a funny thing to be doing. With nothing much to lose, I ask her if she wants to come along. I would, of course, pay for the gas. She thinks about that for a long time. And during the silence, with just the rain falling and the wipers clicking across the windshield of her car, I have the feeling that we should be speaking in French.

"Ah lahk yer hat," she says. I tip it toward her as "The Virginian" might have done. And a waterfall of caught rain runs right off it. She has a nice Southern belle laugh, and I'm thinking maybe I'm not *really* in such a hurry to get to Siler City. I love the Cowboy-Heroes well enough, but there is something to be said for the rancher's daughter.

"Ah'd lahk to go with you," she says. "It maght be fun, ya

know? But mah damn boy friend maght be comin' in on a later plane. Anyway, ah don't much lahk cowboy movies."

The brief encounter ends at the bus station. The bus is just about to leave. Perfect timing. But having now to ride the dog alone, I sleep all the way to Siler City.

Siler City is a backwater town in the North Carolina woods. And the water is rising in the downpour. I splash my way over to the City Hall where about 40 people are gathered for the show. It has the air of a revival meeting. Some of the boys are hanging around the hallway where the punch bowl and the coffee are located. Everyone else, some of them women, are sitting in the auditorium talking among themselves about Cowboy-Heroes. It is amazing. They are *all* Front Row Kids. And except for a few preteeners, none of them appears to be under 40. Some obviously go back to Tom Mix Saturday Matinees. There are a few straw Stetsons in the crowd. And one fellow is wearing a giant Tom Tyler Stetson. It is apparently his pride and joy, that hat. It makes my "Wild Bill" look like a beanie with a propeller on top. Half a dozen good ole boys gather around to greet me. And the word spreads quickly through the crowd that "a feller has just come in all the way from Los Angeles. A writer from Hollywood(!?!)" Some folks twist their necks and stare at me as if I had just dropped through the ceiling from another planet. Some are under the impression that I am a celebrity. I am introduced around, although my name is somewhat mangled in their North Carolina backwoods drawls. But in no time at all they are calling me by my first name. As if we are old friends. Southern hospitality. And they know a Front Row Kid when they see one.

Most of them are Western film collectors. It is their hobby and their life. They swap old Ken Maynards for two Tex Ritters and a "Rocky" Lane. They trade photographs and hand-me-down stories of the old Cowboy-Heroes. They are aficionados of B-Westerns. They know the films by heart. All the titles. All the credits. Probably all the dialogue. They talk about Gene and Roy and Tex and Ken and Tim and Tom and Buck and Sunset and "Wild Bill" Elliott as if each one were a close personal friend. And, of course, they are. Even if these boys have never in their lives met any of them. Or especially because they haven't. Every few months they gather for an afternoon of Western movie-watching and swap the latest news and rumors about their favorite stars. Some of them come from 100 miles away. It is their way of keeping the Faith. I am delighted to see it. And to know that I am not the only Front Row Kid left alive.

I tell them about my roundup. When I say I've seen Gene Autry, it is as if I have seen God. Eyes water over. And they want to know if I've seen Bob Steele, Russell Hayden, Charles Starrett, Don Barry, Randolph Scott, John Wayne, Roy Rogers, Tim McCoy. They seem to know who's alive.

"Ah've seen some of those boys over ta another convention," one of the fellows says. "They is really fahn fellers, ya know. Nevah did see Gene Autry. We got Sunset heah today. Ya wanna meet him?"

Do I want to meet him? Do bears shit in the woods? Is the Pope Catholic? Do GIs love pussy? Do Front Row Kids love Cowboy-Heroes? Lead the way!

Sunset Carson is down at the other end of the auditorium, behind the movie screen, shaking hands and making small talk with the folks. And hawking Sunset Carson Souvenirs. A 45 rpm record and T-shirts with his name on them. He is as big as a tree, about 6 feet 5 inches. He is dressed in pointy-toed boots, jeans, a red Western shirt, and a black leather vest. And way up in the rafters where his head is, he is wearing a big black Stetson. One of his shoulders slopes noticeably lower than the other. He has bushy black eyebrows, and his eyes squint up when he smiles. He shuffles around, shifting his weight from one leg to the other. He reminds me of a great big friendly bear. One of the boys introduces me as "the writer feller from Hollywood." Sunset looks down from his great height on me and my "Wild Bill Hickok" and says, "Howdy, pardner, maghty nice to meetcha."

If Gene Autry is at home with millionaires and Presidents in well-appointed offices, Sunset Carson is right in his element down among the good ole boys. And he seems genuinely glad to meet anyone who is glad to meet him.

They are about to show another film. An early *Three Mesquiteers* with John Wayne. And after that, it is announced, they will be showing the last reel of a Sunset Carson picture.

"Whaddya say we go out to the front hall there so we kin talk," Sunset suggests, "seein' as ya come all this way. And we kin git ourselves some coffee."

We make our way up the aisle, with some of the boys following. On the way, he stops to sign a woman's autograph book.

"I'm happy to come down here for these folks," he tells me when we are outside in the hallway. "They really appreciate it, ya know? Not like those other sonsabitches." Before he can go on about "those other sonsabitches," some of the boys gather around us to listen to what Sunset has to say. He begins to tell us about the Wild West Show he is with, Tommy Scott's Show. Tim McCoy was its headliner for 13 years, until he was 84, but then he got sick and quit and Sunset was asked to take his place.

"We're on the road two hundred days a year," Sunset says. "Going out again in February. I've been showin' in circuses most of my life. Been born and raised on a small ranch twenty miles outside Plainview, Texas. I rode a horse to school and carried my own lunch, biscuits and bacon or ham, you know, and a bottle of milk in the saddlebag. In the winter time the milk would freeze, you know, practically have ice cream. From the time that I saw my first Tom Mix Western, that was the first Western I ever seen, I made up my mind what I was goin' to be. There was only one thing in Sunset's heart, Western and cowboy. Well, one time I was in New Mexico at a rodeo. I started out in rodeo, you know. And Tom Mix seen me and offered me a job. I rode in the Tom Mix Circus, trick ridin' and such as that, and I loaded his guns and so on and so forth for his shootin' act, which I do the same thing now with live ammunition. Shootin' balloons outta folks' mouths and off the top of their heads. That's the main act I do with Tommy Scott. Been doin' it for years in circuses. Since my accident, the doctor says I oughta rest up, but I'm goin' out again on the road in February. Ya know, there's only four cowboys in the Circus Hall of Fame at Baraboo, Wisconsin. Ya had to headline the

Greatest Show on Earth for at least two seasons to qualify. There's only four Cowboys in it," he says and counts them off on his fingers. "Tom Mix, Buck Jones, Tim McCoy, and Sunset Carson." And he grins with intense pride, being able to include himself in that honor roll. "I been all over the world showin' with the circus. England, Germany, Siam, the Philippines, Australia. But ya know," he says. "if it so happens that I'm free and folks like these here want me to come down to a gatherin', why, if I can do it for 'em, I will." And the boys standing around listening nod appreciatively. I want to ask Sunset some questions, but they are all talking at once.

After a few minutes I suggest that perhaps we could talk later, and he says that's fine with him. He's going to be around the whole weekend. I take my coffee into the auditorium and watch the movies. The *Three Mesquiteers* has a very young and boyish John Wayne in it. And the folks are cheering and howling and applauding all the action, the punch-ups and the galloping as though it is the old Saturday Matinee and we are all 10 years old. During the Sunset Carson reel, the folks go wild with delight when a tall and lean and almost baby-faced Sunset Carson wins a fist fight and a shoot-out. I wonder if Sunset has come in to watch himself as he was, 30 years younger. I turn toward the back. Sunset is standing just inside the door, holding his Stetson in his hands, eyes fixed on the screen, something close to a frown on his 53-year-old face. He acknowledges the cheers for the young Cowboy-Hero he once was with a little shrug and a wrinkled brow. His eyes shift from the screen to the ceiling to his boot tops. For a few moments, until everyone settles down to await the next bit of action on the screen, Sunset Carson is made to feel uncomfortable and conspicuous by demon time.

After the show and a final round of Front Row Kid cheering, the official gathering of B-Western freaks is over. Except for the results of a poll that was taken to find who was the favorite Cowboy-Hero of the folks who had come to cheer. Sunset Carson came in second. The winner and number-one favorite was . . . Gene Autry.

I have dinner with Sunset and a few of the good ole boys, including the guy in the Tom Tyler Stetson, at a local truck-stop café. The hamburger gives me heart burn. Sunset says very little. His 6 feet 5 inch bulk is wedged into the booth between two of the boys, and he has a hard time maneuvering his knife and fork. He seems tired and a bit shy. But he cheers up some when one of the waitresses asks for his autograph. He does not seem to notice that the girl has to read what he has written to find out who he is. And even then the name doesn't really ring a bell. I wonder if she hasn't mistaken him for John Wayne.

Sunset Carson might, yesterday and today, have been as big a Western star as John Wayne. He came to Republic Pictures in the middle forties and made over 30 films for Herbert J. Yates. He was just a boy at the time. About 24 years old. His films were an instant success. After Autry and Rogers, he was probably the most popular Cowboy on the Republic range. Even the girls liked Sunset. He was handsome as hell and had a presence on the screen. He might have had a chance with a major studio. But Sunset was, perhaps, too young and too much a country boy to make the most of his chance. They say he was wild and happy-go-lucky. That he drank to the point of outrage. And finally to oblivion. They say he threw it all away. Yet he was very good. You could see that clearly in the reel they showed at the City Hall. He could move. He could ride. He could handle himself. He could even act a bit. You could not say the same for Gene Autry. Sunset rose quickly in the ranks of Cowboy-Heroes. And fell out just as fast and was washed up in pictures. But he remained a cowboy, which was what he knew best. And for 25 years he had been a Wild West Show Cowboy-Hero. Playing to the Front Row Kids with long memories and to the kids of those Front Row Kids who want to see what a real cowboy-type looks like. And in his shooting act, like Buffalo Bill before him, he "breaks onetwo-threefourfive pigeons just like that." He may not be doing well, but he seems to be doing fine.

After dinner we go in Sunset's big old Cadillac out to the back woods to a place called Collins Pond to call on one of the local film collectors and visit the fellow's "Memory Mobile," a fixed trailer with a sign above the door that reads: "Return again to those golden days of yesteryear." The trailer is a time warp. The walls are covered with old film stills and theater posters of every Cowboy-Hero you can think of. Over in the corner is the collector's pride and prize possession. A saddle that once belonged to Fred Thomson. It is a fine, heavy leather saddle. Thomson leaped in and out of it in over 20 films. The collector says it once had diamonds studded in it, but they are long gone. It was worth about $8,000. To a dedicated Front Row Kid, though, it is priceless.

It is the custom of this collector to invite some of the boys over after the gatherings to carry on watching B-Westerns that he projects on a small screen in the trailer. Sunset has come out because he cannot say no to these people, who are as happy as Kids to talk with him and sit next to him and call him by his first name, but he looks quite exhausted. His shoulder is sloping even more than it had been earlier. He does not say much, but he stays on just the same, sipping a beer, which he says he is not supposed to be drinking on account of his accident.

We sit through one film. *Outlaws of the Prairies,* starring Charles Starrett. It dates back to about 1936. It is a revenge story about a Cowboy-Hero in search of the Bad Guys who killed his father and cut off his trigger finger when he was just a boy. That bizarre twist is grisly indeed. Surprising for a B-Western. Charles Starrett in his all-black outfit with a big white Stetson and a large flowing white neckerchief is terrific. He is not supposed to have a trigger finger, so he wears a glove with two fingers folded under. When he draws his six-gun, he has to fan the hammer to fire it. And, of course, he is fast as lightning.

"Great Western!" the good ole boys shout, as excited as Kids. "Tough Western, boy. He's somethin' else. And there's ole Dick Curtis, mean as a rattlesnake. There's old Art Mix, mean as a rattlesnake. Boy, that Charlie Starrett's the best." They seem to have forgotten, in their excitement, that another Cowboy-Hero, Sunset Carson, is sitting in the trailer, listening to them cheer Charles Starrett. But they are lost in the fantasy. True Front Row Kids reacting to the screen action as if it were real and actually happening before their very eyes. It is a weird thing to see.

The rain is still coming down as we head out in Sunset's Cadillac. The back seat is full of his gear, cowboy suits, a big leather scrap book, boxes of "Sunset Carson" T-shirts and souvenir booklets. He says he has a deal with a small fashion-textile outfit in North Carolina to make and sell "Sunset Carson" cowboy-style suits and shirts. And that a local TV station in Hickory puts on a weekly *Sunset Carson Show.* Not exactly big deals. But Sunset works his Cowboy-Hero image as best he can.

"They're real sincere folks here," he says, trying to make out the road in front of him, borrowing my Oshkosh B'Gosh hand-kerchief to wipe the windshield clear, his worn face il-luminated by the lights on the dash of his Cadillac. "Real sincere about their collecting. Not like that other outfit. Nothin' like that." The outfit he refers to is another group that holds a B-Western convention every year in a nearby state. A much bigger operation than Siler City's. Collectors come from all over, and the promoters try to get the old Cowboy-Heroes to come in for it. "They've got a con goin'," Sunset says. "They con the boys into comin' down there. They don't pay any expenses, but they charge the collectors thirty dollars a ticket to see the stars. I've been down there three times. They talked me into it. I drive down there and it's five, six tanks of gas and eighteen dollars for the motel. The last time I was down there was when I had my hit-and-run accident. And while I was lyin' up there in the hospital, I had about two thousand records, a thousand photos, and a mess of shirts, 'Sunset Carson' T-shirts, and they come up and said, 'Let us take this stuff down to the hall for ya and sell 'em. Help ya pay the hospital bill.' So I said sure. And you know, I never saw a red cent of that money. Maybe fifty dollars. They said the stuff got lost! It was at least a pickup truck load of stuff. It ain't possible. Well, I had to pay all my own expenses. And to be robbed on top of that . . . I'll never go back down to that place. I shouldn'ta gone back this year, but I went because of the collectors. They see your name in the program and some of 'em come a thousand miles just to shake your hand. I'm not goin' to disappoint those little people. But these boys here, where we were today, I'll drive over four hours to come here if I'm free and they're havin' a gatherin' 'cos they're nice folks, friendly, sincere, and they get such a kick outta having you here."

We stop along the way for gas at an open station. The guy who owns the station has no arms. He operates from a special booth, taking the money and making change with a contraption he works with his feet.

"He's got some fake arms," Sunset says as we drive away. "But he don't hardly never use 'em. And his wife's blind."

And he talks about how much he enjoyed seeing some of the old Hollywood Cowboys who came down to that ripoff convention.

"I saw 'Lash' there, too," he says. "After my accident he came down to the hospital to see me. He walked right into the operating room. I recognized his voice, but I wasn't sure if I was hearing things. He come in, clean cut and he looked terrific. He said, 'The good Lord's brought you back for something. It's not your time to go. He's got something lined out for you to do on this earth.' And he took out his Bible and said a prayer, and then he left. He came back again about three days later with a box of fruit and stuff and some pictures for the nurses. And that was the last I saw him."

"He's got a little trouble down in Georgia," I say.

"Yeah, I know. Ole 'Lash' just won't leave off the dope and stuff. I guess he just likes it too much. Ya know, 'Lash' is the only cowboy star to be in a X-rated movie. I never saw it, but it's called, wouldn't ya know, *Hard on Trail.* That's just like 'Lash.' But he's a good ole boy."

The next morning, Sunday, we meet for breakfast and talk some more. As long as I came all this way, Sunset says, he'll give me as much time as I need, and I can ask him anything I want to about the old days. It is more than I expected.

This morning, he is dressed in a Sunday-go-to-meeting beige-white cowboy-style suit with brown piping. What that fashion place turns out for a Sunset Carson concession. His boots today are the color of bull's blood. His Stetson matches his suit. He is still as big as a tree, but he is a well-dressed tree. When he takes off his Stetson, I notice he combs the black hair on a balding head forward to cover the baldness. It is possible that the black hair is a tint job. A small vanity for a Cowboy-Hero who never became John Wayne.

After breakfast we go back to my room at the Howard Johnson's Motor Inn, and Sunset brings in his scrapbook of clippings and photographs in a giant hand-tooled leather folder. The scrapbook is six inches thick with stuff. Photos of Sunset in fancy show-biz cowboy gear surrounded by orphans and old folks and performing his sharp-shooting. And there are pictures of some of the other Cowboy-Heroes, including Ken Maynard as he looked shortly before he died, appearing in a film Sunset produced. The film was called *Marshal of Windy Hollow*. It will very likely never see the light of day.

"It come about through talking to film collectors and everything," Sunset says. "And everyone wanting that type of Western to come back. So I got the boys together and produced *Marshal of Windy Hollow*. I did my own stunts and brought Ken Maynard in and Bill Cody and some of the stunt boys from the coast. And we had thirty-five covered wagons, mules, beautiful locations, a beautiful Western town, and we had television people come out from Louisville and Indiana, and it's a heck of a good Western. But we had one wise guy who stole the negative of it. It was cattle rustlin', you know what I mean? This is the first time I ever seen it happen on a Western where a guy actually stole the negative. There's been lawsuits tryin' to get him around, and we got subpoenas served on him, but he's got it hid out someplace. He's bought out four or five of the stockholders and got releases from the rest of them. But I'll see the thing rot before I sign a release for it because I put my blood into it."

And then he sits back in a Howard Johnson's Motor Inn naugahyde easy chair, puts his size 14 boots up on the end of the bed, and talks for three hours about the old days at Republic Pictures. About how he got started. His days at the

Pasadena Playhouse with Alan Ladd and Rory Calhoun when they were so broke they were lucky to get a couple of hamburgers a week. And how, when he first went to Republic, they told him he wasn't ready and should come back in a couple of years. And after he came back from World War II and was in a Warner Brothers film, Yates signed him up. And he tells me how, after he left Republic, he made some films for Astor Pictures, low-budget jobs that didn't seem to come out the way he would have wanted them to. And then TV came along and closed out the little theaters that would buy Astor's films. And that was the end of that. He does not mention the business of his drinking and getting wild. And I don't bring it up because there really doesn't seem to be any point in it. He has his story down the way he wants it and the way he can live with it. We all rewrite our own history books a little bit to soften past humiliations and bad breaks. He does say that Western movies and his years as a Hollywood Cowboy were wonderful. And then he tells me about his accident.

"I was up at the house of one of those promoter guys. We were watching a couple old Westerns. They took me back to my motel about eleven, and I hadn't eaten all day, and I seen this sign across from the motel, hamburgers, bar-b-que, milk shakes." He speaks in a very low voice as if the memory is painful. "So I waited for the light to change and went across. One car stopped and another one. And then another one. I heard him coming, and I turned and got hit. I threw my arms up across my chest. He hit me. Run me over. Run over my arm. Three or four people picked me up and put me in a car and took me to the hospital. My heart was bruised, my chest was swollen from the inside, one lung was full of liquid, my arm was completely crushed, and my shoulder was powdered. It was about three weeks before they could get my lungs to work so they could operate. They took 7 inches of bone from my hip and put it into my arm to rebuild my arm. And on the other side they rebuilt my shoulder. After they put me back together, I took pneumonia and then double pneumonia. And they cut me open and found a hole punctured in my liver. They fixed that up and the son-of-a-bitch is working pretty good now. It's a funny thing. The doctor told me, 'You had to be in perfect condition to come out of it, and you can thank the good Lord for your rodeo days because instinctively, as many times as you've been thrown from broncs and horses, you knew how to land. Even though you were unconscious, you knew exactly how to fall!' "

Later he says about Western movies and Cowboy-Heroes:

"Yeah, I guess everybody was shootin' to be John Wayne and would have liked to get into bigger budget Westerns. But if you follow it back, you'll see that the guys that make it in the big ones are all already forty-five or fifty, so they're seasoned enough to make that kind of Western. Look at Randolph Scott. Look at Duke. He was fifty before he was really ripe enough to know what the heck he was doing and how to do it. And then the book was open. You finally learn."

By the time we finish talking, I've missed the plane back to L.A. So we go back to where he is staying to watch some more old Westerns. His friend is a collector. There are films all over the house. On the floor, in the closet, out in a locked shed. And what you can see is only part of what there is. His friend says he has lots more in other hiding places and locked sheds.

"I love 'em," his friend says. "I don't just look at them. I get right in there with 'em. We've got no leaders, no heroes anymore. But I've got my movies, and I love 'em."

Sunset tells me that this good ole boy shows Westerns to himself all night long. And so he does. This night I stay up with him. (Sunset crashes in the back room about midnight.) Watching Johnny Mack Brown, Tex Ritter, Tim McCoy, "Lash" LaRue, Gene Autry. Wonderful old B-Westerns. And by 4 A.M., the good ole boy is drunk on whiskey and Westerns. Playing, over and over again, a short film clip of Dick Foran singing "Give Me My Boots and Saddle" and a clip of Ray Whiteley singing "Trail Dreaming." And the good ole boy's eyes are watering, and he's singing along.

"Bring it back," he says. "Bring back yesterday. Where did they all go? Money can't buy 'em. God damn, I love 'em!"

At 7 in the morning we are still up watching television. My

head is ringing and echoing with gunshots and galloping. My plane is due to leave in an hour. Outside the air is crisp and clear and fresh. The sun is shining.

As Sunset pulls his big old Cadillac out of the driveway to take me to the airport, I look back and see the good ole boy, Front Row Kid and film collector, standing in the doorway, waving. And I can still hear Ray Whiteley, at top volume, singing out "Trail Dreaming."

"That ole George, he really loves them Westerns," Sunset says on the way to the airport. "I'll bet you didn't expect to find folks like this when you came out from Los Angeles."

"I had no idea," I say.

"There's thousands of 'em," he says. "They're the ones that keep me goin'. Ya can't disappoint them. No sir, no way. I would never do that. I mean, where would us boys be without them?"

"Tell that to Gene Autry and Roy Rogers," I say. "Tell that to John Wayne." And Sunset just laughs.

The Durango Kid

Rrrrriiiinnnngggg!

Somewhere just out of reach of my senses, I hear a ringing. A long way off. But coming closer. Sometimes when you go to sleep stoned and exhausted, you wake up the next morning still stoned. With no memory of having dreamed. In the long run, it is probably not good for you. Nights without dreams are like days without memory. Run a few of these nights together and you begin to feel cut off from your imagination.

Rrrrriiiinnnngggg!

The sound is coming closer. Coming down on me as I crawl uphill to meet it. We connect somewhere in the middle of sleep and waking. It is the damn telephone.

"Mister Horwitz?"

I know that voice. It is deep and full. A cross between New England and "Home on the Range." I *know* that voice. From a long time ago. From just the other day.

"Wha? Huh?" Come on brain. Do your stuff.

"Mister Horwitz, this is Charles Starrett."

Charles Starrett. The Durango Kid. Of course! The Front Row Kid does not forget a Cowboy-Hero's voice. A picture of Charles Starrett, dressed all in black, fanning his six-gun, flashes across my mind. I am instantly wide awake. Terrific.

"Terrific."

"I received your letter the other day," the voice of The Durango Kid says. "The Screen Actor's Guild sent it to an old address of mine. I was a founding member of the Guild. You'd think they would have the correct address. But I guess that's typical. Anyway, I finally did get your letter, and I just wanted

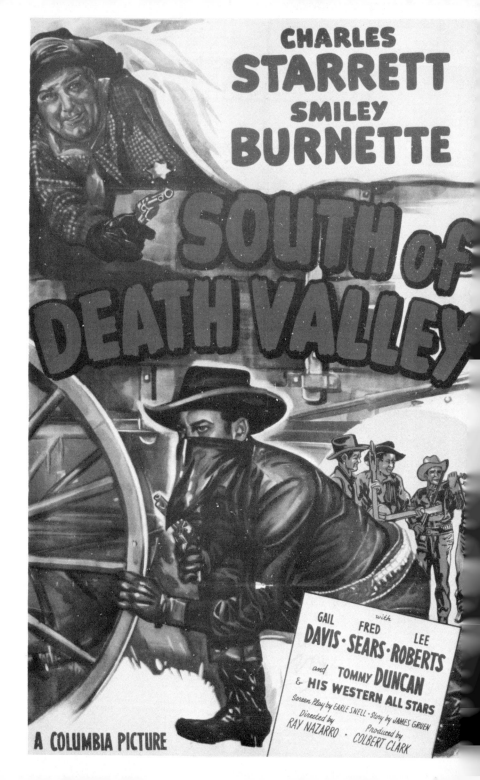

to call and tell you that I'd be glad to talk to you. I sure would. Why don't you come down the early part of next week. We'll have lunch together and visit. I live in Laguna. I'm not really a city person, you know, but Laguna Beach isn't too far from where you live in Los Angeles."

"Terrific. I'm really glad you called. I was beginning to think my letter had been lost at sea."

"Well, when I read it, I said I've got to get in touch with this fellow and invite him down. I liked your idea of wanting to meet the individual cowboy stars. You know, we were all a little different. We all tried to be a little different, with our own personalities and everything. So if you want to come down, I'd be happy to talk to you."

We fix the time for Wednesday at one o'clock.

"I'm really glad you called," I say. "And I'll be there."

"Well," he says, just before hanging up, "I've been out of the business a long time now, but it's always nice to be remembered."

Charles Starrett was Columbia's B-Western big gun from the middle of the Thirties until B-features went out of the picture in the Fifties. John Wayne made one film for Columbia and swore he would never again work for Harry Cohn. But Charles Starrett was to remain at Columbia for 17 years. And most of that time as one of the top four Cowboy-Heroes of that era. Just behind Autry, Rogers, Hopalong Cassidy. A Front Row Kid would more quickly forget the names of all the Presidents of the United States than forget Charles Starrett, The Durango Kid.

As The Durango Kid, Starrett was a Cowboy-Hero cross between Superman and Robin Hood. Until the time came for action, he was just an ordinary handsome cowpoke named "Steve." But when the Bad Guys threatened, and somebody had to get the goods on them, "Steve" would disappear from the scene, and The Durango Kid, dressed all in black, with a black bandanna covering his face, would suddenly appear as if from nowhere. The Bad Guys never had a chance after that. And never knew what hit them. The Front Row Kids, of course, knew all along who the man behind the mask was. In that way, Durango was better than The Lone Ranger. Who was that masked man? We never knew. There was only (and always) the mask. Even now, The Lone Ranger will not unmask. But The Durango Kid, Charles Starrett, will invite a Front Row Kid to lunch.

Laguna Beach, an hour's monotonous drive down the San Diego Freeway from Los Angeles, once had a reputation as an "art colony," and there is a casualness about the place. During the Sixties the Brotherhood of Eternal Love had their LSD ranch there. And the district attorney and the Feds kicked down doors day and night. But now the pressure is off Laguna Beach except for the hammerlock being applied by the real estate developers.

Charles Starrett lives down one of the small roads that lead to the beach off the Pacific Coast Highway. At one time he probably had a clear view of the ocean from his terrace, but now there are too many big houses packed into the cul-de-sac. As I am camouflaging my old Dodge in the bushes, he comes out onto his terrace, looks down, and waves. In California, it seems, you are what you drive, and he guessed right away that a Front Row Kid would be driving a 1961 Dodge Seneca, if not a 1948 Studebaker. And being a Front Row Kid, I half expected to see The Durango Kid, in full gear, mask and all, waving his black Stetson from the terrace. But it is not The Durango Kid I see before me, but Charles Starrett, in his late sixties, with white hair and a friendly Basset-hound face that resembles the old Cowboy-Hero around the mouth but with bags of time under the eyes. The handsomeness of the Cowboy-Hero is gone, but you can see where it once was. No youth, but the eyes are still laughing. And Starrett's enthusiasm is as bright as the red golfing sweater and red trousers he is wearing.

Lunch with The Durango Kid at the Five Crowns. One of those pleasant naugahyde restaurants along the Pacific Coast Highway where the food is not bad, the waitresses cute and toothy. The kind of place an executive briefcase who is slippin' around might take his bimbo to lunch if he's got a whole afternoon to kill and wants to drive an hour out of L.A. to a place where he is not likely to meet anyone who knows him. The place also caters to luncheon parties thrown by blue-haired Orange County matrons. The bartender mixes dynamite Bloody Marys.

"The Mrs. suggested we come here," says Starrett. "We could go somewhere else if you want to." A hen party of about 20 O.C. matrons chatters away across the dining room. The Five Crowns suits me fine. Where do we begin?

"Well, I was born in Massachusetts, went to Worcester Academy there and Dartmouth College, where I played varsity fullback for three years," Starrett says, beginning at the beginning. "I was acting in the theater before I started making pictures. I had been in New York, on Broadway. In those days, when sound was just coming in, Paramount had an Eastern studio in Flushing. I made my first picture there. It was called *Damaged Love*, which sounds like a pornographic picture, but it wasn't. Then I made a picture called *Fast and Loose* with Carol Lombard and Miriam Hopkins. We were unknown in those days. Nobody knew us in Keokuk and St. Louis and Tucson. But we were active on Broadway. A year later, when I went out to Hollywood, Carol Lombard was already a big star. For the first few years out here I made films like *The Mask of Fu Manchu*, *Touchdown*, *The Sweethearts of Sigma Chi*. I never dreamed I'd be doing Westerns. But I did them for seventeen years."

From these rather unlikely Cowboy-Hero beginnings, Charles Starrett became one of the best of the Thirties and Forties breed. He readily admits that he was, in many respects, merely a product of the Hollywood fantasy factory at a time when images were determined and fixed in the front office. The Cowboy-Hero just went along for the ride.

"In the days that I knew Hollywood and was under contract," he says, "they decided, the publicity department and the studio heads decided, since you were a piece of property, that they were going to mold you into an image that they wanted, not necessarily what you wanted. And if that image clicked at the box office, you were landed with it, and it was

very tough to break out of it. Once you got typed, that was it."
He does not speak of Hollywood's way of doing things with any
regrets that it was so but as simply a fact of life in those days.
"I only agreed to do the Westerns for two years, but they
caught on, and it went on for seventeen years. I sat out the
waltz one year, thinking I'd like to make a change away from
Westerns. That waltz cost me sixty thousand dollars. But you
know when you're raising a family, I had two young boys,
twins, you can't always do what you want to do. And it's very
enticing to know that you're going to be paid forty weeks a
year, whether you work or not. That's a pretty good enticing
thing. And I think an actor's life is very much like an athlete's.
It's youth. You've got to make it while you can. So after that
year, I went back and went along with it. I agreed to do this
Robin Hood on horseback I call it, this Durango Kid series. I
did that for five years. I did about fifty or sixty of them. And
you know, after the first ten it was like doing the same story
over again. But that's what they liked. If I'd have said no, they
would have fought me, and I would have lost out. You were
like a ball player, and you did what the manager said." No
regrets. No illusions.

Charles Starrett was an action cowboy. "You couldn't do
anything at normal speed. You don't do over 100 Westerns and
come out with no bumps and bruises. I got busted up. I went
to the hospital a few times. Of course the studio didn't want
the leading actor to do any of the heavy stunts. But I did the
fights. I did so many fights with one fellow I had with me, Dick
Curtis, it got to be called 'The Never Ending Fight.' I used to
box a bit, and my reflexes and timing were good. I think out
of a thousand picture fights, I only hit two guys. One guy, my
elbow hit the door and threw my timing off, and I really
clobbered him. He went down, and I felt so bad about it. I gave
him a case of Scotch. And he took it, too."

I tell him about the Charles Starrett Western I saw down in
North Carolina. *The Outlaws of the Prairies.* Where the Bad
Guys cut off his fingers.

"Gee," he says, "that one goes way back. I always liked that
one. You know, I've had so many people come up to me over

the years and ask me if there are any that stand out in my mind. Well, how can you remember when you've made so many, one hundred and twenty. But that was one I remembered. You see, I never knew the titles of the pictures. They always called them Production 1256 or something and put the titles on later. I think the studio would take votes among the secretaries and pay fifteen dollars for the best title. That's how they named my horse. For the movies they would come up with things like *West of Tombstone* or *North of Montana* or *South of the Border*. I think they were really just boxing the compass. But when you say the one where I got my trigger finger cut off and had to wear that glove and learn to fan a gun, I remember that one from the standpoint that it was a legitimate revenge motive. After we made that picture, the PTA and the church, the Catholic Church, put up a big fuss. They didn't want to see that revenge motive any more than they wanted to see us heroes smoke or drink."

Speaking of drinking, the cute and toothy waitress comes over as if on cue and takes another order of Bloody Marys from us. The PTA and the Catholic Legion of Decency no longer have anything to say about it. The irony is not lost on The Durango Kid.

"I'll tell you a story about that," he says. "About the PTA not wanting this and not wanting that. When we first did those films, I used to go up to the bar in a saloon scene, and the bartender said, 'What'll it be, gents?' And I'd say 'whiskey.' And pretty soon they said, 'Cut that out,' the PTA. So the next picture, the bartender says, 'What'll it be, gents?' and I say, 'Beer, please,' and how many miles to Laredo or something like that. And then finally they cut out the beer. So I walk into the bar through the two swinging doors and slap two bits on the bar, and he'd say, 'What'll it be, gents?' and you'd say, 'Buy *yourself* a drink. How many miles to Laredo?' They cut out the drinking and the smoking and the revenge motive."

I drink a silent salute to the PTA and the Catholic Legion of Decency. I couldn't speak for the Cowboy-Hero, but the Front Row Kid was getting a bit dizzy, pleasantly plastered. And I do not say no when the Bloody Marys come around again. But the PTA would have been proud of The Durango Kid. For lunch he has an omelet and a glass of milk! How many miles to Laredo?

Charles Starrett has been retired now for 22 years. He was still a relatively young man when his show closed. But, he says, an action cowboy shows his age like an athlete. He has done nothing in the way of show business business since he retired from the life in the Fifties.

His passion now is for traveling and taking it easy. He is a free man. And a lover of islands. The Greek Islands. The Canary Islands. Bora Bora. It is a long way from the prairies of the Wild West. There are no Cowboy-Heroes there.

And as the afternoon slips by, and the dining room of the Five Crowns becomes quiet and almost deserted, the old Cowboy-Hero talks about heroes.

"I don't have a lot of hero worship," he says, "but I do have a lot of what you might call boyhood admiration for certain types of men. I'm a great admirer of skill. I'm a great admirer of courage when the two are combined. You find that in some men and women. I have almost a boy's admiration for that. But in most walks of life, jeeze, there's nothing left for us. There's nothing left for the kids. When I was a boy up in Maine, my brother and I would go down to watch this little narrow gauge train go by. And every time that we were on this bluff, we would wave to the engineer. And he would blow the whistle for us. And the little train going up there, gee, I wanted to be an engineer. I wanted to be an engineer so badly. I thought it would be the greatest thing to sit up there and blow the whistle and run that train. I mean, that guy, I didn't even know him, and he was a hero to me. Maybe that's what it's all about," he says. "I think we need to have some illusions like that."

The Durango Kid drives me back to pick up my car. And as we stand in the road in front of his house saying adios, he sounds the note one last time. "An old college buddy of mine put it this way," he says. "Even if we lose everything else, we must hold onto the illusions."

Bull's eye, Durango. Illusions and hero fantasies. You were one of my Cowboy-Heroes. And even if you never were what you seemed to be on the screen at the Saturday Matinee, you were good enough to make us believe in the possibilities of being a hero. And we were eager to believe. It was better than a poke in the eye with a blunt stick.

"Thanks for coming down," he says. "As I said before, it's been a long time, and it's nice to be remembered."

I leave the old Cowboy-Hero waving in the unclear light of dusk. When I play the sound of his voice back in my head, I can still see The Durango Kid of years ago. Perhaps even more vividly than the man I have just left.

Being only 10 miles from San Clemente, I consider for a moment driving over to check out the Bad Guy who lives there. As long as I am in the neighborhood. But then decide, the hell with that. Why spoil a Cowboy-Hero afternoon?

Russell Hayden
in Pioneertown

Russell Hayden was "Lucky." In all those Hopalong Cassidy films he was the one who did the strenuous fighting that Hoppy was too old and fat to handle himself. He was the symbol of boyish energy and enthusiasm. And the one who usually fell head over bootheels for the rancher's daughter. And sometimes Hoppy and the old codger, "Windy" Hayes, had to rescue him from a fate worse than death. Russell Hayden, the "young whippersnapper" of the Bar 20 trio, is still lucky. He is the last survivor of those Hopalong Cassidy Westerns. The only one left alive.

"I don't know if you know or not," Russell "Lucky" Hayden says when I call him, "but I had a heart attack a while back, and I don't like to go very far from home. Why don't you come out here?"

"Out here" is Pioneertown. A 2 1/2-hour drive in the old Dodge out of Los Angeles, past the soulless shopping center communities of Pomona, Azusa, and Ontario toward the High Desert not far from Joshua Tree. It is a painfully boring ride, but the last leg is fine. Once you hit the desert, the scenery changes drastically to clear blue skies, sandy hills, and in the distance, snow-capped mountains. There is almost no traffic. It is the edge of the Mojave void. It is a long way from the corner of Hollywood and Vine.

Pioneertown looks like a ghost town in the dust. Dried out. Nothing and no one seems to be alive and moving about the place. But someone seems to think the future lies ahead. And has put up a sign to announce its coming.

About this corner we are building an Old West town. We hope it will be more authentic than most you see. Our little town won't grow over nite but we hope you'll visit us by foot, horse, bike, auto or wagon anytime.

Russell "Lucky" Hayden's spread is up a dirt road. It looks like an abandoned Western movie set, with a little red schoolhouse, some barns and empty corrals, and an ancient buckboard and some wagon wheels in view. "Lucky" and his wife, Mousie, live in the "Trading Post."

Russell Hayden greets me at the front porch and ushers me into the living room. It is done out in pioneer style. The ceiling lamps are mounted on wagon wheels. There are plaques and Western pictures on the walls, including one of Hoot Gibson. In one corner there is a saddle with some holsters hanging over the horn. The stove is acting up, and the place smells like a smokehouse, which only adds to the pioneer flavor. There is a kind of Old West primitiveness about the place. It is a long way from Beverly Hills.

"Lucky" is dressed in a pair of baggy chinos and a brown striped shirt. His hair is gray, close to white, and his face is weathered and worn. Crusty. More the look of a desert prospector than the "young whippersnapper" of memory.

"Most of my old friends are dead," he says in a voice that is also crusty. "Saw Tex Ritter a while back, and Christ, he ups and dies of a heart attack."

I tell him of some of the old Cowboy-Heroes I have seen, like Sunset Carson, who gave me Hayden's number in the first place, and Charles Starrett. And of those I have not seen because they are hard to find, although not yet dead, like "Lash" LaRue and Bob Steele and Roy Rogers.

"How is Sunset?"

"He's all right. Had that accident, but expects to be going back on the road with that circus."

"They all expect something to happen," says Hayden in a voice that has a fair edge of sarcasm. "I don't expect anything to happen. It's all happened to me. I don't expect to do a damn thing but just sit. I gave up, you know. When you get this

certain age, you sort of forget about it. Hooter's dead, Hoot
Gibson. He was just about my best friend. And Gary Cooper's
dead. And Hopalong Cassidy and Andy Clyde, 'California.'
And 'Windy' Hayes. You kind of get lost from the crowd 'cause
it's thinning out. And old Tex Ritter. It kind of thins out, so you
make up your mind to sit around and watch the sun rise and
watch it set."

And then he explains that he couldn't do anything even if
he wanted to because he is going blind.

"I've had my eye problem with trouble seeing," he says,
"and so I can't read scripts, and even if I had the opportunity,
I'd be embarrassed to death. So I've just retired, and I raise
some pheasants, and I've got ninety acres here. It keeps me
busy. Not this time of year but during the summertime. My
wife and I built every building here, and we built it as authentic as we could within the period of about 1890. I had all this
equipment that I had when I was making the television shows
I produced and directed, *26 Men, Judge Roy Bean,* and *Cowboy G-Men,* so a lot of this equipment I owned, and I just
bought it up here and laid it around and that's what it amounts
to."

At one time, he tells me, he and a few other cowboys, Roy
Rogers, the Sons of the Pioneers, Dick Curtis, the Western
movie Bad Guy, and Frank MacDonald, the old B-Western
director, formed a partnership and had big ideas about Pioneertown and the surrounding High Desert emptiness. They
were going to turn it into a Western movie location like Chatsworth and Lone Pine and Corriganville. They hoped to hire
the spread out to studios looking for authentic Wild West
locations and to catch the tourist trade and the holiday-makers
who had to pass this way to get to the resorts up at Big Bear.
They almost called it "Rogersville" but decided on Pioneertown so nobody would get top billing. In this particular venture, Lucky Hayden was less than lucky.

"I owned this property for thirty years," he says. "We
bought 32,000 acres. But we couldn't put it together. We had
it together at one time, but we had to have more money.
There was a lack of water, and 32,000 acres without water isn't

worth a damn. It's like the Sahara Desert. So we lost it to the finance company." Hayden managed to hold onto ninety acres, and this is where he plans to make his last stand. "But I'm not anxious to do anything. We don't have a hell of a lot of money, but I've got enough to live on. So, now, what would you like to know? What would you like me to tell you?"

He begins to pace around the room. He says he gets "all stove up just sitting, sitting, sitting." And I tell him I would like to know something of how it was back in the days of Hopalong Cassidy.

"I worked for Harry Sherman. I was a production man at the time. And he had Jimmy Ellison in the Hopalong Cassidy pictures playing the young part. Anyway, Ellison left for some reason, and so he decided to make me an actor for no reason that I could ever think of. One day, Harry Sherman said, 'Hey, Russ, you ever been an actor?' I said no. And he said, 'Would you like to be?' And I said not particularly. And he said, 'Well, you can do it. I know you can do it because I've seen you ride. You want to try it? I'll pay you a thousand dollars a picture.' So I went over, and he bought me a shirt and bought me a Western hat and a scarf that he liked, and I had a Western outfit. I'll never forget, it cost seventeen dollars for a brand-new tailor-made shirt and the hat cost seven dollars brand-new, and I don't know what the scarf cost, and I wore my own jeans and boots and made my first picture. I was scared to death, but for a thousand bucks I didn't mind being scared to death. And that's the way it started."

The first picture with Russell Hayden in the part of Lucky Jenkins was *The Hills of Old Wyoming*. Hayden liked it enough to continue the role for six years and appear in 36 Hopalong Cassidy Westerns. It was never bad, but it was not always easy.

"Bill Boyd was a tough guy to work with. Finally George Hayes said he couldn't stand it anymore, so he went to work at Republic with Roy Rogers. Me, I always got along well enough with Bill, but he was always the star. He had been a star before with DeMille, and he had that attitude about it. I mean his mind was different thinking, and he didn't like his scripts, and he didn't like this, and he didn't like that. And especially he didn't like Harry Sherman. Of course it was mutual. Harry Sherman didn't like him. But Sherman needed him for Hopalong Cassidy, and he needed Sherman for Hopalong Cassidy. Harry Sherman always thought he was doing him a favor putting him in the part, and of course Boyd thought he was doing Harry Sherman a favor by taking it. What the hell difference did it make? Anyway, there was always that conflict."

Hayden managed to get along with both of them. Especially Harry "Pop" Sherman.

"I just loved Harry Sherman. He was one of the best men I've ever known in my life and the cleanest, nicest, fairest. I never had a contract with him. We just shook hands on it, and he said if we didn't like each other, we'll skip it. With everyone else he had big contracts. But I never needed one with him. If he said I was going to get X amount of dollars on my next picture, then I got it. That's the way it worked. He and I became very very dear friends."

But if Russell Hayden had no contract with Harry Sherman, Clarence E. Mulford had a very strange one indeed.

"Sherman had read the Hopalong Cassidy books year before," Hayden says. "And when he was in New York, and he met Mulford, he made him a deal. They signed the contract on a piece of toilet paper. Went to the men's room and got a piece of toilet paper and signed the contract. And they both lived up to their part of it. Harry kept the piece of toilet paper. I saw it."

Harry Sherman may have made the contracts, but Boyd chose the clothes. "Boyd hated the singing cowboys because he couldn't sing," Hayden says about that. "He thought it was a gimmick and thought the monkey-suit deal was, too. He used to say, 'Look at those idiots, they got their monkey suits on.' And he was the biggest monkey in the world actually, when you start to analyze it, what he wore. A black hat, a black outfit with white hair and a white horse, a silver mounted saddle. Now, how corny can you get?"

Bill Boyd had his way with that. And also wanted his way on

everything else. The Cowboy-Hero and the producer, "Pop" Sherman, fought constantly for 10 years. And according to Hayden, when Boyd didn't get his way, which he didn't most of the time, then he'd grumble. After a while people on the set just avoided him. And, as Hayden tells it, the Sherman-Boyd relationship finally ended more or less as it had begun.

"When they came to their parting of the ways," Hayden says, " 'Pop' sold Bill all the old pictures he had interest in, and I imagine Boyd made himself five to eight million when he put them on television. But he died unhappy. When he stopped making pictures for television, he got grumpy again, and he invested a lot of money down at an amusement park in Santa Monica, and it folded. I guess he just kind of gave up. So what else is new? Everybody goes through that."

And whatever happened to Harry "Pop" Sherman after he stopped making Hopalong Cassidy pictures?

"Well, Pop was waiting for somebody, like everybody wants to wait their life out, he was waiting for someone to come along and offer him a good deal. He didn't want to make those slop pictures, you know, not slop but B pictures, he wanted to make A pictures. I think what killed Pop Sherman was a broken heart, in my honest opinion. Just died of a broken heart sitting in his beautiful home in Bel Air. I think it just got to the point where he just gave up. I don't think he was crying for money. He was crying for recognition. He had a big deal when he made *Buffalo Bill* with Joel McCrea. It was a good picture. And he did another one with McCrea. They were good pictures. But all of a sudden nothing happened. The studios never called him again. He used to say to me, I saw him a month before he died, he used to say, 'Just give me one or two more pictures, one or two more good stories, and everything will be all right, I'll feel great.' And I'd say, 'Pop, who cares about two more pictures? Why don't you just relax and take a trip around the world?' And he'd just sit there and brood. So one day he has a heart attack and dies. I always thought it was the brooding caused it. He used to go back and forth to New York and wear his poor old soul out trying to get someone to listen to a new story. But he didn't have a good story. Pop did not have good stories. Pop was never a story man. The stories were no good. If he'd had some good stories, it might have been different for him."

Russell "Lucky" Hayden stayed in the Hopalong Cassidy-Bar 20 trio until 1941. Then he went over to Columbia to co-star with Charles Starrett in the Durango Kid series. And to make a series of his own. He made one film at Republic but says he couldn't stand it there and left. Except for that one picture, all the B-Westerns he made—the Hoppys, the Starretts and his own—were, if not great, certainly enjoyable to make. "I never made a picture in my life that I didn't enjoy starting the picture and hate like hell to have to finish. I could hardly wait to start in the morning, and at night I didn't want to go to bed. I never had a picture I was dying to get out of. There was always so many interesting things happening all the time. It was exciting."

And when television came in, he produced three Western series. *Cowboy G-Men,* in which he starred with Jackie Coogan. *Judge Roy Bean* with old Edgar Buchanan. And *26 Men,* a series about the Arizona Rangers. "I think that was the best thing I did, *26 Men,* "Hayden says. "I did 105 of those for ABC. Of course, the money was a lot less, but they worked out fine."

As a boy and a Front Row Kid himself, he never imagined that he would actually become a Cowboy-Hero in the movies. But it did seem natural and inevitable that he would be in the movie business because he was born and raised in Hollywood, and Hollywood is a company town, a one-industry town. The studios were where the work was, and during the Depression, when Hayden was coming up, you went where the work was. If he had been born in Detroit, he says matter-of-factly, he would have gone to work for General Motors on some assembly line. But once having been a Cowboy-Hero, he would not have wanted to be a straight actor. "Hell," he says, "I wouldn't give you a dime to be a straight actor. I made four or five straight pictures, and I never liked them at all, never liked the pictures. I just thought it was a hell of a lot of fun to read a couple of lines and get on a horse and ride off."

Russell Hayden puts on a jacket and a battered old Stetson,

and we go out to take a look around the yard. The air is getting cold as the afternoon goes off into the sunset. We walk by the wagons to get a closer look. "I painted all the wagons myself. Haven't got started on the buggies. There's a guy coming up here, and we're going to put in a pipeline." He takes me over to an old-fashioned well he built and an open-air dance floor he put up. And we go into the saloon/shed to get out of the wind, which is beginning to whip up, and we lean against an old long bar. "This bar goes back to the Hoppy films," he says. "They all stood up against the bar. Hoppy, Roy Rogers, you name it. I got it when Pop Sherman died.

"It's all gonna take time," Hayden says, once again outside, looking around his once-and-future frontier town. "But as I say, we're not going anywhere. I don't like to come into town too often. It's too crowded for me now. I can't see the traffic, and the horns bother me and people screaming and yelling. And as for passing the time, there's no time to pass. I got a lot of work to do out here. And when we get this place fixed up, if someone wants to come out here for a location, why, that'll be all right. I'll just sit there on the front porch and watch."

And then it is time for me to be away. Back to the traffic that Russell Hayden can't see and is not missing. He is at home in his Pioneertown. He may never get his spread together, but it does not seem to bother him. He is in his own Old West World out in the High Desert. And he has been lucky so far.

Joel McCrea

The thing is, there are more days in the week than there are living Cowboy-Heroes to see. And there is something about Los Angeles that makes me sleep a lot during the day. And to watch television late into the night, fitfully. The guy who sells the used cars during the late shows, Cal Worthington by name, is so frenzied and insistent in his pitch. I am tempted to go out to his used-car lot in Long Beach and see if he really will eat a bug or stand on his head to sell me a used car. Or maybe I will just kick him in the nuts. Eventually a fellow could go crazy. The Late Show continues to come to my rescue with Randolph Scott and John Wayne and Joel McCrea oldies.

They are fine men, my old Cowboy-Heroes. But they are old and past it now. And it is beginning to depress me, to make me feel slightly ghoulish. Wanting them to dig up their pasts for my Front Row Kid curiosity. But the wish to see them is more compelling than the Late Show. And so, on a sunny afternoon when I have no Cowboy-Heroes to see, I check out some places where they might have been 30 years ago.

With my freeway map folded open on the passenger seat, I take a run out to Chatsworth, the old Wild West location. Where more Western movies were made than probably anywhere else in the world. The Iverson Ranch was out there. And Corriganville. And the Spahn Movie Ranch. Where the Cowboy-Heroes chased Bad Guys and runaway buckboards from sunup to sunset before whirring cameras. Where perhaps half a thousand posses rode. Where, after you have seen enough old Westerns, you begin to recognize the rock formations, the clump of bushes, the hill in the background. Every

Hollywood Cowboy who ever rode in the Saturday Matinees must have left a hoofprint in the dirt of Chatsworth. Perhaps there was still something of them out there that will tell a Front Row Kid a thing or two about the way it was.

But time has done for Chatsworth what it has done for everything else. A drive through the Santa Susana Pass reveals a mobile home park where the old wide-open spaces used to be. It is impossible to visualize a Cowboy-Hero galloping hell-for-leather through *that*. Most of the old range that was so familiar in all those Westerns is now fenced off Rocket-Dyne Aerospace Private Property Keep Out. If there are any vibrations at all coming from this once-famous location, it is an unsettling that comes from the knowledge that Charlie Manson and his band of ghoulies lived at the Spahn Movie Ranch. Driving their stolen cars and dune buggies over the hills where Cowboy-Heroes once galloped. Living in the bunk houses and the ranch house where the Good Guy came a-courting the rancher's daughter. Some time after the Manson Family was rounded up by the posse, the old sets of the movie ranch caught fire and burned to the ground. The place gives me the creeps. I do not stay long.

On another afternoon, just as sunny, I decide it is time to knock on Randolph Scott's door. Direct action. And to go to John Wayne's office for a showdown. I have nothing to lose. They can only say no. They would not be the first.

Batjac, Duke's production company, is on Wilshire Boulevard in Beverly Hills. The directory in the lobby lists almost a dozen John Wayne enterprises that get their mail there. True Grit Cattle Co. Red River Land Co. Rio Bravo Ranches. Red Eye Farms. J-W Cattle Co. Buckshot Cattle Co. Battle Ltd. Batjac. This must be the place. I ride up the elevator, accompanied by Muzak. The brushoff from Duke's mail opener is swift and direct. "No chance," she says. "Absolutely no chance." I am back in the elevator, going down to the lobby before Muzak even changes tunes.

Randolph Scott's office is nearby. His listing is more discreet. G. R. Scott. Nothing more. The word is that this fine old Cowboy-Hero is in the oil and gas business these days. And wealthy beyond counting. His office is on the third floor. Tucked away in a corner. It is a two-room suite. Large and bright. He is not in it, as far as I can tell. Unless he is hiding under the desk. His secretary is friendlier than I have come to expect. But no less firm in her refusal than all the other secretaries I have encountered. "Mr. Scott is completely retired from show business," she says. "And he has made it a policy for some years now not to give any interviews whatsoever. He just doesn't do it. Not for friends or fans or anybody. You know, he's 77 years old now, and he simply wants to lead a private life. I'm very sorry, but that's sort of a rule he has and he has stuck to it since he retired." So much for Randolph Scott. I admire his last firm stand. It is, in fact, what I would have expected from this straight-faced Lonesome Cowboy. He hung up his spurs and that Stetson hat with the chin strap for the last time back in '62. And he has, so to speak, stuck to his guns. See ya later, Randolph Scott. On the Late Show.

There is still Joel McCrea. He died gloriously in the gunfight in *Ride the High Country.* But that was only a movie. Joel McCrea is still alive. Whatever happened to Joel McCrea?

Another early-morning phone call from another familiar voice has me tooling along the freeways again. This time to Westlake Village, just over the Ventura County line. For lunch with the Good Guy, Joel McCrea.

Westlake Village is a new town, the realization of some property developer's dream. The architect was probably his brother-in-law. Every house looks the same. Crypto-Mexican. But no *barrio,* that's for sure. It is a model city of wholesome middle-class affluent family living. There appears to be no-body alive in the whole town. Joel McCrea, now a gentleman rancher, has a ranch nearby. We have arranged to meet at the Westlake Inn, a motel-golf course-restaurant-Standard station complex on the edge of town. I am early. The hostess shows me to the reserved table by the window. I sit with my back to the door, like Wild Bill Hickok on that day in Deadwood when Black Jack Macoll put his lights out, looking out the window onto the golf course and the duck pond. But not really seeing them.

A few nights before I had seen *Ramrod* on the Late Show. It was one of the very best Joel McCreas. It is a story of cattle-ranch feuding. With a villainous and unscrupulous cattle baron on one side and Joel McCrea, utterly scrupulous and ultimately deadly as a rattlesnake, on the other. It has all the good stuff in it. Shoot-outs and showdowns and plenty of galloping. And best of all, it has that almost patented, archetypal Joel McCrea Good Guy. Wry and a little reluctant but so fine-looking on horseback you would think he was born in that saddle.

I have a lingering vision of a particular moment when he comes riding in full tilt and steps off his horse as casual and easy as if he were stepping off and walking on water or a cloud. And the horse is still moving! It is a dance of considerable grace and style. The whole movement only lasts a few seconds on the screen. But it is an image to conjure with. And I want to hold onto it until the very last moment when Joel McCrea will suddenly appear behind me, as if out of nowhere, or out of my imagination. It is a good way of taking the warp out of time and playing a trick on the years.

Joel McCrea arrives. It is almost as if he has just stepped off that horse and left him tied to the hitching post outside. He is wearing cowboy boots. And in his big hand he carries a Stetson. He is older than he was in *Ramrod* by more than 20 years. His hair is white. And he wears wire-rimmed glasses. And a brown cord cattleman's jacket. His shirt is *not* buttoned at the top. But he is big, and his face is tanned and weathered. He still has the look of a Cowboy-Hero about him. Owen Wister might have created Joel McCrea. He is *The Virginian,* 70 years on.

"I've always kind of tried to keep that Western thing," he says in a voice that is still deep and clear as a bell, speaking with the same slowness and hesitancy that characterized so many of his portrayals. "I can't speak for anyone else, but I, frankly, that was the image I wanted to portray. I wasn't trying to prove that I was the greatest actor in the world, but I tried to prove that I was legitimate and authentic in what I was doing, whether it was with horses or whatever. And I have kind of tried to maintain the integrity of that image. Anyway, I've always been interested in Westerns and Western things. The real thing. I feel more at home in it because I was a cowboy before I entered pictures. I've been ranching since 1934."

McCrea says he bought his first horse from Rex Bell, who later became a mediocre cowboy star, married Clara Bow, and went on to be lieutenant governor of Nevada.

"We both went to Hollywood High School, and he came to school one day and told me he had to get rid of his horse. I said, 'Gee, how much do you want for it?' He said he had a horse, a saddle, a buggy, and a harness, and he said he'd take eighty dollars for it. I didn't have eighty dollars, but I said I'd see if I could raise it. So I went home, and my mother gave me forty dollars, and I had forty dollars, so I bought it. And that started me on the horse thing. And then I'd go see the Westerns, and I'd go out to an empty lot in Hollywood and try what I'd seen and do different things. Since then I've always had horses. Sometimes fourteen of them and sometimes three or four. I didn't do it just for the movies, you know, I did it because I liked it. If I hadn't made it in the movies, I would still have been running a ranch and cowboying."

He says he always found William S. Hart more to his liking as a Western model than, say, Tom Mix. And his good friend was Gary Cooper, a man whose Cowboy-Hero image was, perhaps, even more like *The Virginian* than his own. They both played the Wister character in the movies. Cooper was the first. He says Coop used to often come out to his ranch to sit and whittle and talk things over. What a conversation must have taken place between the two reticent Cowboy-Heroes. Howdy, Coop. Howdy, Joel. Whaddya reckon, Coop? Well, I reckon. Yup. Whaddya reckon, Joel? Mebbe. Yup? Nope, mebbe. Mebbe? Yup. Well, I reckoned that's what you reckon. I reckon. Yup. Well, so long pardner. See ya later. Mebbe. Yup. Adios.

"Cooper was an ideal type," Joel McCrea says, "because he

looked like a cowboy. He had been one, and he liked it. He wasn't what we would call a 'Palm Springs Cowboy.' " And Joel McCrea ought to know because he wasn't one, either. McCrea, like Cooper, really knew what he was doing. The difference between making it and faking it. And whether he learned his cowboying or it came to him on the air he breathed in his boyhood Hollywood, he seems to have worn it well through the years. It suits him.

But the man who really influenced Joel McCrea, who gave him a leg up and taught him by example about cowboying was, yup, Will Rogers. I reckon.

"I graduated from college in 1928 and then worked extra for 1929 and 1930, and then they took me to do this *Silver Horde* thing, which I did for RKO," McCrea says, talking slow but getting there. "Then Will Rogers and Henry King picked me to do *Lightning*. During *Lightning* we became friends. I'd get him to do rope tricks and show me because, well, I could rope a little, like on a ranch, but he was a magnificient roper. And after I did the picture with him, he went to Winnie Sheehan, who was running Fox, and said, 'I'd like this boy to be with me on all my pictures because he'd fit.' So Will helped me to get started. And of course I knew that if I didn't do the things authentically, if I didn't create the right Western image, that he would be disappointed. While he never said anything, I just had the feeling that I must do it, you know. And the thing that impressed me was his great integrity toward whatever he did and his showmanship. When you were around him, you just didn't dare to be a little phony. He was just about the most unphony man that I ever knew."

But even with Will Rogers's encouraging words and his own natural inclination toward cowboying, McCrea still has to talk the moguls into letting him do Westerns. He was tall and good-looking and charming, and they wanted to make a lounge lizard out of him.

"I was in these pictures co-starring Constance Bennett," he says, listing the titles of several less than memorable films. "I was a young artist or aviator or something sophisticated, and I had to wear tails. I didn't even have tails, and I didn't have enough money, so the studio had to buy them for me. But I said I wanted to do Westerns. They had a couple of New York juveniles doing Westerns who didn't know which side of the horse to get on. But I never got the chance to do them until Howard Hawks and Sam Goldwyn put me into *Barbary Coast.* And once they saw me do that, then DeMille put me in *Union Pacific,* and Frank Lloyd put me in *Wells Fargo,* and I was off. And once I did that, then the only things that came along were Westerns. And I just kept on doing them because that's what I really liked. I made eighty-two pictures, and I'd say at least sixty of them were Westerns. And in the period in which I was most active, the Thirties, Forties, and Fifties, the Western movies kind of told the American story. And I always tried to stick to the realistic things as much as I could. In the Western field I knew what I wanted to do, so I would turn down things that I felt were pretty corny or, you know, illegitimate in some way. Like the fellow says, You either have to be honest about it, or you're not. Like this one fellow said, You can't be a little bit pregnant."

He did take a little time out of the saddle in those years to star in a couple of Preston Sturges comedies, a George Stevens comedy, and Hitchcock's *Foreign Correspondent.* And although he beat Cary Grant out of the part because Hitchcock fought the producer, Walter Wanger, to give McCrea the job, McCrea would be the first to admit that he was never a Cary Grant. He took those pictures mainly, he says, because it was a chance to work with three of the best directors in the business.

"And, of course, there weren't that many good Westerns that would come in," he says. "See, I had considerable competition then. Coop was kind of number one. Then after *Stagecoach,* Wayne was kind of number two. Then Randy and I came in. There was kind of the four of us. So these things came along at a time when it was a challenge to see if I could do them. But I wouldn't have done them if I thought I was miscast."

He says he never looked down on the B-Westerns that some of the studios cranked out (although he thought the singing cowboys "were pretty remote from reality"), and he got a kick out of Hopalong Cassidy. As far as television is concerned, he agrees wholeheartedly with me that it is poison on the hoof. And that it is ironic that the medium that did so much to put the Western out of business should now be filling up so much of its viewing hours with, of all things, the old Westerns of Joel McCrea and John Wayne and Randolph Scott.

And we talk for a while over half-eaten lunches about *Ramrod* and *Saddle Tramp* and *Four Faces West* and the other fine Joel McCrea Westerns that are worth staying up late for. He manages to see one once in a while. Recently he saw *Four Faces West* when a friend of his phoned and told him it was on. And he found it had been fairly brutalized by some mad cutter to make room for commercials.

"There is one scene where Charles Bickford is following me and tracking my horse, and I'm trying to throw him off the track. I ride up to an old windmill, we made this in New Mexico, and the cattle are there drinking, some longhorned cattle there and everything. Well, in the picture I roped a steer, snubbed him up to a post, took my saddle off my horse, put it on the steer, and then rode off. And the steer tracks were going off in all directions. Well, in the television version they see me ride up and look around at the cattle, and then they cut, and I'm in the saddle riding off on a steer. You never see me rope it. You never see how I do it. And I said to myself, it wouldn't take thirty seconds to show it, and it would show how it worked, and people would like to see that. If they wanted to cut, they could almost take a big chunk, you know, of some of the long rides I did in the picture or something."

But on the other hand, it is those great riding sequences in Joel McCrea Westerns, with all the good background and action that make the old Westerns so much better than the talking heads they call television Westerns, the shit where Matt Dillon and those boys never leave the saloon and never shut up. Without the action, I say, and McCrea agrees, you might as well be listening to it on the radio.

"That's right," McCrea says. "That's the reason I've stayed away from a lot of television series I've been offered. I felt why go backwards. You started out on a big scale and started out with big panorama backgrounds, and that had to do with the whole idea of the Western. Television just doesn't do that sort of thing. Television is good for making money and for exposure. But I figure I've had enough exposure and have enough money, so I didn't need to do it. So what I did was to go get a ranch and get out in the wide-open spaces and rope the steers when they needed to be roped and sometimes when they didn't, just for the practice and to keep the feel of it."

The thing about fellows like Joel McCrea and Randolph Scott and Wayne that sets them apart from the Autry and Rogers and Tom Mix Cowboy-Heroes was the way they grew older in their roles and got better as they got older. McCrea seems to feel that, considering the character he played and the fact that he had been going on for 30 years, *Ride the High Country* was a good one to go out on. And it was sweet to his ego to get the best reviews of his career on that one.

"It was kind of tying the knot. I died in the end of the picture, and I felt it was kind of the end of the era. The wind-up of the Western and the wind-up for Randy and me, the whole era and style. I still get calls from people when something like *Four Faces West* is on. They still want to see that. They talk about it. They say, 'Why don't you make a picture?' Why do they care whether I make a picture? After all, I've been around a long time, and I tell them I don't really have to work anymore. I've got ranches. I've got kids. I have plenty of interests. But by the same token, if they bring a thing along by some young writer who says, 'Gee, you're exactly the one for this,' I have to read it, you know. And a lot of times it doesn't work out for one reason or another. But if it were something that came out of the blue like *Ride the High Country,* I don't want to miss it. I've been talking to a fellow about a film they want to do. It's a really complete Western story, with a good character and terrific scenic value and tremendous animal things. I think it would please the younger generation. It would be uplifting to them. And also it would bring back what you remember as a kid. It might work out. But I don't really care if I ever do another picture."

Joel McCrea and I say adios in the parking lot of the West-lake Inn. I follow behind him out onto the road through town and out to the freeway overpass. And as I turn off to go to the freeway, Joel McCrea toots his horn, waves his Stetson, and literally drives off into the sunset.

Some months later, the trades carry a small item in their list of film productions in progress. A Western doing location shooting in Alberta, Canada. Its title: *Mustang Country*. Its star and Cowboy-Hero: Joel McCrea. Good news for old Front Row Kids and insomniacs of the future. It means Joel McCrea is once again riding the high country. And there will be a new Joel McCrea Western for the Late Show in 1984.

The Last
Singing Cowboys

Gene and Roy were the best singing cowboys. Rex Allen and Jimmy Wakeley were the last. As the weeks go by, and the L.A. Freeway mileage adds up, I am beginning to think Roy Rogers is just a figment of my imagination. If a Front Row Kid can't get in to see Roy Rogers, then who can? Come to think of it, who else but a Front Row Kid would want to? According to his manager and main man, I had to get in line behind about seven million guys from *Time Magazine,* the *Village Voice,* the *L.A. Free Press, Country Music Magazine, Rona Barrett's Hollywood,* ABC-TV and the *Polish Daily Zgoda.* The word was that Roy was just about as busy as those Chinese coolies who built the Union Pacific. Planning a comeback. And when he wasn't busy, he was bowling. Twice a week, in a league out in Apple Valley. A friend of mine who is sympathetic suggests I go out there in disguise and catch him unawares. "Disguised as what?" I said. "A ten pin?"

But I cannot wait. The Cowboy-Heroes who are still alive are not getting any younger. I feel I am in a race with Mister Death. It is not a happy thought for a Front Row Kid. Death and old age were never a part of the fantasy. Chasing ghosts along L.A. Freeways is not my idea of a good time. If Gene has little to say, and Roy wants to play hard to get, Rex Allen and Jimmy Wakeley will give some time to a Front Row Kid. They are neither bowlers nor ball-club owners. But they are still singing for their supper.

Rex Allen was billed at Republic Pictures as "The Arizona Singing Cowboy." He came to Westerns late in the day. His first film was *Arizona Cowboy* (what else?) in 1949. He stayed on until the end, which came pretty soon. Around 1954. He had a good, deep country voice. He was young and good-looking. He could sit a horse. He could handle himself well in the action. He was no stiff. He was, in fact, very good. Only thing was, he was too good too late. Too bad.

Out on his Diamond X Ranch, Rex Allen is doing O.K. There are some horses fenced in but otherwise free to roam. A hired hand is watering an expanse of green lawn that looks hand-painted. In the driveway next to the big ranch house there is a trailer that has seen some bad weather, a Ford Pinto and a Mercedes. At the top of a hill overlooking the ranch there is a horse, with white mane and tail, striking a picturesque pose against the sky. It looks like Rex Allen's old horse, "Koko." But the pose is held, unmoving, beyond the point of physical endurance (even for a horse), and you realize it is a statue.

Rex Allen, "The Arizona Singing Cowboy," greets the Front Row Kid at the side door.

"Howdy, pardner," he says. And, again, the voice of an old Cowboy-Hero is what you remember it to have been. Very deep and clear, with a noticeable slow-going Western drawl. But unlike, say, Gene Autry, Rex Allen is still a relatively young man of 52, and except for a paunch and a bit more chin, looks recognizably like the Singing Cowboy of the old movies. To enhance the deja vu, he is dressed cowboy style in sky-blue Western trousers, a pink rodeo shirt and string tie, and a pair of big old pointy-toed cowboy boots. And in case anyone might mistake him for Roy Rogers, his belt buckle reads: ARIZONA COWBOY.

For Rex Allen, living the image means more than just wearing the gear. He has retained a total philosophy that is in keeping with the old Republic Pictures Cowboy-Hero contract, complete with morals clause, in which the Good Guy's public image was a reflection of the role he portrayed on the screen. No smokin'. No drinkin'. No cussin'. No unpatriotic or discouraging words. No shit on the bootheels. No city-slicker suits.

"It was never tough for me to live it," Rex Allen says in a slow drawl. "In fact, it's a damn good way of life, and it's still my way. It's still the biggest thing in my life. I've been associated all my life with that element of show business. When I first started out in radio, I worked for WLS in Chicago, which was a very conservative bunch of people. National Barn Dance. Then when I came to Republic, the same set of rules applied there. And the last 12 years I've been associated with Walt Disney Studios, where the same thing carries through. It's been good for all the fellows who've stuck with it over the years and played the game right. There is no better thing in the world than to be established as a Western star. Some of the fellows were just lost when the Westerns finished for them. There was nothing they could do, and they probably never realized it was over. They just got bitter and disappeared. Now me, being a singing cowboy, there was still plenty I could do. And the thing never did end for me. I still live it. I love it. I don't even own a pair of shoes. I can't even walk a golf course in flat heels. I play golf in a pair of cowboy boots with cleats on them. It's a beautiful way to live, and I can't find any better way. Who wouldn't want to live it? It's still as beautiful as the day I walked in on it."

Rex Allen points out the bay window to the hill beyond and the horse on it. "That's a replica of the horse I used to ride," he says. And he explains how, with so many Western stars riding through the Saturday Matinees for 50 years, he had had to really hunt to find things to make his Cowboy-Hero different from the others. And the biggest problem was finding a horse.

"It wasn't easy," he says. "Roy rode a palomino, so that was out. Autry rode a sorrel. Mix rode a black. First thing you know, I'm out of colors. So I went looking. I found this stud who was 10 years old. He was dark chocolate with a snow white mane and tail. I had never seen any regular saddle horses that color, so I decided to use him. Anyway, what I failed to take into account was that shooting these pictures as fast as you did, you couldn't take your lead horse and just run him to death. You had to have doubles so you could double that horse on long shots and save your main horse for close-ups where you didn't want him to look all lathered up and dirty and lousy. I spent six years hunting for a double. I never did find one. Never did."

That one and only horse of his is dead now and buried in Rex's home town of Wilcox, Arizona, where some of the singing cowboy's memorabilia is on display for the tourists who pass through on the way to someplace else. The horse is not stuffed and standing on that hill.

He could have used a double for himself. Especially during the days of endless road shows promoting his pictures on the trail that Gene Autry first blazed.

"Oh my God," he says, "we were doing four shows a day. Playing Seattle one night and Portland the next. I went to 190 cities in one year. I played 15 theaters in Baltimore in one day. Started at 6 in the morning and got through about midnight. This was at the time Roy was leaving and the studio didn't have anybody. You couldn't very well send 'Rocky' Lane out on a tour like that? What would he do? Say hi, spin his guns, and sign autographs? But me being a singing cowboy, an entertainer, I had that act, see?"

It was "that act," of course, that saved Rex Allen from the glue factory when the B-Western went that-a-way. He kept it on the road, working auditoriums, rodeos, fairs, making records. And for rainy-day insurance he went into diverse businesses, real estate, radio stations, hotels, a film company to produce commercials. He would like to have gone on into bigger A-Westerns, but it didn't work out that way. "Then there was this thing," he says, "I had been typed as a B-Western actor. Very few of them ever got out of that. Roy never did. Gene never did. Jimmy Wakeley couldn't. Once you were typed, you stayed that."

After Rex Allen answers a few phone calls about a commercial he is making the next day and gives some instructions to the Mexican maid in pretty fluent Spanish, I cannot resist a last potshot question. What does an old morally pure, quick-on-the-draw, white-hat Cowboy-Hero Good Guy make of something like Watergate and old Tricky's complete corruption? They say he enjoyed a good Western movie now and then. Take it away, Rex.

"I think it is a very shocking thing," he says. "But I feel an overreacting press made a world issue out of a two-bit robbery. I can't condone the cover-up by the President. That I can't condone. But you tell me why this should throw all these people in jail, why it should topple the Presidency? Those tapes. These were conversations that were thought to be confidential between two or three good friends, and the guy says kill the thing, get it done, pay off whoever you have to, let's get on with our life and business. And the press wouldn't let him do it. This has probably overshadowed one of the best Presidents that ever walked into that office. He did more for peace than any President in my lifetime."

Ironically Rex Allen, the Arizona Singing Cowboy, once made a Western, *Thunder in God's Country,* in which he gets the goods on the Bad Guys by slipping a microphone through the window of their hideout and recording their conversation! I wonder, did Nixon ever see *that* Western?

Jimmy Wakeley lives in North Hollywood, the other side of the hills, the edge of the San Fernando Valley, in a pink ranch-style house with a "Tom Sawyer" picket fence. He comes to the door in a pair of casual slacks and a lumberjacket shirt. His reddish hair is beginning to creep back behind a wide forehead. He has a sharp chin. His eyes are very blue. He uses a cigarette holder for smoking. And his accent is soft-spoken Southwestern states. Okie with a hint of Arkansas razorback. He is not a big man compared to some Cowboy-Heroes. He looks a few years younger than his age. He speaks modestly of his singing cowboy days. He never did make it to the Top. Rather, he was one of the many. But certainly not the worst. He came in late and did most of his work for Monogram Pictures. He has no illusions about what his career might have been. And no regrets over what it was.

"Monogram was a place where stars were born and stars went out of the scene," Jimmy Wakeley says in his quiet drawl. "You got your break there because they couldn't afford much money, and so they would get beginners. And those that had gone over the hill would come there to make movies because

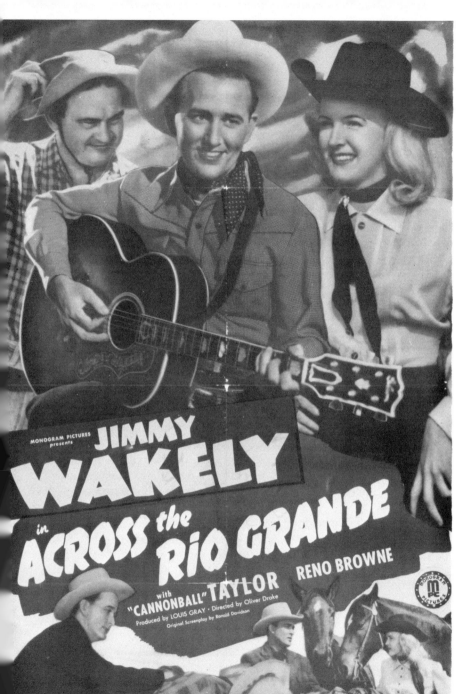

MONOGRAM PICTURES presents

JIMMY WAKELY

in ACROSS the RIO GRANDE

with "CANNONBALL" TAYLOR   RENO BROWNE

Produced by LOUIS GRAY · Directed by Oliver Drake
Original Screenplay by Ronald Davidson

they couldn't get jobs at the big studios. You might say Monogram was the before and after studio. I came to Monogram to get going, and fellows like Johnny Mack Brown went there to die."

Some of Wakeley's critics during his Western movie days accused him of being a Gene Autry copycat, of patterning his act too much after Autry and consequently failing to distinguish himself as anything more than a bargain-basement version of the original Singing Cowboy. Wakeley's answer to that put-down is: "Everybody reminds you of somebody until *they* are somebody. And I would rather be compared to Gene Autry than anyone else. He was number one. He was the greatest. I worshiped the guy. I sat through his pictures three times so I could learn his songs and put them in my radio show. And he was one of the best friends I ever had. He still is."

Autry, it seems, really gave Wakeley his start. Wakeley had a singing group called "The Bellboys" and a radio show in Oklahoma City. When the group came out to Hollywood, with Autry's encouragement, Gene put them on his own radio show, *Melody Ranch.* And they worked in his pictures. In those early scuffling days, Wakeley got his good break playing the second lead in seven Charles Starrett-Durango Kid films, where he got a chance to be on camera singing solos and doing some acting instead of being just one of the singers around the campfire. From there he went over to Monogram. From 1944 to 1949. After that he quit. Today Autry and Wakeley are in business together in a mail-order record-distribution operation.

In all, he made about 24 Jimmy Wakeley Singing Cowboy Westerns. And when it was over, he went right on singing and performing. He has written almost 300 songs. Has a gold-record million seller to his credit. And a few other C&W and easy listening hits, including the old Christmas song, "Silver Bells." He says he never even considered trying to carry on in Westerns. It would have meant starting over again in bit parts and character roles. He didn't want that and didn't need it. He was doing fine. And he hated to see the old Cowboy-Heroes trying to make it in minor roles.

"It kind of hurt me to see a fellow like Johnny Mack Brown trying to do that," he says. "He was a hero to me while I was still a cotton picker in Oklahoma. And then I came out and worked with him, and he was still a star. A terrific guy. And I hated the way he looked later in those secondary roles. It diminishes the image that was in my mind of the star he once was. And I think that image should stay there. The way it was.

"A lot of people come up to me because they remember me in Westerns," he says. "They see I'm playing somewhere, in some club, and they don't know what to expect. Is he going to show up in chaps or what? Or his spurs? Is he going to have his horse? Is he going to be singing cowboy songs or is he going to play hillbilly music? They really don't know for sure. I sometimes will put on a Western suit just for kicks. I'm still in show business, with an outlet for my ambitions, but in a different way. Now if you said to me today, 'Jimmy, I'd like to make a series, and I want you to be the star,' I'd say, 'You're crazy!' I don't need to go where I've already been."

The business has changed a great deal since he was a singing cowboy. In those days it was romantic. And he was poor and hungry. For him it was a way up and out.

"You came in and made a movie," he says, sticking a cigarette in his holder and lighting up, "and you knew from the day you made that movie that you would never again have to pick cotton, you would never have to pitch hay, you would never have to brand cows, you would never have to walk in mud feeding hogs. You knew that you were off the farm and that you were in a business, show business, and you knew when you made that first picture you had arrived. You might not be the biggest in the world, but you were working at your favorite craft. And you were glad to have a job."

And Jimmy Wakeley finishes off the conversation about the old days with a touch of country-boy Cowboy-Hero Evangelism. And the Oklahoma drawl sparks with the fervor of the old values. So there is no mistaking where this old Singing Cowboy stands on the subject.

"There's the Bible," he says. "And there is wrong and right in all of us. If, through the media of motion pictures and television, we can be stripped of the children's respect for the family circle, if we can be stripped of our belief in a Supreme Being or a hereafter, if we can be stripped of our heritage, of our belief in our country and any right things we might have done, if we can be stripped of our historical values, if they can get us to where we don't believe in anything, this whole country will fall apart like a bag of cookies. If we make a youngster think that everybody's rotten, that everybody's bums, then what's he got to live for? Then he has no conscience, so he'll go out and rob a filling station. But you make him believe in a Supreme Being and a hereafter, and he has a good moral conscience to adhere to, then his conscience will keep him straight."

Jimmy Wakeley, too, is still singing the old songs. Home home on the range/ where the deer and the antelope play/ where seldom is heard/ a discouraging word/ And the skies are not cloudy all day.

But what to do about Roy Rogers? Must I wait until the cows come home? I had seen him on television doing commercials. But do commercials really count for anything? Does anyone even buy the crap? Even if Roy and Dale are selling it? As far as I could make out, Roy was working salad dressing and toilet bowl disinfectant. I had never heard of the salad dressing. I had also seen him on one of those early-morning wake-up-and-jabber programs, plugging his record, "Hoppy, Gene and Me." He looked to me less than comfortable plugging himself. He seemed more confident pushing salad dressing. As if the thought was in his mind that this was just a wee-bit degrading for the old King of the Cowboys to be doing. And the certain knowledge that most of the early-morning risers who had tuned in were, at that very moment, either shaving, spitting gargle, or perhaps having a wake-me-up fuck with the TV set on could not have made it any easier for him. But in the way of a repeat performance for anyone who had overslept that morning, he turned up several weeks later for the good-night crowd on the Johnny Carson's "Tonight Show." Alas, poor Roy. He did a comedy sketch with Carson that must have taken a small but expensive toll on his good nature and dignity. And Johnny should have apologized to all Front Row Kids in the audience for degrading Roy Rogers in that way. And if that wasn't enough for a Front Row Kid to endure and for Roy's soul to bear, Buddy Hackett bombarded him during the chitchat session with an endless and tasteless stream of horse-manure jokes.

No doubt Roy Rogers was busy these days. But I could not help thinking that he might have more decently exposed himself on the Dinah Shore show in the middle of the afternoon. Or perhaps on the radio. The King of the Cowboys looked so uncomfortable. I had never seen him look that way on a horse.

The only thing I could tell with any certainty from seeing Roy Rogers on television was that he appeared to be in better shape than Gene Autry. In fact he looked to be in pretty good trim for a 64-year-old Cowboy-Hero who had been out of the movies for 21 years and had suffered a heart attack a few years back. And his face, resembling as it did a Chinese baby with his tiny eyes like slits and the high cheekbones, did not come near to showing his age.

I would like to have seen Roy face to face. Television was no substitute for life. The next best and probably only thing to do was to go out to the Roy Rogers Museum in Apple Valley.

Apple Valley lies on the edge of the Mojave Desert. It is 189 miles from Las Vegas, about 5 miles off the main Interstate, and is fairly barren of living souls. At the Roy Rogers Museum there is a distinct feeling of being in the middle of Nowhere.

The museum is on the far side of town. The first thing you see is a giant statue of Trigger up on his hind legs on the roof. The building itself is designed like one of those forts you might see in Frontierland, with colored pennants, the Golden Bear, and the Stars and Stripes flying from roof-top flagpoles. Apparently it was, at one time, a bowling alley. Next door on one side there is a "historical" sheriff's office, which is actually a real estate office in disguise. And on the other side is the Apple Valley Post Office, a bank, and a couple more real estate offices. In the distance rise the hills of the High Mojave. There are a few cars, Winnebago trailers, and campers in the parking lot. And a battered old Chevy Caprice station wagon with "Roy Rogers Museum" painted on its flanks in bold lariat-type lettering. This must be the place.

I pay my $1.50 at the ticket window and enter.

On the wall is a picture of Roy in fancy, frilly Western gear, a blue shirt emblazoned with eagles. And Dale Evans in red-and-white apple dress. On one side of a long corridor a visitor can go to the "Happy Trails" Snack Bar or buy souvenirs in the gift shop. On the floor, arrows point the way to see Roy Rogers's monument to himself.

The Roy Rogers Museum consists of an almost incredible collection of Roy Rogers and Dale Evans memorabilia and trivia. It is staggering. It is also more than a little grotesque. The Pharaohs of ancient Egypt could not have filled their tombs in the Great Pyramids with more personal belongings and symbols of their glory than Roy Rogers has managed to pack into his museum. For Roy Rogers freaks, this is as close to heaven as they will ever get. For a Front Row Kid whose favorite Cowboy-Hero was someone else—Gene Autry, Tim McCoy, Joel McCrea, John Wayne, Ken Maynard, anyone but Roy Rogers—he has come to the wrong place. Gathered together in this huge room are countless displays, exhibits, photographs, souvenirs, trophies, plaques, awards, and the Lord only knows what else, covering the life and career of Roy Rogers and Dale Evans. A kind of living scrapbook of photos and objects labeled: "My first boots" . . . "My first guitar" . . . "Me and my first horse" . . . "Roy and his 4-H prize hog" . . . "Mom and Roy" . . . "Dale's first evening dress" . . . "Dale age 6" . . . "My first job in a shoe factory" . . . "My first holster" . . . "My second holster."

There are special glass display cases dedicated to the memory of each member of the Rogers family who has died. His mother, their baby girl, Robin, who died at the age of 2, the adopted Korean girl, Deborah Lee Rogers, who was killed in a bus crash, their adopted son "Sandy," who died in Germany while in the army. Each exhibit has some of their personal things in it. The little girl's baby shoes, her birth certificate complete with footprint, a tiny stuffed white horse, the little girl Debbie's Bible and her school certificates, "Sandy" Rogers's old catcher's mitt, a letter he wrote from military school, a .22 calibre rifle, the flag that was used to cover his coffin. And in each case there is a copy of the book Dale Evans wrote to commemorate that child. *Angel Unaware. Dearest Debbie. Salute to Sandy.* The memorials could be quite moving. But seen altogether and with everything else in this place there is something overwhelmingly morbid and ghoulish about them. A kind of death-freak fascination.

Farther on, a Front Row Kid passes hundreds more Roy Rogers photographs, a display dedicated to the Shriners, the saddle Roy used in all 188 Republic Westerns and TV shows, the 1923 Dodge truck he drove to California when he first came out in 1930, the original ridiculous jeep, "Nellybelle," from the Roy Rogers television series, a Westernized 1963 Pontiac covered in ornamental guns and cattle horns. And more photographs.

There is another astonishing display case diorama called: "Our American Religious Heritage." It is a schizophrenic collection of neon religious artifacts of Judaism, Christianity (Protestant and Catholic), and Dale Evans Orange County Evangelism. There is a Jewish window with Jesus coming in a door, a Torah, a crucifix or two, a Last Supper that looks to have been catered by McDonald's. Doubtless another sincere exhibit, it is heavy with religious-nut frenzy and confusion.

Over in the corner there is a glass-enclosed mini-room containing memorabilia of other Cowboy-Heroes. A Tom Mix six-gun and Stetson. A Buck Jones saddle. Hoot Gibson's piano. Portraits of Hart, Will Rogers, Buck Jones, and Tom Mix. A picture of Roy and Gene Autry putting on golf shoes. One of Charles Starrett. A Republic group publicity photo of Roy, Bill Elliott, Sunset Carson, "Rocky" Lane, "Red" Barry, and Bob Livingston. But the mini-room is overwhelmed by all the Roy Rogers displays. If you went through the place on roller skates, you would miss it completely.

Following the arrows and picking up the "oohs" and "aahs" of some of the other visitors who are slowly making their voyage of discovery, you come to a Vietnam exhibit that would make General Westmoreland, whose picture is prominently displayed, get up and dance. And would make the late Senator Wayne Morse turn over in his grave. Captured guns and rifles, military insignia, certificates naming Roy and Dale honorary lifetime members of the 9th Infantry Division Advisory Detachment and Honorary Air Commandos. Hot damn, Vietnam. The one the Indians won.

And there is more. Much more. Collections of arrowheads, autographed baseballs, Indian trinkets, hand-tooled shotguns, pistols, honorary sheriff's badges, saddles and tack, rocks, cowboy boots, elaborate cowboy duds designed by Nudie of North Hollywood, spurs, Roy Rogers comic books. Against a wall there is a cabinet holding a complete collection of blue Shirley Temple glassware.

I am dizzy from looking at all these things. Almost mindboggled by the sheer accumulation of Roy Rogers stuff. And I am only halfway to the end of it. It is impossible to sort it out and take it all in. It batters you senseless. Each single item seems to lose whatever individual significance or interest it might have. It all screams: ROY ROGERS!

And then, out of all the thousands of things collected here in the Roy Rogers Museum, I see a tiny item that is almost certainly insignificant and almost an accidental inclusion among all the Roy Rogers memorabilia. It seems to me greater and more important as a Front Row Kid memory jolter than anything I have seen. Next to this small thing, all the rest is junk to me and meaningless. Standing on its own on a shelf below the Shirley Temple glassware, there is a Hopalong Cassidy drinking glass! I haven't seen one like it since I stopped drinking my milk out of them about a million years ago.

It was the Front Row Kid's most prized possession. He could almost hear his mother's hands tapping out that galloping ta-ta-tump ta-ta-taump on the dinner table as he gulped the dreaded milk down and emptied the glass. He thought he would never see one again. A Hopalong Cassidy drinking glass. Oh, God. For one brief moment he was lost in time and events and did not know where he was. And then he thought: I'm going to steal it!

He thought about that for a long time. He looked closely at the glass. The picture of Hopalong Cassidy and Topper painted on the side of it. He almost could not believe what he was seeing. He could just as easily be only imagining it. But no, there it was all right. He could reach out and take it. In a flash. Who would know? Who would care?

And then he decided. No. Leave it there, where it is. It is the best thing in the place. It belongs here. Standing up against this mountainous collection of totems and monuments to Roy Rogers's ego-vision of himself. And let it stand for the Front Row Kid that Roy Rogers was too busy to see. Gotcha, Roy!

I leave the shelf where the Hopalong Cassidy glass is standing. And walk into the valley of Death. Roy Rogers's collection of wild animal trophies. His kill collection. Stuffed and mounted dead animals. Elephants, lions, antelopes, gazelles, bushbucks, wart hogs, hippos, rhinos, elk, moose, wolves, foxes, a baby seal, a giant polar bear, all sorts of small game. A sailfish he hooked. They are quite impressive as a collection. Roy Rogers must, indeed, be a crack shot. But it is also grisly seeing all these dead heads. This museum is intended to sum up the life of Roy Rogers, his accomplishments and successes, his Cowboy-Hero glory. But it feels like a mausoleum. There is more than a touch of the vampire about the place, with its memorials and exhibits of the past and dead things.

But the weirdest is yet to come. Following the arrow through the zoo and around a corner. I come to the bell ringer, the Grand Finale, the Final Touch, the Freaker-Outer.

TRIGGER 1932–1965
in 188 movies

Inside a glass display case, rearing up on his hind legs in front of a painted scenic background, carrying an empty silver mounted saddle, frozen in dead motion, stands "The Smartest Horse in the Movies." Trigger. Stuffed! And what I want to know is how do you like your golden palomino, Mister Death.

An old lady is standing in front of the glass case with her back to it. "I can't remember if Trigger is alive or dead," she says to the young boy with her. As if she has not yet seen or cannot believe what is inside the case, what this display is all about. Or perhaps her confusion has, indeed, gone right to the core of this exhibit. In the Roy Rogers Museum, Trigger is neither alive nor dead. He is both at the same time. And so is the Roy Rogers Museum. I have seen enough.

At the Roy Rogers Museum in Apple Valley, the riderless horse awaits only the Cowboy-Hero . . .

Oh Ceesco! Oh Pancho!

"The Cisco Kid had killed six men in more or less fair scrimmage, had murdered twice as many (mostly Mexicans), and had winged a large number whom he modestly forebore to count. Therefore a woman loved him.

"The Kid was twenty-five, looked twenty; and a careful insurance company would have estimated the probable time of his demise at, say, twenty-six. His habitat was anywhere between the Frio and the Rio Grande. He killed for the love of it—because he was quick-tempered—to· avoid arrest—for his own amusement—any reason that came to his mind would suffice. He had escaped capture because he could shoot five-sixths of a second sooner than any sheriff or ranger in the service, and because he rode a speckled roan horse that knew every cowpath in the mesquite and pear thickets from San Antone to Matamoras."

So began the Wild West Tale "The Caballero's Way," in which the great and peculiar short-story writer O. Henry introduced the character who would eventually be transformed into one of the most fabulous and romantic and amusing Cowboy-Heroes of them all. The Cisco Kid.

I would have read on. But the guy who owned the second-hand bookstore over in the no man's land part of Hollywood Boulevard shouted at me from behind a small mountain of out-of-date movie magazines: "This ain't a library!" It was an intimidating bellow, much like the one a porn shop night manager puts on when he wants to shake up the bent-legged beaver browsers. Read 'em at home, fellas. This ain't a library. And the browsers self-consciously shift their weight from one foot to the other. And some of them slink away. The second-hand book dealer did not seem to give any consideration to the fact that only the other day I had bought from him a fine 1904 edition of Wister's *The Virginian* that had been collecting dust on his shelf, and that I was in the market to buy the complete works of Balzac. A 35-volume set!

I had seen the O. Henry volume with this particular short story in it. I didn't want to buy the whole book for just one story, so I began to read "The Caballero's Way" as fast as I could. I am not a speed reader and did not get very far.

The Cisco Kid. O. Henry's Robin Hood of the Old West. What I managed to read did not exactly sound like the Cisco Kid the Front Row Kids knew and loved. The Cisco Kid a hot-blooded killer (albeit mostly of Mexicans)? Impossible. The Cisco Kid we grew up on, the Latino Cowboy-Hero and his sidekick Pancho were, next to The Lone Ranger and Tonto, the most fabulous and fantastic pair of Good Guys on the range. Cisco. Dashing and colorful in his hand-tooled and elaborate South-of-the border gear and big old white ten-gallon sombrero. Riding his painted pony, Diablo. Fighting for Law and Order in a Wild West time when words like that did not mean "keep the niggers and spics in their place." Chasing down Bad Guys with tricks and ploys and hoodwinks. Ending each Wild West Tale with a good-natured joke and the unforgettable exchange: "Oh Pancho! Oh Ceesco! Oh Ho Ho!" And galloping off to new adventures.

As in all O. Henry short stories, there must have been a twist in the tail of "The Caballero's Way." Something to change the gunslinger into a Cowboy-Hero. I didn't wait around to find out what it was.

Everybody remembers The Cisco Kid. Even 20 years after the TV series closed down. Can anyone recall even one episode when The Cisco Kid actually killed a Bad Guy? *Billy* the Kid certainly did many a man that way. But The *Cisco* Kid? Never. Not as far as I can remember. And I remember The Cisco Kid.

So does the redhead in the Pink Flamingo Massage Parlor. The Cisco Kid and Audie Murphy are the only Cowboy-

Heroes she does remember. But then she is quite young. Most of the Cowboy-Heroes were before her time. And she is not now nor has she ever been a Front Row Kid. She is working her way through college, and her specialities are marine biology and below-the-belt meanderings. Call her the Finger-Tip Kid. The Pink Flamingo is not the sort of place you would normally go to talk about The Cisco Kid. But that is one of the things about 3 A.M. on the Strip. You never can tell.

"How do I know you're not a cop?" The Finger-Tip Kid said, standing there, green-bikinied, next to the "operating table" but with her hands behind her back.

"Take my word for it. Do I look like a cop?"

"Cops don't always look like cops. I can't afford to get busted."

"Who can?"

"Yeah. Well, if you're not a cop, d'ya mind telling me what you do do?"

"I'm out here searching for old movie cowboys. Roy Rogers, Gene Autry, Randolph Scott, "Lash" LaRue, The Lone Ranger, guys like that."

"Really?" One hand appears from behind her back. She brushes her hair out of her eyes. The truth is sometimes the best answer. No undercover vice cop could have come up with a line like that. Movie cowboys?

"Would I lie to you?" I would, of course, but I was beginning to feel a bit cold on that slab.

"No kidding? You mean like Audie Murphy and The Cisco Kid?"

"Well, Audie Murphy's dead," I said. "But I'm still looking for The Cisco Kid."

"They're the only ones I remember from when I was a little girl," she said. It seemed as though I had rung a bell in the Finger-Tip Kid's girlhood past. She moved into groping range. Both hands were out in front now. I could see there was nothing up her sleeve.

"The only reason I know about Audie Murphy," she was saying, "is because my father was in the army with him and told me about him. Then I saw a movie with him in it, and I thought he was so cute. I kind of had a crush on him for a long time. I used to cut his picture out of the movie magazines and put them up in my room. He was sort of my favorite actor, you know?" She was finger-tip-toeing and talking at the same time. And, I sensed, more interested in what she was saying than in what she was supposed to be doing. "And I remember The Cisco Kid and Pancho because I used to watch it all the time on TV. I used to love The Cisco Kid. He always wore that great outfit, that kind of Mexican stuff, you know, that was, like, designed and all fancy. And I remember his horse was named Diablo. Ya wanna turn over?"

"Why not?" I was only here for the beer.

"Who was it played The Cisco Kid? Duncan something." She stopped what she was doing to plumb the depths of her memory.

"Duncan Renaldo," I said.

"Oh, yeah. Duncan Renaldo. I remember now. And Leo Carillo was Pancho. I bet you must have heard that song by War, you know, about Cisco Kid and Pancho?"

"The Cisco Kid was a friend of mine. Yeah." It had been a million seller. Number one. It was a better song than Olivia Newton-John's stuff but not one of my favorites.

"Yeah, that's the one." She began to sing it, really get into it. I couldn't believe what was happening. I was beginning to forget why I had come in there in the first place. "Cisco Kid was a friend of mine," she sang. "Cisco Kid was a friend of mine. He drink whiskey, Pancho drinkin' wine." Her voice was not as good as her touch. And she was losing her touch. Finger-tapping more than finger-tipping. My time was running out. And then she wanted to talk about the other movie cowboys I had seen. And was I *really* going to see The Cisco Kid?

"If I can find him," I said. "Do you ever take that thing off?"

"That's extra. You got $20 for a tip?"

"What do I get for it? Another song?"

"Nooo," she laughed. "A topless hand job."

Oh Ceesco! Oh Pancho!

O. Henry's caballero of fiction was the first Cisco Kid. And
Duncan Renaldo was the best as far as the Front Row Kids
were concerned. But in the time between there had been
other Cisco Kids. As a Cowboy-Hero, The Cisco Kid has been
around, in various versions, even longer than The Lone
Ranger. Four years before George W. Trendle even dreamed
up the masked man, Front Row Kids were watching The Cisco
Kid gallop across the screen. He was the hero of Raoul Walsh's
early days talkie, *In Old Arizona*. It was the picture that cost
that director his eye. And won Warner Baxter the Academy
Award for Best Actor. Baxter was so good as the Kid, the
moguls took him out of Westerns and put him in the Big Time.
But he had established the character as a Cowboy-Hero to
reckon with.

When Baxter moved up from Cisco, the role was taken over
by Caesar Romero, with Chris Pin-Martin as Pancho. Romero,
who was no cowboy, but one of those Brill-creamed Latin
lover types, played the Kid as a smarmy dandy and fop, while
Chris Pin-Martin's Pancho was a gut-bucket slob. Latin America's
macho sensibilities were mortally offended by this highly
unlikely duo. An international incident very nearly occurred.
Diplomatic cables flew back and forth between Latin America
and the State Department. The Cisco Kid, as portrayed by
Romero, was, so to speak, queering America's South-of-the-
border foreign policy. Darryl Zanuck, the mogul at Fox, was
more or less ordered by Washington to change Cisco's style or
stop making the pictures. He decided to drop the series altogether. And the character fell into oblivion for a while.

It was resurrected in the forties by Monogram. This time
Gilbert Roland had a go at the part. And this time, Cisco was
no Romero poof but a typical Rolandesque cigarillo-smoking,
hot-sweat-of-passion, *cojones*-all-the-way, Latin ladies man. A
lusty, hairy, mucho macho caballero. The films bombed out.

It was Duncan Renaldo who really put the style and charm
into The Cisco Kid. The Renaldo-Carillo team made 12 pictures at Monogram and later for United Artists. And 156 half-
hour television shows. Winding it up in 1955. The Cisco Kid of
Renaldo's fashioning was an elegant hombre, stylish, humor-

ous, daredevilish, exciting, and no killer of men. As a Cowboy-Hero, he was more than a Good Guy. He was a Good Spirit.

But if Duncan was The Cisco Kid everyone remembers, the trail to that good fortune and everlasting glory was a long one. It held more than a few ambushes and road blocks and unexpected detours marked Bad Luck, Misfortune, and Go Directly to Jail.

He fell down his darkest hole when he was right on the verge of stepping into the bright marquee lights of Hollywood stardom. He had been around the business since the early twenties, had played his first big role in *The Bridge of San Luis Rey* in '29, and had spent two years in Africa making *Trader Horn,* in which he starred with Harry Carey. It was almost a sure thing that Duncan Renaldo would become a big deal in Hollywood on the strength of that film. But it didn't work out that way. On January 17, 1931, on the verge of the gala premiere of *Trader Horn* at Grauman's Chinese Theater, Duncan Renaldo was arrested and charged with being an illegal immigrant and of making false statements about his birthplace to obtain a passport. It was not exactly the crime of the century. But it was the beginning of a hellish ordeal for the future Cisco Kid. The next six years would see Duncan Renaldo indicted by a Grand Jury, hauled into court for trial, slapped with more contempt of court citations than the Chicago 7, convicted of perjury and making false statements, sentenced to two years in the Federal slammer (he served 18 months on McNeil Island), then hounded out of the country by Immigration authorities who wanted to deport him to Rumania, which resulted in his having to live on a friend's boat out beyond the 3-mile limit because neither the United States nor Mexico (nor Rumania) would let him land, and finally in 1936, after he had done his time and eaten more than his fair share of shit, he was granted an unconditional Presidential pardon by FDR. And allowed to return to the land of the living.

Essentially it was all a case of mistaken identity. Nobody seemed to know for sure who Duncan Renaldo was (if, indeed, that was his name) or where he came from. It came down to multiple choice and your-guess-is-as-good-as-mine. According to the government, he was supposed to be either Basil Couyanos, Renault B. Gugliamos, Vasile Dumitree Cuchieanas, Renalt Duncan, or Duncan Renaldo. One of the above. All of the above. None of the above. Any combination of the above. Take your pick. And he was allegedly born in Rumania. Or was it Spain? Mexico? How about Camden, New Jersey? The only thing Duncan Renaldo knew for sure was that he was up on a bum rap. He hadn't a clue who his parents were, or where he had been born. As far as he knew, he was an orphan with distant memories of Spain. For Duncan Renaldo, the whole affair was total Kafkaesque weirdness. And before it had run its bizarre course, it fairly ruined him.

Back again in Hollywood in 1936, he got work at Republic Studios. But not as an actor. He was put to work sweeping up around the place! Having been run over by the wheels of justice, he swallowed this new humiliation with stoicism (at least it was better than jail) and pushed that broom across sound stages where less talented men were acting. Until Herbert J. Yates got wind of the situation. Yates, to his credit, immediately put Renaldo in the saddle and in front of the cameras. Finally Duncan Renaldo was back in business. For the next five years he played in Republic Westerns.

And then, with new and fresh ideas about The Cisco Kid and how he should be played, and having picked up the rights to the character from Doubleday, O. Henry's publisher, Duncan Renaldo went over to Monogram, became The Cisco Kid, and took his place among the best and most adventuresome Cowboy-Heroes of Front Row Kid fantasy. It had been a long time coming. But for Renaldo and the Front Row Kids it had been well worth the wait. Perhaps because he had paid such high dues in time, money, and plain hell, he could bring an enthusiasm and style to his characterization of Cisco that a mincing Caesar Romero or a lecherous Gilbert Roland could not have done on the best day of their lives. If The Cisco Kid, as Renaldo played him, was a man of unusual qualities, it was because Duncan Renaldo himself was a man of quality. As any Front Row Kid, sitting cross-legged and cross-eyed in front of the television set, could plainly see.

The Cisco Kid was young and lean and dark-haired and Spanish handsome back in those television days. I remembered him clearly. As if it were only yesterday. Riding that splendid pinto pony. Dressed in that fabulous caballero costume. Will I recognize him now, I wondered as I waited for Duncan Renaldo at high noon in a parking lot of a Santa Barbara shopping center. It would be too much to expect him to come down in his sombrero. I would just trust to my Front Row Kid instincts and keep my eyes peeled. Just look out for the 71-year-old man who looks like he's looking for someone.

The Cisco Kid spotted me first. I guess it must have been my "Wild Bill Hickok." Just as well because I would not have picked The Cisco Kid out of a crowd as easily as I could have spotted Joel McCrea or Rex Allen. I would have known the voice, though. That mellow, South-of-the-border accent with a hint of laughter around the edges. To hear him speak, I would not have mistaken him for Caesar Romero or Gilbert Roland.

Duncan Renaldo, The Cisco Kid of my memory, is white-haired now. His face, lined and well worn and pouched, shows his age. He can no longer climb aboard a horse, as his legs are those of a 71-year-old ex-Cowboy-Hero who rode too hard in his younger days and took too much battering from all that jumping and stunting. He is wearing a blue suit with a white shirt that is open at the neck. There is a bandage on his hand. And there is a mellowness about him that goes beyond his accent. He does not look like he is from around here, rather like a European gentleman. French, possibly, or Spanish or even, yes, Rumanian.

We drive out to his new house in Santa Barbara and settle down to talk in the study/office/library, which when it is finally fixed up, will be his special room. Some of his Cisco Kid mementos are already on display. The rest will be. Eventually. On a stand across the room there is a big, handsome Mexican saddle. The one The Cisco Kid rode in all those exciting episodes.

"The Cisco Kid never killed anybody," Duncan Renaldo says. "We tricked the bandits into killing each other off instead of our doing it. We manhandled them a lot, but we always turned them over to the sheriff. In The Cisco Kid we developed a format where we'd have an awful lot of action but as little violence from the standpoint of the protagonists as possible. And a lot of comedy. It was a romantic character and at the same time an action character. After the trouble Fox had with The Cisco Kid series, we didn't want that to happen to us. So I spent three weeks in Mexico at the Inter-American Relations Committee to find a format that would be acceptable to them. And finally out of desperation I said, 'Look, why don't we pattern The Cisco Kid after Don Quixote and Sancho Panza? Only The Cisco Kid is a more sane human being. Instead of fighting windmills, he fights the windmills of trouble of humanity. And his partner Pancho is a goodhearted man. He loves everybody and wants to help everybody. And he does. To the point that he gets his partner in trouble all the time.' And they loved that. That was the format, and it became very successful."

To illustrate his point, Renaldo tells the story of a writer on the series who came to him with a vengeance and violence story that Renaldo didn't want to do because it wasn't right for The Cisco Kid. And the writer, in a quandary, wondered what to do. Renaldo, inspired, suggested he write about two ducks and somehow they would get a story out of it for Cisco Kid and Pancho. Quack. Quack.

"So we started just for the fun of it," he says. "To see what we could come up with. We fooled around with it the whole afternoon, and we spent the whole night. We never went to bed. And the next morning we came up with a story about two ducks. A male duck and a female duck that belong to two different families. And you know, we ended up with a picture that was the most successful of the whole series. Primarily, it was about two ducks."

Duncan Renaldo says he doesn't know what the devil is happening in the motion picture business today. Particularly television.

"You know, it goes into people's homes, with little children, and it's mayhem," he says. "It's fearful, the death and the killings. It doesn't make sense. After 1955 in TV something happened—like a disease set in, and people began to shoot everybody. The minute they had the slightest altercation, the first thing, a gun came out, and at least five people dropped dead. The fun has gone out of it. And warped thinking has taken its place."

To Duncan Renaldo's way of thinking, the heritage of the West is of brave and decent folks who settled in the wilderness, cleared the land with their own muscle and an axe, not a bulldozer, built their homes and towns and worked hard at it. They did not have time to go around gunning each other down. He thinks it is shameful to give children the idea that the West was just a wild place full of con men and gunfighters and prostitutes, although he concedes there were some of those types out there. "The development of this country," he says, with the patriotic fervor of a naturalized citizen, "was a fantastic social upheaval that the world has never experienced before or since. And the greatest thing that happened was the form of government we have, this constitutional government." But that government, he feels, has been fooled around with and holes have been made in it "so it looks like a Swiss cheese."

"When the Warren Court began to give arbitrary decisions," he says, sounding more like Ronald Reagan than The Cisco Kid, "they lost track of it. Nowadays, it's just like you're in a stagecoach with 4-ups, you know, and you have no reins, so you're going all over the place in all directions, wherever the horses want to go. That's why we have the confusion in this country and the hysteria. It's fantastic. It's one thing to punish people for doing wrong. And another thing to keep them from doing wrong in the first place."

And he tells the story of Dick Turpin, olde Englande highwayman, and a British Justice by the name of Cruikshank, the Hanging Judge, who decreed that any highwayman caught in the act was to be strung up by the neck to the nearest tree. No trial. No nothing. And anybody who cut down the body was liable to 30 years in prison without parole.

"That's a bit harsh," I say. I think The Cisco Kid would not have approved.

"It was harsh," Renaldo agrees. "But in six weeks time, people all over England could leave their doors open. They only strung three. That's all. I'm not advocating that. But really it needs some very drastic action to stop all this hysteria."

The sermonette begs the question: How do you feel about Dick Nixon, Cisco?

"I knew Nixon very well before he became anything," Renaldo says. "And then I saw him in Washington years later and his head had become so big. I said, 'Dick, it's just like show business. One day you're important and a celebrity, and the next day you can walk down the street and nobody will even spit on you.' Now this Watergate business, I think Nixon must have become mentally deficient over the years. That's the only way to explain his actions, the terrible way he acted, the skullduggery and the larceny."

"Where are the Good Guys?" I ask.

"They're all gone," The Cisco Kid says.

And then, having said this about that and having made himself perfectly clear, Duncan Renaldo goes through the story of his own life and his ups and downs in show business.

He began in the business in 1923. His first picture in the silent days was with Richard Barthelmes and Bill Powell. He also played in a film with Lionel Barrymore. "And I had the good fortune of playing about six characters in the *Music Masters* series," he says. "I played Beethoven, Mozart, Wagner, Schumann. It gave me a start. And from there I became an assistant cameraman, and I carted an old hand-cranked Pathe camera on my back. Then I started to do a little writing. I wrote a couple of scripts which I sold. And directed a picture which turned out very bad because I wasn't capable. In the course of events I came out to Hollywood in 1924. In '25 they had this earthquake that chased us out, and I went back East again and played in some pictures in Fort Lee, New Jersey. I struggled up and down the ladder, you know."

When he came back to Hollywood, it was both an up and a down. It seems he owned the rights to the book *The Bridge of San Luis Rey,* but he was going to lose it because he couldn't afford to make the option payment. Theda Bara's husband, a director, happened to see him one day at a restaurant on

Hollywood Boulevard. Renaldo was feeling awful about the prospect of losing the rights to the book when this director offered to buy them from him for what he owed. Then he turned around and sold it to M-G-M. That was a down. The up came when Irving Thalberg, who knew Renaldo was interested in the book, gave him the part of Esteban in the movie. After that came the big up and down. *Trader Horn* and his arrest.

"It was a very monotonous piece of business," he says. "And I had to spend a lot of my . . . I went broke entirely spending money with lawyers and arriving noplace. Finally the Supreme Court held with me that I was right and they were wrong, but in the meantime we lost all that time. And then in 1941 I was allowed to apply for citizenship and renounce *each* and *any* country that I might have been subject to. The Supreme Court gave me special dispensation. I told them, 'If you want me to be Chinese, I'll be Chinese. I don't care which one it will be, but just let me live my own life.' So they said, 'Presumably you are from Rumania.' But I'm not from Rumania. At the trials they produced five different birth certificates for me. I said that was ludicrous. I could not have been born five times in five different places. It was one of those idiotic paradoxes. Had I known where I was born, I wouldn't have had the trouble."

He says Herbert J. Yates saved his life. Renaldo was lucky. He might just as easily have been left for dead, because Hollywood can be merciless, not unlike wolves in the wilderness. As Renaldo puts it, "When there are wolves around, you must be careful never to get scratched."

In 1943, having the rights to The Cisco Kid, he made his deal with Monogram. And tailored his own image.

"I devised the costume myself, and I tried to make it signify in some way each of the Latin countries. For example, the belts were Argentine and Ecuadorian. The hat was Mexican. By the time I got through with it, the whole thing was an amalgam of representation from each of the countries." It seems The Cisco Kid was not only a Good Guy but a diplomat.

"It was all for entertainment," he says. "For fun and for

comedy. After all, if you can give people pleasure, that's a thing that's almost divine because you can't buy that for money. To me that's the greatest psychiatry in the world. And we used to have this thing at the end where Leo used to come to me and give me a bromide that didn't make any sense. And I would say, 'Oh, Pancho, how could you?' and he would say, 'Oh, Cisco.' And both of us would laugh and ride away. That little gimmick I invented for this one reason. If we had a laugh at the end of the pictures, then the kids who watched those pictures, instead of being confused, would laugh with us at the end. Leo used to say we were baby-sitters for the whole country at one time."

The TV show ended for Duncan Renaldo in 1955. But it still pops up on television 20 years later. He does not make a penny from the reruns, although he still gets plenty of fan mail from places like Indiana, Massachusetts, and Ghana. He still does an occasional personal appearance. But the splendid outfit that was so much a symbol of The Cisco Kid no longer fits him.

"I have 2 percent interest in the television sales," he says. "But this company that is distributing the show is disregarding me. So I'm about to sue them. Not so much for the money as it is . . . damn, I hate people who break contracts." Duncan Renaldo is apparently still having his ups and downs in that way.

For the rest, he says, he still keeps pretty busy. He gives speeches at colleges and Rotary Club luncheons. He tends his garden. He does a little writing. He reads history and listens to classical music. He is thinking of taking up painting again. When he was in Africa on *Trader Horn,* he painted a portrait of an African queen that Eleanor Roosevelt liked so much she hung it in the White House. It now hangs in Duncan Renaldo's own living room. When he gets a chance, he says, he goes to visit his horse, Diablo, who is boarded at a friend's ranch. In fact, there are two Diablos. One is 36 years old and the other is 33. There were, at one time, five. They pick Cisco's pocket for sugar when he goes visiting.

Thinking of the Finger-Tip Kid, I ask him one last goofy question: Did he ever hear that hit song "Cisco Kid?"

"Oh, yes," he says. "And I raised the dickens with those boys because in it they say Cisco drank whiskey and Pancho drank wine. Now Leo could not drink. He was highly allergic to liquor. If he drank even a thimbleful, he'd get red in the face and break out. People used to think he was drunk, but that was because he was always in high spirits. I called it that he had an effervescent personality. He was a wonderful man. He bubbled all the time. But those boys went ahead and used the names, anyway. The song was quite a big hit."

Finally and too soon, it is time for me to hit the trail.

Unlike, say, Clayton Moore, who has apparently given up his own identity completely to The Lone Ranger, as if there is no Moore but only The Lone Ranger, Duncan Renaldo is his own man. "The Cisco Kid was a characterization to me, and I delineated it along certain lines, and that's all it was," he says.

Tim McCoy

Tim McCoy is alive and well. And living in Nogales, Arizona.

That was the word according to the tumbleweed connection. Someone who knew someone who knew. And, yes, I could look him up. If I wanted to drive all the way down to Nogales. Tumbling tumbleweeds! I would have walked to Nogales to see Tim McCoy.

Tim McCoy was "The One." The last of the first and best Cowboy-Heroes. The only surviving Miracle Rider and rival to Tom Mix. The last of the Big Four. The real McCoy. Not just another Cowboy-Hero. To this Front Row Kid, Colonel Tim McCoy was the keeper of the Wild West Hero tradition, something of a symbol of what this whole Saturday Matinee Cowboy-Hero fantasy business was all about. Wyoming cowboy. Indian Agent and sign-talker, army officer in two wars, Saturday Matinee "Man of Destiny" dressed all in black, quick-on-the-draw and stylish beyond compare, Wild West Show Headliner and Cowboy-Hero until he was 84 years old. A genuine original. I would rather see Tim McCoy than even Tom Mix himself. You could take John Wayne and Gene Autry and Roy Rogers and all the others and put them in the corral. As long as Tim McCoy is alive, they are second features. And a drive to Nogales to see Tim McCoy was more than just another trip. It was, to me, almost a pilgrimage. A base you had to touch on the way to home or else the whole voyage backward wouldn't count for anything.

I hit the San Diego Freeway heading south in high excitement. If my old wheels held up all right, I would do the 800-mile run to Nogales in one go, nonstop. The evening rush-hour jam-up had already begun. A million cars were doing an elephant walk from L.A. to San Diego. You could almost walk on car roofs all the way without touching the road. I didn't mind. I hardly noticed it. For once, I was immune to all the blinking taillights in front of me and the Southern California ugliness all around. The line that led back to the old Cowboy-Hero fantasies was hard enough to find out here without having to suffer the gross intrusion of all those hamburger stands and used-car lots. It was like having somebody standing behind you in an elevator whistling off key. If you could not shut it out, it would drive you crazy. But this was a joy-ride. For a change.

Tim McCoy, Cowboy-Hero, had cut a trail across time. From the days of the open range to the day before yesterday. I could think about that all the way to Nogales. All through the night. I had about 47 million questions I wanted to ask him that nobody else could possibly know the answers to. About the Indians and the Cowboys. About *The Covered Wagon* and Jesse Lasky. About Thalberg's M-G-M. About Sam Katzman's shoestring productions. About *The Rough Riders.* And the *Man of Destiny.* About the Wild West Shows. About what it all meant. Or if, indeed, it has any meaning at all. What makes a Cowboy-Hero carry on with the show until he is 84 years old? Is it just show business to him? Or something more? Something to do with the old Wild West Tale and Cowboy-Hero fantasy that goes way back through Buffalo Bill to the very roots of the tradition? And what do you have to say about time and events, Colonel McCoy? What is the Ultimate Truth?

There was, of course, the possibility that he would have nothing to say about anything. That he would not be able to tell a Front Row Kid anything the Kid didn't already know or could not have guessed for himself. Would that make the trip a waste of time? I did not think so. Tim McCoy was still a Cowboy-Hero. And I was still the Front Row Kid. I would travel 800 miles just to say "howdy."

I drove all night. East along the California-Mexico border. Through Yuma, Arizona, and Gila Bend toward Tucson. For hours and many miles, there were no other cars on the road. The desert was all around. But I couldn't see it. I kept myself company. And sometimes I listened to the car radio.

I made Nogales much sooner than I thought I would.
Nogales is a border town. Its atmosphere is neither here nor
there. It is neither as American as apple pie nor as Mexican as
a jumping bean. Tim McCoy's hacienda was back along
Nogales Road on the edge of town. I missed the turnoff twice
and began to curse. I didn't want to be late. Not even one
minute. And when I finally found the place, I wasn't altogether certain that was it. But it was the only house near
where his was supposed to be. I walked all the way around the
house. I could not see any signs of life. I knocked at the big
wooden door. No reply. Had he left town? Or worse? Fallen
ill? Died? I was seized with a momentary anxiety attack. The
thought came to me that I had driven all this way for nothing.
That I had missed him. If so, then I was through with my
Cowboy-Hero roundup. The end. I would leave the freeways
to those who had to drive them. I would go to China or someplace. The hell with it. Fuck it. I was beginning to feel bad.

Then I heard the sound of someone trying to unlock the
door from the inside. And not having much luck. I thought I
heard a voice. But couldn't be sure. The door was thick as a
brick. Like something they used to have in Crusader castles.
If you couldn't unlock it, then you couldn't open it at all without dynamite.

Finally the lock turned over, and the big door opened, and
Tim McCoy was standing there, just inside the doorway, his
blue eyes twinkling just as they had done in 200 Western
movies, and he was cursing in his mellow-smooth voice at the
trickiness of some locks.

Tim McCoy was dressed in a blue jumpsuit. What Winston
Churchill used to call a "siren suit." The color matched his
eyes. He wore an ascot around his neck. His hair was white.
There was a small liver spot on his face. He was a small man.
Smaller than I thought he would be. Under 6 feet. But not
altogether frail. You could see right off that he had been tough
as old boots at one time. His movements were slow and careful, but he still stood straight as the army officer he had once
been. He may be 85 years old. But he did not look a day older
than, say, 79.

I had to refocus. It was the same for all the Cowboy-Heroes

I had seen. In my mind they were always as they had been. In cowboy outfits and Stetson hats. Looking as they had looked in the Saturday Matinees. I always half expected to see *that* Cowboy-Hero. Although I knew it was impossible and that I would find, instead, old men in their sixties and seventies. It was always a jolt. Putting my mind through strange time twists. I always had to readjust. With Tim McCoy it was slightly different. I had been seeing in my mind the dashing, handsome, and cool Cowboy-Hero. And now with my eyes I saw the old man. But it was all right, in a way. Tim McCoy was, to me, the one Cowboy-Hero, so much older now and having survived so long, who had grown in my mind even larger than life than he had once seemed to be. This charming old man with the bright blue eyes. I had the strange sensation of being in the presence of something magical. For once I did not feel let down.

Tim McCoy greeted me and showed me into his hacienda. The house itself was wrapped around an open Spanish-style courtyard with a fountain in the center of it. Off the courtyard on one side was a living room with stained-glass windows, antique furniture, and paintings on the wall. The room was absolutely spotless and quite elegant. I hoped we wouldn't be talking in here. It was a room meant for elegant old-fashioned gentlemen to take tea in with beautiful gentle women in high-necked dresses, who would talk to them of music. Standing in the middle of it in my jeans and boots, I feel like a lumberjack.

"Should we go across to my suite?" McCoy says, leading the way out and across the open foyer. "I think it'll be more comfortable. It's where I spend most of my time when I'm at home."

McCoy's suite was more like it. A large, wood-paneled combination bedroom-sitting room, with plaques and photographs and a portrait of his late wife on the walls. There was a large bed at the back and easy chairs and a small coffee table in front of the tiled fireplace. In one corner there were books on a shelf and a television set.

"That's my Emmy over there," Tim McCoy says proudly, pointing to it on the book shelf. "I got that for my television show. I had a television show for about five years down in Hollywood. And up there is the trophy from the Cowboy Hall of Fame. I got that last year.

"I'll tell you," he says. "I don't like telling my life story. To begin at the beginning? Well, I just don't have the heart to do that anymore."

We sit down in front of the fireplace, which is not lighted. I am still a bit Front Row Kid-awed to be actually sitting here with Tim McCoy. And I don't know which of my 47 million questions to ask first. Or if, indeed, to ask any of them. So I tell him I have seen Sunset Carson and that he said to say hello.

"How is the old boy?" McCoy asks quite cheerfully. "He sort of got banged up last year. The last I heard he was in bad shape."

"He's all right now. Getting around."

"He's a nice fellow. I never knew him very well. In fact, I'd never met him until he came to take my place with Tommy Scott when I got sick." Tim McCoy had stuck with the Wild West Show for 13 years. Until he was almost 84 years old. Doing a bullwhip act as the headlining Cowboy-Hero. Finally he decided to hang it up. "You see I was thrown into the hospital with this damn back. I couldn't walk. It was a slipped disc. So then I said, 'The hell with it. This is it. I'm going to quit. I'm going home. I've had enough punishment. I'm going home.' And Tommy said, 'What about next season?' And I said, 'No, I've done my last season.'"

Tim McCoy may have quit the Wild West Show business. And he may be 85 years old. But he is not yet ready to settle down to a rocking chair. He says he has just returned from a trip to England to see his daughter. And is planning to leave in a few weeks for a vacation in Hawaii. It is really quite extraordinary that Tim McCoy has kept on going while so many others, much younger than he is, have slowed to a crawl and retired to oblivion.

"Well," he says, "they were just not versatile enough. I think that's the answer to it. They could do the old thing of getting on the horse and riding, and when they got through with that, they were finished. When I came back from the war, the

Western thing was practically gone. But instead of saying, 'Well, this is the end of things, I'm through professionally,' I just lowered my head and charged and batted around and got my way into television, got my own television show. I had the prime time on Saturday night on CBS. Seven o'clock on Saturday night. But one man with Indian stuff and historical things couldn't expect to hold that. The business got too big. The spot that I was in was taken over by Jackie Gleason. So when that petered out, and they offered me the job to come into the circus, I went into the circus for five years. And then after that, Tommy Scott, who'd been after me for quite some time to join him, came out to see me at the circus, and we chatted. I was building this house then, and I said, 'I'll tell you what I'll do. I'm building my house now, but when I get through with that, I'll come out and join you. I'll join you for 13 weeks, and if we're both happy, and we're both making money, why, I'll finish the season with you.' Thirteen weeks? I stayed with him for 13 years! And I think I'd still be doing it if my wife hadn't died. That pulled the rug out from under me." McCoy's voice falters for a moment. "That just . . . whipped me . . . I didn't think anything would have ever happened to her . . . but I've somehow gotten . . . now the thing to do is not to stagnate here. I've got my house, this beautiful house here, and I love living in it. But the thing is, having been as active as I have, why, I can't just sit here and let the rocking chair get me down. Anything I've got a notion to do, I do."

McCoy then goes into a funny story, complete with Irish accents, about his recent trip where he stopped off in Ireland and old McCoy kin met him and told him about how his grandfather had left the old country "on a sailin' ship" and not one of the McCoys had ever come back until Tim did. He was the real McCoy. And he says how surprised he was that the Irish McCoys knew all about him and had followed his career.

"I got to thinking of it the other day," McCoy said. "And it's 53 years ago that I came into this show business. I was sitting here in front of the fire thinking about it the other day. When I brought the Indians for *The Covered Wagon,* that was 53 years ago. It seems impossible . . . but you see, time flies. And now at the end of the string, after all my years in pictures, and I see what's happened to so many others, some of them even more successful than I was, but I lasted longer, apparently, than any of them. And to be able to sit back and say, Well, I'm able to take care of myself for the rest of my days. I don't have a damn worry financially. I'm not a wealthy man, but I've got enough so I don't have to worry what's going to happen to me if I live another five years, and I can live in my life style until the end of my days. I think that at the end of the road, after you've been in this business for a long time, it's more or less of an accomplishment."

Being the Cowboy-Hero who goes back farther than any other that I have seen and wanting him to "begin at the beginning," although I know he doesn't want to, I ask him what it was like 53 years ago when he came out with his Indians.

"Oh, it was a totally different business," he says. "Vine Street was covered with pepper trees. And everybody was friendly. Everybody knew one another, and you visited around. It was like a club."

"Hollywood must have been just a village," I say.

"It was. Hollywood was very small. There was just a street-car out from Los Angeles. And I had all my Indians camped, had their tepees and all camped on a beautiful level spot right along the streetcar line there in the hills with the trees all around it. And I stayed there with the Indians. And we brought them in on a big bus to Grauman's theater, it was the Egyptian Theater right on Hollywood Boulevard. I'd gotten up this prologue for *The Covered Wagon,* and I used to come out on stage and introduce these Indians. And we brought covered wagons right up there on the stage with the horses and all. We did that for eight or nine months. And then Jesse Lasky called me in and said he was opening the picture in London, and he wasn't sure how it would go over, but he thought if I brought my Indians over to Europe, that would really give it some ballyhoo . . ."

McCoy's story is interrupted as his oldest son, Ronnie, a big, strapping fellow, comes into the room to tell him there is a guy outside who wants to know if McCoy wants to buy a cord of oak for $45. McCoy says he'll have to go out and take a look at his wood pile. He returns a few moments later, the owner of a cord of oak for his wood pile.

"I've frozen here before," he says. "So I figure, what the hell, if I don't use it this winter, I'll use it next winter. I like to light a fire here every night. They light a fire for me, and every evening I like to sit back here if anybody drops in . . . only a few people do drop in because I don't, I'm not a loner exactly, but I suppose I've been around so much and have had to be with people so much that it's, uh, I don't have to be gregarious. I have one or two close friends that do drop in. But I can sit here by the fire with a book and read. Hell, I don't need anybody around me. I've got enough stuff tucked away inside me, and I've got enough interests. That, and a good television set, and heavens, I don't need anything else." And he says about his upcoming trip to Hawaii that he is getting a cottage right by the ocean, and he's just going to sit back there and listen to the waves come in. "It recharges your batteries, you know. There's something about the sound of the waves, the energy it generates, that does something to you, if you're receptive, that just relaxes you."

McCoy sits back in his chair for a moment, listening to those waves. And then he carries on with his story about the old days and his Indians.

"So I gathered up 50 Indians and headed to London, and they were a great hit over there. I remember going to get their passports. There was only two of them who could speak English. They were all longhairs, and I had changed the names of some of them because some of them didn't want to go. They were afraid to go across the Great Water. So I had to substitute somebody else for them. We were in New York for a couple of days, and I had their tepees pitched on the grounds of the Museum of Natural History. Well, when we went to get the passports, we left one of them asleep in his tepee. I knew that would cause trouble, so I told one of the other Indians in sign language to go back outside the passport office and put on a war bonnet and then come back. I knew the passport people couldn't tell one Indian from another. So we got them all through. And we got them over to London and pitched their tepees on the grounds of the Crystal Palace. They stayed in London for nine months and over in Paris for three months. After that I went to M-G-M."

When M-G-M called him, they had never made any Westerns or had a contract Western star. McCoy recalls coming down to Hollywood from his Wyoming ranch to make a screen test for Irving Thalberg.

"I came into the projection room with Irving Thalberg and two or three others," he says, "to watch these rushes. And later on outside, Thalberg called at me, and he said, 'Well, what do you think of it?' And I said, 'I wouldn't pay a dime to go across the street and look at that fellow.' But Thalberg said, 'Maybe we've got some different ideas about it. Come on over to the office. I want to talk to you.' So we did, and the result was I signed a contract with M-G-M."

McCoy and the director Woody Van Dyke worked up his first Western between them because nobody at M-G-M really had any idea about how to go about making Westerns. The first film, *War Paint,* was shot on his own home grounds in Wyoming, with his own Indians in the background. He then went on to make more Westerns and the costumed "historical" dramas. He recalls one film that was made simply because Thalberg happened to see him working out on the lot with Australian bullwhips.

"We'd work out all the time," McCoy says. "I mean you had to keep in shape, in physical shape. I'd have my horse brought over there to the hills where UCLA is now, and I'd ride him for an hour or so and then go over to the lot and work out in the gymnasium every day. And one day I was out on the big lawn where the sound stages were, working out with these Australian whips. And Irving came over and saw me tossing these whips and said, 'Let me hold one of those.' And I said, 'No, no, careful, because these things will jump right at you. You can't fool with these.' So he took one and cracked it, and it came right back and hit him. Then he went back up to his office and had a couple of writers come in and write a story for me about the Australian bush so I could use the whips in it.

That's the way the business was then. He wasn't screwing around. He had the story written for me just because he'd seen me using the whips. Those were the good days in the business."

McCoy says that although he was the resident cowboy at M-G-M, he was treated just like all the other big stars there.

"There were only seven stars on that M-G-M lot, and you were one of them," McCoy says with a mixture of pride and modesty. "You got the same treatment anybody else did. There was John Gilbert, he was number one, Ramon Navarro, Buster Keaton, Marion Davies, Lillian Gish, Lon Chaney, and myself. We were the seven M-G-M stars at that time. Then when Garbo came there, she wasn't a star but what they called a Leading Lady. And there was Lionel Barrymore. I would have the same supporting casts as John Gilbert. And dressing rooms, I dressed between Lon Chaney on one side and Lionel Barrymore on the other. And if you weren't working on a picture, you came over there for lunch every day, damned near. It was your club, and these were your friends."

Did Tim McCoy ever cross paths with the other great Cowboy-Heroes of the day? Tom Mix? Buck Jones? Hoot Gibson? Ken Maynard?

"No. I never knew them very well. Oh, I knew Hoot and Mix fairly well. I didn't know Buck Jones then. You see, I moved in a different group entirely. While I was at M-G-M, my real friends were Ronnie Coleman, who was my very closest friend, and my son is named after him, Bill Powell, Richard Barthelmes, and Warner Baxter. That was my group. So I never saw much of the other cowboys at all. Well, to put it smugly, it was sort of a different social strata. I often think of when a big soiree was held, by God, you came in white tie and tails. Not in a sweat shirt and a pair of old broughs like these birds do today, a pair of torn Levis and a pair of dirty old shoes."

And I wondered: Is he looking at my jeans? Is there shit on my boots?

"That was the Hollywood in my heyday," he says. "I wouldn't trade it for what they have now."

When sound came in, Tim McCoy's option was not picked up by M-G-M. They told him they wouldn't be making any outdoor pictures because sound was so primitive they were not able to record outdoors. So Westerns were dropped from their plans. And McCoy along with them. McCoy just said, "Forget it," and went over to Paris for a year with his first wife and their kids.

"I was out of work for a year when I came back. Everything was musicals. When I came back, I was the forgotten man." He went to his ranch in Wyoming, expecting to stay there and never get back in pictures. Until old Uncle Carl Laemmle called him back for the Universal serial *The Indians Are Coming*. It seems that for years Uncle Carl wanted to make a picture called *The Indians Are Coming*. But the Indians never seemed to come.

" 'Zis time da Indians gotta come!' " Tim McCoy says, mimicking Uncle Carl's German accent. "That's the way he put it. So I came down from the ranch and did that, the first talking serial. And I was back in business again."

McCoy didn't have to bring his own Indians for this one because by that time, he says, Hollywood was full of Indians. "They were filing in from all over the reservations to work in Western movies. I called them 'Cahuenga Indians' because they used to hang out over there on Cahuenga Boulevard just off Hollywood, where a lot of cowboys used to hang out. It was called 'The Water Hole.' There was a saddle shop and a boot shop and things of that sort."

Being back in business meant riding the range for smaller outfits than he had been accustomed to in his M-G-M days. There were Columbia and Universal. But there were also Puritan and Monogram. It was a bit of a comedown. "But they always treated me very well, those smaller companies I worked for," McCoy says about that. "I was always treated with proper respect, and I think that made it easier for me. They always gave me the deference I felt I was entitled to. And for that reason I was always quite happy with them. I enjoyed them and had a very good time."

And about the "Man of Destiny," the black-outfitted Cowboy-Hero he developed in those days, McCoy says: "That was my own idea. The black outfit. I was the first one. Hoppy copied it later. I liked it because I felt it was outstanding. All that fancy gear, I never wore that, anyway. That black, that solid figure was more menacing and had more strength to it than all the checkered shirts, all that junk you could put on." As for the Tim McCoy trademark of the "steely gaze" and the sideways glance, he says that was just one of those accidental things that was quite effective for playing certain kinds of scenes, and so he kept it up.

When he finally did quit the picture business, it was to go to World War II. Because his real love was the military life, and he wanted to fight the war where it was happening, not, like some Hollywood stars, on a studio back lot.

"I walked out of a contract with Monogram because the war was on. I used to say at the time that any guy who was physically fit to do the things we had to do in Western pictures ought to be in there doing his stuff. We had a war going on. And not playing Indians. So I sent 'em a telegram and walked right off. They said they could have me deferred. Deferred my eye! The War Department would have been glad to defer me. They didn't want a bunch of old full colonels getting in the way of promotions for a lot of young guys. And besides that, I was way past the age of anybody else. I was 50 years old when I came back for World War II. I was determined to go overseas. They offered me a job as commander of a glider-pilot school down in Kentucky, but I turned it down, and a short time after that I went overseas." While serving in France and Germany, he often ran into soldiers who recognized him from the Saturday Matinee and would say "howdy" and tell him how it had been a big thrill to root for him against the Bad Guys on all those Saturday afternoons.

"I got a big kick out of that," he says. "One day we put down in the Azores, I think it was, on a flight back to Washington and the sergeant in charge of the ground crew came up to me and saluted and said, 'Pardon me, but aren't you Colonel McCoy?' And I said I was. Well, he said, 'I've helped you a lot. I've done a lot of things for you.' And I said, 'Oh, is that so? Where did you serve with me? I don't seem to recall you.' 'Oh,' he said, 'I never served with you, but the little town in Ohio where I grew up had a little picture house with a balcony, and we kids used to get right up there in the front row of the balcony. And I had a slingshot and a pocketful of iron staples and any time the outlaws got anywhere near you, I shot the hell out of them.' . . . In the middle of a war this comes out! I got a big kick out of that."

And, yes, he still gets fan mail, although he has been out of the movie business for over 30 years.

"They say to me how we were their heroes and gave them a mark to shoot at. And they're very complimentary to me about the fact that they looked up to me because, you see, I was always so clean and neat and turned out and didn't have a look like a tramp. It's surprising that they remember all those details. And they say, 'Those were some of the things that gave us a mark to shoot at, something to live up to, that we wanted to be heroes, too. You gave us a good example.' Well, that's very gratifying to me. It doesn't affect me one way or the other, but I'm just grateful I was able to do these things. It has no effect on my vanity. My vanity was taken care of long ago, but it is gratifying that I was able through all these years to give these youngsters an example, a decent example. I'm very pleased about that. As for taking it seriously as to consider myself a hero, no. That was a Hollywood manufactured thing."

He says, "It was damn well done" the way Hollywood manufactured its heroes in the old days but that he feels it is just the reverse today. "They've turned it around. They've made the image something totally different. It's the tough guy who's the hero, not the fine upstanding fellow. And then the sickness that's coming into them now. Gracious, films are filled with nothing but filth and pornography and profanity. They have to fall back on that just to give people a thrill. Well, heavens, it's no thrill to go around and listen to words you used to see written on the fences. You can't get violent enough these days. It reminds me of what's going on down on Skid Row in Los Angeles. That's the dangedest thing that's happened since Jack the Ripper."

"You mean the 'Slasher'?"

Someone was going around cutting the throats of old winos in L.A. and giving the city a chill. The *Los Angeles Times* was keeping score. The "Slasher" had done in about 11 men before he was either caught or took a vacation.

"And that Manson fellow," McCoy says. "That was the goldangedest thing. What did they do? Did they finally execute him?"

"No," I say. "He's doing life at San Quentin."

"To me, the terrible thing behind all of this is narcotics. They're all weirdos, way out. Hell, they don't live in this world at all. And think of those girls that followed Manson. Whooo! Makes you shiver, doesn't it? I'll tell you, I wouldn't live near a big city for the world. That's why I came out here. All I wanted was room enough to build a house, that's all. And this place was ideal. But, God, deliver me from big cities. Just to go through them. I don't want to have anything to do with it."

Getting up steam, Tim McCoy says that the world has really turned since the days of the Cowboy-Heroes. And although he's an old soldier, he feels that wars have become nothing but vulgar brawls.

"Heavens, my younger boy Terry was in Vietnam. Now what the hell relation has that got to any of the wars that I've seen? The last war of chivalry was probably our Civil War. From there it kept deteriorating. World War I was bad enough. And World War II was worse. And when they got over to Vietnam, heavens alive, that was no war. That was murder. That's what that was, just murder."

And speaking of heroes and villains, McCoy has a few choice words to say about the erstwhile Richard Nixon.

"Just look at what this Nixon administration has done to this country," he says, "and you can't blame the younger generation. If the President of the United States has no integrity . . . here I am a hard-rock Republican, always have been . . . and that Nixon administration has done more to undermine the decency of this country than anything that has ever happened to it since it beginnings. It has destroyed all sense of integrity, all sense of honesty and decency. I think it has been a terrible thing for this country. There's no place else to go after that."

Hooray for Tim McCoy! Take that, John Wayne!

Then, having said, already, much more about his life than I expected he would when he told me he didn't have the heart to do it anymore, Tim McCoy talks a bit more about how he built this house himself, was his own architect, and chose the spot because there were a number of retired army officers he knew who lived around here.

"The only thing I need now, since my wife died, is either Terry or Ronnie to take care of the gardening and a maid to come in about three times a week to keep the place clean and policed up. We don't want her to·cook. Hell, no! I do my own cooking. Now my wife was the same way. She wouldn't let 'em cook. Nobody I know around here does. My wife had been a writer in Hollywood before I married her. She'd been a columnist, writer. And perfectly beautiful."

And then he begins to talk about his wife, more, I sense, to himself than to me. That she had been brought up in Denmark, was a marvelous cook, and a very intelligent and cultured woman. That Louis B. Mayer wanted to make a star out of her, but she simply couldn't be bothered with that. That she was one of the few beautiful women Tim McCoy had ever known who was completely without vanity. That they had had a marvelous 27 years together. And although she was 23 years younger than he was, there really was no age gap. It was just that it seemed naturally on the cards that he would have gone before she did.

"But that was that," he says. "Just a year ago she died . . . but we had a remarkable life together, and it couldn't have been nicer. And I think it's a little easier for me to be here without her than it would have been for her to be here without me. Although I didn't think I would ever recover . . . but she used to have an expression . . . I always had my boots made without pull-on straps in them, and I had the habit of wetting my thumbs to pull on the boots. So when anything was going rough, she would say, 'Well, cowboy, spit on your boot straps and pull 'em up.' That was her great expression. 'Spit on your boot straps and pull 'em up.' So that's what I had to do . . . So I can say I've had a most interesting life. I've had a wonderful marriage. I have a lovely home. And can't say if I kick off tomorrow it's in the flush of my youth. I have no regrets, I'm pretty well satisfied with what life has done to me and what it's been. There's nothing to be bitter about. There's nothing to be dissatisfied about. I've been a very very fortunate man. And that sums up my life for you."

And so it does. I had 47 million questions to ask Tim McCoy when I arrived. There was nothing further, really, that I could ask him that would not be just plain stupid. He had said everything that he wanted to say about himself and his life. Tim McCoy is alive and well. And that's the main thing that a Front Row Kid needed to know.

As I drove north toward the Interstate between Tuscon and Phoenix in the late afternoon, I felt depressed as well as elated. I had seen some old Cowboy-Heroes. And missed some others. Some had been willing to see a Front Row Kid. Some had simply turned me down flat. Some were dead, and I would never know about them. I had gone looking for the old Cowboy-Heroes, not knowing where to find them. And had asked them to dig around their past for me. To go back 30 or 40 or, in Tim McCoy's case, 50 years into the well of their memories. For a date, a fact, an incident or two about their days as Saturday Matinee Cowboys. For something trivial or something important that would help me to remember my own memories. I had spent an hour or two here and there. Up one freeway and down another. Given my old Front Row Kid memories a jolt or two in the process. But really there was not enough time. There never would be. For Tim McCoy to cover his 85 years would take . . . 85 more years. To find out everything I would like to know would take the rest of my life. And for everything I would come to learn, some old thing would be forgotten, crowded out by time and events. Exactly as it had been with my old Cowboy-Heroes. They had forgotten their best stories and their worst times. I think they did not really want to think too hard about those old days anymore.

And what for? Except to remember some past thing when they were younger men and at the center of the screen, with certain hopes and fantasies of their own. And as everyone does, they kept their secrets to themselves. The ones who had already died, "Broncho Billy," Hart, Mix, Maynard, Buck Jones, Hoot and Hoppy, Bill Elliott, "Rocky" Lane, Tex Ritter, Johnny Mack, Audie Murphy, so many others, had already taken their stories with them to Boot Hill. The others would be going in their own time and soon enough. What they have chosen to forget or what has slipped beyond their memory by accident or age has already gone to Boot Hill ahead of them.

Charles Starrett, "The Durango Kid," had said that it's always nice to be remembered. And so it is. And also to remember. But memory is one thing. And going back to the places of memory is quite another. An impossible thing. That can only turn your head around. And as clearly as I could remember what it was like to sit in that front row and cheer my Cowboy-Heroes like crazy, I could not go back to that front-row seat. The theater isn't playing those films anymore. And even if I am still the Front Row Kid, I am not *that* Front Row Kid. Nor is Gene Autry, with his strangled voice and paunch and millions, *that* Cowboy-Hero. Nor is 85-year-old Tim McCoy any longer the "Man of Destiny." And I cannot dismiss the feeling that what my old Cowboy-Heroes and I were doing in the time I spent with them was standing over a dead body and talking about it. It is, really, a hard thing to ask anybody to do. Especially when it is your own dead body you are talking about, someone you may once have been but are not any longer. There is more than a touch of melancholy in that trip.

Tim McCoy is 85 years old. He is the last of the original Moving Picture Cowboys. I had seen him, and that was fine. I would rather have seen him than not. I did not have to see any others after him. The Cowboy-Heroes I had seen, I would remember. Those I had missed, I would have to do without. I would remember them just as clearly as I would remember the others. Because really what I remember best is not what they are but what they were. In the time since those days when they were Cowboy-Heroes and I was the Front Row

Kid, the picture has changed. They have ridden out of it.
Which way did they go? They went thataway.

Outside Tucson, I detoured to Route 80. A road that is not
much traveled since the Interstate 10 cut up the scenery between Tucson and Phoenix. Along Route 80 there are cactus
plants growing that are higher than a car. In the dusk they look
like cowboys in round-crowned Stetsons standing with their
hands up. Beaten to the draw by some other cowboy you
cannot see.

About 18 miles outside Florence I found the spot I was looking for. The spot where Tom Mix went off the road in his
custom-built Cord. Full-throttle to death. The dry wash his car
plowed through before turning over is now called Tom Mix
Wash. There is a sign next to the road. A little farther along
is the Tom Mix Memorial Monument. It is a small rest area on
the left side of the road as you're heading toward Florence.
The ground has been cleared for 50 feet around. There are
picnic benches there and firestone bar-b-que pits for travelers
to roast hot dots and marshmallows. And some wire baskets for
litter. In the very center of the rest area is the Tom Mix
Memorial Monument. A small stone monument with a metal
cut-out figure of a horse on top, his head bent down toward the
grass, and with an empty saddle on his back. At the base of the
monument there is a plaque with Tom Mix's dates. Jan. 6,
1880–Oct. 12, 1940. And an engraved inscription:

In the memory of
TOM MIX
Whose spirit left his body on this spot and whose characterizations and portrayals in life served to better fix
memories of the Old West in the minds of living men.

I read it in the light of my old car's headlights. The horse on
the monument was in perfect silhouette against the sky,
which, only moments before, had been streaked with orange
and purple and blue in the sunset. In the distance, across the
wide-open spaces, you could make out the mountains. A half
moon had jumped up, dangling the evening star. The air was
cool and smelled of country. All around there was stillness and

silence. Broken only occasionally by the crackle of the under-brush and the sound of crickets and some cattle, carried on the wind from some place out of sight. The sun was down now. Completely. And when I turned out the headlights, the whole place was dark as absence and things forgotten.

I went around to the trunk of my old Dodge and fetched out my old, small, cracked-leather Front Row Kid cowboy boots that I had galloped around my back-yard cowtown in, playing Cowboy-Hero in the days of Saturday Matinees. And that I had been lugging around with me for all these miles. I tied them together at the pull-up straps with a piece of string. The old spurs were so rusted with time and ac-cumulated basement damp and dust they would not spin. I rubbed up the curled pointy toes of those small boots with my coat sleeve. But more than that and spit and polish would be needed to ever get a shine on them. And then I put the boots down at the base of the Tom Mix Memorial Monu-ment. And left them there. It was as good a place as any for those old boots. I had outgrown them years ago. I couldn't fit into them now as hard as I might try.

I stood there for a moment in the dark. Trying to think of something. But my head was empty. Which way did the Front Row Kid go?

Then I got into my old Dodge, started her up, and drove off into what would have been the sunset. Except the sun was already down.

We have all gone thataway.